THE EDUCATION OF SEBASTIAN

The Education Series: Book 1

JANE HARVEY-BERRICK

HARVEY
BERRICK
PUBLISHING

ISBN 9780955315077

Harvey Berrick Publishing

www.janeharveyberrick.com

Cover design by Hang Le

Cover photographs by Shutterstock

Thanks for permission to EMI Music Publishing to reproduce lyrics from 'Martha's Harbour', All About Eve in 'The Education of Caroline'

Acknowledgement to 'How to Avoid Being Killed in a War Zone' by Rosie Garthwaite and

'One Dog at a Time: Saving the Strays of Helmand' by Pen Farthing

'High Flight', John Gillespie Magee, Jr. (1922—1941)

✸ Created with Vellum

To Lisa Ashmore, for telling me to write this series
To Sheena Lumsden, for her humour and energy and loyalty
To Audrey Orielle, for loving Sebastian so much

Thank you.
JHB

PROLOGUE

I'VE OFTEN WONDERED WHY BRIDES-TO-BE SPEAK WITH SUCH excitement of their wedding day *—the best day of their lives*. Doesn't that imply that it's all downhill from then on?

My own wedding day was the culmination of the briefest of romances, if you could call it that. My husband was not a romantic man. He was not many things. Perhaps if he had been many, perhaps if he had been more, things might have turned out differently between us. Then again, perhaps it would have been exactly the same.

Despite what happened later, I can't bring myself to regret the events of that summer.

〜

I think it was the uniform. My husband dazzled me in his US Navy whites and with his flashy sports car that was so low to the ground, it seemed to skim along the road like a pebble on a lake.

David was a medical officer in the US Navy, newly promoted to Lieutenant Commander and assigned as a flight surgeon. He was II years older than me. He seemed urbane and sophisticated and to a girl from nowhere who had seen nothing, he was every wish fulfilled.

My mother smelled a good catch and my dear, sweet father was talked over and down by the two women in his life who vied for his attention.

Competition with my mother was relatively new. She had always been rather ashamed of her plain, gawky daughter, who seemed to have no breeding and no wish for it, but at the age of 17, I blossomed, quite literally, growing breasts almost overnight, and attracting the attention of young men who had formerly cast their glassy-eyed looks at my elegant and glossy mother. Suddenly, I was interesting, the sexy one, and she loathed it. Of course, she couldn't and wouldn't admit to that, so we fought. My father hated it and would descend to the basement to listen to Puccini or Rossini, and wonder why his 'two best girls' were at each other's throats.

So when David came along to sweep me off my feet, my mother couldn't help a quick shove to speed the process and send me on my way.

She'd never thought of college as an option for me—consequently there was no college fund. She'd always told my father I wouldn't last a single semester: 'too weak', apparently. Besides, marriage was supposed to save me from all that tedious studying.

"He's too good for you, of course, Caroline," she said, "but we'll do the best we can." *Well, I'll do my best to make you attractive, although 'pretty' is too much to hope for.* "Oh, you look so much like your father."

My father was short and dark and very Italian. I inherited his bright hazel eyes, thick, uncooperative hair that rippled in waves down my back, his olive skin and quick, passionate temper. I also inherited certain hirsute qualities that meant I was waxing my legs from the age of 10 and my armpits from the age of 12. But for all that, I blessed the deity who made me, that I had inherited little from my mother except her slender build, and height.

I used to wonder why she and my father had ever married because she undoubtedly despised his immigrant Italian ancestry and flaunted her own WASPishness at every opportunity. Her hair was blonde and coiffed, her eyes blue and sharp, her complexion strawberries and cream.

It didn't surprise anyone, least of all me, when I jumped the moment I was pushed, and found myself a bride at the age of 19. The year was 1990.

What David saw in me is less easy to understand. A young wife with European aspirations perhaps, fluent in Italian and with an appreciation of wine that was unexpected and, later, unwelcome. I was different enough from the other Navy wives to mark him out for distinction, and myself for alienation and loneliness.

The other wives tried very hard to include me in their artificial social whirl—coffee mornings, lunch dates, baby-sitting, play dates for children I didn't have, and 'drinks with the girls'.

They weren't unkind, merely satisfied with their lives, happy at home and fulfilled with their roles in a way I could never be. I was too young, too myopic and too self-contained to see the pitfalls of my willful isolation. I went to their book club once, but when I found they preferred bestsellers and romances to the chilling wildness of Hemingway, or the maverick prose of Nabokov, I had nothing to say and we merely stared at each other with fragrant disdain.

There was one thing about me that pleased my husband—I was athletic. He taught me to sail a dinghy and later a yacht, I could shoot almost as well as the Corps' best marksman, I was fearless of heights and I could dive from the top diving board at the Base swimming pool.

Those were the only things he liked about me, and even that was limited to the first twenty months of our marriage. He hated the way I dressed, the way I spoke, what I spoke about and the things that interested me to speak about. In the end, the irony was that he wanted me to be more like the other wives, while relishing my alienness. It was confusing and wearying and I didn't know how to be myself. I think that during those early years I forgot how. So I wore the clothes he liked and kept my mouth shut ... a slow descent into silence.

By the time we realized that children weren't going to happen for us, well, for him, I had undergone a number of invasive and unpleasant examinations and, blaming each other, we had both lost interest in procreation, fortuitous happenstance, I suppose. Sex was desultory and uninspiring. I was uninspired. I was dull.

After two years of marriage, David was transferred to the Naval Medical Center in San Diego and he very much wished me to be friends with the wife of his new CO. Estelle was everything that I was not—poised, charming and perfect. She was also cold, controlling, and a snob. I loathed her. The feeling was mutual. But for the sake of appearance, we cultivated a chilly friendship. It was easy for her to fake, less so for me. I pitied her child, perhaps feeling some kinship with his loneliness. Sebastian was eight years old, I was 21.

He was cursed with sensitivity, and with his bitch of a mom and his monster of a dad, he was damned twice.

Between us there arose a sweet and gentle friendship. Sebastian got into the habit of dropping by after school to tell me about his day. I'd pour him an alcohol-free *limoncello* made from Sorrento lemons, when I could find them, syrup and soda. We talked about books that he'd read, and I would suggest stories he might enjoy—the stories I had read as a child that were far removed from the anodyne books his mother thought suitable. Together we worked our way through the casual brutality of the Brothers Grimm and easy psychopathy of Hans Christian Andersen, whose little mermaid felt the pain of knives slicing into her feet when she walked, and whose angelic voice was bargained away for love.

At about this time, my dear father came to stay. My mother, of course, was too busy—involved with her clubs, her Bridge, and her good deeds for everyone but her family. It was a relief to us all, although David was determined to remind us of, and lament her absence at every meal. *Such a fine woman.*

Sebastian and my father adored each other, and happily spent hours together making model airplanes and blowing them up with the powder extracted from fireworks. David disapproved, of course, so—from him—they hid most of their activities. It was their special time, innocent and childish, if typically destructive play.

One day, Sebastian entered my kitchen when we failed to hear his knock. 'Madame Butterfly' was playing at full volume and my father and I were wailing along to the wonderful lyrics of '*Un Bel Di*'.

"What are you singing?"

"*Sto cantando in onore di Dio, giovanotto*," said my father.

Sebastian frowned and my father looked puzzled. "I don't understand what Papa Ven is saying."

"You're speaking in Italian, papa," I said, smiling. I turned to Sebastian. "He says he's singing to God."

"Ah, *cara! Italiano!* The language of Dante! The language of cooking! The language of love!"

Thereafter, every day of my father's visit, Sebastian learned a few more words of Italian, not all of them were entirely suitable for a child of his young years, but my father had a wicked streak in him. As it turned out, one that I inherited.

I was reasonably happy in San Diego. I became involved with the Base's magazine and helped out on open house days at the Base or the hospital. I had even put in an application to go to evening classes in journalism, one of the few individual forays I had ever made. It was at this time that David informed me he'd been assigned to Camp Lejeune in North Carolina, and that we were leaving. It was another sideways move for an officer who had failed to live up to his early promise. David chose to see it as a promotion, but then he would.

Within 48 hours, David had disappeared to the far side of the continent, and I had a week to watch the contents of our little home being packed into containers.

Sebastian came to see me every day, every day he cried.

And then, on a Tuesday in September, I was gone.

CHAPTER ONE

THE SUN WAS WARM ON MY SKIN, AND THE BOOK HAD BECOME heavy in my hands. I'd missed the California sun, it felt good to be back, even under these less than ideal circumstances.

I tossed the book aside, pushed my sunglasses up to my hair, and rested my head on my arms, soothed by the warmth of late morning.

I wasn't entirely sure I'd wanted to make this return journey with David. I had friends in North Carolina independent of Navy life, I had a job I enjoyed as an administrative assistant on a small but respectable local newspaper, and had finally gotten my English Lit degree after six years of night school.

But at the same time, I was feeling restless and ready for a change. Turning 30 had shifted my world view somewhat, and I was a little surprised to find myself still married. I felt ready to try something new ... or something old, as it turned out, because we were back in San Diego. It was a prized location and considered a step up from Camp Lejeune. In any event, David was happier, which made my life easier. We'd found a way to coexist that was not unpleasant. He wasn't always an unkind man, or so I told myself, and I wasn't a faithless wife, we were just fundamentally unsuited to each other. We'd grown apart.

At least I was enjoying the beach. Point Loma was seven miles from the hospital and patronized by nearly all the Base personnel, a finger of land that separated the ocean from San Diego Bay. The less popular part was at the north end of Adair Street, here, I thought, I was less likely to be disturbed.

Perhaps fate was watching, but I suppose the meeting would have happened sooner or later, if not that day.

"Hello, Mrs. Wilson."

I didn't recognize the light, tenor voice. I twisted around and cupped my hand over my eyes, squinting against the sudden brightness of the sun.

"Yes?"

Two men of about 20 were standing awkwardly a few feet away, and a third was leaning over me, dripping onto my beach towel.

"It's Sebastian."

"Who?"

His radiant smile faltered.

"Sebastian Hunter."

My mind unraveled. *Little Sebastian Hunter—all grown up*.

"Oh, my gosh, Sebastian! I ... I didn't recognize you. Wow!"

I rolled over and sat up.

"I heard you'd come back. I was hoping I'd see you," he said, smiling again.

The sweet, sad-eyed boy of eight had become a truly handsome young man. His light brown hair was long for the son of a Navy officer, curling nearly to his chin, and bleached to a dark gold by the California sun. He was slim, muscled like an athlete, with broad shoulders and narrow hips.

A bright blue surfboard was tucked under one arm and he wore deep red swim shorts that were heavy with seawater, pulled down to show a sliver of paler skin at his waist, highlighting the tan on the rest of his body. The thought passed through my mind, *He must have his pick of girls at school*.

"Look at you, Sebastian. So grown up. It's good to see you. How are you? How are your parents?"

His smile faltered.

"Oh, they're fine."

I didn't know what to say, it was so strange to see him again after all these years. With a stretch of the imagination, I could just see the child I had known in the young man before me.

"Well ... that's great. I'm sure I'll see you around the Base. Um ... do you guys need a ride back?"

I looked uncertainly toward his friends, unsure how I'd manage to load three full sized surfboards on top of my old Ford.

"No, we're good thanks. Ches has got a van." He nodded to one of the boys. "And we're going to catch some more waves. When I saw you, I just wanted to ... come say hi."

"Okay, well, good seeing you, Sebastian."

He smiled again, hovering tentatively. "I'll see you again, Mrs. Wilson?"

His voice held a question.

"Yes, I expect so. *Ciao*, Sebastian."

He beamed. "*Ciao*, Mrs. Wilson."

I watched him walk away, drops of seawater dewing on his muscled back. Good Heavens! Little Sebastian Hunter—and not so little. How old was he? Seventeen? Eighteen? Certainly not twenty. I frowned, trying to do the math. He'd really grown into a fine young man. Amazing, considering his wretched parents.

Oh, God, I'd probably have to see the rancid Estelle and the monstrous father, Donald. The gloomy thought killed my good mood, and I scowled at the writhing, hissing ocean.

Sebastian and his friends strolled toward another group of surfers hovering on the shoreline. I could see they were laughing at him about something, I guessed it was to do with me. I shook my head—teenage boys ... they don't change.

I watched as they paddled out, a small flock of brightly plumed beach rats, disappearing abruptly behind the rising surf. I could just pick out a bright blue board weaving along the leading edge of a breaking wave. I gasped as the rushing water suddenly swallowed the boy, then relaxed when I saw his head break the surface, and he swam back to his board, paddling again toward the line-up.

For perhaps half an hour I continued to watch as they took

turns racing across the hills of green water before being engulfed by the roiling froth, then paddling back to chase the next wave, over and over. It was pointless and beautiful and utterly mesmerizing.

Reluctantly, I checked my watch, time to head back to the Base. I was expecting a delivery of some more of our belongings. I couldn't be late, it wasn't worth the ensuing argument if all was not ship-shape before David returned from the hospital.

I slipped a yellow sundress over my bikini and headed back to the car. It was super-heated, of course, the air inside arid. I rolled down all the windows and drove back, singing along to Figaro's aria on my temperamental CD player.

When I pulled up, the delivery guy was pounding on my door, frustrated by the lack of response.

"Sorry! Sorry! I'm here now."

He glowered at me. I smiled pleasantly and offered him a cold beer.

"Well, ma'am, I wouldn't say no to a cold soda if you've got one."

He stood and poured it down his throat in one swallow, wiping sweat from his glowing face. Then he happily deposited two large crates in the garage and drove away.

I stared sourly at the boxes, wondering if my withering gaze would force them to unpack themselves. But no.

Three hours later, dirty and sweaty, and with aching muscles, I admitted defeat with one-and-a half crates still left to unpack. Tomorrow would have to do, although I knew it would mean a fight. But I just didn't have the energy.

At 6PM David drove up in his pride and joy—a newly purchased silver Camaro, vivid symbol of his promotion. He frowned at the unpacked crates, and I waited for the dissection of my day—where had I been, what had I done, who had I seen. But instead he tapped his watch, a habitual gesture of irritation.

"We're due at the Vorstadts' in an hour, and you're not dressed."

"Who?"

"Captain Vorstadt has invited us for drinks."

"You didn't say."

"I put it on the calendar, Caroline. Didn't you check the schedule?"

No, sir. Sorry, sir.

"I thought you might have mentioned it, that's all, David."

"I want to leave at 1850. Wear the green cocktail dress."

I hated it when he ordered me around—which was most of the time, admittedly. But it was really grating on me.

"I'm tired, David. I've been unpacking crates for the last three hours—it's exhausting."

"Making life and death decisions all day is exhausting, Caroline. For once, could you just do something to support me? I don't ask for much, considering the lifestyle I give you."

I bit back the retort that sprang forward. What was the point? We'd been here before. I'd never won an argument with him yet. It was so damn tiring to even try.

"Fine. I'll go shower."

I dressed quickly, applied a little eyeliner, mascara and some clear lipstick: the minimum makeup I could get away with. David liked women 'to look like women'—that meant heels and make-up. Not really my look, inasmuch as I had one. He wore his favorite sports jacket and an open-necked shirt. He still looked handsome, I suppose.

"What did you do today?" he said, breaking the silence as we drove the short distance to the party.

"Before I spent three hours unpacking crates?"

"Just half a crate, I noticed."

Pedantic ass.

"I read a book at the beach. Before the crates were delivered. Oh, I bumped into Sebastian."

"Who?"

"The Hunters' boy. You know, from last time we were here."

He grunted, which could mean anything, but I suspect it meant he didn't remember. David wasn't good at remembering people, something of a handicap for a doctor. It gave the impression he was cold.

"Who's going to be there tonight?"

"I wasn't given the guest list, Caroline."

Jeez, I was only asking.

Mrs. Vorstadt met us at the door of her townhouse.

"David, how lovely. And you must be Caroline. I'm Donna."

Donna was a strong-looking, attractive woman in her fifties. She kissed me on the cheek. Her breath smelled of gin and tonic.

"Do come in."

The room was crowded and noisy, people spilling out into the large yard at the rear of the house. A barbecue was spitting away under an awning—men gathered in little groups drinking beer from bottles and laughing loudly, women huddled together sipping Manhattans, their high heels sinking into the recently watered turf. I was glad I'd worn flats, despite David's frown of disapproval.

I mentally prepared myself for an evening of tedium. But it was worse than that.

Donna furnished us with the mandatory beer for David and cocktail for me, then ushered us toward a couple who seemed vaguely familiar. When the blonde turned, I recognized her icy smile.

"I believe you know the Hunters from last time you were in San Diego."

"Caroline, dear," said Estelle in a cool voice. "And David, you haven't aged a day."

We air-kissed insincerely, the men shook hands and Donald wandered off to speak to some of the other officers.

"Hello, Estelle." I spoke mildly without inflection. "I saw your son today."

She stared at me in disbelief. "Sebastian?"

"Yes. At the beach. It was a nice surprise."

"He was at the beach?"

For God's sake, I'm not talking Serbo-Croat.

"Yes."

Her eyes narrowed, and I had the distinct impression that I'd somehow given away his secret.

"Sebastian!" Her clipped vowels carried across the yard, and several people turned around to stare.

I followed her eyes and saw him again, leaning against the deck, by himself. He was taller than I'd realized now that I was standing, too: as tall as his father, taller than David. This time Sebastian was more formally dressed in khaki chinos, a white shirt, sleeves rolled up his strong forearms, and a loose, black tie around his neck. He still looked more casual than the majority of the men.

"Mother?" he said, his eyes wary.

"Caroline said you were at the beach today."

He smiled suddenly and walked over to join us, his expression lightening as he saw me. "Hello, Mrs. Wilson. I said we'd meet again."

"You were right. How was the surf?"

"Great, thanks! We..."

"Sebastian!" interrupted Estelle in a low, furious voice. "You were supposed to be studying for your advanced placement tests. You need to pass these if you're going to be a semester ahead, for God's sake. You've got your college credits to think about. Do you want your Associate degree early or not?"

He shrugged nonchalantly in that infuriating way that most teenagers learn simply to annoy their parents, but I could see that he was anxious, too.

"I studied this afternoon," he replied softly. "There was a good swell this morning, Ches..."

"We'll talk later," she hissed. "Your father will want to hear about this."

She marched away, leaving an embarrassed silence behind her. Donna steered David away, and I was left with Sebastian.

"I'm so sorry about that—I wouldn't have said anything if I'd realized I was going to make trouble for you."

He shrugged again and smiled. "I'm always in trouble, so it doesn't make any difference."

"Oh, well then ... here's to trouble!" I raised my glass in an ironic toast.

Sebastian grinned at me, his eyes crinkling happily. I

realized they were blue-green, the color of the ocean. I'd forgotten.

"Have you been surfing long? You looked pretty good."

"Did you see me?" he seemed delighted. "There were some really gnarly tubes."

"I have no idea what that means! But I did watch for quite a while, you looked very graceful."

He blushed suddenly and looked down.

"How's school?" I asked, changing the subject.

"Oh, okay. I graduate a week from Thursday..."

That would make him 18, I guessed.

"And then off to college in the fall?"

"Maybe. Dad wants me to enlist, but Mom wants me to get my degree first."

"What do you want?"

He looked surprised, as if no one had asked him that question. Then he smiled wickedly.

"I want to surf."

"Of course. The perfect career path—a beach bum. Perhaps we should drink to the endless summer."

He laughed, a carefree sound that had me grinning back at him.

"I could drink to one of your special *limoncellos*."

I must have looked puzzled because he clarified his comment immediately.

"You used to make them for me—alcohol-free!"

"Oh, yes. When you were a kid."

He frowned, as if something about what I said didn't please him, but he quickly threw off the thought.

"Do you go to the beach a lot?" he asked, his eyes surprisingly intense.

"I did in North Carolina, although I had a job, too. But we've only been back here a week, so today was my first chance. I still have a lot of unpacking to do."

I shuddered at the thought of those one-and-a-half crates in the garage.

"I could help you. Unpack, I mean. Carrying things."

"Oh, well, thank you. But I expect I'll manage, it's not that much really."

"I'd like to help. It's great having you back."

I was nonplussed by his offer and his comment, although part of me acknowledged it would be useful to have someone to do all the carrying. No, he had studying to do, it wouldn't be fair.

Over his shoulder, I saw Donald Hunter stalking toward us and a shiver ran through me: he looked furious.

My expression must have alerted Sebastian because he turned to see what had caught my attention.

"Your mother says you were at the beach again this morning," barked Sebastian's father, without preamble. He gripped Sebastian's arm, spinning him around to face his wrath.

Sebastian blanched. "Yes, but..."

"I fucking warned you what I'd do if you did that again when you should be studying."

I was utterly shocked that this foul man would speak to his son like that in front of me, a virtual stranger.

"Dad, I..."

"Quiet!" he snarled.

People were staring. And I was caught in a horrifying paralysis, unable to tear my eyes from this nasty little family drama.

"You can kiss your surfboard goodbye—and no more beach. No son of mine is going to waste his life being a beach bum."

Sebastian tugged his arm free and faced down his father.

"I studied in the afternoon, Dad. And I paid for that surfboard, I worked for it. It's mine. You can't touch it."

Donald's face turned an ugly puce, and I thought he was going to hit his son. At the last second he realized that people were staring.

"This isn't over," he hissed, then marched away.

Sebastian stared at the ground, humiliation and anger vying for dominance on his face.

I felt terribly guilty, this was all my fault.

"I'm so sorry, Sebastian," I whispered. "I had no idea..." My words trailed off lamely.

He shook his head. "He's just an asshole. I really hate him. I can't wait to leave home," he said, fiercely. "The sooner the better."

I didn't know what to say to that. I just nodded sympathetically. After all, hadn't I left as soon as I could to get away from my mother? I searched desperately for a change of topic, but my brain was unwilling to cooperate. Donna returned quickly, looking suitably irritated at Donald's outburst. *Such bad manners*, I could see the thought flickering across her face.

"Can I refresh your glass, Caroline?"

Without realizing it, I'd downed the cocktail already.

"Oh, yes, thank you."

"Sebastian, more soda?"

"No, thank you, Mrs. Vorstadt," he muttered, then left abruptly, his expression mortified.

Donna shook her head. "That poor boy. What he has to put up with."

"Is his father always like that?" I was still shocked.

Clearly the answer was 'yes' but Donna didn't want to commit herself to anything too definite—or damning.

"Oh, well, Donald is Donald. I'm sure you must remember."

I stared after Sebastian, recalling other instances of Donald's bullying from when his son was a boy. I was amazed Sebastian hadn't turned into a monster himself. He seemed just as gentle and sweet as when I'd known him all those years ago.

The rest of the evening passed with uninteresting small talk, as usual. I stayed away from Estelle and Donald, Sebastian seemed to have disappeared, and David and I ignored each other, as usual.

I was relieved when he decided it was the right time to return home.

CHAPTER TWO

THE NEXT MORNING THE DAMN CRATES HADN'T miraculously unpacked themselves. I was staring at them with antipathy when I heard a car pull up.

Donna Vorstadt stepped out of her new Chevy and waved when she saw me.

"Hello, Caroline, dear, I thought I'd just come and see how you're settling in. Goodness, I think you've got your work cut out there."

She smiled, commiserating, and I warmed to her a little more.

"Do you time for a cup of coffee, Donna?"

I didn't usually feel the need to socialize with the wives of my husband's fellow officers, but she seemed genuine, and I still knew how to follow some of the niceties of Base behavior.

"Sure, that would be great."

I realized too late that the breakfast dishes were still scattered across the counter. Oh well, I'd blown my chance of pretending I was perfect.

"Cream and sugar?"

"Just the cream. Do you have skim milk?"

I cleared a space, and we sat down to drink our coffees.

"So, how are you settling in? It's a pain moving, isn't it?"

"I don't mind the physical aspects of moving ... it's just ... I had a job I really liked back in North Carolina." *Oh, too personal.* "Mind you, those crates won't unpack themselves."

I sighed and she looked sympathetic.

"I have to run to the shops now, but I could come by this afternoon and help if you like."

Before I could reply, there was a knock at the front door. I hoped to hell it wasn't another wife come to help by drinking my coffee.

"Hi, Mrs. Wilson."

Smiling hugely, Sebastian stood there, dressed in torn jeans and a plain, white t-shirt.

"Oh, hello! It's nice to see you again, Sebastian. What can I do for you?"

"You said you had to unpack crates, I thought I could help."

I was taken aback by his offer.

"That's very sweet of you, Sebastian, but I don't think your parents would be happy if they knew you were here instead of studying."

"I'm taking a break," he said, his lovely smile slipping at the mention of his parents.

"I'm sure they won't object to Sebastian helping a neighbor," said Donna, appearing behind me. "That's very thoughtful of you, Sebastian," she continued, kindly.

Sebastian reddened when he saw her, and he looked down.

"Well, I could certainly use some help," I said, feeling flustered.

"Great!" said Sebastian, his smile returning. "I'll get started."

"Thank you," I muttered to his back.

Donna winked at me. "I think you have got admirer there," she whispered. "Thanks for the coffee. Call me if you need anything."

I watched her drive away, and then headed for the garage. Sebastian had already made inroads into the second half of crate number one.

"You really don't have to do this, you know," I said, shaking my head in bewilderment.

"I want to," he said simply.

I decided I'd let him help for half an hour, then kick him out and send him back to his parents before I caused any more trouble for him.

It was useful having him there—he heaved tables and chests and boxes full of who knows what, and before I knew it, two hours had flown by.

"Oh crap! It's nearly lunchtime." I said, looking at my watch, horrified.

"Do you have to be somewhere?" Sebastian asked, looking concerned.

"No, no, I'm worried about you. Your parents ... your studying."

He shrugged. "No sweat."

"Look, I'm not going to be responsible for you flunking out. I'll fix you some lunch and then you must go study. Deal?"

"Okay, deal!" he said happily.

He followed me into the house and I showed him where he could wash his hands. I was stretching up to get some of the tall glasses when I heard him come into the kitchen.

"I'll get those for you," he said.

His sudden proximity behind made me jump as if an electric shock had jolted through me. It was the strangest feeling, I suddenly felt almost nervous as he reached past my shoulder, lightly brushing against my back. I took a step away and turned to find him staring at me, a glass in each hand.

"Thank you," I said, awkwardly.

He didn't reply and I had to look away first. The intensity of his gaze made me feel uncomfortable—and in my own home, too, damn it! Yes, and annoyed. I took refuge, hunting through the refrigerator, trying to restore some equilibrium.

"I have soda or a lemon *pressé*," my voice was half swallowed by the fridge.

"I've never had a lemon *pressé*. What's that?"

"Oh well, just lemon juice and sparkling mineral water."

"I'll try that, please, Mrs. Wilson."

The tension left my body and I smiled at him.

"Sebastian, you can call me Caroline. Mrs. Wilson is so formal ... and it makes me feel ancient."

"Okay, Caroline," he grinned at me.

"Now, I can make you a chicken salad sub or ... tricolored salad."

"*Insalata tricolore, per favore*."

I turned to him in surprise.

"I've been learning Italian," he announced proudly. "A correspondence course. My high school only offered Spanish."

"Really? *Molto bene!*"

"And I've been listening to opera, too. I like Verdi."

"The fallen woman."

"Excuse me?" he gasped.

"*La Traviata*: I presume that's what you mean when you say you like Verdi. Or maybe *Aïda*? *Rigoletto*?"

He let his breath out in a gust. "Yeah, all of those."

"I thought teenage boys only listened to heavy rock music," I teased him.

He looked wounded and I regretted my comment. He was obviously trying to impress me.

"I'm glad you like opera, my father loved it."

"I remember. I remember you and him singing opera in your kitchen."

"Really, you remember that?"

He nodded, serious. "I remember everything."

I sighed. "That was a great visit when Papa came to stay."

Sebastian smiled. "Yeah, he was fun. We blew up a lot of things."

I rolled my eyes at the memory. "Yes, David wasn't very happy about it."

Why I mentioned David at that moment, I couldn't say.

Sebastian frowned. "How is your dad?"

And the painful memory lanced through me. My dear father, lying shrunken and in pain, tiny and helpless in a hospital bed, the morphine failing to tame the pain of cancer that devoured him whole.

"He passed away—two years ago."

I could barely speak the words, taken by surprise at the crushing force of the memory. I felt tears hot in my eyes. *Ridiculous, I scolded myself.*

"I'm sorry. I didn't know," Sebastian whispered.

He looked like he wanted to say something else, but now I was craving his absence. I heartily wished I hadn't offered him lunch.

"Thank you for your help this morning, Sebastian. It was really very thoughtful of you, but I'm going to have to insist that you go and do some studying as soon as we've eaten. I don't want to get you into any more trouble."

He pouted, suddenly looking his age. It made me want to laugh, but I truly didn't want to hurt his feelings. Especially not when he'd been so helpful. I changed the subject.

"Will you go surfing with your friends again soon?"

He sighed. "Maybe. I'll have to borrow a board."

"Oh, what happened to the blue one?"

"Dad trashed it—snapped it in half. Said I wasn't to waste any more time surfing."

He said the words casually, but I could hear the anger and hurt beneath them, and I remembered his father's threat at the barbecue.

"That's awful. And it's all my fault. I should never have said..."

He interrupted me, speaking softly. "It's not your fault that my father is a sadistic bastard, Caroline."

My hand fled to my mouth as he spoke, my eyes fixed on his.

"I'm so sorry." My words were whispered and faint.

He shrugged. "No big deal. I'm used to it."

"I must buy you a new board, Sebastian. That's all there is to it."

I tried to lighten the mood.

"Thanks, Caroline, but it's cool. I can always borrow one of Ches's. His dad surfs, too."

"Well, let me give you a ride home after we've eaten. It's the least I can do."

He grinned at me, and the tense moment had dissolved.

I sliced some mozzarella and tomatoes, diced the avocado, drizzled virgin olive oil, and ground some black pepper. I was irritated that I hadn't had time to buy any fresh basil to shred over it. It would have to do.

I found some bread I was going to use for bruschetta, and put a plate in the middle of the table. I imagined a teenage boy would eat a lot more than me.

He tucked in with gusto, swallowing everything in sight.

"Boy, you really can cook, Caroline."

I laughed at his enthusiasm. "This isn't cooking, Sebastian."

"Mom never cooks anything," he said, raising his eyebrows at me. "Dad thinks she does, but it's all store bought."

"Hmm ... well, anything you say or do can and will be held against you in a court of law."

He looked horrified. "Don't tell her I told you!"

"What's it worth?" I teased him.

"My ass!" he said, forcefully.

The expression on his face made me laugh out loud.

"Oh, Sebastian, you've left yourself open to blackmail now."

"You can blackmail me anytime, Caroline," he said huskily.

His eyes were suddenly intense, and I blinked at him in surprise.

"Time to go," I said blandly, and began to stack the dishes.

He stood and watched me uncertainly for a moment, then helped me clear the kitchen table.

"That insalata was good," he said, shyly.

"Thanks. Glad you liked it."

I looked at my watch, a not very subtle gesture. "I'll get my car keys."

I played the same CD that I'd listened to yesterday, but I didn't feel like singing now, the atmosphere in the car was uncomfortable again. I was having trouble keeping up with Sebastian's mood swings. It must be a nightmare living with a teenager, I reasoned, even one as seemingly mature as

Sebastian. Or maybe it was just men in general—David's mood swings could almost be set by a metronome. The thought made me grimace.

"Can you drop me here?" Sebastian said suddenly.

"But we're not at your place yet?" I said, confused by the request.

He twisted his mouth in the semblance of a smile. "There'll be fewer questions this way," he said.

I felt guilty again—he'd spent the whole morning helping me when he should have been studying. And it was obvious his mother had no idea what he'd been doing. I hoped Donna didn't mention anything to her.

I pulled the car to the curb and waited for him to get out.

He sat for a moment, fiddling with his seatbelt.

"Will I see you again?" he said.

I frowned, puzzled by his odd question. "I expect so. Everyone bumps into everyone on the Base. Now, promise me you'll study this afternoon."

He forced a muted smile. "Okay, Caroline. See you later."

"Bye, Sebastian."

I drove away. I couldn't help glancing in the rear-view mirror —he was still watching.

Donna's words came back to me: *You've got an admirer there*.

Oh hell. Just what I didn't need—a teenager with a crush on me.

Irritated, I returned to my duties in the garage. By the time everything was put away and each assorted oddment had been found a home, I was bone weary. I was grateful to Sebastian—I would never have finished so soon without his help. I didn't have much experience of boys his age even when I *was* his age, but in my opinion he seemed different ... more mature than I would have expected. I wondered if he really did like opera, or whether that was just for my benefit.

God, what it must have been like growing up with those parents. Although Estelle was disturbingly like my own mother, at least I had one parent who'd loved me unconditionally.

I poured myself a glass of water, and took it to the yard to sit in the sun for a few moments of peace. I felt curiously adrift, as if the ties to my life were unraveling one by one. My mother, long absent by mutual choice, my father dead, my job gone, even David was AWOL in spirit.

And I was a shadow.

Oh, stop being so melodramatic.

I blamed my father: the Italian genes.

I needed to get out of the house, off the Base, and do something.

I threw myself in the shower, washing off the grime, and pulled on jeans and a t-shirt. That was deliberate—David hated seeing me in jeans, but today, right now, I wanted to feel like me —just for a few, precious hours.

I pulled out of the driveway and drove, too fast, down the road and past the hospital. From the corner of my eye, I recognized the figure walking away from me. I almost drove on, but something made me stop.

I leaned over and rolled down the passenger window.

"Hi. You need a ride somewhere?"

Sebastian's face lit up.

"Yeah, thanks."

He climbed in, folding his long legs into my compact Pinto, and grinned. I waited for him to give me directions, but he just leaned back in his seat and smiled.

"So, where can I take you?"

He shrugged. "Anywhere."

"Excuse me?"

"I just needed to get out of the house—you know, get some space. Mom is ... well, Mom."

"Oh, okay."

I felt awkward. I wouldn't have offered him a ride if I'd imagined he was just out for a walk.

"Did you finish your work?"

I really didn't want to be responsible for him neglecting his studies twice in one day.

"Yeah, I guess."

"Well, I was going to go downtown. You want to come?"

Part of me hoped he wouldn't, things were already awkward enough.

"Sure, that'd be great, Caroline."

There was a short pause while I thought of something to say. We'd chatted so easily this morning in the garage, but now I felt awkward. Maybe it was the memory of his intense gaze, the way his body had pressed against mine as he'd reached for the drinking glasses. I shook my head to clear it.

"How is the studying going?"

He shrugged, as if bored of that topic.

"Not a problem. On practice tests, I've scored high. It's all good."

"What AP classes are you doing?"

He glanced sideways at me. "Math, English Lit ... and Italian."

"Oh, well ... that's good."

I knew I ought to ask why those particular subjects—except I could guess, one of them at least.

"I want to do an Associate of Arts degree. It's only two years."

"So I understand," I said, briskly.

He looked like he wanted to say more, but instead turned to gaze out of the window.

"Why don't you put the radio on?" I said, hoping it would provide a suitable diversion.

"Okay," he said evenly.

It's ridiculous that this 18-year-old boy is more at ease than I am. Come on, Venzi, pull yourself together. Even after 11 years of marriage, there were times when Caroline Wilson was still Carolina, feisty daughter of the immigrant Marco Venzi.

The radio hissed and crackled until Sebastian found a reasonably clear signal—Blue Grass. His choice surprised me—from Verdi to this? It made me smile.

"You like Doc Watson?"

"I like all kinds of music."

I parked in a lot on Harbor Drive and we wandered up the hill to Little Italy, talking about music and food. I remembered this area from when I'd lived here before. There was a Mercarto every Saturday, and I looked forward to being able to buy Italian specialty oils and vegetables that weren't stocked in regular stores.

"Do you want to grab a coffee?" Sebastian said, sounding hopeful.

Mmm. Good Italian coffee. "Oh, a real espresso. Yes, that would be lovely."

Too much enthusiasm. Don't encourage him—no mixed signals.

But the day was too beautiful to be half-hearted, and I found myself delighted with all the pretty cafés, gelateria, and ristorantes.

We stopped at a tiny coffee shop just off India Street. The owner's wife came out to serve us and was ecstatic when I spoke to her in Italian. She kissed me on both cheeks and summoned the rest of her family to come out and meet me. Sebastian looked overwhelmed, then offered a few careful Italian phrases and was engulfed in the bosom of the family. I couldn't help laughing—their exuberance reminded me so much of my father.

They rattled out Italian like peanuts, with such speed and vigor, each talking over one another so that I struggled to catch everything they said. Sebastian probably only caught one word in fifty, but he sat there grinning, only wincing when the owner's mother, a little, round *nonna* of about eighty, grabbed him with both hands and kissed him repeatedly.

Then they all pulled up chairs and surrounded our small table, which soon overflowed with affection. Someone fetched half-a-dozen espresso cups and I sipped happily at the thick, bitter coffee. I was amused to see that Sebastian added several spoonfuls of sugar before he found the rich brew palatable.

Eventually some more patrons arrived and the family scattered, returning to their various roles of cook, cleaner, chef and bottle-washer.

"Whoa! That was something else," said Sebastian, as we were left to our own devices.

"Wonderful, wasn't it?"

"They kind of reminded me of your dad."

I sighed and leaned back in the uncomfortable chair.

"Yes, crazy—just like Papa."

"I'm sorry," he said softly, "I didn't mean to make you sad."

Then he laid his hand on mine and I felt his gentle touch. My eyes flew open in surprise and I jerked my hand away.

"I'm sorry," he said again, his cheeks heating.

"No, that was rude of me. I was just..."

Tension returned and to my horror, I found my hands were shaking. I fumbled in my wallet for some money and placed the bills on the table under an abandoned coffee cup.

"I have money," he said, awkwardly.

"No, it's fine. I've got it," I muttered. "I have to get back now."

Sebastian stood in silence, then followed me back onto the main street.

"*Aspetti, signor!*"

The coffee shop owner had followed us and was waving the notes I'd left on the table.

I stared, bewildered as he forced the bills into Sebastian's hand.

"No, please. You and your beautiful wife must come again. You are like family. Please!"

Refusing to keep the money, he kissed us both and trotted away smiling.

Sebastian's bemusement turned into a broad grin as he passed the money to me. "For you, *signora*. Beautiful wife, huh? Well, he was half right."

It was my turn to flush, but I tried to laugh it off. "Free coffee always tastes the best."

"Yeah! We should definitely do this again."

I couldn't return his puppyish enthusiasm, I simply smiled weakly.

"You know," he said thoughtfully, "I only got about one

27

word in every sentence. I thought my Italian was better than that. Hell, I've been studying it for four years. Maybe you could teach me, I mean, just some Italian conversation practice. That would be awesome!"

My automatic response was a big NO, but I didn't get the chance.

"Hey, Seb. What's up?"

Sebastian's face froze.

"What do you want, Jack?"

"Who's your cute friend?"

A look of anger and deep dislike crossed Sebastian's face.

"Ah, come on, dude! I'm just saying."

I was pretty certain Jack was one of the surf rats that I'd seen with Sebastian the day before. He was slightly older than Sebastian and his friends, with dark hair and dark, feral eyes. I disliked him from the first sentence he spoke.

"Caroline Wilson," I said, hoping to defuse the sudden tension.

"Howdy, *Mrs.* Wilson," he said slyly, his eyes swiveling from my wedding rings to my cleavage.

We both looked at Sebastian, who seemed very ill at ease.

"Well, it was nice bumping into you again, Sebastian. Do you want a ride back to the Base or perhaps you'd prefer to stay with your *friend*."

I waited less than a second before I fixed an insincere smile to my face.

"See you around then. *Ciao*."

And I walked away.

I was furious with myself. Why had I pretended we'd just bumped into each other? It had all been perfectly innocent, so why lie?

And then I remembered the touch of his hand on mine and my ridiculous over-reaction.

Oh, this was not good, not good at all.

My temper was free-wheeling by the time I got back to the car. I was angry with Sebastian, with myself, with the loathsome Jack: stupid, pathetic little shit. He'd made me feel ... guilty, and

I hadn't done anything. I was used to David making me feel guilty, but this was insufferable.

I wound down the windows before I got in, to let the heat escape, feeling some release of pent-up energy in the trivial task.

When I heard footsteps behind me, I didn't need to turn to see who it was.

"Caroline, I'm sorry, I..." his words trailed off.

"What? What!"

The words came out more forcefully than I'd meant. He stared at me, wounded. I badly wanted to kick something.

I took a deep breath, and reminded myself it wasn't his fault.

"Do you want a ride back?"

He nodded, still looking hurt.

I drove in a quiet rage. After a few minutes, I felt calm enough to risk a glance at Sebastian, he was gazing out of the window.

Eventually, he broke the heavy silence.

"I'm sorry about Jack and what he said." There was a brief pause, then he added, "The guy's an asshole."

I exhaled slowly, forcing some of the tension and irritation from my body in one long breath.

"Yes, he is, but don't worry about it."

He looked at me hopefully. "So, will you help me with my Italian? We could..."

"Sebastian, no. I don't think that would be a good idea."

"Why not?"

"It just isn't."

We sat mutely for several more minutes before he said softly, "I had fun today."

So did I.

But I didn't reply.

~

I dropped Sebastian off near his house and drove home, feeling irritated and petulant.

I stomped around, finding places for the final pieces of detritus from our marriage, items that didn't seem to fit were unceremoniously shoved into a closet in the guest room, metaphorically as well as literally.

Out of some guilty urge, I fixed David his favorite meal: lasagna and green salad, with a heavy dessert of apple pie and ice cream that he'd have to eat alone. I sat on the porch facing out into the yard and stared moodily at the yellowing grass. It needed watering, another chore. It was one of those days when I wished I'd taken up smoking years ago just to have something meaningful to do with my hands—and a purpose for being outside.

What was it about that boy? He really got under my skin. It had been simple when he was a child, and I'd enjoyed his uncomplicated company. Things had certainly changed. I'd enjoyed his company today, until Jack showed up. The thought was unwelcome.

When I heard David's Camaro outside, I pushed all thoughts of Sebastian Hunter from my mind.

"Mmm ... something smells good."

"Lasagna and apple pie."

David looked pleased. "It was the right decision coming out here again, Caroline."

If you say so.

"So what did you do with your day?"

"Puttered, mostly. Finished putting things away. I thought I might see if I could get some work—maybe writing. I'd like to use my degree. There's a cool, local newspaper, *City Beat* ... maybe I..."

"Good girl. Well done."

And that was the end of the conversation about me. Instead, I listened to a blow-by-blow description of his day at the hospital. Despite his snide comment about making life and death decisions while I played the little woman, most of his work was with orthopedic medicine.

After the meal, he leaned back in his chair and folded his hands over his stomach.

"I was talking to Donald Hunter today. Seems that son of his is running with a bad crowd."

"Sebastian? Is that likely? He seems such a nice boy."

David frowned. He didn't like having his story interrupted. I stood up quickly to clear the dishes—I didn't have the energy for either a fight or a lecture.

"He's spending all his time at the beach, surfing." He sneered the last word. "He's wearing his hair long, and Donald thinks he's probably smoking pot—he caught him with a lighter."

I hid a smile. Didn't most high-schoolers do things like that? It hardly seemed the crime of the century. But David's mantra was that rules were to be obeyed. I preferred my Papa's version: 'Rules are for the obedience of fools and the guidance of wise men'. A version which covered a multitude of small sins.

"He says he'll have to put his foot down."

"What does that mean?"

"He wants him to enlist—sooner rather than later. I think it's a good idea. A young man out of control—he needs some discipline. It made a man out of me."

I didn't want to start an argument so I stayed quiet, for a moment, seething inside, before I said, "Oh, I got the impression Estelle wanted him to go to college first."

David's frown deepened. "Well, Donald's the one paying the bills, so he's the one calling the shots."

And this was what it always came down to. I became even more determined to get some work—writing, if possible. I wouldn't mind serving in a shop or a bar, but David would never allow that. Pursuing my writing was acceptable, a suitable hobby for an officer's wife.

I loaded the dirty plates into the dishwasher and stacked the pans by the sink. I liked doing the dishes, it meant I could stay busy while David filled me in on more of the dull trivia that completed his day. I'd have washed the plates, too, except then he'd complain about me not using the household appliances properly.

I felt sorry for Sebastian. He'd seemed so happy and carefree as we'd wandered through Little Italy. It must be awful living with a controlling bastard like Donald Hunter—and Estelle, so cold and heartless. Well, I didn't have to guess how it felt to have a mother like that: I knew exactly.

Perhaps it would be a good thing if he enlisted, if only to get away from his damn parents.

I realized I was spending way too much time thinking about Sebastian, and I had enough concerns of my own. I resolved to get my résumé up-to-date, and to contact *City Beat* in the morning. And then I had an idea—it was something that might help Sebastian—and it would definitely wind up his father at the same time. Undoubtedly it would irritate David, too, that was practically a given.

Pleased with my idea, I finished up in the kitchen and hunted down my notepad. I wanted to sketch out my thoughts while they were still fresh in my mind.

I sat cross-legged on the bed and began to make some notes. I really needed internet access, but we hadn't yet got around to hooking up DSL. David expected me to take care of things like that, for once I was in agreement with him. In the meantime, I'd have to find a café with Wi-Fi, or head to the library.

"What are you doing?"

Sometimes I wondered if it would be simpler if I just gave David an itinerary of my day rather than answer his endless questions on how every hour had been spent, or was going to be spent.

"Just jotting down some notes, I had an idea for an article."

"You look tan, it suits you."

I looked up, recognizing the tone in David's voice: he wanted sex.

He took the notepad and pencil out of my hands and tossed them on the floor.

"Come here."

Dutifully, I stood up and went to him. He unzipped my dress and lifted it over my head, dropping it on top of my notepad.

I started to unbutton his shirt, but he brushed my hands away.

"Turn around."

I followed his instruction and he unhooked my bra, then briskly yanked my panties down.

"Lie on the bed. No, face down. You really have gotten some nice color today, I can see your tan lines."

I felt the bed shift as he lay down next to me.

"I've always liked you with a tan, Caroline."

He ran his hand down my spine and stroked my ass several times. I heard him undo his zipper and I rolled onto my side as he stroked himself, steadily encouraging his erection.

"Do you want me to do that?"

"Okay."

I carried on, watching his eyes close and his mouth slacken.

"Okay, that's enough."

Then he lay down on top of me, his weight forcing me into the bed, and entered me carefully. He thrust half a dozen times, shuddered, then stopped.

"Mmm!"

He lay back on the bed, smiling. I stared at the sheets. I'd have to wash those in the morning.

"What are your plans for tomorrow, Caroline?"

"I'm going to get my résumé together and then contact that newspaper I mentioned. Oh, and I'll call the telephone company to get DSL hooked up."

"Good idea. I'd like to throw a little party for the guys at the hospital—a week from this Saturday okay? About 7PM."

"Sure. Canapés and red wine?"

"Better get some beer, too. And that fancy *pressé* you like, for the wives. Maybe some of those little ... what do you call them ... cannelloni?"

"Oh, *cannoli siciliani?* Sure."

Damn it. It would take me all morning to make those.

"Great. Thanks, honey."

He heaved himself off the bed and strolled into the bathroom. I heard him pissing into the toilet bowl and, a moment later, running the faucet to brush his teeth. He flushed the toilet afterwards—that had always irritated me.

I knew from experience that I'd find his uniform tossed onto the floor. I pulled my nightgown out from under the pillow, picked up my dress and notepad, waiting for him to finish.

CHAPTER THREE

David was up and out early. Getting that promotion had made the world spin his way, for a while at least. I hoped the good mood would last. He was easier to live with when he wasn't mad at me all the time.

I wasn't keen on the idea of a party, but it was something that was expected. I looked forward to these little soirées with the enthusiasm of someone going for root canal.

I cleaned up the kitchen just in case anyone decided to drop in for coffee, then finished off the notes I'd started last night. I wasn't entirely happy with the necessity of asking Sebastian for his help, but I suspected he'd get a kick out of my idea for an article.

When I'd cornered the laptop and intimidated it into crawling into action, I updated my résumé. It certainly looked a lot better than last time I'd had to do this. Now I had solid experience under my belt, sort of, not as much perhaps as many women my age, but enough—I hoped. I also knew that the fact of my being a military wife garnered enough cachet to get me through the door. Civilians were always intrigued by the idea of a world within a world: nearby, but closed.

I called the phone company and they agreed that I'd be hooked up by Friday, and they were usually pretty good at attending to military folk. It made them feel patriotic.

Having ticked off all my chores but one, I was now faced with the tricky prospect of contacting Sebastian without raising his hopes—or getting him into more trouble with his parents. I had no idea how I was going to do that. But, unwittingly, Donna Vorstadt was kind enough to help me out.

The phone rang, loud and demanding.

"Hello?"

"Hi Caroline, it's Donna. I just thought I'd ask, if you're not too busy unpacking, some of the girls and I usually get together on a Monday afternoon and have coffee ... chew the fat. I was wondering if you'd like to join us? You'll know some of them: Penny Bishop, Estelle Hunter, Margarite Schiner."

"Oh, that's so kind of you, Donna, but I'm just up to my ears in jobs. I have to call the phone company to get DSL, David is on my case about that. And I have a thousand and one things to do. Did he mention we're having a few friends over for drinks a week from this Saturday? About 7PM. Maybe we could catch up then. And coffee another time—for sure."

She accepted my excuses with good humor and said she was looking forward to Saturday. We hung up on good terms after she gave me Estelle's number, obviously surprised by my request. Donna was easy company—I was beginning to feel she was a woman I could like.

Estelle, however, was something else altogether.

I started to dial her number and, to my surprise and chagrin, I felt a nervous knot in my stomach. *Oh, for crying out loud. You're a woman of 30!* I really didn't like having to ask her for help.

Irritated, I dialed the number.

"Hunter residence. May I help you?"

Sebastian's voice was cool and polite. I was so surprised, I couldn't speak immediately. I'd assumed he'd be at school.

"Hello?" he said again.

"Hi, Sebastian ... it's Caroline," I stuttered.

Over the phone I heard him take a sudden, sharp breath.

"Caroline, hi! How are you?"

"Good, thanks. I was expecting to reach your mother..."

"I had a free period—and I'm graduating on Thursday anyway," he reminded me.

"Oh, well, as luck would have it … I wondered if you could help me—with an article I'm writing?"

"Sure, anything!"

I tried to ignore the obvious delight in his voice.

"Well, when we were talking at the barbecue the other day, you mentioned that your friend's dad surfed—I think you said his name was Ches? Well, I wondered if you could give me his number, I'd like to speak to him."

There was a short pause.

"You want to speak to Ches?"

He sounded hurt.

"Well, I really wanted to talk to Ches's dad," I said hurriedly. "I'm writing an article about Base personnel who go surfing. I thought it would make a great piece for *City Beat*."

"Oh, right." He sounded ridiculously relieved. "Sure, I can get you that. We were going to hang out at the beach this afternoon. There's a swell coming in off the Pacific that looks awesome. Mitch was going to ride with us. You want to come, too?"

"Mitch?"

"That's Ches's dad. He's a Staff Sergeant."

"Well, that would be great. What time were you going to go?"

"About 3:45PM. We could pick you up?"

"Um … are you going to Point Loma again?"

"Maybe … we were going to sort of drive around till we found the best break."

Oh, well…

"In that case, yes, I'd love a ride. Are you sure it'll be okay with Mitch and your friends?"

"Sure!"

He answered so quickly I couldn't help a small chuckle escaping. "Well, okay, but I'd feel happier if I could talk to Mitch first."

With some reluctance that had me smiling to myself,

Sebastian gave me his friend's number and confirmed three times that he'd see me after school at 3:45PM.

I hung up, still smiling. Then I redialed for Sergeant Peters. A woman answered.

"Hi there, Peters' residence."

"Oh, good morning. My name is Caroline Wilson—I'm Commander David Wilson's wife. I was wondering if I could talk to Sergeant Peters."

"Oh. Good morning, Mrs. Wilson. This is Shirley Peters. I'm afraid Mitch isn't available at present. May I take a message?"

"Yes, thank you. This will probably sound a little odd, but I understand Mitch is taking the boys surfing this afternoon and I wondered if I could tag along."

She hesitated long enough to let me know that this sounded more than just a little odd. I rushed to fill in the blanks for her.

"It's just that I used to write some stories for the local paper back east," I said, exaggerating slightly, "and I hoped to try and do the same here—I thought an article on Base personnel who go surfing would be interesting. I was hoping your husband could give me some tips."

"Oh, I see. Well, I'm sure that Mitch will be just fine about that, Mrs. Wilson."

She still sounded surprised and I knew why—officers' wives didn't have much to do with the families of the enlisted ranks. A distinction that had always bothered me.

In the end, we agreed that Mitch would call me if there was a problem, otherwise I was to be ready to go at 3:45PM.

"Um, Mrs. Wilson, that van is pretty old, and the boys use it for all their surf stuff. It's got half the beach in there. Well, I wouldn't want you to ruin any of your clothes."

I was touched by her thoughtfulness.

"Thank you, Mrs. Peters. I'll wear an old beach dress then. Thank you so much."

After that, I felt full of energy, delighted with how the day was panning out. I drove over to the library, got online to check up on the local surf spots, and also to find out more about what kind of stories *City Beat* ran.

I just had time to stop by the Kwik Shop to stock up on groceries for supper and, as an afterthought, picked up a dozen focaccia rolls before running home to change into my old, yellow sundress and pick up my notebook.

I filled the rolls with pastrami, lettuce and tomatoes, and was finishing wrapping them up in kitchen paper and loading them into a cardboard box when I heard a horn honk outside. I grabbed my camera and notebook, swiped a bottle of *pressé* from the refrigerator and scooted out to meet my surf Svengalis.

Sebastian had already leapt out of the van, smiling hugely.

"Hi, Caroline!"

He looked so thrilled to see me, I didn't have the heart to be cool.

"Hello, Sebastian. Could you help me with this? I brought some sandwiches for you and your friends."

"Wow, thanks!"

He tucked the box under one arm and opened the passenger door. "This is Mitch, um, Staff Sergeant Peters."

Mitch Peters was a thick-set man of medium height with the trademark Marine buzz-cut. "Mrs. Wilson, pleased to meet you."

"Oh, call me Caroline, please. You're doing me the favor. I really appreciate you letting me crash your surf safari."

He smiled and his face immediately relaxed. "No problem, Caroline. It'll make these beach bums mind their manners. Right, boys?"

Then he introduced me to his son Ches, Sebastian's friend, whom I recognized from a few days back, Bill, Mitch's buddy, and another boy they called Fido, for some reason.

I sat in the front, sandwiched between Mitch and Bill, and the boys crowded into the back of the van among a motley collection of surfboards, body boards, wetsuits, and strange, shiny t-shirts that I was told were rash vests.

"To stop the wetsuits rubbing around the neck and under

the arms when you're paddling out," explained Mitch. "We won't need them today—the water at this time of year is around 63°F."

I made a note of that and snapped a quick photo of the back of the van with all the boys pulling faces and flipping the bird.

"Caroline brought food," Sebastian announced happily.

They must have all been starving because the rolls evaporated like water in the desert, and the *pressé* was passed around between them. I was sure I could have brought twice as much food, and it would have disappeared the same way.

We drove across the spectacular Coronado Bridge, then headed south, stopping occasionally for a surf check.

Mitch explained that they were looking for a steady swell and offshore breeze to hold up the waves, the best conditions for producing long, workable rides.

In the end, Mitch pulled up at the side of the road near Cays Park and the boys spilled out of the back, their reckless enthusiasm catching. Mitch and Bill were somewhat more circumspect, but I couldn't tell whether that was because of their seniority, or because I was inhibiting them from the whole male-bonding ritual.

"Just forget I'm here," I added, somewhat helplessly. "I'll just watch and soak up the vibe."

"Yes, ma'am," said Bill, smiling at me, as he tugged off his t-shirt to reveal a barrel chest, thickly coated with reddish-brown hair.

Out of the corner of my eye, I saw Sebastian scowl at him, yanking off his own t-shirt. His skin was the same beautiful, golden color that I remembered, but I hadn't noticed before how well muscled he was. All those hours of surfing had left him with long, lithe muscles, and a marvelously toned body. In fact all of them were in great shape. I wondered if I should get into surfing, although 63°F didn't sound that warm to me.

Mitch handed Sebastian a garish red and yellow board, smiling kindly. It was then I remembered that Sebastian's own father had destroyed the blue surfboard I'd first seen him with.

I took some more snaps as they posed for the camera, and then watched as they sprinted into the water and paddled out beyond where the waves were breaking. I knew from my half-hour of research that this was called the line-up. They sat there, a gaudy flock, waiting for their wave. As the swell approached, they all started paddling, their arms stroking through the sea, the green water lifting them up, they raced down the shoulder of the wave, so graceful, so powerful. It took my breath away to watch them. Then, inevitably, the wave broke and they all dived off in different directions, bobbing to the surface seconds later.

After I'd watched for a while, Sebastian caught a wave that carried him into the beach, and he jogged over to join me, flicking his hair out of his eyes, skin glistening.

"You finished already?"

"I thought it might help if I explained some more—for your article."

"That would be great—it all looks kind of the same to me."

He laughed lightly. "Not really. See, Mitch is using a long board with a rounded nose. He can work the smaller waves with that, and do some hippy shit like hang ten. Ches is riding a short board, so he can slash across the wave, catch some air and do the more radical stuff."

I had no idea what he'd just said to me—it was like learning a foreign language, but for some reason his words made me smile.

"What sort of board do you have—have you borrowed?"

"This is a short board, a thruster, same as Ches and Fido. See how fast they're going there? You can't do that on a long board."

I began to see what Sebastian meant about the surfing styles as he patiently pointed out the differences, then named and described the different maneuvers. I made copious notes and was pretty sure I could turn this into a workable article.

"How many guys on the Base surf?"

"Quite a few: once you've got your board, the ocean is free. You can be an individual out here—you know, different from military stuff."

I understood what he meant immediately: there were no rules out here, no regulations, no one barking orders at you.

"Well, there are some rules," Sebastian said, seriously. "First, you don't drop in and steal someone's wave. That's bad etiquette. The guy who takes off first—that's his wave."

"And the second?"

"You go help anyone in trouble."

Obvious, when you think about it.

"Sebastian, don't let me keep you from your friends. I'm quite happy to sit here and watch."

He shook his head and looked at me intently.

"I can surf anytime, I'd rather be here with you."

I stared down at my notepad, unsure what to say, but absolutely certain that if I looked up I'd be caught in the net of his blue-green gaze. But I also needed to be clear.

"I wish you wouldn't say things like that, Sebastian. I'm a married woman. It makes me ... uncomfortable."

I still hadn't been able to look up. I dug my toes further into the sand, as if burying one small part of my body could hide me from him.

"I really like you, Caroline," he said softly.

I felt his hand touch my arm, he was trembling.

I had to look up. His face held such an expression of longing, mixed with anxiety. I slid my sunglasses from my hair to cover my face and stood up, abruptly.

Walking along the beach and breathing deeply helped restore some of my stolen equilibrium.

Why the hell did he have such an effect on me?

But I knew why: I was attracted to him. He was beautiful and sweet and kind—and he liked me. I had no idea why. I mean, I was nothing special—just an insipid, boring woman who lived down the road from him. What on earth was there to interest someone like him?

Why had he touched me like that? He said he *liked* me— what did that mean? What did he want?

I was irritated with myself as I stalked up the beach. It was beyond ridiculous. *I* was beyond ridiculous.

He's just a kid. Write your damned article and you won't see him again.

The thoughts were a warning siren blaring through my skull.

I was relieved when Mitch paddled toward the shore. I made certain I asked him endless questions, about surfing being so resolutely non-military and a way for Base personnel to relax. I wasn't giving anyone else a chance to talk to me—certainly not Sebastian.

"Well, the thing is, Caroline, there's just *no point* to surfing," said Mitch thoughtfully. "It isn't like skiing, you can't use it for anything. You might get military skiers like they have in those Nordic countries, but the military doesn't have any use for surfing. Plus there's a certain kind of rebelliousness to surfers. Call it individualism or what you will, but some people sure don't like it."

"Donald Hunter?" I said quietly.

Mitch's eyes narrowed and he looked around quickly to make sure Sebastian couldn't overhear him.

"He'd be on the list," he said shortly.

I knew better than to pursue that line of questioning.

I glanced at my watch and realized with horror that it was already 6 PM. I couldn't believe how the time had flown. David would be on his way home, he wouldn't be pleased to find an empty house. With a sinking feeling I realized that he'd also loathe the fact that I'd been spending time with a non-commissioned officer. He felt it reflected badly on him in some way.

"You okay, Caroline?" said Mitch. "You look kinda worried."

He was too observant.

"Oh, not really. I just realized how late it had gotten. Enjoying myself too much." I gave him a weak smile. He understood me instantly.

"We'll get you home, on the double," he said good-naturedly.

He yelled toward the ocean, parade-ground loud, and gave the time-honored time-out signal.

Ches was the last to surf in, complaining bitterly that he just wanted to catch one more wave.

"We've got to get Mrs. Wilson home," said Mitch, looking pointedly at his son.

The look and his tone was enough.

We walked back to the van together, Sebastian unnaturally quiet, while the rest analyzed the afternoon's surf, talking about tubes, green rooms and wipe outs. I turned my back while they peeled off their surf-shorts and dried themselves with old beach towels, pulling on t-shirts and jeans for the drive back.

I could barely listen to their cheerful banter, tension filling me up like an overflowing drain. I did manage to pull myself together enough to ask Mitch if he would read through my article once I'd written it.

"Oh no!" he shook his head laughing. "I don't do words, Caroline, not reading and writing words. You should ask one of the boys—that's more their thing."

"Sebastian will do it," said Ches, throwing a teasing look at his friend.

Fido snickered quietly while Sebastian scowled.

"Okay with you, Seb?" asked Mitch, restoring order swiftly.

"Sure," said Sebastian quietly. "Whenever you like, Caroline."

I felt bad, he looked so miserable, but better like this than ... I couldn't bring myself to think of the alternative.

Twenty minutes later Mitch dropped me off. I raised my hand in a quick wave and sprinted to the house. The small burst of speed didn't make any difference because David's Camaro was already parked in the driveway.

I fished in my beach purse for the key and tentatively unlocked the door.

"Caroline?"

Who else?

"Hello, David. Sorry I'm late getting home."

He was waiting for me at the kitchen table. He didn't look happy—irritation rolled off him in waves.

"Where have you been? Your car was parked out front."

"Sergeant Peters gave me a ride. He was helping me out with an article I'm writing for *City Beat*."

"Peters? Which one is he?"

"Um, he lives out on Murray Ridge. He's a Staff Sergeant. His wife is Shirley."

"You know I don't like you mixing with the non-coms, Caroline," he said, with finality. "When will you understand that it undermines my authority if my wife hobnobs with the enlisted men—and their wives?"

"I'm sorry, David, but he really was very helpful. He..."

"I'm not interested in your excuses, Caroline."

I felt the control on my temper starting to slip.

"I'm not making excuses. I'm very grateful for Staff Sergeant Peters' help today."

A chilly silence descended.

"I'll go make supper," I muttered.

"Don't bother," he said sharply. "While you were absent, I made other arrangements. I'm meeting one of my colleagues in the mess. Don't wait up."

He strode out of the house and I heard the Camaro screech down the road.

I knew what this meant: David was going on one of his rare drinking binges. He'd probably be falling out of a taxi at two in the morning, breathing his beery fumes in my face.

I was glad when he went, but I knew I'd have to face his wrath at some point.

I tried to settle down and type up my notes, but the yawning absence of his disapproving presence made me restless.

It was starting to get dark, with stars appearing in the east. I dug a coat from the closet, pulled on some sneakers and headed out for a walk.

I took a circular route, wandering toward the park, when I realized that it might not be the most sensible place to be as darkness approached. I looked across and could see a man sitting on one of the benches, his sweatshirt hood pulled over his head.

I was alert but not overly worried, not yet. The quickest way home was to walk past. I debated whether this was the smart thing to do and, in the end, decided that as he wasn't looking at me, I'd risk the most direct route.

As I got closer I realized the silent figure was Sebastian. What was he doing out here by himself? I almost walked past. I really didn't need another uncomfortable encounter with him. I had enough on my plate dealing with David's petulance. But he looked so alone, that I decided to risk a quick word and make sure he was okay. I wondered if he'd had another fight with his father. I hoped it wasn't because of me again. Or, rather, because of the surfing.

"Sebastian?"

His head jerked up and he looked directly at me before dropping his eyes to the ground.

I gasped. He had a bruise across one cheek, and his lower lip was split.

"Oh, my God! Are you all right?"

What a dumb question. Any fool could see he wasn't all right.

"What happened?"

He didn't answer, but hunched his shoulders and carried on staring at the ground, as if the answer would spring from between the scraggy blades of grass.

Without any conscious decision, I raised my hand and lifted his head carefully.

He jerked his face away. "Don't look at me," he whispered.

"Did your father do this to you?"

He nodded, and a slow burning anger began to build in me.

"Sebastian, let me see. I want to make sure you're not hurt too badly."

"I'm okay," he said in a hollow voice. "I've been hurt worse than this."

The pain in his voice was more than I could bear.

I stroked his face and felt tears beneath my fingertips.

"Don't cry, Sebastian. It'll be okay."

I didn't feel any force behind my words, we both knew they were empty.

I walked around to stand in front of him. Finally he looked up and met my eyes.

"Come back to the house. I'll fix you up and drive you home. Okay?"

My words seemed to sink in slowly. He stared for a moment longer, then stood up.

He walked as if dazed, in silence, unseeing. Twice I had to stop him before he plowed into the road at an intersection. His behavior was starting to make me really worried.

When we finally got back, the house was dark. I was intensely grateful for David's continuing absence, I was certain he would have insisted on phoning Sebastian's parents had he been there—and no way would anything good result from that.

I opened the door, switching on lights as I went and led him into the kitchen. I pulled out a chair and, after a moment's hesitation, he sat down.

I had to search through several drawers before I could remember where I'd put the antiseptic cream. More urgently, I needed a cloth to fill with ice to try and take down some of the swelling. I smashed the ice tray on the counter and saw Sebastian jump.

"Oh, sorry!" I said softly. He still didn't speak.

Gently, I placed the ice pack against his cheek and lifted his hand for him to hold it in place.

I pulled down the hood of his sweatshirt and an involuntary gasp escaped. Someone—Donald, I guessed—had hacked off chunks of Sebastian's hair.

"Your father?"

He nodded, his eyes flicking to mine briefly, then away.

Fury coursed through me.

"Because of the surfing?"

He closed his eyes and nodded again.

"Because of me?" I said, my voice a whisper.

His eyes blinked open. "No, it would have happened anyway. I'd already planned to go out with Ches and Mitch today. It's not your fault..."

But it felt like my fault—I felt guilty.

"Do you want me to fix it for you?"

He didn't seem to understand my question.

"Do you want me to turn it into a buzz-cut?"

It was the only viable option, short of shaving his head completely.

"Okay."

I led him upstairs, through the bedroom and into our bathroom, pulling out a chair for him to sit facing the mirror.

"I don't want to look at myself," he said, angling the chair away so he couldn't see his reflection.

David's shaver was in the cupboard. I'd trimmed up his crew cut many times and for once I was grateful that I could perform this simple task well.

The buzzing sound filled the small room as I ran the shaver over Sebastian's head. His sun-bleached hair fell to the floor in unhappy clumps. When I'd finished I took my towel and dusted away the small hairs frosting his face and neck.

He looked older, harder, and I didn't know if this was simply the result of his new haircut or something resolving inside him.

"All done," I said hoarsely, unshed tears making my voice rough.

His head sank to his chest as if a great weight pulled it down. I was desperately tempted to run my fingers over his short, soft hair, to soothe him in some way.

"It'll be okay," I murmured pathetically.

He looked up, his eyes meeting mine. "Will it?"

"Yes. When you leave home. You won't have to see him again—either of them."

He nodded slowly, as if the thought were difficult to process.

"Would you like me to get the ice?" I said gently.

He shook his head.

"Let me look."

Gently, I lifted his chin so I could examine his cheek, the bruise was coming through darkly but his swollen lip was looking better.

Then he laid his hand over mine and I felt the shock of his touch surge through me.

"Please don't," I whispered. But there was no force behind my words.

He stood, still holding my hand.

"I love you, Caroline."

He spoke softly but the words were clear, spoken without expectation and with little hope. His eyes were wide with anxiety and I could see the rapid rise and fall of his chest beneath the sweatshirt.

Whether it was these simple words, or the look on his face, his vulnerability, or my weakness, I couldn't say.

I lifted my empty hand and stroked his cheek, then ran my fingers over the fine bristles of his hair and around to the back of his neck, pulling his head toward me.

His lips were warm and soft and a small whimper escaped me as he increased the pressure against mine.

Tentatively I let my tongue explore, gently probing his split lip, and he opened his mouth gratefully. I felt his tongue enter and desire swept through me, fanned from small flames into a raging forest fire, greedy and unstoppable. I gripped his neck with my free hand and slid my fingers from his cheek, down his throat, to his chest.

His hands hovered over my waist, and then locked themselves around me, pulling me tight, closing me in.

Every piece of my carefully constructed restraint was washed away in the flood of unfamiliar sensations.

Abruptly, I pulled back from him, my heart thundering, caged by my ribs. Fear reflected itself in his eyes and his arms hung rejected at his sides.

Could I have stopped at that point? Perhaps. A very weak, stillborn perhaps.

I was married, yes, but it wasn't much of a marriage. Everything I did or said seemed to irritate David—his habitual expression was a frown of sour discontent, a tone of annoyance whenever he spoke to me—perhaps even dislike. If there had once been love between us, it was long gone.

Uncertain of so many things about myself, about my life, I knew that I wanted Sebastian. I wanted him very badly.

My hands fastened around the hem of his sweatshirt, my intention clear. Amazement flickered across his face, followed by a heated passion that I'd never seen, never experienced before.

He raised his arms willingly and I pulled the sweatshirt over his head, letting it drop where it may.

His white t-shirt hugged his chest snugly, and I indulged in a moment of sheer pleasure, feeling his muscles through the fabric beneath my bold fingers.

I let my hand drift down to the material's edge and gently skated my fingers over the smooth, warm skin of his stomach.

He inhaled deeply and rested his hands on my upper arms, his eyes wide and wondering.

I retraced my route upwards, this time my fingers tented under the t-shirt, enjoying the ripple of muscles and the undulations of his now shallow breathing.

I stroked his skin, my eyes still fixed on his, then let my hand steal downwards toward the waistband of his jeans. My fingers drifted around the edge and a shiver ran through him.

Taking a step back, I seized the hem of his t-shirt and ripped it upwards, pulling it over his head, and kneading it in my hands before dropping it to the floor.

I took a deep breath as I allowed my eyes to drink him in, his youth, his beauty, the desire flaring in his eyes. I reached out and hooked one hand into a belt loop and let the other trace the outline of his erection, so evident through the denim.

He swallowed and closed his eyes briefly. When he opened them, I took a step forward so my breasts brushed his chest.

One hand reached up to his bruised cheek, the other an adventurer in a foreign land, continued stroking him.

Tentatively, his hands crept around my waist, so gently that they barely touched me. I pulled his face down and kissed him again. And this time he kissed me back more urgently, his tongue driving into my mouth, and I felt his hands tightening around me. Encouraged, I slipped my hand inside his jeans, and his body tensed. I could feel his heat, his nakedness beneath the denim was doubly arousing. He moaned, a long drawn out sigh of desire.

"Undo my zipper," I ordered quietly.

Fumbling slightly, he pulled down the zipper of my dress. I shrugged my shoulders, watching with distant surprise as it fluttered to the floor.

For the length of a heartbeat, Sebastian paused, and then he stepped toward me again, his hands moving from my hips to my waist, then hovering uncertainly over my breasts.

"Yes. Touch me."

I threaded my fingers through his and slowly lifted his right hand to my breast, moving in a slow circle, showing him what pleased me, letting him explore my body as I shivered beneath his touch. The sensation of flesh on flesh.

He curled his left hand behind me, slowly drifting upwards, then pressed the palm flat against my spine, his right hand now cupping my breast. He kissed me again. My own heart rate escalated and I was aware that my whole being was responding to his touch.

"Kick off your shoes. I want to undress you."

He hesitated briefly, allowing the instruction to soak into his flooded brain, then he toed off his sneakers. His feet were beautifully bare.

I pulled him toward me again and undid the button on his jeans. His eyes were huge, gazing at me with unmistakable lust. I didn't dare stop to analyze how I felt. Boldly, I unzipped his jeans and pushed the denim off his hips. I surprised him by sinking down to pull the material from his legs.

His erection was freed, and I was surprised and slightly appalled. He was so much bigger than David. I'd never been with another man before or since my marriage. I was disconcerted, knowing that Sebastian was counting on me to continue taking the lead.

I ran my careful hands up his calves, behind his knees, over and between his thighs, then let my fingers drift through his pubic hair, stroking his erection softly. It was beautiful—soft and silky on the outside, but firm, too. I'd never wanted to spend time looking at David that way: this was different. Sebastian seemed so vulnerable standing there, trusting me. I continued stroking him, gently massaging him, rubbing my fingers along his tip.

His entire body quivered, and he squeezed his eyes shut.

I stood up and undid my bra as he watched me with stunned disbelief. I took a deep breath, then hooked my fingers into my panties, pulling them off my hips and stepping out of them.

For a moment, time seemed to billow outwards as we stood and stared at each other, drinking in our nakedness.

I held out my hand and Sebastian took a step toward me. Suddenly, it was as if a switch had been flicked on inside him and he wrapped his body around me—his hands on my breasts, my shoulders, my buttocks, my thighs, his tongue in my mouth, on my neck, between my breasts, overwhelming me everywhere.

I grabbed hold of him almost violently, pushing my fingers hard against his length, I heard his breath hiss through his teeth.

I pulled his erection once again, my fingers wrapped firmly around his sweet skin. He exploded suddenly, his body shuddering. I felt the dampness on my thigh and looked down to see the pale, creamy fluid.

A familiar feeling of disappointment trickled through me. But the look on his face halted my thoughts.

Crushed by the weight of further humiliation, he shattered, falling to the floor, weeping brokenly.

"I'm sorry! I'm sorry! I'm sorry!"

He heaved out the words again and again, his face hidden in his hands.

"No, don't. It doesn't matter. It's okay," I whispered, stroking the soft, golden skin of his back.

How many times had I said those words before without meaning them? Until now.

I sank to the floor and held him in my arms, rocking him to and fro, crooning wordlessly as his sobs wracked him.

Eventually he stilled but refused to look at me.

"Sebastian, it's okay."

There was no response.

"Sebastian. Look at me."

"I'm sorry," he muttered again, his face turned away.

I wasn't sure what to do, how to show him that it didn't matter, or, at least, that I didn't think any less of him because of what had happened, or rather, not happened.

I pulled one hand away from his tear-stained face.

"Come on."

He finally looked at me, utterly bewildered.

Gently, I tugged his hand.

"Come."

CHAPTER FOUR

Sebastian looked confused as I led him back into the bedroom.

I pulled the sheets away and tried to erase the thought that this was David's side of the bed.

"Lie down."

He lay back, his beautiful eyes watching my every move. I walked around the bed to lie on my side next to him, pulling the sheet up and around us, cocooning us, protecting him.

I reached out to stroke his cheek, and his lips parted. I traced the outline of his mouth with one finger and then leaned over to kiss him, tasting salty tears.

I moved down to his throat, gentle butterfly kisses, my hair sweeping across his chest. Hesitantly, he lifted one hand, skimming along my arm to my shoulder and then, more boldly, down to my breast.

His thumb circled my nipple and I gasped with pleasure. He immediately lifted his hand away.

"No, don't stop."

I continued kissing him across his chest and down to his stomach. His hand moved to my ass, stroking it carefully.

His erection was stirring again so I kissed him there, feeling his body tremble beneath my feather-light touch.

I lay back down beside him and moved his hand to my thighs.

"You can touch me."

I guided his hand closer. Folding my fingers over his, I massaged myself with his hand, tilting my hips upwards, sucking in a deep breath when he found my most sensitive place.

"Yes, that's right. Like that."

It was pleasurable for a few moments, but I wanted more. I took his hand, folding the shorter fingers toward his palm, and slid his index finger inside me.

"Slowly. Yes, in and out."

He followed my instructions carefully, the gentle assault making me moan and writhe. I angled my hips slightly, and moved his thumb so it made sweet circles around my clitoris. I let out a long sigh of pleasure. His warm lips kissed my throat as his hand continued its steady motion.

I didn't want to have thoughts of David in my overwhelmed brain, but I couldn't help comparing ... this love-making with the selfish sexual demands usually made of me.

I reached down and stroked him, now so firm and erect. I longed to feel him inside me, but I was afraid of rushing him again.

I trapped his hand between my thighs and sat up. He looked surprised and suddenly unsure of himself. I leaned over and kissed him, more forcefully this time, rocking onto him. With his free hand, he wound his fingers through my hair and kissed me back, letting himself go further and take more.

Then he ran his hand over my breasts, and gently pulled on one nipple. The sensation was overwhelming and shocking, an orgasm taking me by surprise. His fingers must have felt the ripples of my pleasure, and he could see the way my body arched and stiffened. So unexpected, so confusing. For me, orgasms were a solitary pursuit, this was new.

"Are you okay?" he asked hesitantly.

It took me a moment to find my voice. "Yes. Very okay. Very, very okay."

And for the first time that evening, he smiled.

I'd guessed, and I think I'd guessed right, that this was all new to Sebastian, but he made me feel things I'd never experienced before—love and passion. I just hadn't realized ... I didn't know it could be like this.

"Now your turn," I said.

A quizzical expression crossed his face. Then a look of understanding as I sat up and kneeled across him. I leaned down to kiss him as his hands snaked around my back, pulling me toward him. He moaned against my mouth, and I pushed myself upright again.

This time I raised my hips and used my hands to guide him inside me. Slowly, I sank down onto him, my eyes closed, I heard him gasp.

At last I could feel every inch of him inside. I took his hands and pressed them against my belly.

"Can you feel yourself inside me?"

His face was filled with amazement.

"Yes," he whispered. "I can."

I leaned forward again, my hands resting on his chest, moving my hips up and down in a steady rhythm. He pushed his head back into the pillow, his mouth open, absorbing the new sensation. I felt his body flexing into mine, pushing himself deep inside me.

He began to move faster, more confidently, more desperately, and I let the feeling carry me with him.

I opened my eyes to find his locked on mine, almost feral in their intensity. I moved faster, meeting each movement he made, grinding down as he squeezed his eyes shut, his hands locked over mine. He came quietly as his body quivered inside me. I fell forward onto his chest, breathless and relieved.

We lay peacefully for a few minutes, and I listened to the sound of his heart, slowing to its normal rhythm. Then I slid off him and lay on my back. I think I was smiling.

I felt the bed move, and I opened one eye. He was leaning on his elbow looking down at me.

"Hi," I said, almost shyly. "You okay?"

He nodded solemnly. "That was ... that was..."

"Yes, it was."

I stroked his cheek, and his eyes closed with a sigh. Then he turned his lips toward my hand and kissed the palm. The unexpected, intimate gesture took me by surprise.

"I love you, Caroline. I always have. My whole life."

I smothered a delighted laugh.

"That's a very long time," I teased him. "You're only 18—your whole life isn't that much, really."

He smiled. "It feels like it sometimes. Anyway, I'm not 18 for another four months, I'll let you know then."

As I processed his words, cold shock rushed through me, and a look of abject horror etched itself on my face.

"What?" I couldn't believe the words he'd just said.

He looked at me, puzzled.

"You ... you're *only seventeen?*"

He nodded, his expression anxious.

"For God's sake, Sebastian! *Seventeen?*"

Shit! Shit! Shit!

He looked at me nervously. "What's the matter?"

I threw my arm over my eyes, unable to look at him. *What had I done?*

"Please, Caroline. You're scaring me."

I took a deep breath and turned to glare at him, needing to take my sudden panic and anger out on him.

"The matter, Sebastian, is that you're a minor. What we've just done ... what *I've* just done ... it's against the law. It's a felony, for God's sake!"

"But I love you."

I wanted to scream.

"Sebastian: it's *statutory rape!* Do you know what that means? I could go to prison. If anyone found out..."

"I won't tell anyone. I love..."

"Don't say it! Do *not* say it!"

sI shouted the words and he flinched.

I ran to the bathroom, afraid I was going to be sick. I held my hand over my mouth as dry heaves raked me. Tears sprang to my eyes, and I felt him hovering uncertainly behind me.

"Caroline, please."

I held my hand out like a traffic cop, stopping him from coming any closer.

What had I done?

The words echoed emptily.

"Please!" His voice was begging, desperate, but I couldn't look at him.

My skin felt icy-cold then hot with shame, as a torrent of emotion engulfed me. I staggered to the bathroom door, plucked my robe off the hook and wrapped it around me, as if the thin material could hide my crime.

I tried to push past him to the bedroom, but he blocked my way.

"Oh, God, please, Caroline!" and he tried to pull me to him.

"No!"

I made it as far as the bed before my knees gave way and I sat down, gasping.

"What have I done? What have I done?"

I hid my head in my hands and tried to fight the rising panic.

I knew he was watching me but I couldn't look. Silently, he sat down next to me.

"I'm not sorry," he whispered. "That was the best experience of my whole life. I love you, I can't help it."

And he pulled me against his chest, wrapping his arms around me, taking care of me, soothing me.

Slowly the shock wore off, and finally I was able to sit up, pushing his arms away.

"I apologize, Sebastian. It isn't your fault. Please forgive my ... behavior." I spoke coldly, formally, afraid to give way to further emotion. "I think you'd better leave now."

"Please. Don't send me away."

His voice was husky.

When I didn't reply, he stood up and walked into the bathroom, his eyes downcast, searching the floor for an answer that wasn't there. I could hear the soft rustle of material and I knew he was getting dressed.

I hurried into the kitchen, needing activity to stop my hands from shaking. I cleared away a puddle of melting ice, and threw the antiseptic cream into the nearest drawer.

Then I leaned over the sink, trying to force some coherent thought into my befuddled brain. I heard his quiet footsteps on the linoleum and, taking a deep breath to calm my nerves, I turned to face him.

The expression on his face shocked me: he looked so broken.

"Oh, Sebastian!"

And I started to cry.

Half a heartbeat later I was in his arms, my cheek against his chest, and he was stroking my hair.

"Don't be sad, Caroline, I love you. It'll be okay."

I was crying and laughing and crying. How ridiculous. Of course it wasn't going to be okay. How ridiculously happy and terrified and happy I felt.

I lifted my head, aware that I was red-eyed and hideous.

He wiped my tears with his thumbs.

I thought he was going to speak, but then we heard the sound of a car outside.

"David!"

Panic lanced through me.

"You have to go! Quickly! Out through the backyard. Go!"

He turned to run to the door, then skidded to a halt. "When will I see you again?"

"I don't know! Go! Go!"

"Promise I'll see you again! Promise me!"

"Okay, I promise!" I said desperately, staring aghast at the front door.

He pulled me to him, kissing me fiercely. And then he was gone.

Trying to breathe naturally, I ran to the bedroom, straightening the sheets, plumping up the pillows where Sebastian had been just a few minutes before. There was no time to change the sheets and I felt faintly appalled by the thought of David sleeping where Sebastian and I had made love.

I heard his key in the lock, and then remembered that I'd shaved Sebastian's hair in the bathroom. I raced in and fell to my knees, sweeping up the sun-blond hair with my hands and tossing it down into the toilet bowl.

A sudden desire to have something of Sebastian made me pick up one lock and shove it deep inside the pocket of my robe. Then I pulled the handle and watched fascinated as the rest of the hair was swirled away. I splashed some water on my face and ran a brush through my knotted hair.

I heard a crash in the living room. As I'd expected, David was drunk.

"Car'line ... Car'line."

He saw me and licked his lips.

"Beau'ful Car'line. *Bella, bella!*"

I tried to lift one of his arms over my shoulder so I could help him to the bedroom, but he pushed me off, tugging open my robe. He ran his hands over my breasts as I tried again to steer him stumbling toward the bedroom.

"Come on, David, give me some help here."

"What I'd like to give you, Car'line. C'mere."

He tried to grab me again but missed and fell face first onto the bed. He was asleep instantly.

With relief, I straightened my robe and then pulled off his shoes and socks. His uniform would be un-wearable in the morning.

Glad of something to do, I hunted around in the closet until I found a clean shirt and the rest of his spare service summer whites. The pants would need pressing.

I'd tucked the portable ironing board into a closet in the utility room. I pulled it out, wincing when a mop clattered to the floor. But David didn't stir.

I set the iron to 'hot', finding some equilibrium in the familiar drudgery.

I was appalled by what I'd done. What part of 'forsaking all others' wasn't clear? And with a *child!* Dear God! I deserved to burn in purgatory for all eternity. But I couldn't think of Sebastian as a child, even though the law defined him as such. He'd made love to me, we'd made love together.

I knew it was wrong: I knew it was right.

I'd have to leave. I'd have to persuade David to take an assignment somewhere else. But what excuse could I give? That I missed my friends on the east coast? No, that wouldn't even give him pause for thought during the length of a coffee break. That I wanted to be nearer to my mother? No, he'd never believe that. My brain was empty of further excuses.

Maybe *I* could leave? Leave David, start again somewhere else—no job, no home, no money? It was a terrifying prospect. I'd never been alone my whole life, I didn't know how to do it.

Miserable, pathetic, *whore!*

And then a new fear threatened to derail me—I hadn't used any contraception.

"NO!"

I wailed out loud, then threw a hand over my mouth. "Shit! SHIT!" David grunted but carried on snoring.

I wasn't on the pill, I had no need—David was as infertile as the Gobi desert. But Sebastian ... oh God!

I tried to organize a list of urgent jobs for the morning but all I could think was, *what if I'm pregnant?* For the briefest of moments I imagined an alternative universe where I was the mother of a blond-haired child with eyes the color of the ocean, with a husband who loved me. But that's all it was: a moment.

Plan B Emergency Contraceptive—that was my priority. At least I could buy it over the counter. I'd have to drive into the city or somewhere I wasn't known.

How could I be so stupid?

Everything I'd done in the last 12 hours had been lunacy. What on earth was wrong with me?

I realized belatedly that I'd ironed David's pants to within an inch of their shiny-ass life. I let the iron cool and tiptoed into the bedroom to lay out the rest of the uniform. David was K-O-ed. I stared down at the man who was my husband, for better or worse. I gazed for so long, my eyes were dry. How curious. I couldn't put a name to what I felt when I looked at him. Maybe something, maybe nothing. My emotional gauge was running on empty, I think it had been that way for a long time. Until Sebastian ... no. Must not think. Must not think like that.

Back in the kitchen I fixed myself a coffee which I didn't drink, and waited solemnly for dawn.

As the sun's first light filtered weakly through the windows, I had resolved nothing. Go or stay? Stay or go? The devil I knew or the deep blue sea? Go or stay? Stay or go? Endlessly repeated through the torpor of my mind.

The doleful ring of the bedside alarm made me jump. David snorted awake, and I hurried to make breakfast. He liked it hot and greasy after a bender. Luckily, yesterday's sprint to the store had furnished the refrigerator with bacon and maple syrup. I whipped up some pancake mix and put a dab of oil in the pan.

He arrived at the breakfast table with military precision and in a full-on sulk.

"Nice to see some food for a change," he muttered.

"How many pancakes do you want?"

"Two."

Silently I served him the guilty-wife special: three pieces of bacon, two eggs sunny-side up, two pancakes, syrup on the side and coffee.

"This plate's cold."

"You want me to heat it up?"

"I haven't got time for that. Christ, Caroline! Can't you do anything right?"

No. Probably not.

He left the house without a word. I wondered how long his sulk would last—nine days was the record.

Belatedly, it occurred to me that Sebastian would probably come looking for me once he was sure David had gone to work. I knew it was cowardly and unfair, and I was *supposed* to be the adult—but I just couldn't face him.

I showered on the double and ran out of the house without

bothering to dry my hair, scooping up my notebook from the hall table as I passed. I couldn't say why—perhaps some atavistic memory of needing to write, from a time when life was simple.

As I drove away, I refused to look in the rear-view mirror. I had an almost superstitious belief that if I looked, Sebastian would appear. Cowardly to the last, it seemed.

I was ridiculously grateful to find an out-of-town mall with a drugstore sign in cheerful neon, the 'Good Morning Pharmacy'. *Not for me.*

The woman serving was sympathetic until she happened to see my wedding ring, then the shutters of disapproval came crashing down and I slunk out, clasping my paper bag.

I hunted for a coffee shop and sat hunched in the corner to order a double espresso and a glass of water.

The Plan B Emergency Contraceptive packaging scolded:

'Side effects may include changes in your period, nausea, lower abdominal pain, fatigue, headache and dizziness.'

I don't care! Just don't let me be pregnant!

I swallowed the pill quickly, then tore up the packaging into postage stamp-sized pieces. My hands were shaking as I sipped the espresso. I probably looked like another caffeine junkie after my fix.

I had to find a way to channel the flurry of half-formed thoughts that gushed through me. Eventually I pulled out my notepad, trying to make sense of the scrawled words and phrases. Working slowly and carefully, I started to plan my article. It felt important, somehow, that of the complete fuck-up I'd made of my life, that I do this one thing well.

I realized I'd been working for over an hour when the irritated waitress asked me if I wanted anything else.

Yes, a life! Oddly enough, that's not something waitresses served up on a regular basis. I removed myself from her baleful gaze, leaving a larger than deserved tip. *Coward.*

I hid in my car and wondered what to do next. If I went home, I knew Sebastian would be waiting for me. I didn't know what to say, and I was afraid of how much more damage I'd done.

"Are you all right, miss?"

A worried looking man in a Padres baseball cap knocked on my car window, making me jump.

I wound the window down halfway.

"Oh, thank you. I'm fine, really."

"You were sitting there for so long I was starting to get worried. You sure you're okay?"

What was it about the kindness of strangers that made me want to weep?

"I've just got a few things on my mind, but I'll be okay. Thank you for your concern. That was very sweet of you."

He nodded, smiled uncertainly and ambled off.

The car engine started with a roar, and I was soothed by the familiar grating sound the gear shift made as I reversed out of the parking space. I drove without a destination, idly wondering what problems troubled other drivers locked in their glass and metal worlds, individual and isolated. Were they pondering the meaning of life, itemizing shopping lists in their heads, or simply idling in traffic, minds full of happy non-thoughts?

The June gloom of early morning had given way to hazy sunshine as I found myself driving along a quiet stretch of Pacific coast. It seemed as good a place as any to brood. The air was mild and a light breeze stirred the stubby grass that tried to maintain a foothold among the dunes.

I kicked off my sandals and felt the fine grit beneath my toes. My thoughts turned inward as I wrapped my arms around my knees and gazed out toward the ocean. Had I reached a turning point in my life, or was this merely a blip on a long and bleak horizon? Was leaping from a failed relationship to a doomed one the most sensible action for a woman of thirty? Rationally, no. But the feel of Sebastian's body against mine, inside mine, his sweetness, his gentleness. Could I really say that meant nothing? Were those feelings so abundant in my life that I could count them worthless?

The only real love I'd known in my life had been from my dear, chaotic father. Sebastian hadn't even had that. He was hungry for love.

Could I help him? Answer: I couldn't. I would only hold him back from all the wonderful things he deserved from life. So I had to let him go.

But where did that leave me? Contemplating leaving everything I had ever known because of one ill-advised hour of passionate lunacy. If I left David, I was well aware I would have nothing, not even my reputation. I had never lived on my own, never lived on what I could earn, never lived without the say-so of someone else. The unknowingness was terrifying.

I sat and stared until I realized with vague surprise that the shadows were beginning to lengthen around me.

I unclamped my hands and stood up stiffly, watching with fascination as blood flowed back toward my white knuckles. I'd wasted a whole day and resolved little—except that Sebastian deserved better than me.

Dread settled like a toad in my stomach. I didn't know how I could face David after what I'd done. I'd got away with it in so far as he hadn't caught us, caught me, last night, but I'd never kept a secret from him before—I had no idea how I was going to start. How could I school my face to stone in the next 30 minutes?

I made it home shortly before six, his usual home-time, unsure if I was relieved or disappointed that the house stood silent, untroubled by either friendly or malign presence.

I threw myself into cooking: spaghetti alla puttanesca— tomatoes, olives, chili pepper, capers, garlic. It seemed appropriate—the Whore's Spaghetti. Odd to think I'd planned that meal yesterday, when I was still an honest wife.

Hearing David's car in the driveway brought me sharply back to the present.

Set the table. Place the napkins. Open his beer. Pour it in a glass. Wash the salad. Act normal.

"Hi, supper is nearly ready," I said as brightly as I could manage, my voice sounding shrill and insincere to my ears.

He ignored me entirely. Oh, of course, he was still sulking. That made things easier.

We ate in silence. I cleared the plates without a word. He retired to his study. Not a syllable had passed our lips.

I was grateful to him. It made things so much simpler.

To my bemusement, I was able to concentrate on writing up my surfing story that I hoped *City Beat* would publish. The words flowed and it was therapeutic to spend the evening in a happier place.

At 11PM, David exited his study and headed for the bedroom. *I wish I'd remembered to wash the sheets today. Whore.*

I observed dispassionately that he deliberately balled up his clothes and flung them onto my side of the bed, knowing I'd have to get up early to press the pants—again.

He returned from the bathroom marching with stiff, military precision in his ironed PJs. I had an almost irresistible urge to laugh.

The sheets were thrown back with disdain and he turned sharply, hauling the bedspread onto his side. How marvelously childish.

Smiling to myself, I slid between the sheets and dared myself to feel hopeful.

~

By morning I knew I couldn't put off facing Sebastian any longer. I suspected that if I waited at home long enough, he'd appear. I probably had a few minutes to dash to the store to buy milk, vegetables and candy.

I didn't linger over my purchases, but even so, when I turned into the driveway, there he was, sitting huddled in my porch. At least he was hidden from the road.

My stomach flipped over.

His eyes lit up when he saw me, and he went to stand. I shook my head quickly and luckily he understood.

As soon as I opened the door, he slid inside unobtrusively. I still hadn't planned what I was going to say to him. I wasn't even sure it was possible to plan.

We stood looking at each other, the door unyielding against my back.

"Are you okay?" he said at last.

I nodded slowly. "I guess. You?"

"I ... I had to see you."

"Come in," I said, somewhat reluctantly, pointing to the kitchen. "Can I get you a coffee?"

He shook his head.

This was harder than I'd expected and I'd barely said a word. I sank into a kitchen chair while he continued to stand.

"I tried to see you yesterday. What happened after I went? Was it ... okay?"

His voice was low, hesitant.

"David didn't suspect, if that's what you mean."

By contrast my voice was unnecessarily harsh.

Sebastian's eyes reflected his hurt.

"Don't look at me like that," I said coldly.

You can do this. You can let him go.

"Caroline..."

"What?"

He took a deep breath.

"I've been thinking about you ever since..." His words came out in a rush. "We can go back east if you like, wherever you want. I can get a job."

I stared at him, stunned.

"We can be together," he whispered. "Forever."

I didn't know whether to laugh or cry, instead I continued to sit and stare.

"Caro?"

Caro? Oh, I liked that ... what a lovely dream.

"Caro!" he said, sounding panicked.

But just a dream.

I sat at the table and rested my head in my hands. This wasn't what I'd expected, it certainly wasn't how I'd planned the course of the conversation. Where was my resolve to end this?

I heard a chair scrape across the floor and he sat down next to me.

His beautiful face, so earnest, was just inches from mine. I straightened up and looked at him directly.

"Sebastian, I think you're very sweet but..."

He cringed as if I'd slapped him.

"Give me a chance—I know we can make it work, Caro."

"No, we can't. You're only 17 ... I could be arrested. I *should* be arrested! No, listen to me! The other night was..." I hesitated, unable to find the right word. "But the point is, it was wrong."

"Not for me."

I sighed. Again I recalled the sensation of his body against mine, how good it had felt. Good, bad, wrong, right.

"Then we'll wait until I'm 18," he said defiantly. "It's not so long. We can be together and no one can stop us."

Stupidly tempting.

"I'm married, Sebastian." *You were married two nights ago. Whore!*

"You don't love him, Caro."

My eyes darted to his. *How did he know?*

He sensed a small victory and pursued his advantage, grasping my hand.

"I love you. I'll ... I'll do anything, go anywhere. You can do your writing—we'll be happy."

So, so tempting. And his touch: flesh on flesh.

My traitorous mind filled with images of our sweet, gentle, glorious love-making. I'd never been touched like that before—it had been an education, a delicious, dangerous awakening.

He could sense the feebleness of my will. His lovely eyes were unclouded, free of all doubt, confident and reassuring. And when he leaned forward pressing his lips lightly against mine, it was a peaceful moment at the heart of a whirling pool of emotions. It was an electric moment, the eye of the storm.

I tried to understand the feelings that filled me, making me lighter than air. I felt beautiful for the first time in my life, safe and secure.

Loved.

Cherished.

He gathered me to him and I clung to the protective circle of his arms, feeling the warmth of his body, and listened to the steady beating of his heart.

Had David ever told me that he loved me? I couldn't remember that far back. I knew he was cold and controlling, and I knew that he didn't love me. Sometimes it felt like I was utterly despised.

And finally my poor, starved heart caught up with what Sebastian had been saying: he loved me. He'd always loved me. Such a balm to my shrunken soul. My damascene moment hit me with extraordinary clarity.

I loved him, too.

CHAPTER FIVE

A SUMMER OF STOLEN HAPPINESS—THAT'S HOW I REMEMBERED the days that followed. The storm clouds gathered in the distance while my days with Sebastian were filled with light.

We knew we had to be careful. The military was a close-knit family and, like all families, the whisper of disapproval was never far away.

Daytime was easier. David worked until 6PM most days and every third weekend, but now Sebastian had finished with school for good, his time was his own. Estelle had persuaded Donald of the benefits of a college education for their only child and, as far as they knew, Sebastian was due to start at UCSD in the fall. Only his mother had reluctantly attended his graduation, Donald being far too busy to attend such a trivial event, and Sebastian had shyly shown me the formal photograph of himself in his cap and gown. My own graduation seemed a shadow in another lifetime.

The hard part was knowing that we couldn't be together intimately—I was quite clear about that. But the more I saw him, the more I spent time with him, the harder it became. He was beautiful inside and out. I loved the way he looked at the world, with such zest and enthusiasm, despite the coldness of his parental home. He soaked up every smile, every hesitant touch that I could give him. But I knew he wanted more, and so did I. Pandora's Box had been opened, and it was proving very hard to keep the lid closed. No matter how hard I tried to ignore it, the intense memory of our night of love-making was ever present in my thoughts, I was pretty certain Sebastian felt the same.

We were sitting huddled together, sheltered by a sand dune, while a short shower clouded the horizon, a picnic blanket swaddling us.

"Caro, you know you talked about wanting to go back east —did you mean North Carolina or Maryland?"

"Not Maryland," I said, shuddering at the thought of being in the same state as my mother. "I was just thinking about getting as far away from here as possible. No, it doesn't have to be there or North Carolina. Why? Did you have somewhere in mind?"

"Well," he said hesitantly, "I was thinking maybe we could go to New York City. It should be easy to get work there, right?"

"I guess."

I wasn't sure I wanted to live in a city that size but after a moment's thought, I could definitely see the benefits. For one thing, we'd be harder to track. Sebastian was right about the increased chances of finding work. But I was also rather intimidated by the sheer scale of what we'd be undertaking. I'd been there twice, and each time had quailed at the speed at which everything happened. I was afraid I'd be lost. But ... with Sebastian? I wouldn't have to face it alone. I wouldn't have to face anything alone ever again.

"I looked at some courses at NYU," he said, in a voice that was just one shade too casual to be believable.

"And?"

"Nothing, really. I just thought it would be cool—you and me in the Big Apple."

"Sebastian, I don't mind where we go. If you want to go to New York, if you've seen some courses that interest you, then that's what we'll do."

"Really?"

He beamed at me.

"Of course! It's just as much your future as mine." *Or more.*

In secrecy, we planned for Sebastian to apply to NYU with his courses starting in the spring semester. We—and I delighted in that small pronoun—would leave California as soon as he was 18 on October 2nd, and hoped to hide in the anonymity of the gray metropolis. I would, of course, find work as a journalist, and undoubtedly we would be happy.

I was swept up in that delicious dream. I couldn't fully hide my happiness, someone was bound to notice.

"Caroline!"

Donna Vorstadt's voice interrupted my happy musings in the Kwik Shop.

"How are you? Johan and I are really looking forward to your little soirée tomorrow."

My brain lurched to attention. Had she seen me arrive with Sebastian? No, she was still smiling, acting normally—unlike me.

"Oh, yes, of course! Sorry, my mind was elsewhere."

So true.

"It must have been somewhere lovely—I called your name three times!"

I flushed uncomfortably and she raised an eyebrow, but was kind enough not to pursue the point.

"David told Johan that you'll be making some of your delicious little Italian delicacies."

She glanced, puzzled, at my cart. A milk carton and bottle of olive oil blinked back at her.

"I prefer to cook everything from fresh," I muttered, improvising wretchedly.

"Of course," she smiled. "Well, I'll leave you to it. Oh, look! There's the Hunters' boy over by the cold meat counter. He's cut his hair. Goodness! Sebastian! Yoo-hoo!"

A brief expression of horror swept over his face before he schooled his features into blankness. He walked toward us, warily.

"Hi, Mrs. Vorstadt." He paused. "Mrs. Wilson," he muttered.

"Hello, Sebastian," she said, eyeing his buzz-cut. "Are you shopping for your mother?"

"Um..."

"That's awfully good of you. I wish I could get my boys to do chores around the house. They think food just materializes into the refrigerator."

I laughed weakly and Sebastian smiled, giving a vague, non-committal answer.

"Can I give you a ride home, Sebastian?" Donna offered kindly.

"No, thanks, Mrs. Vorstadt, I'm good."

She smiled. "Well ... see you tomorrow, Caroline."

"Bye."

Eventually she disappeared behind the frozen goods and I let out a sigh of relief. I didn't realize I'd been holding my breath.

"We must be more careful," I whispered.

Sebastian nodded solemnly, but there was a glint of amusement in his eyes.

"What?!"

He shook his head, a small smile escaping. "Let's get out of here."

I abandoned my few goods with the shopping cart, much to the irritation of the staff, no doubt, and headed for the parking lot. Our exit was certainly more discreet than our shopping expedition.

I slipped into the driver's seat feeling elated and guilty at the same time.

Sebastian let his fingers drift down my neck, a shiver ran through me.

"Not here!"

"Where then?"

"Let's go to the beach."

He grinned. "Perfect."

As I drove, he fiddled with the radio and picked up a station playing cool, ambient jazz.

"Mom and Dad have been on my case about getting a summer job," he said casually.

My heart sank—if he worked all day, I'd never see him. I couldn't go out in the evenings, not without facing the inquisition from David.

"What sort of job?"

He shrugged. "Ches says I could get a job bussing tables at the place he works—the country club out at La Jolla."

"That sounds ... fun."

"Mostly evening shifts, Caro. I'll still be free during the days."

I smiled with relief. "By the way, I'd like you to read my surfing article, just to make sure it's okay."

"You finished it?"

He sounded surprised.

"Sure! What else is there to do in the evenings?" I said, teasing.

He scowled. "I hate you going home to that asshole."

I sighed. "Me, too, but it's not for much longer."

The truth was that I found David's brittle company almost unbearable. I honestly didn't know if I'd be able to last four months. I'd been turning over in my mind the possibility of moving out—but I was scared and had little money of my own.

I banished the thought of David: here and now was for Sebastian.

"Which beach should we go to?"

"There's a place I know not far from here. There's a beach shack, too, so we should be able to get some food."

I smiled to myself—the boy could *eat*.

No, not a boy, I snarled.

But the part of my brain where I parked all my miscreant thoughts was getting pretty damn crowded.

We drove with the windows down, Sebastian leaning back lazily, singing along softly to the radio, while the wind tangled my hair.

Sebastian was showing me a side of San Diego that I'd never seen before—the chilled out, laidback beach community that would have given David hives.

The girl working the counter of the beach shack eyed Sebastian with interest. I watched her follow his progress around the store. She was pretty, a stereotypical California girl with long, blonde hair, long tanned legs, and long, false eyelashes. To my amusement and delight, Sebastian didn't appear to notice her.

"What do you want to eat, Caro? They've got tuna on wheat or meatloaf on rye."

"I'll just have a soda and a small bag of chips."

He frowned. "That's not very healthy."

He looked so serious, standing there in his cut-offs and surfer t-shirt, I couldn't help a broad smile.

"Then I'd better have the tuna, kind sir."

"Are you laughing at me?"

"Just a little, but in a good way. You're so sweet!"

He looked like he wasn't sure whether or not that was a compliment, but shrugged it off.

I paid for the food, irritated with myself for recalling that the money came from the housekeeping David so grudgingly gave me. To hell with it! I earned every penny: cooking, cleaning, ironing his damn pants—even entertaining his colleagues.

The cashier loaded our purchases into a carrier which Sebastian tucked under one arm, with the briefest of smiles at her. Then he took my hand.

He took my hand!

David never held my hand. Well, perhaps once—the day of our marriage, when my father had given it to him. Not since then, not that I could remember.

It felt wonderful and terrifying, strolling along the beach, our fingers learning the lines and shapes of each other's hands.

We found the perfect dune, a concave dip among the marram grass. It gave us some slight protection from the prevailing wind, although it was gentle today, but, more importantly, it gave us privacy from anyone watching from the beach.

Shyly, I pulled a copy of my surfing article out of my bag.

"This is it."

He sank down to the sand and sat cross-legged. I watched his face anxiously as he read. It was the first time I'd shown anyone my writing. I badly wanted him to like it. I felt like I'd launched a baby out into the world and was waiting for someone to tell me whether or not I had an ugly child.

Once or twice Sebastian smiled as read through the pages, then he looked up.

"It's really good."

I looked at him, skeptically.

"It is! I really liked the joke about the Hawaiian Surfers Marine Corps storming up the beach to invade, but deciding to catch one more wave first."

"You really liked it?

"It's good, Caro."

"You'd say that anyway."

He smiled.

"Probably, but I mean it. It gives people an insight into surfing and the Military way of doing things. It's clever. There's just one thing..."

I knew it.

"You've got a spelling mistake there: you've put 'truster' instead of 'thruster'."

"Where? Show me."

He laughed. "Just kidding."

I raised an eyebrow. "Hmm, imagine getting the thrusting wrong."

He gaped at me as I lay back on the warm sand, basking in the sudden heat of his gaze.

"You are so beautiful, Caro," he whispered, unwinding his long legs so he was stretched out next to me.

I grinned stupidly at him.

"You are!" he insisted.

He was leaning on one elbow, his head resting on his hand. Out here, his eyes looked slate-green and his skin glowed gold in the sun.

"You're the beautiful one, Sebastian. Beautiful inside and out."

He blinked, surprised at my words, then smiled. Another chip of ice dropped from my heart.

"I think you should kiss me."

The words were out before I knew what I'd said. I really meant them.

"I thought we weren't going to ... you know ... until I was 18."

"That's right, but that doesn't mean you can't kiss me."

"Really?" He looked delighted.

"Perhaps you'd prefer a written invitation?"

"Not necessarily," he whispered.

I wrapped my arms around his neck and pulled his head down toward me, stroking his short, silky hair. His gentle lips touched mine and desire exploded inside me, rushing through my veins like quicksilver. A soft, wordless sound escaped him, and my tongue was in his mouth, savoring his taste, tasting his own desire.

My hands ran down his back and greedily pulled up his t-shirt. My fingers turned to claws as I raked my nails down his back, making him gasp. He leaned away abruptly and tugged the material over his head, then his naked chest was pressing into me, forcing me into the sand. Against my belly, his erection was taut.

God! How I wanted him. To renew the sensation of him inside me, to understand, to feel that I was desired and loved and needed.

He forced one leg between mine and ran his hand along my bare skin, up my knee, my hip, teasing the material of my panties, before moving up to my waist and then running his hand over my breast and squeezing gently.

I was desperate to take it further but I was held back by the thin edge of reason, and the knowledge that one more step would tip me into the darkness.

"We have to stop," I groaned against his lips.

"No," he gasped.

His hand moved determinedly under the thin fabric of my strappy t-shirt, stroking and caressing my breasts.

My breathing was becoming ragged, as if I was running.

Summoning my final ounce of will power, I pushed feebly against his chest.

"No, Sebastian."

He stopped instantly, and with a soft moan, rolled onto his back.

"I want you, Caro," he breathed out. "I want to make love to you. I want to make love to you forever."

My breath caught in my throat.

I want that, too. So much.

I didn't answer, but lay unmoving, feeling my body float back to earth.

Out of the corner of my eye, I saw him adjust himself. I felt guilty for making him uncomfortable.

Hell, was there anything I didn't *feel guilty about?*

"Is this what it's going to be like for the next four months?" he said, sounding aggrieved.

"Or I could join a convent," I muttered, almost to myself.

"I'd still find you," he said darkly.

I smiled.

"Okay, no convents. Or monasteries, come to think of it."

I fished around for a new topic of conversation.

"Tell me about this job you mentioned. When do you start?"

"I haven't applied for it yet."

"Why not?"

"I wanted to make sure it was okay with you first, Caro."

I was surprised. Yes, that was the word, surprised and plain amazed.

"You ... you were waiting for ... what, my permission?"

"Well, not exactly." He sounded puzzled. "So we could discuss it together and then decide."

Oh. Like a real couple.

David never discussed anything with me, I simply received his Decree from on high.

"And you'll be working the late shift? Well, that sounds fine to me."

"Great!" he said and turned on his side to look at me, smiling. "I'll have to do some day shifts, maybe. The pay is shit but Ches said the tips are pretty good, especially from older women."

I winced and his expression froze.

"I didn't mean ... I don't think of you like that! Caro, no!"

But the genie was out of the bottle, a vintage one at that.

"It's not far off the mark, Sebastian."

He sat up, his face alarmed.

"Don't say that! I love you so much, Caro. I ... what I feel for you ... I've never..."

He grabbed my hand and held the palm against his cheek.

I sat up, too, shaking sand from my hair.

"It is what it is, Sebastian."

We sat in silence for some minutes.

I could tell he was mortified, wishing his candid words unsaid.

"So," I said at last, my tone deliberately light, "no girls at high school who grabbed your attention? No cheerleaders waving their pompoms at you?"

He smiled ruefully, relieved, I thought for yet another change of topic.

"Not really."

"Not really isn't not at all. Tell me, I'm curious."

He sighed. "They didn't mean anything."

I couldn't help laughing. "I'm not jealous, Sebastian!"

But even as I said the words, I wasn't entirely sure they were true. I remembered the hungry look of the surf shack girl and how much I'd wanted to punch her vapid smile into the back of her throat.

"What do you want to know?" he said in a resigned voice.

"It's not important, honestly, I was just curious."

He lay back on the sand, his eyes closed.

"It's always been you, Caro. The first time I saw you, I thought you were the most beautiful girl that I'd ever seen. I thought you must be a princess, like Cinderella. It's only ever been you."

I was stunned by his reply.

Yes, a fairy tale. That's what this was—a lovely fantasy. But somehow I couldn't bring myself to care. I longed to run my fingers down his smooth skin, over his bare chest, across the defined muscles of his stomach. My gaze lingered on the waistband of his cut-offs.

"What about you?" he said, his eyes still closed.

"What about me what?"

"Did you go out with anyone before ... before David?"

I didn't really want to hear David's name and certainly not from Sebastian's lips, but it was a fair question.

"I dated a few times in high school—movies, bowling, that sort of thing. I met David when I was in my senior year."

"My age," he said softly.

"Yes."

Where was he going with this?

"Did you ... did you ... sleep with him then?"

I really didn't want to go there.

"Yes."

"But you won't sleep with me?"

"Oh, Sebastian! Please don't do this!"

"But I don't understand. You were my age. You just said so. How can it have been right then and wrong now?"

He sounded really angry and he turned his head away from me.

"Please don't, Sebastian."

My voice was suddenly hoarse with tears.

He didn't reply.

I swallowed and took a deep breath.

"Because we were in Maryland and the age of consent is 16. It wasn't illegal."

"And that's the only reason?" he muttered.

"Of course!"

He paused and then said,

"Are you still sleeping with him?"

"What?" I choked the word out.

His voice was barely a whisper. "Are you still sleeping with him? Now, I mean."

This was ghastly.

"We share a bed, Sebastian, but we haven't … had sex. Not since … you … since us."

I thought that would be enough, but I was wrong.

"Are you going to sleep with him? While you're still living there?"

He turned toward me, his face desperate.

"Will you, Caro?"

Appalled by the direction of his interrogation, I closed my eyes and spoke with a cold, controlled voice.

"The thought of David touching me is utterly repellent, Sebastian … but my husband is not a patient man."

I heard him gasp.

"You mean he'd *force* you?"

Sebastian's voice was horrified. I saw rage flare in his eyes, his expression scared me.

"No, not the way you mean…"

"You can't, Caro! You can't let him! Promise me you won't let him touch you."

How on earth could I keep that promise? I wanted to, desperately.

"I'll try."

He looked like he wanted to say more.

"Sebastian, it's a beautiful day, we have a few precious hours left, please let's not spend it fighting." *Or talking about David.*

He took a deep breath. "When I think of him touching you, I just…"

"Please, don't."

"I'm sorry."

We paused, our lives at opposite sides of a gorge, a delicate tightrope stretched between us.

He reached over and pulled me to him, so I was splayed across his chest.

"That's better," he said. "You were too far away."

I smiled sadly. His words were truer than he knew. But I was where I wanted to be, in the enchanted circle of his arms.

He nuzzled my neck, the tickling sensation making me squirm.

"You're all sandy," he murmured against my throat.

"I wonder why? Could it be because we're at the beach?" I tried to match his playful tone.

"You'll have to wash it off," he said, his voice soft and seductive.

"Mmm, I suppose I should."

He sat up quickly so I was cradled in his lap.

"I want to help with that," he said, his eyes glinting with mischief.

He stood up with me in his arms and started striding toward the sea.

"Sebastian! Don't you dare!" I half-screamed, half-laughed.

"I'm helping!" he said, smiling broadly.

And he dunked me in the sea, fully dressed.

"Aagh!"

The water was shockingly cold.

"Sebastian!" I gasped, spitting out seawater, "I'm soaking!"

"Mmm, I've always wanted to see a wet t-shirt competition."

"Sebastian!" I yelled, trying to maintain some shreds of dignity as I struggled back to the dry sand. "Just look at me! I'm furious with you!"

"What are you going to do, spank me?" he said with a wicked grin.

My mouth dropped open in shock.

"I'll think of something," I huffed ineffectually.

"Bring it on!" he replied, his tone amused.

I dripped back to our cozy dune and stripped off my strappy t-shirt and summer skirt, draping them across the long grass.

The material of both was thin so there was a good chance they'd dry out before I had to go home. If not, well, David hadn't looked in the laundry hamper in the 11 years we'd been married.

I turned to watch Sebastian. He dove through the waves, swimming strongly. I caught glimpses of him, silvery in the sea as he bodysurfed back to the beach. He saw me watching him, waved once and disappeared into the ocean again.

I lay back in the sand, a strange sensation of happiness filling me.

My underwear, however, was uncomfortably damp. I slipped off my bra and spread it out in the sunshine, then lay on my front, the coarse sand doing a better job of exfoliation than any expensive beauty salon.

The sun was deliciously warm on my back and I began to doze, lulled by the rhythm of the waves.

"You look so beautiful like that."

Sebastian's words roused me gently. His hands, however, were chilly.

"Whoa! Cold hands!"

He laughed out loud, a happy carefree sound.

"Sorry, I couldn't help it."

"You didn't try," I muttered petulantly.

"No, not really," he admitted. Then his voice was serious. "I want to touch you, Caro."

"I know. I want that, too. But we have to wait."

He groaned. "I'm going to go crazy!"

"And it's not even a full moon."

"I'd love to see you in moonlight," he said, softly.

His sudden change of tone made me look up. *What his words did to me.* No one had ever spoken to me like that. It was all so new, I was adrift in a sea of unfamiliar feelings, as innocent as Sebastian in one way at least.

I shifted my shoulders and rolled them awkwardly, I'd been lying on my front for some time.

"Are you okay?"

"Just a little stiff."

"Should I give you a massage?"

"I don't think that's a good idea."

"Why not?"

"You *know* why," I said, patiently.

"I think I'll risk it," he said and reached out, sweeping my hair from my neck, massaging my shoulders and back, running his strong, supple fingers along my spine.

The feelings that his touch ignited.

Then he knelt across me and pressed down with more force, loosening my tight muscles but stoking the flames that burned within me.

Without warning he leaned forward, kissing the nape of my neck.

I groaned and his weight pinned me down. I could feel the cool skin of his chest on my back, the chilly dampness of his sea-soaked cut-offs against my backside.

"Oh, hell!" he said suddenly, throwing himself down next to me and squeezing his eyes shut.

"What's the matter?" I said, concerned.

"Nothing," he muttered.

"Tell me!"

"I have another boner," he admitted, sounding embarrassed.

I laughed with relief. "I did warn you."

"Yeah, yeah." He paused. "Are you sure we couldn't...?"

I groaned again. "Stop trying to tempt me. When you talk like that ... I feel like there should be a booming voice coming down from the sky pointing a fiery finger at me saying, 'The devil is at your elbow, my child'."

"Oh, come on, Caro! Four months, I mean ... *four months!*"

He had a point. But so did I, and the thought made me miserable.

"Let's eat something," I said brusquely. "Could you pass me my bra, please?"

He didn't reply.

"Sebastian?"

"No," he said.

"Excuse me?"

"I don't want to give you your bra."

"Oh for goodness sake. Fine!"

I sat up and brushed sand off my breasts, stomach and arms, aware that his gaze was pinned to me.

My bra was still damp and my nipples hardened automatically as I slipped it on. I glanced across to see Sebastian's eyes wide and wanting. It made me feel like a goddess.

"You might want to put your eyes back in before they roll down the beach," I said sarcastically.

"It would be worth it," he said, his tone matching mine.

I shook my head to hide a smile, he really was incorrigible.

We ate our subs which, by this time, were rather warm and limp. The sweet soda set my teeth on edge. A bottle of chilled Sauvignon Blanc would have been perfect. Then it occurred to me that Sebastian wasn't even allowed to drink alcohol for another three years.

His youth and our age difference kept booby-trapping my happy thoughts. Everything had a price: every glance, every kiss, every stolen touch. It seemed desperately unfair—I didn't want to live without love. Why should I?

"Hey, where did you go just now?" he said softly.

"Nowhere as nice as here and now," I said honestly, and sighed.

"It'll be okay, Caro, I promise," he said.

Don't make promises you can't keep.

"I think it's time to leave," I said sadly. "I have to buy some groceries and..." my words trailed off.

I didn't want to taint him with the dreary trivia of my life with David.

"Okay," he said, trying hard to keep his voice neutral.

He stood up and offered me his hand. But he took me by surprise when he crushed me to his chest and kissed me fiercely, an edge of desperation in the way his hands tightened around my waist. I kissed him back, matching his urgency, the specter of separation hanging over us, our own invisible sword of Damocles.

When he released me, when I could bring myself to let him go, there were no words. Solemnly I reached for my wrinkled clothes and Sebastian pulled his t-shirt over his head, then collected up the abandoned food wrappers to deposit in the nearest trashcan.

It was a strangely domestic scene, at odds with the sudden tension we both felt.

We walked back to my car, each wrapped in the emptiness of our thoughts.

"So, I'll see the guy about that job with Ches?" he said at last.

"Yes, good idea," I murmured, trying to dispel the image of large tips from *older women*.

"Do you still want me to read your ideas for some more articles?" he said hesitantly.

"Oh, yes, please. I'll email them to you."

I frowned.

"What?"

"Maybe that's not a good idea. What if your parents saw that I'd been emailing you?"

He shook his head. "Mom doesn't know how to program the washing machine, let alone check my email. And Dad," he glowered, "he doesn't know my password."

"Well, okay, then," I said, reassured.

"What about David?" he said. "Does he read your email?"

I had a horrible thought that he probably did and Sebastian saw the doubt reflected on my face.

"Bastard!" he said viciously. "Set up a Gmail account, Caro, and email me from there."

"Okay," I said faintly.

"And you'd better turn your phone off when he's there so I can still text you, or he'll want to know who's sending messages. Then check in when you can."

I was so bad at the practicalities of an affair. I wondered absently where Sebastian had learned such expertise. But then, I supposed, with two controlling parents, evasive tactics were fundamental to survival.

He looked at me, frowning.

"Are you okay, Caro?"

I nearly laughed.

"It's just that I've never ... done anything like this."

"Like this?"

"Had an affair." I blushed saying the words.

"Don't say that," he said heatedly. "That's not how I think about us, Caro."

I sighed. "Neither do I—but that's what people would call it, if they knew."

"I don't care about anyone else," he said, fiercely. "Just you."

I wrapped my arms around his neck and leaned my head on his shoulder. I felt his body relax slightly.

"It's going to be a long weekend," he muttered, "not being able to see you."

"You could come to our soirée." I laughed mirthlessly. "Your parents will be there. David has invited all the *right* people."

"Perhaps I will," he said, quietly.

I looked up at him, horrified. "No! I was teasing. You mustn't. I couldn't ... if you were there I know I'd give myself away."

"But I could make sure that the asshole doesn't touch you," he snarled.

"Sebastian, no. I mean it."

He scowled at me belligerently.

"I'm not afraid of him."

"Stop it!" I said, trying to pull away, but he wouldn't let me go.

"I can't wait four months, Caro," he said, almost desperately.

I felt panicky, but at the same time, aroused by his need.

"We have to," I said, barely able to think coherently. "You know what they'd do to me."

He sighed and pulled me closer.

We'd survived another 24 hours, but it was getting harder.

I drove back with one hand in his. That small connection meant so much.

As was fast becoming our routine, I dropped him off several blocks from his home. I hated that moment of desolation when he slammed shut the passenger door and I accelerated away from him: it felt so wrong.

David's sulk had finally come to an end. Whether this was because he was over his irritation or because we had a social engagement to live up to, I couldn't say. It made things both easier and harder.

I dreaded the nights the most, that moment when he sank onto the bed. If he picked up one of his journals I could relax, if he didn't...

After dinner and after he'd spent a couple of hours in his study doing God knows what, evening had passed into night.

I was already in my nightgown when he strolled out of the bathroom and eased himself onto the bed. The journal remained on his bedside table. He looked at me expectantly.

I tried to ignore him and he frowned.

"Is everything ready for tomorrow, Caroline?"

"I need to go to the store in the morning for a few things." *Everything, in fact.*

"That doesn't sound very organized."

"I wanted the ingredients to be as fresh as possible."

He grunted, then moved his hand down to his dick, pulling it out of his PJ pants and stroking it suggestively.

"I'm a little tired tonight, David," I said, trying to stay calm.

"So am I. I'll sleep better and so will you. Come here."

I took a deep breath. "No, David. Not tonight."

He looked irritated. "Well, the least you can do is relieve me, Caroline."

I closed my eyes, but closing my mind to the sounds and sensations was not so easy.

When he was finished, I walked into the bathroom to wash my hands and stared at my impassive reflection in the mirror. David was already asleep by the time I could face going back. I stood looking down at him, wondering: who was this man I'd married? Why had he married me? Had there ever been love? I knew I had never felt this way before, the way I felt when I was with Sebastian. Was David happy? I knew he was frustrated by not having climbed the career ladder with the speed and success of other men. He didn't have friends, he networked with people who could be useful.

I lay awake for a long time, refusing to cry. I'd made my bed.

~

Saturday started with a guilty dash to the large, out-of-town grocery store.

David had enticed his colleagues with promises of fine Italian cuisine—I doubted it was his sunny personality and winning ways that made so many people desirous of attending our supper party—so fine cuisine was what I had to supply. All homemade. David wouldn't allow anything pre-prepared—he liked to see me busy in the kitchen.

I checked my phone as soon as I left the house but there were no messages from Sebastian. I decided to text while I was out and hoped that'd he'd reply quickly while I dared to leave my phone on.

Am shopping but thinking of you. Cx

I was stupidly happy when he replied immediately.

I think of you all the time x

I read the simple message three times and then, with a sigh, deleted it. Now I had groceries to buy: I had to be *that* person —David's wife.

Ninety minutes later I staggered into the house, bowed under the weight of a multitude of loaves and fishes, and unloaded all the grocery bags into the kitchen. David was doing something in his study—he was too busy and important to help me. I hoped I'd bought enough for the 35 people I was expected to feed.

At noon I made him a quick sandwich and delivered it

express. I surprised him. He snapped shut the lid of his laptop as I entered, but not before I'd seen that he was playing card games. Yeah, too busy to help me. Not that I cared anymore, but it was another irritant. I realized my tolerance levels were being eroded—every moment I spent with Sebastian made the long hours with David more unbearable.

By early evening I was exhausted. I'd been standing in the kitchen all day and I felt tired and bad-tempered. David wandered in fresh from the shower and eyed the buffet table with the air of a lord surveying his fiefdom.

"You're not ready," he said, gazing at me in my flour-stained, rumpled apron.

"I've just spent seven hours cooking, David."

"You look like it."

I turned on my heel. He couldn't even bring himself to say a simple 'thank you' or that the food looked damn fine, which it did. Bastard.

I thought again about Sebastian's words: *four months*. I was beginning to think I wouldn't last that long either.

Then I saw that the dress I'd laid out to wear tonight had slid off the bed. David would have had to step over it three or four times as he'd moved around the bedroom, but he'd left it in a crumpled heap.

His pettiness filled me with sudden fury. I supposed his childish behavior was punishment for not fully attending to his *needs* last night. Whatever the reason, I felt a small kernel of real dislike hardening in the pit of my stomach.

I showered quickly, running through all the angry words I wanted to spit in his face, words that were getting harder to bite back.

Once I'd dried my hair, I swept it up into a simple chignon —one of the few arts of graceful dressing that I learned from my mom—then slipped on my favorite, if slightly wrinkled, terracotta cocktail dress, and cream pumps.

I was applying some gloss lipstick when I heard the first car pull up outside, followed by David's hysterical yell for me to be front and center in the living room.

Tempted as I was to keep him waiting, it just wasn't worth his prima donna overreaction later. He always found a way to exorcise his pique. It occurred to me that over the next few months it would behove me to be a model wife—it would certainly make life easier, but I severely doubted I was up to the challenge. But not when I felt like stabbing him with a pastry fork.

The early arrivals were a Commander Dawson and his wife Bette, a well-dressed couple in their mid-thirties who radiated curiosity, looking at me, the food, the house, our fixtures and fittings with such avid eyes, I wondered if they'd try to sell it on the home-shopping channel.

Then four people arrived together: two single officers and a couple called the Bennetts who were friendly and easy-going, greeting me kindly and ooh-ing and ah-ing over the food.

By the time Donna and Johan arrived, the house was filling up and people spilled out into the yard, the pleasant hum of chat drifting on the summer air.

"Darling Caroline. You look beautiful, as always," said Donna, kissing me on the cheek and holding my hands. "It's so good of you to have everyone over so soon after moving in."

I felt she was trying to convey some sort of message with her words, but I just smiled and nodded, and accepted a quick peck from Johan, whose eyes were fixed expectantly on the buffet.

Donna hooked her arm through mine and asked how I was settling back into the old neighborhood.

"I hear you're taking up your journalism again," she said.

"Oh?" I was surprised. I hadn't broadcast the fact and I doubted David would have mentioned it to anyone.

She winked at me. "No secrets on the Base, you should know that, Caroline. I just happened to run into Shirley Peters and she told me you'd been out with Mitch and the boys."

"Oh, I see."

Donna didn't mind mixing with the wives of enlisted men. Good.

The doorbell rang again and I was saved from having to move the subject away from Mitch and surfing.

"Duty calls," I said, rather too glumly.

Donna flashed a warm smile and released my arm, promising that we'd 'catch up' later. I was sorry that I'd have to avoid her instead—I liked Donna, but I couldn't afford to be friends with her. Not now.

Sebastian's parents were standing at the door when I opened it, Estelle's face set in the rictus smile she reserved for social occasions, Donald muttered some platitude and pushed his way inside.

Over Estelle's shoulder, I saw Sebastian sitting behind the wheel of the Hunters' car. I was caught off-guard and something about my expression caused Estelle to turn to see what I was looking at. She smirked.

"It seems that having a child can be useful after all," she said. "Who knew? Anyway, it saved us a fight over who got to drink tonight."

"Is he going to wait outside all evening?" I asked, the concern a little too evident in my voice.

"Oh no," she said, off-handedly. "He'll come when we call him."

He's not a pet dog!

She turned away and walked into the house, Sebastian and I were left to stare at each other across the expanse of driveway.

He gave me the briefest of smiles then reluctantly pulled his eyes away from mine. I watched until the car had disappeared from sight. My heart was racing and I felt dizzy. I took a deep breath to steady myself, and walked back inside.

I spent the rest of the evening being polite and a good hostess, but anxiety strained my nerves to the point where I felt I'd scream.

"Are you all right, Caroline?" said Donna sympathetically. "You seem a little out-of-sorts."

I laughed, trying to control the quaver in my voice. "It's just been a long day. I feel like I've been cooking forever."

It was a lame excuse and I didn't think she'd fallen for it. But, thoughtful as ever, she accepted my words at face value.

"Well, I'm afraid you've set the standard now. It's all

absolutely delicious. I don't know how you do it: cook, write, and look after David."

She glanced over to where he was holding court, extolling the virtues of white Port over other fortified wines. I knew for a fact he'd looked up the salient points earlier that day on the internet … in between playing cards. David knew nothing about wine. He hated the fact that I did. Was there anything he liked about me? Oh yes, my cooking.

I heard a loud crash and turned in time to see the remains of the food I'd so carefully prepared cascade to the floor in a shower of crumbs and broken pastry.

The worse for wear, Donald Hunter had blundered into the buffet table and was being supported by Commander Bennett and one of the officers whose name I couldn't remember.

The room was equally divided between those who stared at Donald and those who stared at me to measure my reaction.

"I guess that's what you call laying on the buffet," I said, with a resigned shrug.

A ripple of laughter eased the sudden tension in the room and Donald was escorted into the yard, presumably to sober up.

Donna squeezed my arm. "I didn't know you were mistress of the one-liner, Caroline."

Mistress? If only you knew.

"Let me help you clear that mess," she continued.

Several of the women and a few of the men volunteered to help shovel up the ruined food. Not David, of course. Nor Estelle, who stood with her back to the scene her husband had caused.

"What a waste," said Donna, sighing. "I admit I had my eyes on a box of take-out."

I smiled ruefully and was about to reply when we heard raised voices out in the yard. Donna's eyes hardened, and she shook her head with annoyance. I saw her exchange a look with her husband, who nodded slightly and headed outside.

"The Hunters," she said, confirming my suspicions. "Donald never could hold his liquor. I wonder how they're getting home."

"Estelle said that Sebastian was driving them." I answered a fraction too quickly and Donna threw me a quizzical look.

"Hmm. I'd better give him a call," she said, pulling a cell phone from her purse and scrolling through the numbers.

I couldn't control the riot of emotions that flooded through me: *I would see him. Soon.*

The argument outside ended abruptly. I suspected Johan had managed somehow to calm the situation, I knew it wouldn't have been David. He was far too cowardly to go up against a man like Donald Hunter.

During a tense few minutes while the Hunters snarled at each other across the barbecue pit, I chewed anxiously on my lip. I wasn't the only one—several guests looked dubious, as if the latent violence, so evident in the couple's venomous scowls, would erupt at any moment.

For different reasons, we were all relieved when the Hunters' car drove up and Sebastian climbed out.

Seeing his beautiful face, drawn for now with a serious expression, some of the tension left me. Just having him so close, albeit untouchable, made me feel safe.

"Well, if it isn't my son and heir," sneered Donald. "Although it's not son and hair anymore, is it, son?"

Donna snorted with disgust and my hands clenched involuntarily. I wanted to rip Donald's vile tongue from his head.

"Just get in the car, Dad," said Sebastian, quietly.

I was probably the only one there who could hear the tone of suppressed rage.

"Don't fucking tell me what to do!" snarled Donald, lurching toward his son, his fist raised.

Johan grabbed his arm but Sebastian didn't move an inch—he just continued to look at his father impassively.

"Take it easy, Don," said Johan. The note of authority in his voice might have had some effect on someone who'd had less to drink.

Donald just laughed mirthlessly.

"You're lucky you haven't got a fucking useless deadbeat for a son, Johan," he spat.

"Maybe that's because he takes after his father," slurred Estelle spitefully.

"It's all your fault!" shouted Donald. "You're too fucking soft on him! You've turned him into a fucking faggot! English Lit and Italian: that's what he wants to study at college, for fuck's sake!"

Johan gripped Donald's arm and, with the help of another guest whose name I couldn't remember, steered him toward the car. Estelle wobbled after him, still throwing barbed comments.

Sebastian's expression hadn't changed, but his cheeks burned with a tell-tale flush of anger.

"Show's over," said Donna. "We'll let these folks go take a nap."

But the ill-tempered display had cooled the party mood and the other guests started to make their apologies and leave. I wasn't sorry to see them go.

I stared at Sebastian, desperate to be with him, but unable to move. I simply hoped he knew how much I wanted to.

The ghost of a smile touched his beautiful mouth and then he turned to help load his inebriated parents into the family car.

Donna joined me, watching the unpleasant display as the senior Hunters continued to snipe and bicker.

"Gee, I'm sorry about your party, Caroline."

"At least no one will forget it," I sighed, shrugging my shoulders.

She smiled. "No, I guess not. You okay?"

"Yes, I'm fine. Really," I added, seeing the skeptical look on her face. "Please thank Johan for ... well ... everything. You, too."

She squeezed my arm. "Our pleasure, Caroline. You be well now."

$\sim$

It was only when the final guest had left and I'd cleared the last of the debris from the kitchen that I realized how drunk David was.

"What a fucking disaster, Car'line," he said, leaning against the door frame, watching me.

"It was fine except for the Hunters' little scene," I said reassuringly. "And no one will worry about that."

"You really are stupid, aren't you, Car'line? I'll be a fucking laughing stock. At least you're good for one thing."

He tried to grab me but I dodged out of his reach.

He frowned, trying to comprehend what had just happened.

"Come here," he ordered.

"I think you need to sleep now, David," I said, my heart beginning to sprint as adrenaline flooded through me.

"What I need, Car'line, is a fuck. And you're my wife."

I tried to swallow but my mouth was suddenly dry.

He took another step toward me. I turned and ran into the darkened yard, listening to his curses, a loud crash, and then sudden silence.

Cautiously, I peered into the pool of light spilling out from the kitchen. David was sprawled on the floor and across the doorway: out cold. I breathed a sigh of relief.

I tugged at his arm, trying to pull him across the threshold so I could close the door to the yard. He grunted, but his dead weight was too much for me. I stared down at him, wondering how the hell I'd move him.

Nervously, I stepped over his prone body then ran into the bedroom to get my cell. I hesitated briefly before pressing 'call'.

He answered instantly.

"Caro! Are you okay?"

My answer was a slightly hysterical laugh.

"Yes, I'm fine, but David is out cold and I can't move him. Will you come? Can you get away? Are Donald and Estelle...?"

"Sleeping it off," he said with disgust. "I'll be there in five minutes." He paused. "I'm glad you called me, Caro."

He hung up before I could reply.

With my adrenaline rush over, my knees gave way and I sagged to the floor and sat staring warily at David.

When I heard a car outside, I pushed myself up and staggered to the door.

I opened it, and without speaking Sebastian gathered me into his arms. I leaned weakly against his chest as he stroked my hair. I felt both calmed and reassured.

"Are you sure you're okay?" he said, his voice a soft murmur against my ear.

"I am now."

He sighed then straightened up. "Where's the asshole?"

I nodded toward the kitchen and followed him into the house.

David was snoring loudly.

"Just like my parents," he said, his voice hot with dislike. "Where do you want me to put him?"

"Can you help me get him to the couch?"

"Sure."

Sebastian rolled him into a sitting position and hooked his hands under David's arms. I grabbed his legs awkwardly and together we managed to half-carry, half-drag him into the living room and deposit him on the couch.

While Sebastian arranged my comatose husband into the recovery position, I fetched a spare blanket from the closet and threw it over him loosely.

"That's more than he deserves," muttered Sebastian. I wasn't sure if he meant for me to hear.

Then he looked directly at me, such a burning, scorching look that I couldn't breathe. He stepped forward.

"Not here," I whispered. "Not with him here."

Sebastian didn't take his eyes from mine but he nodded slowly.

"Where?"

I hesitated. "Can we take your car?"

"Of course. My parents won't miss it." His lips curled with distaste. "They'll be out for hours. As well as..."

He didn't need to finish the sentence.

Gently, he took my hand and led me to the car, opening the door and leaning across to fasten my seatbelt. He kissed me softly on the lips and grinned at my startled expression.

For the first time that evening, I smiled a genuine, happy smile.

"So, where to, ma'am?"

I shook my head. "Anywhere. Nowhere. Somewhere. I don't care—just as long as it's with you."

"The beach?"

"Perfect."

We drove in silence through the night, the tension slowly mounting between us.

Fate had thrown us together: who was I to deny it? No, that wasn't right. I simply no longer cared. I had chosen—willingly, knowingly, deliberately. I chose love over law. And I didn't care.

Finally, Sebastian stopped the car on a remote stretch of road and cut the engine.

"I always wanted to see you in the moonlight," he said softly. "I didn't think you could look more beautiful."

He reached over and touched my cheek, running one cool finger down the line of my jaw.

I captured his finger in my mouth and bit it gently, teasing him with my teeth. He gasped, then held his breath, his eyes closing.

"Oh, God, Caro!"

Air hissed through his lips.

The sound was beyond arousing. I wanted him. I needed him.

I unbuckled my seatbelt and his, sliding onto his lap, taking him by surprise again. I ran my fingers over the soft bristles of his hair as he wrapped his arms behind my back and pulled me to him. I kissed him deeply, my tongue pushing between his lips, stroking his, and he returned the kiss with ferocity. I felt him hardening beneath me and I knew I wasn't going to deny him again—or deny myself.

His tongue was urgent in my mouth, tension and ardor in equal amounts, pouring out of him.

When I pulled away I was breathless.

I couldn't, damn it! I'd already taken Plan B once, I didn't want to have to take it again—especially not so soon after the last time. Was I ever going to remember the basics?

"Caro!" he moaned.

"I know. I want you, too. But we can't. I'm not on the pill."

His eyes flared and he reached for me again, then stopped.

"You're not? But..."

"No ... I ... took care of ... last time."

"What?"

"I got some emergency contraception, Sebastian."

"Oh."

It was clear he didn't know what to say to that. I dropped my gaze and shifted uncomfortably. He winced.

"Sorry," I whispered.

I tried to move off him, but he broke the awkward silence first.

"I... I have condoms," he said, his voice uncertain.

I blinked in surprise. Had he been expecting this to happen —or just hoping? I decided either way, it didn't matter. I wanted him.

"Oh, right. Good."

I scrambled off his lap and leaned back on my seat, my eyes wide. He reached inside his jeans pocket and pulled out a small pack, then stopped again.

I didn't know what to do. I knew what I *wanted* to do but I'd never put a condom on a man in my life. My uncertainty turned to pity as I stared at the stricken expression on Sebastian's face.

I leaned toward him and ran my hand up his thigh, feeling the denim worn smooth with a thousand washes, then over his erection, tracing the outline greedily. He closed his eyes and took a deep breath.

I unbuttoned his jeans, and his eyelids fluttered but remained closed. I licked my lips, and slowly tugged down the zipper. He moaned softly as I let my hand explore through his boxer briefs. Then I pulled him free and ran my hand down his length. When I looked up, his eyes were burning into me, hot with desire.

Emboldened, beyond bold, I leaned forward, resting my hands on his thighs. I took him in my mouth and moved down, taking him deeper in my throat.

He cried out softly, his hands gripping my shoulders.

I sucked gently and felt his fingers tighten, but it wasn't enough for me, I wanted more. I sat up slowly.

"I want you inside me, Sebastian," I whispered.

He nodded, wordless, his eyes blazing and naked.

In the darkness I felt around on the floor until my fingers touched the packet of condoms that he'd dropped moments before.

"I've never done this," I said quietly.

I ripped open the packet and felt the smooth, slightly tacky, almost powdery texture. I frowned, wondering what that would feel like inside me.

"I'll do it," he said, his voice barely more than a whisper.

I looked up, surprised. "You know how to?"

He looked embarrassed. "Just ... you know ... for practice. Not with a girl or anything."

"Oh. Okay." I didn't know how to respond to that. Under the circumstances, being prepared was coming in handy.

He reached down to his jeans.

"Wait, I want to see you."

I tugged at the hem of his outer garments to emphasize my point.

I saw his throat move as he swallowed and he closed his eyes briefly, then with ones swift move he hauled his t-shirt and sweatshirt over his head, and tossed them onto the rear seat. He kicked off his sneakers, lifted his hips quickly and pulled his jeans and briefs out of the way.

His skin was silver in the moonlight and I longed to run my hands over every inch of him. But, patiently, if greedily, I watched as he pinched the nipple of the condom with one hand, placing it at his tip, then, he held it firmly in place, and rolled it down his length with the other.

He looked so beautiful and so vulnerable, gloriously naked and trusting. I reached under my dress, pulled my panties down, and wriggled out of them.

Taking a deep breath, I climbed awkwardly onto his lap, facing him, and rested my hands on his shoulders. The steering wheel dug in my back and I wondered briefly if this would be easier on the passenger side, but I didn't want to unsettle him, us, with more fumbling. And I wanted him. Oh, God, I wanted him.

I ran my right hand down his chest and he shivered under my touch. I could feel his heart beating a frantic tattoo and I knew he wanted me just as badly as I wanted him. God, what a feeling.

Moving as carefully as I could in the cramped conditions, I positioned myself over him. Our eyes locked for a second, then I reached down and gripped his erection with one hand, and lowered myself down onto him.

He groaned loudly but I was lost in the sensation of feeling him deep inside me once more. I clenched around him and he gasped, a fleeting look of astonishment on his face. I gripped him again and his eyes flew open.

"Oh, God, Caro!"

I kissed him deeply and his responding ardor scorched me. He ran his hands up my thighs, bunching the material of my dress around my waist so he was cradling my ass, caressing the flesh with his fingers.

Moving my hands to his shoulders, I raised myself off him and watched with delight as his eyes closed and he groaned again. As I slid back onto him, he flexed his hips upwards and I gasped as he thrust into me.

Every nerve ending in my body felt aroused and needy and grateful. I rose and fell again, more urgently, and with each movement he thrust into me.

Sweat broke out across my body as I moved faster and faster. My thigh muscles burned from the awkwardness of the position, but I was barely aware of the discomfort. My body began to tremble but then Sebastian called out, thrust deeply and stilled, burying his face against my chest, his hands still gripping my ass.

We sat locked together for some moments before his eyes opened and he looked up at me. He smiled. It was like seeing a sunburst in the darkness, and my heart leapt.

"Caro," he said.

Then, still smiling, he closed his eyes and leaned back, pulling me to him. We lay wrapped in silence.

CHAPTER SIX

RELUCTANTLY, WE DISENTANGLED OURSELVES AND I SHUFFLED back to my own seat, tugging my dress down to cover what wasn't left of my modesty.

Sebastian pulled on his jeans and reached onto the back seat for his t-shirt.

"Leave it off," I said. "I like to look at you."

"Yes, ma'am," he grinned back at me.

The windows were steamed up and the car smelled of sex. The moon cast a bluish light across the dunes and the ocean was an icy gray. I shivered.

"Are you cold?"

"No, not really. Are you?"

He shook his head, a wide grin threatening to break out again.

"Are you going to stop smiling at any point?" I asked, amused.

"Nope. Shouldn't think so."

"Do you want to go for a walk?"

"A walk?" He looked longingly at the back seat and I knew what he was thinking because I was thinking it, too. But there was something else I wanted to do first.

"Yes, a walk: perambulation, a stroll, an amble, a short journey made on foot."

"Oh. That sort of walk. Okay, I guess."

He half-fell out of the car and scooted around to open my door.

"My gallant knight."

"Your anything," he said seriously. "But I want to be your everything."

Oh, Sebastian. You already are.

"I want to make love to you again," he said softly.

"So do I." It was important to reassure him. "But I want to walk on the beach with you. I want to walk on the beach with you and hold your hand and to not be afraid that someone will see us."

My smile was sad and he leaned down to kiss me softly. He wasn't the only one who needed reassurance.

The breeze was cool in the night air so I insisted that Sebastian wear his sweatshirt, in spite of my selfish desire to watch the ripple and play of his muscles as he moved.

I'd left the house in just my summer cocktail dress but luckily the car had a picnic blanket in the trunk. Sebastian draped it carefully around my shoulders.

The tide was a long way out, the shoreline stretching almost to the horizon, we wandered along the cold, flat sand, under the moonlight, leaving the footprints of lovers. I couldn't help staring up at him as we walked hand-in-hand. His strong, clear profile, and soft, sensuous lips were thrown into relief by the moon's light, he was beautiful. And for now, he was mine.

"What?" he said, looking down at me, amused.

"You're so beautiful, Sebastian. And when I look at you I feel ... happy."

He swallowed and turned to face me.

"I want to make you happy, Caro. You look so sad most of the time."

"Do I?"

He nodded and ran his thumbs across my cheeks before leaning down to kiss me.

His lips were so gentle, his kisses so sweet. I pulled him

closer, wrapping the blanket around both of us so were shrouded under the moon.

Desire blazed through me again. I hadn't known it could be so consuming, so devastating, so utterly impossible to think of anything but consummation. And seeing Sebastian so desperate for me, I was aroused beyond belief.

"Let's find our dune," I said.

He grabbed my hand and started dragging me up the beach.

"I can't keep up!" I shouted at him, half-laughing, unable to match his long strides.

But he didn't slow down, instead he swept me into his arms and staggered toward the nearest dune where he carefully stood me on my feet.

"Here," he said, his voice commanding.

"Yes, sir!" I threw him a quick salute and a reluctant smile spread across his face.

"Sorry," he said. "I just really want you."

I threw the blanket at him and he caught it one-handed.

"Don't be sorry," I said. "Let's have a picnic."

"We haven't got any food." He looked puzzled.

"I was planning on eating you."

His eyes widened with shock then a dazzling smile lit up his lovely face.

"Okay," he said shyly.

For a moment the blanket floated above the sand as he spread it out, a matador with his cape.

I sat down rather inelegantly and watched him sink down beside me. I lay back and held up my arms to him in invitation. Accepting, his heat and weight pressed me into the blanket, his hands greedy on my body.

His touch was becoming braver and more confident and I celebrated in that, because I'd been the one to teach him. And there was no doubt that I was learning from him, too. I was beginning to understand what it meant to be loved. It was terrifying.

He rolled onto his back and pulled me on top so he could unzip my dress. His fingers were hasty, fumbling deliciously. He pulled the dress open at the back and ran the palms of his hands across my bare skin. I groaned into his throat and slid my teeth to his neck, biting more sharply than I'd meant.

Suddenly the dress seemed constricting. I pushed away from him, knelt up and pulled it off. For the second time in a few hours it was thrown to the ground, this time I didn't care.

I unhooked my bra and dropped it to the sand, my nipples hardening in the cool air. He sat up, his eyes wide and needy, then tugged his sweatshirt over his head.

"You're still wearing too many clothes," I said, raising an eyebrow. "I think I should undress you. Lie down."

He obeyed immediately and I knelt across him feeling wanton with need. His hands skimmed up my thighs, over my hips, crossing my stomach until they rested on my breasts, stroking them, caressing them. A sound like purring came from deep within his throat and he sat up, the hard muscles of his stomach contracting, and he nuzzled his face between my breasts. Then, angling his head to one side, he sucked my left nipple, hard. I gasped and his eyes flickered up but his mouth didn't move away, his tongue teasing me, flicking from side to side. I arched my spine, throwing my head back. He ran his nails lightly across my skin then cupped my buttocks and squeezed them. His erection was hard, trapped by his jeans, pushing against the material as if it was trying to climb through the denim to reach me.

I pulled my breast out of his mouth and winced as I felt the sharp raking of his teeth.

I sat further back on his thighs and undid the single button of his jeans. I fixed my eyes on his, wanting to savor his expression as I unzipped his pants.

He leaned up on his elbows, his mouth slightly open, his breathing unsteady.

Almost more slowly than either of us could bear, I pulled the zipper down. Then, running my fingers over his sweet skin, I bent down to kiss him below his waistband.

He tasted different, not so good as before and I realized the odd, rubbery taste was from the condom we'd used earlier. *Oh well, live and learn. Now time for the next lesson.*

"Take off your pants and pass me a condom," I ordered, my voice low and brittle.

He reached into his jeans pocket and passed me a foil packet. I rolled to one side and examined the little packet curiously while he kicked off his pants.

"Weird things, aren't they?" I said.

"I guess," he replied, his mind obviously elsewhere, as he reached over to run his hand up between my thighs and pushing his thumb against my clitoris the way I'd shown him. I convulsed so hard I nearly levitated off the blanket.

"Oh, God!"

"You okay?" he said, his voice concerned as he looked up.

"Aah!" I gasped, utterly incoherent.

I saw his expression change from concern to lust. He sank two fingers inside me, pushing slowly in and out, and continued circling my clitoris. Definitely a fast learner. My hands clawed the blanket as his other hand pulled roughly on my nipple.

"Can I kiss you, down there?" he asked, hesitantly.

I didn't really want that. David had never showed any interest in performing oral sex on me—he'd made it sound dirty, sordid—unless, of course, he was the one receiving the pleasure. I wasn't sure I wanted to start now, but I couldn't say no to Sebastian either. If he'd asked me to fly to the moon naked on the back of a broomstick it wouldn't have seemed an unreasonable request.

"Okay, I guess," I said quietly.

He kissed my stomach, running his tongue down to my navel and biting my hip bone. Then he sat up, trailing one hand down my body and crawled between my legs. He pushed my knees up and curled his hands around them before his head disappeared between my thighs.

Dear God! The feeling of his hot mouth down there, kissing me, nuzzling my pubic hair. It was a strange, alien feeling, disconcerting almost. But then he slid his tongue inside me and my hips bucked involuntarily. His hands glided up to my thighs and pushed my legs more widely open. I ran my fingers over his hair as he kneaded my thighs, unsure if I wanted to pull his head away or push him more deeply inside me.

Then his tongue flicked against my sweet spot unexpectedly, and I exploded around him, calling out, sounds without words.

I had no idea. I had no idea!

My body continued to send a tsunami of tremors through me, the most powerful and unexpected orgasm I'd ever had.

"I want to be inside you, Caro," he said, his voice tight with urgency.

I couldn't speak, I think I nodded.

He leaned over me and picked up the condom packet from where I'd dropped it, my fingers nerveless. I watched mesmerized as he rolled the thin latex down his powerful erection, his own breathing equally rapid.

He grasped himself in one hand then positioned the tip.

"Please!" I gasped.

He thrust deeply into me and groaned, my name, I think.

I lifted my hips and wrapped my legs around his waist, crossing my ankles over his fine ass, and gripped him tightly.

Each powerful thrust pushed me further and further up the blanket, and further and further into another dimension. My nails raked his back, his shoulders and biceps. I forced my eyes to open and gazed into his face, contorted, stripped bare—there was just me, just him and the endless ocean.

I screamed his name as loudly as I could, needing to voice my love for him just once.

Too quickly, his body shuddered deeply inside me, his muscles contracting, sending waves of pleasure rippling through me.

He collapsed and I pulled him tighter inside, milking every last inch of him. He moaned and lay with his head nestled into my neck, breathing hard.

After several minutes locked together without moving, he reluctantly pulled out of me, making me gasp.

I was cold without the heat of his body and I shivered slightly.

He pulled the edges of the blanket around us and we curled up together, sated briefly. I half expected him to fall asleep, it was what David always did, but I was learning that they were different in so many ways.

Sebastian continued to run his fingers up and down my arm, gently stroking my skin. It was comforting.

"Sebastian, can I ask you something?"

"Of course—anything."

I was glad it was dark because just thinking the question, let alone asking it, was making me blush.

"What is it, Caro?"

"Well, I was just wondering ... that was really ... nice ... when you ... you know ... kissed me ... down there."

He nuzzled my shoulder.

"Good."

"How ... how did you know what to do?"

His body was suddenly still, and his hand froze on my arm. I regretted my impulsive question immediately.

"It's okay. You don't have to tell me. I was just wondering..."

"It's not what you think, Caro," he said, quietly. "I've never ... you know I've never been with anyone else. I've never ... done that before."

"So, how did you know? Because it was amazing."

"Amazing? Really?"

He sounded pleased.

"Oh, believe me: I know what 'amazing' means, and that definitely qualifies."

He chuckled quietly.

"Cool!"

"So ... come on ... how did you know what to do? Or maybe you're just a natural."

I sensed there was something he wasn't telling me.

"Come on, Hunter. Fess up. Other than being God's gift to women..."

"Okay, but promise not to laugh."

"Cross my heart."

He sighed heavily.

"I looked it up."

"Excuse me?"

"Online. I looked it up. There are websites where you can ... find out stuff."

I was astonished. It would never have occurred to me in a million years.

"So ... did you just do an internet search on 'oral sex'?"

I heard his quiet laugh again.

"Kinda, yeah. A couple of years ago me and Ches were on my dad's computer when he was out, he'd only turned off the screen so when we turned it on again it was on some porno site. Someone had posted a question about ... that. I think it freaked us out at the time but I was thinking about it the other day after we ... and I just thought ... I just wanted ... if we did it again ... I just wanted to please you. I know I'm not very good at this and ... well ... after what happened that first time, I thought it might be good to ... you know ... pick up some tips."

I was so overwhelmed—not only had he done this for me, to please me, but that he was so open and honest.

"Sebastian ... I think you're a wonderful lover. The things I feel when I'm with you ... the things you make me feel ... I've never, *never* felt like that."

I pulled his mouth to mine, trying to show through my kiss that I meant every word.

"You're very special, Sebastian," I murmured onto his lips.

"I love you so much, Caro," he said huskily.

We lay quietly for some minutes and I began to drift off to sleep. But then, in a hesitant voice, he spoke again.

"Caro, can I ask you something?"

"Of course. What is it?"

My brain was happily disconnected from my body, and my voice sounded dream-laden.

He hesitated and I stroked his chest to reassure him.

"Why did you change your mind?"

"About what?"

"About us."

"I haven't. Oh, you mean ... this."

"Yes. I mean, I'm glad you did—I was just wondering why."

I wasn't sure I knew how to answer that. In fact I didn't want to be reminded that this was ... wrong.

"I didn't really change my mind: it's still ... dangerous for us, for me."

He wrapped the blanket more tightly around us as if that could protect me from the disapproval of the world.

"I was too weak to stay away from you," I whispered. "And today was so ... I've never felt like this before. You make me feel alive. But that doesn't mean it isn't wrong and..."

"How can you say that?" he said angrily, his body suddenly too still. "How can you say it's wrong? How..."

He stumbled, trying to find the words, and I gasped with pain.

"Don't be angry with me, Sebastian."

I couldn't bear it if you left me now.

"Just ... just please don't say it's wrong. I can't hear you say that."

His hands were bunched into fists against the rough blanket.

I sat up alarmed.

"I'm sorry! I'm so sorry, I didn't mean it like that but *nothing has changed.* You're still only 17 and I'm ... still breaking the law. In the eyes of the world, I'm some disgusting, depraved sexual predator ... a vile, awful..."

"Don't!" He shouted, his eyes furious.

Abruptly, he pulled away from me, his fists pressed against his forehead.

His sudden anger scared me. I was used to anger from David and it rarely touched me—but this ... I felt torn in half.

"Sebastian!"

I tried to pull his hands away from his face, but he was too strong and refused to look at me.

"Sebastian," I spoke more gently. "You asked me why and I've tried to explain. This isn't going to be easy. You know this."

I stroked his shoulder.

"Please?"

Eventually he turned toward me, although he still couldn't meet my eyes. He let me take one of his hands in mine.

"Sorry," he muttered softly.

"Me, too."

He moved gently, wrapped me in his arms again and pulled me down so we were lying, a tangle of arms and legs and coarse wool.

He kissed me with sudden ferocity, covering my face and throat with hard, burning kisses. His weight pinned me down as I ran my hands across the taut muscles of his back and shoulders.

"I love you," he growled. "That's all that matters."

I badly wanted to believe he was right, I knew he was wrong.

But I let his words, his hands and his body sweep me away. I realized with dim surprise that he'd grown hard again and his erection was probing between my legs. I wished I could just allow him to slide inside me without fear or consequence but the small, unquiet voice of reason was just about audible.

I felt his wet tip push again against my thighs. I laid my hand firmly against his chest.

"Sebastian," I said, a warning in my voice.

He groaned and rolled onto his back, then fumbled around while I waited, growing impatient.

"I can't find the fucking condoms!"

"What?"

"They were in my jeans' pocket, but I can't find them now."

What?

We scrambled around in the dark, frustration mounting. I grabbed handfuls of sand, sieving it through my fingers, trying to find the small packet.

"Oh, for fuck's sake!" he yelled suddenly and threw himself back down on the blanket.

He looked so wretched and, well, kind of uncomfortable, that I couldn't help smiling. I was really trying hard not to laugh but the situation was so ridiculous.

"Oh dear," I said, the humor obvious in my voice. "What are we going to do now?"

He ignored my tone. I really hoped he wasn't going to sulk. But I had a solution in mind.

I stroked his satiny skin, still stretched tight over his erection. He groaned and turned his eyes toward me.

I held him firmly, sliding my hand up and down him several times. His hips arched underneath me while his hands lay limply at his sides.

Slowly, my intent now obvious, I knelt at his side and stared down at him.

"Oh, fuck!" he breathed.

Well, not quite, but this will have to do for now.

Gently, I pulled his erection back toward my mouth and ran my tongue around the skin. I tried to ignore the rubbery flavor and hoped it would wear off soon. I decided to do some more wearing off using my tongue and teeth and, with great satisfaction, I watched him writhe and pant under my touch. I massaged his balls with one hand and spread my other hand out on his stomach, pressing him down into the blanket.

"Caro!" he moaned.

Hearing my name on his lips was extraordinarily arousing. For the first time ever, I really wanted to do this, to take him all the way.

I moved my mouth faster and sucked harder. I could feel him all the way to the back of my throat so I made sure I relaxed, then stroked my mouth up and down him rapidly. I felt Sebastian's hands weave themselves through my hair and with a sound that was more animal than human, he shuddered and stilled.

I swallowed quickly, trying not to think about the salty taste too much, then crawled over to curl up next to him. I was cold and the heat of his body was welcoming. I pulled the blanket around us and felt his arms sweep down my back.

As I snuggled up to him, I felt something dig into my hip.

I pulled out the packet of condoms that had gone AWOL, and held it up.

"Look what I found."

Sebastian's eyes opened sleepily. "What? Are you kidding? Oh well, that was pretty fucking amazing anyway." He laughed in astonishment. "I mean, just fucking sensational!" Then he paused, "But keep that packet where we can find it."

Now it was my turn to be amazed. "You want more?!"

His voice was suddenly serious, all humor gone.

"It could be weeks, months even before I get to spend the whole night with you again, Caro. Whereas that fucking asshole..."

I held my finger over his mouth then kissed him. "But tonight is still ours."

And I didn't want to waste the hours by uttering David's name.

As dawn began to leak through the darkness, Sebastian slept. His head rested on my chest and his arms and legs were wrapped around me. I could feel his warm breath on my skin as my fingers rhythmically stroked his back.

It was a peaceful moment tinged with sadness for me. I didn't want it to be over, but with each minute the dark faded, and I knew it was time to go.

I'd never known a night like it, I'd never known it could be that way. I finally understood what my dear Papa had tried to tell me when I'd announced that I was marrying David.

"You're so young, *mia cara*. You have so much life ahead of you. You don't have to decide now. See a little of the world first."

Of course I hadn't listened. Children never listen to their parents, do they? Not about life, not about love ... or what I'd thought was love.

"Sebastian," I whispered, rubbing his arm. "We have to go."

He mumbled something and tightened his grip. His reaction made me smile.

"Come on. Wake up."

"I *am* awake," he said, and to make his point he took my nipple in his mouth and tugged gently.

I swatted his shoulder even as my body shuddered with desire.

"Stop it! We have to go."

"Yep, I'm ready," he said, pushing his growing erection into my hip.

Good God! He really was insatiable, I'd always thought that must be a myth. I was very grateful that David had always been easily appeased. The thought spoiled my good mood.

"No, it's time to go," I said, feeling grumpy and turned on at the same time.

Sebastian sighed. "We're out of condoms anyway," he said sadly.

We got through a whole box of condoms? No wonder my legs felt like I'd never be able to cross them again. Yes, well used—that was the sensation. I wondered idly if Sebastian felt the same. I didn't know though, could men be sore from, um, extended usage?

I was about to ask him when I realized the sky was lighter with pink streaks glowing in the east. I sat up in a panic, looking around for my clothes, I *had* to get back before David woke up.

"What's the matter?" said Sebastian, sitting up, frowning.

"I really have to go!" I hissed, feeling angry and tearful at the same time.

"Caro!" Sebastian tried to capture my hand.

"No! What part of that don't you understand?" I snapped.

He didn't reply but his hurt expression said it all. He stood up and pulled on his jeans and sweatshirt in silence, then shook the sand off the blanket and folded it under his arm.

I'd found my dress, which looked more like a rag than anything else, but my bra was missing in action. The panties, well, I assumed they were still somewhere on the floor of the Hunters' car.

I stepped into the dress and almost jumped when I felt

Sebastian's hands on my spine, pulling up the zipper. He kissed my neck quickly and held out his hand.

I took it, feeling rather ashamed of my outburst, but too anxious to apologize.

When we reached the car, I fished out my panties from under the driver's seat, shyly stepped into them and wriggled them up my hips. Sebastian was gentleman enough to turn his back during this awkward procedure. How ridiculous of me, after everything we'd done several times last night and twice this morning.

Sebastian drove barefoot, but I tried to brush sand off my feet and push them into my pumps. The sky grew lighter each minute and I was terrified that someone would see me get out of the Hunters' car or, worse still, that David would be awake and waiting for me.

Sebastian pulled up outside the house and gave my hand a quick squeeze. "Text me later? Let me know you're all right?"

I nodded and pulled my hand away.

I stumbled up the driveway and crept around to the back of the house, peeking in through the window. I breathed a sigh of relief: David was still asleep on the couch and snoring loudly.

I took off my pumps and tiptoed through backdoor, feeling all colors of guilty, but oddly exultant at the same time.

In the bedroom, everything was as I'd left it, a lipstick on the dressing table and a comb abandoned by David's side of the bed, which hadn't been slept in.

It was nearly 7AM and although my body ached for sleep, and really just ached from using muscles that had never before seen the light of day, I ignored the bed and headed for the bathroom. I badly needed to pee. Sebastian had had no qualms about wandering off into the dunes during the night to relieve himself, but I hadn't quite been able to be that free. Luckily, I hadn't drunk much during the evening, so I'd been able to hold on.

I showered quickly, enjoying the hot water on my skin, and washed off the last of the sand that had managed to work itself into a number of interesting crevices.

I wondered if Sebastian's parents would comment on his absence—or the fact that the car had been missing all night. But then again, the state they'd been in when he'd taken them home, I doubted they would have noticed much at all. I hoped that was the case.

As I dressed, pulling on a pair of jeans and old shirt, I heard David stirring next door. I didn't know how I was going to do this—to go on deceiving him, to carry on living the lie. I wondered again if I could contemplate the alternative, or could I weather the next four months.

I took a deep breath and walked into the living room. David peered at me through bleary eyes, grunted and rolled into a sitting position.

"Coffee?" I said, a little too brightly.

He eyed me suspiciously. "Where have you been?"

"Showering," I said, breezily.

My hands shook slightly as I put the water on to boil.

"Bacon? Pancakes?"

From the corner of my eye I saw David pull a face and he didn't reply. I couldn't help feeling a sharp sense of satisfaction that he was suffering with a hangover. If things ran true to form, he'd spend the rest of the day in his study.

I hoped Sebastian would be able to get a couple of hours sleep—he started his new job today. It was only bussing tables at a country club outside of La Jolla, but it would keep him out of his parents' way and meant he'd eventually have enough money to buy a car—especially if tips kept up, as Ches had promised.

I had the interesting task of cleaning the house and erasing the evidence of occupation so it would pass David's undoubtedly close inspection later on.

The day dragged almost unbearably. The only bright side was that David stayed out of my way. I managed to send Sebastian a quick text halfway through the morning. David was in the shower and I was vacuuming his study. I had just a few minutes.

I'm ok. Hope all good with you?

I waited anxiously for his reply but my cell stayed ominously silent. When I heard David dressing in the bedroom, I turned it off.

Throughout the day, I checked it intermittently, my anxiety increasing with every hour that passed. I finally got a reply late in the evening.

Sorry, baby. Got called in to start work early. Weird place! Tomorrow? Please say yes

He called me 'baby'!

I wondered why the place was weird. Yes, tomorrow. God, that seemed a long time from now.

I felt better after reading his message, but was sad that I had to delete it immediately. But my sense of well-being evaporated when it was time to go to bed. With my husband.

I was reading a book: well, I was trying to concentrate but the words swam in front of my eyes. I switched off the light and turned on my side, hoping this would protect me. My breathing was shallow and I tried to slow it down to appear as if I were really resting. I felt the bed shift and couldn't help holding my breath. David leaned over and ran his hand over my hip.

"Not tonight, David," I said, trying to speak naturally. "I'm tired. Last night was very late."

Especially for me.

"You're not menstruating—what's wrong with you?"

"Nothing. I'm just tired."

"Hmm."

He didn't say anything else but rolled to his side of the bed. I breathed slowly. Soon he was snoring, but it was much later when I was able to relax enough to sleep.

I was awake before the alarm—occasionally David liked to be jerked off before breakfast and I wanted to avoid that particular scenario.

I made sure his uniform was laid out, coffee was waiting,

bacon and pancakes delivered with military precision on a hot, fucking plate.

But it wasn't enough to earn sos much as a 'good morning', he was making it very easy for me to leave him.

As soon as he was out of the house, I texted Sebastian.

Meet you at the park—30 minutes?

He texted back seconds later.

Not soon enough but I'll be there

My heart lightened immediately.

I ran into the bedroom and dug out the knee-length floaty skirt and strappy top that I'd planned to wear. I'd shoved my hair into a ponytail before breakfast, but now I shook it out and brushed it vigorously. I'd noticed that Sebastian liked to run his hands through it when we made love.

I didn't bother with colored lipstick, just a little gloss, as I wasn't planning on wearing it for long. Just thinking about kissing Sebastian made my heart race ... and other things. Yes, I definitely felt a little moist—best to concentrate on finding sandals that matched.

He was waiting for me. I'd barely stopped the car before he was opening the door and climbing in, a huge smile on his face.

"Hi!"

His eyes glowed with love and something darker. He took my breath away.

"Hi!" I grinned back at him. "So, where do you want to go?"

I pulled out into the road, happiness flooding through me.

"I don't care. Anywhere, as long as it's with you."

"Should we go to our coffee shop in Little Italy?"

He raised his eyebrows. "That's a little public for what I had in mind."

"Which is?" I asked innocently.

He smiled wickedly and without speaking leaned across to bury his head in my lap, biting me softly through the thin material of my skirt and running his hands along my bare legs and up to my panties.

"Sebastian! I'll crash!" I whimpered.

He let his fingers stray a little further and I gasped. Then he sat up slowly, leaving my skirt bunched up around the tops of my thighs.

My breathing had accelerated and my hands were clenched into fists on the steering wheel.

"That was really stupid and reckless!" I said, my voice shaking. "I could have had an accident."

"You were fine," he said, arrogantly.

I shook my head, really rather angry with him.

He just grinned.

Two could play at that game.

I stopped the car, letting it rest at a crazy angle, half-on and half-off the curb. I got out, standing with my hands on my hips.

"Caro?"

He looked at me anxiously then came and stood next to me, worried that he'd really upset me.

I passed him the keys.

"You drive."

"Okay," he said softly, still concerned.

Without speaking, we got back into the car and he pulled away from the curb. I let him drive a short distance before I reached over and squeezed his balls, hard.

The car swerved across the lane and the truck behind honked loudly.

"Fuck!"

"Not so easy to concentrate, is it?" I said.

I'd just contributed an important lesson to his portfolio of life skillss and safety while driving. They should cover it in Drivers' Ed.

Sebastian glanced at me then, as we passed a weed-covered, overgrown and empty lot, he pulled over suddenly.

He cut the engine and the sudden silence whispered out between us.

I felt a tremor of apprehension—I had no idea what he was going to do.

"I have a whole box of condoms."

His voice was quiet but his eyes were blazing. I think my mouth dropped open. *Another whole box? Wow!*

Two long seconds ticked by as we stared at each other. I don't know who moved first, but suddenly we were tearing at each other's clothes.

"Back seat!" I gasped.

I clambered over the seats and felt him bite my ass. Then he forced me down onto the seat, tugging his t-shirt over his head. I ran my hands greedily over his chest and stomach, then pushed my right hand into his jeans pocket and pulled out the condom packet. It was still wrapped in cellophane so I used my teeth to rip it open. It exploded apart and condoms showered down around us.

Sebastian caught one and kneeled up, tearing the foil. I yanked down his zipper.

"Ow! Careful, Caro!"

"Sorry," I breathed. "Let me kiss it better."

There wasn't much room to maneuver in the backseat but I managed to take him briefly in my mouth before he pulled back and shook his head.

"Caro, I'll come in about three seconds if you do that—and I want to be inside you."

"Okay, but let me do the condom, you have all the fun."

He stared at me as if he couldn't believe what I'd said, but passed me the little piece of latex. I pinched the nipple like I'd seen him do and then carefully rolled it all the way down to the hilt. It didn't seem to want to stay in place so I tried tugging it.

Sebastian pushed my hands away, groaning loudly.

"Fuck, Caro!"

The slippery little sucker wouldn't stay put but Sebastian eventually wrestled it into submission, pulling it down. Seeing him touch himself like that drove me crazy.

His eyes were wild as I grabbed his jeans and dragged them down, running my hands over his firm ass-cheeks.

He groaned louder then clawed at my panties, tugging them roughly down my trembling legs. They were still hooked over one sandal, waving like the flag of a defeated army when he plunged into me.

He buried his head in my neck and I clutched him inside and out.

"Ssh, Sebastian. Let me feel all of you."

He drew back slowly and I clenched tightly, making him moan again.

"Yes, like that," I breathed, running my nails over his back.

Twice more he moved inside me slowly, luxuriously, letting me enjoy the delicious sensation, watching my face as I gazed at his. Then he squeezed his eyes shut.

"I can't! I can't!" he moaned. "Please, Caro!"

Without waiting for my reply he started pounding into me. I felt his whole body stiffen suddenly and he cried out softly.

For a second I felt his full, crushing weight, then he propped himself up on his elbows and kissed me deeply, lovingly.

I stroked the short, soft bristles at the back of his head then ran my hands down the length of his spine.

"Sorry," he said, at last, looking shamefaced.

"What for?" I was genuinely confused.

"Well, mostly because I wanted that to last longer for you ... but for nearly making you crash, too. Although you got me back."

I smiled up at him. "Consider it a life lesson, Sebastian."

He kissed me again. "I like your lessons, ma'am."

"Don't call me 'ma'am'," I grumbled at him. "That makes me feel even older."

He silenced me with another kiss then pulled out carefully.

His face was suddenly chalky under his tan.

"What?" I said, struggling to sit up.

"I can't find the condom!" he said, gazing at me in panic.

"What do you mean you can't find it?"

"I mean ... it's not here!"

He pointed to his erection which was still very worth looking at. But he was right: no condom.

"It must have come off when you pulled out," I said, not feeling too worried yet.

"I think ... I think it must be still inside you!" he said, shock and horror mingling on his face.

Oh, what?

"Just ... just close your eyes, Sebastian," I ordered.

"What? Why?"

"Just do it!"

I wasn't going to go searching around *up there* with him watching. But search as I might, I couldn't find anything that felt rubbery.

My cheeks must have been a brilliant, flaming red.

"I think I'm going to need the ladies room," I muttered quietly.

"Do you want me to...?" he offered.

"No!" I said quickly.

But I couldn't help a small laugh escaping.

"What?" he said, half-relieved, half-puzzled.

"We never seem to get a break, do we?" I sighed.

He pulled a face, twisting his mouth into the semblance of a smile. "Other than meeting you in the first place, not really, no."

He finished buttoning up his jeans and gallantly passed me my panties.

"Thanks," I said, a wry expression on my face.

"At your service," he said, trying to stifle a smile.

At this point I decided I was going to have to start taking the contraceptive pill—I couldn't afford anymore fuck-ups, so to speak.

Sebastian drove a couple of miles down the road and we found a mall that had a restroom.

"Are you sure you don't want any help with the ... um ... situation?" he said, a salacious gleam in his eye.

"No, thank you," I said primly.

He laughed and I stalked off to the restrooms.

It was some minutes before I was able to locate the missing

condom. Who would have thought it could disappear so far ... um ... up. At this rate I was going to have dreams about my ovaries being tied in knots by miscreant latex.

When I finally emerged, Sebastian was wearing an expression of dismay. His face cleared instantly when he saw me.

"Everything okay?"

"It's all in hand," I smirked at him.

He squeezed my fingers and whispered, "Next time, *I* want to play hunt the rubber."

I shook my head in disbelief. "Can we please go and get that coffee now?"

He draped his arm around my shoulders, possessively. "Sure, baby."

God, he made me feel like a teenager. Except that I wasn't. I banished the thought and we headed off to Little Italy.

Papa Benzino kissed me warmly on both cheeks and swept Sebastian into a huge bear-hug, which he returned a little shyly. Mama B came running from behind the counter, dabbing at her eyes with an apron as if we were her long, lost family. They chattered away in Italian and I could tell that Sebastian was picking up more of the conversation than before. Perhaps I was doing him some good after all.

The *nonna* issued forth from her room over the shop and held my cheeks while she kissed me and told me I was glowing with love. Then she slapped Sebastian on the chest, felt his biceps and winked at me, repeating something that translated as, 'a fine lover is like a good salami' and threw me a knowing look.

Sebastian blushed, whether from her words or her touching, I couldn't say, but it made me laugh out loud and he gave a grin that was embarrassed and amused at the same time.

A crowd of people on their lunch break came in to order food, sending the family scampering back to work, so we sat outside under a sun umbrella and sipped our coffees: espresso for me, regular for Sebastian.

"You didn't tell me how your first day at work went?"

"Oh, that," he said frowning.

"Was it bad?" I said, surprised.

"It ... well, it wasn't really what I was expecting," he muttered, and for some reason he looked embarrassed again.

I rubbed the tip of my finger over his hand. "Tell me."

"No, it's just dumb."

"Sebastian, you just watched me go fishing for a stray condom, it can't be any dumber than that!"

He smiled wryly. "Yeah, that was pretty funny!"

"It won't be funny if I get pregnant." I reminded him.

He gaped. "Could you?"

"Well, of course I could, but don't worry, I'm going to take care of it. I've decided it's going to be safer to start taking the Pill. I can't afford any more ... accidents."

Sebastian looked totally out of his depth at this sudden conversational segue. I steered us back to less controversial topics.

"You were saying about your first day at the country club?"

He frowned again, and I could tell he was wondering whether or not he should pursue the more serious subject. He shook his head and chose to follow my lead.

"Well, I thought I'd just be bussing tables but ... they wanted me to do other stuff, too."

"Like what?"

He hesitated, drawing patterns on the palm of my hand with his index finger.

"Sebastian?"

"It's just kinda lame."

"Tell me anyway, I won't tell anyone," I said, raising an eyebrow.

"They had me waiting tables," he said finally. "Carrying food and drinks."

"Okay. That doesn't sound so bad. And...?"

"I had to wear a uniform."

"That wasn't a surprise, was it?"

Surely he didn't have a problem with uniforms, he was the son of a Navy officer.

"Shorts and a polo t-shirt, they were a little ... tight."

I was beginning to get the picture.

"Okay: shorts and a tight t-shirt. And...?"

He closed his eyes, a pained expression on his face.

"The women there ... they ... they grabbed me ... *a lot!*"

And I laughed out loud, I couldn't help it.

"So, basically, you're telling me you're a cabana boy—and that all the women were feeling you up."

"I was supposed to be bussing tables!"

He sounded so indignant, it just made me laugh harder.

"I can't blame them." I teased. "Did you get any offers? Any phone numbers dangled in front of you?"

His cheeks reddened, and he stared at the table.

"You did! Sebastian!"

"I said no!"

He grimaced at me and I took pity on him.

"*Tesoro*, I'm not the least bit surprised—those places are notorious for hiring good-looking young men as eye-candy for the diamond-wife brigade. I bet your boss is a woman, right?"

He nodded unhappily.

"And she took one look at you and saw dollar signs. That's all. You'll just have to put up with a bunch of horny, older women shoving dollar bills in your back pocket for the summer. You think you can do that?"

"I guess. It's not as much fun as I thought it would be."

I fell a little bit more in love with him.

I stroked his cheek and rested my free hand on his knee.

"You can always get another job, Sebastian. Besides, they shouldn't really have you serving drinks at your age. Do they know how young ... how old you are?"

He raised his eyebrows. "They do, but I guess I look older than my age."

It was my turn to blush, especially when I remembered my comment about 'horny older women'. On the other hand...

"I think I'll join."

"What?"

"The country club."

"Why?"

"I heard there are a lot of horny, older women there—I thought you might need some protection. Besides, it could be fun."

A slow smile spread across his face.

"Yeah! That would be fun."

"I'd tip well."

"Would you throw me your phone number?"

"I think that could be arranged."

My cell phone rang, interrupting us. It was a number I didn't recognize, which made me nervous.

"Hello?"

"Caroline Wilson?"

"Yes, speaking."

"This is Carl Winters, the editor at *City Beat*. I was just calling to say that I loved your 'Base Line Up' article. I'd like to run it in Thursday's issue. You got some great photos there, too. The fee would be $325. And I'd love any other articles you've got on life out at the Base. Folk around here are real interested in stories on life from a military point of view. Between 1,500 and 2,000 words."

"Wow! That's great! Thank you! Yes, I'm sure I could write any number of articles on military life."

"You've got a very nice writing style, Mrs. Wilson—really draws the reader in. I'm surprised I haven't run across you before."

"Oh, thank you. We just moved here from the east coast."

"I guess that explains it. Well, drop by the news desk sometime and we'll sign you up to one of our standard freelance contracts."

"I'll do that. Thank you, Mr. Winters."

"Call me Carl. It'll be great to meet you, Caroline. And maybe next time we could send out one of our photographers with you."

We hung up and I threw my arms around Sebastian's neck. "*City Beat* is going to print the surfing article." I said into his chest.

To the surprise of both of us, I started to cry.

"Hey! What's the matter? This is good, isn't it?"

"Yes, yes, of course. I'm just being stupid."

He hugged me tightly. "I don't understand."

How could I explain? I wasn't even sure I understood myself.

He stroked my back and kissed my hair, his touch soothing me. When my sobs finally ebbed, he leaned back and brushed the salty tears away with his thumbs, his face lined with concern.

"Caro? Why were you crying?"

I took a deep breath and tried to order my thoughts.

"It's just ... getting one of my stories printed. You know, someone saying that I'm actually *good* at something. I'm ... not used to it. David never..."

I stopped mid-sentence as his face hardened.

"It was just a nice surprise," I finished lamely.

He picked up my hand from the table and kissed it softly. "Yeah, I get that."

We sat in silence for some moments.

"Come on," he said at last. He stood up, still holding my hand.

"Where are we going?"

His expression softened. "To our place."

"Our place?"

"The ocean."

I smiled up at him. "Okay."

CHAPTER SEVEN

THERE'S SOMETHING SO RESTFUL ABOUT THE OCEAN. WHY IS that? Perpetual motion, never still and yet it's a soothing, peaceful, rolling, restless movement. Even the rage of a winter storm has a quality that strips away troubles, if only for a short time.

And it was *our* place—it was where Sebastian and I went to be ourselves for a few, brief, uninterrupted hours.

Even so, we had to be careful.

We walked in silence, away from the vacationing crowds that were beginning to populate the beach, until the nearest were mere pinpricks on the horizon.

Then, hand-in-hand at last, we stopped to find a secluded dune. I sank down into the warm sand and Sebastian pulled me to his side.

"Are you okay now?" he asked, anxiously.

"Yes. Sorry about that."

I was embarrassed by my most recent loss of control. It seemed to happen around him a lot, as if some emotional levee had been breached after a decade, a lifetime of holding back.

Sebastian stroked my hair and said in a low voice, "Don't be sorry. I just hate seeing you unhappy."

I didn't know how to reply so I just let him hold me.

For 19 years I'd been someone's daughter and, for the next

11, someone's wife. But what was I now? Could I have the chance of a career after all? Could I be something different, something else?

"What are you thinking about?"

I shook my head and smiled. "Not much. But I'll have to come up with some more ideas for the *City Beat*—if he really meant what he said."

"Of course he did. You're a brilliant writer."

"Well, thanks, Mr. Bernstein."

His face fell and I immediately regretted my words.

"Sorry, I'm just a little freaked. Maybe you could help me come up with some ideas about life in a military family."

He pulled a face. "Depends on the family."

That was true.

"How are Mitch and Ches?"

It seemed an innocent enough question but Sebastian looked away.

"Okay, I guess. I've only seen Ches at work."

"And?"

I waited for him to continue but he just carried on watching sand run through his fingers. "Sebastian, what's the matter?"

He took a deep breath. "Ches said that he knew I was seeing someone."

I felt the blood draining from my face.

"How?"

Sebastian looked at me anxiously.

"He was ... when I wouldn't tell him anything he started saying that there must be a reason and what was the problem. He kept on and on at me. He was just horsing around but... "

Sebastian didn't need to finish the sentence.

"What made him ... suspect?"

"Well, at first it was because I haven't been hanging out that much. He's been asking me to go surfing with him and the guys, and when I kept on saying no ... I guess he worked it out."

"Then what ... you said 'at first'?"

His expression was evasive.

"Tell me!"

He sighed. "Ches saw me getting changed into my uniform at work."

"So?"

"He noticed ... scratches down my back."

Oh! I remembered doing that.

"What did he say?"

Sebastian shrugged, unable to meet my worried gaze. On second thought, I didn't need to know what Ches had said, I could probably imagine how *that* conversation had gone.

"I told him to drop it but he wouldn't. I got so mad at him..."

"We're not very good at this, are we?" I said softly.

"It's harder than I thought," he agreed quietly.

My heart lurched painfully and I felt a little nauseous.

"Do you want to end it?"

He looked at me, horrified.

"No! Caro, no! Of course not! That's not what I meant! How can you say that?"

"Just ... if it's getting too hard..."

He pulled my face to his and kissed me roughly.

"Don't say that! Please don't say that! We'll work it out somehow. Promise me you won't give up on us, Caro. Promise!"

I felt the edge of desperation in his voice so I kissed him back, trying to pour reassurance into my touch, words that I couldn't say out loud because I was afraid they might not be true.

He pulled me down onto the sand so I was half-lying across his chest. One hand was tangled in my hair and the other pressing into the small of my back. My lips crushed his and he forced his tongue into my mouth, locking us together.

I had to break off the kiss before we went too far, it was still mid-afternoon and I was hyper-aware that someone could stumble across us at any time.

Sebastian was reluctant to let me go and I had to push hard against his chest to make him release me.

I was breathless when we rolled apart. He threw an arm over his face and groaned.

"Fuck, Caro," he said softly, and he turned to stare at me, his sea-green eyes accusing.

"We have to get back," I said, cowardly as ever. "You'll be late for your shift."

I started trudging back up the beach and, reluctantly, he followed me.

"Don't forget to bring me an application form for the country club," I said, trying to lighten his somber mood.

He smiled slightly. "I guess I could take some day shifts, if you're going to be there."

"And maybe you'd better arrange to go out with Ches a few times."

"What for?"

I sighed in exasperation. "To throw him off the scent and..."

"And what?"

"Well, if our plans work out, you won't be seeing him again."

His eyes widened in surprise. He clearly hadn't thought about what he'd be giving up if we did make it to New York.

I looked at him steadily, watching him regain his equilibrium.

"Ches is a good buddy—but I love you. Ysou're where I want to be."

And that was it: his alpha and omega.

~

I drove us back, torn between joy and fear, and wishing the night would race past so we could be together again.

A few blocks from his house, I pulled the car to the curb. He brushed his lips over my hand and got out quickly. "Tomorrow," he said, and his words were not a question but an answer—and a promise.

The house, my so-called home, seemed empty and unwelcoming. It didn't bother me, not really, not anymore, but I couldn't help noticing the emptiness a little more each day.

I set up my laptop at the kitchen table and sketched out some topics for articles. I was pleasantly surprised by how easily the ideas flowed. Then again, after 11 years of being a military spouse, there wasn't much I didn't know about Base life. And David talked so oftens about the hospital that I pretty much wrote out an entire article in one go.

I was enjoying myself too much because I didn't realize how late it had gotten. Suddenly David was standing over me inspecting the kitchen for evidence of a meal, when he realized nothing was ready, his already chilly look became glacial.

"The least you could do is to prepare a meal when I come home, Caroline, instead of playing around on your computer. I should throw the damn thing away."

"I wasn't *playing*," I said sourly. "I'm working on some articles for *City Beat*—they've accepted the one I wrote on surfing and they're publishing it on Thursday with my photographs."

He frowned. "What for?"

"Because they thought it was *good*. It may be a surprise to you, David, but there are some people out there who think I can actually do something useful."

"What would be useful would be for my wife to cook a fucking meal when I come home in the evenings." He paused, staring coolly at me. "I don't know what's gotten into you lately, Caroline. You're forgetful, distracted, disorganized. In fact, I'd say that you've been acting very strangely for some time."

He paused, waiting for his words to sink in. I stared back, afraid he suspected something. For all his faults, my husband was not a stupid man. At least, not in that way.

"I think you should see a doctor. I've made you an appointment to see Dr. Ravel," he said at last, his tone carefully neutral.

"What? There's nothing wrong with me! Who's Dr. Ravel?"

"A competent gynecologist, Caroline. I suspect you're experiencing an early menopause."

I couldn't help gaping at him. He was really unbelievable.

"David, I'm only 30! Most women don't reach the menopause until they're 50."

"Don't be obtuse, Caroline. Early menopause is not uncommon and you have all the symptoms."

"What symptoms, for fuck's sake?"

"Don't use language like that, Caroline. It's unpleasant and unnecessary."

"What symptoms, David?"

"Mood swings, irritability ... loss of libido. Dr. Ravel will undertake a colposcopy to ascertain which stage you're at. They are expecting you at OB-GYN Reception at 10AM. I've already checked that our insurance covers the exam."

"David, I've never heard anything so ridiculous. I..."

"Maybe I should make you an appointment with a psychiatrist instead!"

I was outraged. "How dare you!"

"Then you tell me why you refuse intercourse with your husband!" he snarled.

He turned away from me, his ferocious temper barely in check.

Gingerly, I closed my laptop. My hands shook slightly as I prepared a cold pasta salad, but my brain was working feverishly, desperately trying to come up with a suitable reply, some convincing words. As usual, his molten anger silenced me.

I was furious with myself for not standing up to him. Then again, he'd had 11 years' practice making me feeling inconsequential, there was certainly no reason for him to stop now.

Although he didn't suspect the truth, I couldn't help thinking it would be a case of when, not if. My life, once so gray and certain, was now on shifting sands. Whatever the catalyst, no one had forced me to go in the direction I'd chosen. I wasn't sure what choices I had now, other than to wait until Sebastian was of age. If I went to a lawyer about a divorce tomorrow, how long would it be before my 'affair' became known? That was the crux of the problem. I was committing a crime, David's only crime was to be born an asshole and just grow bigger.

We ate in silence and he didn't speak to me again that evening. Nor did he try to touch me, which was a blessing.

Breakfast passed with the same cheerless routine. Perhaps we both breathed a sigh of relief when it was time for him to go to work. He flung down my appointment card as he left.

At 9.45AM, I presented myself at the OB-GYN reception. The waiting room was already full of pregnant women, toddlers and babies, each trying to make themselves heard above the din. I felt conspicuous and ill at ease. One of the women smiled kindly and raised her eyebrows in acknowledgment of the noise. She probably assumed I was newly pregnant.

What the hell was I doing here? I'd had a Pap smear just six months ago and that had come back clear. I had no menopausal symptoms and I knew David was just using this as a means of exercising his power: and I was letting him. Again.

I was ashamed of myself for being so weak. Part of me wanted to get it over with to appease him for a few more weeks, but another, newer, bolder part was telling me to stand up to him.

Somewhere a door opened and the moving air caused posters tacked to a bulletin board to flutter colorfully. The notice for a women's rights group caught my eye: 'However we dress, wherever we go—yes means yes, and no means no'.

There was something about the simple wording that resonated—perhaps it was my turn, at last, to say no.

I took a deep breath and stood up. The appointment receptionist looked irritated to see me standing in front of her window for a second time.

"Yes, may I help you?" she said curtly, clearly having no wish to help me whatsoever.

"Yes, you may. I had an appointment for 10AM with Dr. Ravel, but I've decided to cancel it."

"Cancel it?"

"That's right. I apologize for wasting Dr. Ravel's time." *But not yours, you sour-faced bitch.*

"Well, that's most irregular. Dr. Ravel is a very busy woman."

"Hence the apology."

"Hmm, well. I can give you another appointment in five weeks and..."

"No, there's no need. No appointment necessary. Thank you."

And I left, leaving her puzzled and annoyed.

Damn, that felt good! Even though I knew I'd have to face David's ire later. What the hell: I was a habitual irritation to him anyway. For the first time, it occurred to me that he might even be a happier man without me in his life. I wasn't sure he'd see it that way, without his cook, cleaner, party organizer and occasional sexual toy, but it might even be true.

I drove out of the hospital parking lot feeling elated and jittery. I'd taken my first baby steps toward independence.

On a roll and feeling unusually daring, I headed out to the country club. I knew Sebastian had taken a double shift. He hadn't been happy at not seeing me in the morning, but when I said I was having a doctor's check-up, he'd acquiesced at once and said he'd work to take his mind off 'things'. He promised to text me on his break but now I was hoping to see him before that: a surprise.

The country club was located at the end of a long, private driveway, fringed by an avenue of mature palm trees. The single story was old Spanish-style—white with tall arches, a wide, cool veranda running around three sides, and frothing with bougainvillea in rich magenta. Wides steps led up to an impressive frontage, and green lawns flowed down toward an 18 hole golf course. Behind the building, I could see the ocean stretching to the horizon, breakers rumbling in the background. Whoever had picked the location had done half the job of selling memberships.

My old Ford looked so out of place I dumped it in the rear parking lot, deftly avoiding the valet service as I walked to the entrance.

It was clear that the dress code was more than advisory: men wore polo shirts with collars, and women's skirts were of a decent length. I couldn't spot an un-tucked shirt anywhere. A handsome young man in uniform smiled at me as I walked up the steps. Sebastian had hinted at the way staff were selected: those I could see were young and attractive, wearing Navy blue shorts and plain, white t-shirts with the club's logo discreetly positioned.

I was glad I'd dressed up for my abortive hospital appointment, otherwise I'd have felt even more intimidated by the grand surroundings.

"May I help you, ma'am?" said the well-dressed young woman at the reception desk.

"Yes, I'd like a membership form, please."

"Certainly, ma'am. Would that be an individual membership, associate member, executive or junior executive member, non-resident membership or social membership?"

"I ... I..."

"The individual membership starts at $1,000 per month, with an initial fee of $4,000 or for a social membership, if you don't wish to play golf..."

"I believe Mrs. Wilson is entitled to the Active Duty Military Membership."

The voice made me jump.

"Of course, Mrs. Vordstadt," said the receptionist, rummaging through her files, then passing over a thick sheaf of paper.

I turned to find Donna standing behind me, smiling at my surprise.

"I didn't figure you for a country club type, Caroline. Or perhaps this is more David's thing?"

I tried to wipe the shock from my face but I don't think I was entirely successful.

"Donna, how ... how nice to see you. Yes, I, um, just came to pick up a membership form—I had no idea there were so many different types." *Or that it would be so expensive.*

"One of the few benefits of military service—and it puts the fee down to a more manageable $500 a month," she whispered conspiratorially.

She took my elbow and led me out to a seating area at the rear. Several women were sipping cocktails, even at this early hour. The view of the ocean was stunning and the club had a large pool overlooking the wavess, peppered with sun loungers and fringed umbrellas. I was far from enjoying it though—foolishly, it hadn't occurred to me that I'd bump into anyone I knew here. And now Donna was ordering coffee for the two of us.

"I'm so glad you're here, Caroline. We haven't had a chance to chat and I did so want to thank you for inviting us to your home on Saturday. I really should have called before now."

"Oh, no, that's fine…"

There was an awkward pause—perhaps we were both remembering how the evening had ended—or our different versions of that.

"Is David a golfer?" she asked at last.

"A little, in Florida," I said, flustered. He'd played a couple of times that I could recall.

"And you?"

"I prefer the beach," I said, truthfully. "Swimming, sailing—anything like that."

"Have you tried surfing?"

I'm sure I blushed beet red: I was thankful that my tan covered it up a little.

"No, I've never tried."

"You should get the boys to teach you," she suggested.

I nearly choked on my coffee.

"I'm sure Mitch Peters wouldn't mind helping out."

I smiled weakly. Clearly the 'boys' she was thinking of were quite different from the ones—the one—I had in mind.

"I thought you might have been tempted," she continued.

I was ready to crawl through the floor—her words laced with unintentional double entendres.

And then I saw Sebastian.

He looked so handsome in his crisp, snug uniform, no one would have guessed he was still only 17. Certainly not me—he looked more like early twenties. It was easy to see how the club could get away with allowing him to serve alcohol. It seemed I suffered from the same hypocrisy.

Donna turned to see what, or rather who, I was staring at.

"Oh, there's the Hunters' boy. I remember Shirley Peters mentioning that her son was going to get him a job here."

She waved to attract his attention, as I sank lower into my chair.

He hesitated for a moment, then strode over.

"Good morning, ladies," he said smoothly.

His audacity brought a small smile to my lips.

"Hello, Sebastian," said Donna.

"Hi," I said, shyly.

"How long have you been working here?" asked Donna.

"Just a few days. Ches Peters got me a job."

"And how are you liking it?"

"It's getting better," he said, glancing at me.

Donna raised her eyebrows and I could tell she was trying not to smile.

I frowned. Sebastian's recklessness was hardly helpful.

"Can I get you ladies anything?" he asked, sounding a little flustered as he correctly interpreted my cool expression.

"No, we're good, thank you. We're just having coffee."

"Well, okay, then ... I'd better get back to work..."

Donna waved him on his way and with a last flicker of his eyes toward me, he headed off.

"He's such a nice boy," said Donna thoughtfully. "Amazing he's turned out so well when you consider..." She paused. "I was very impressed with how he handled his parents last Saturday."

"Yes," I agreed quickly, wanting to get her off the subject but not sure how.

"Of course," continued Donna, "you knew him as a child. What was he like then?"

I couldn't help smiling. "Oh, he was so sweet. He used to come to our house after school. My father was particularly fond of him."

Dear Papa. My smile faded. How he would have loved Sebastian the man, as well as the boy he'd known.

Donna touched my arm. "Sorry, Caroline."

I shrugged.

"So, do you think you and David will join?"

Now that I realized how popular the club was with Base families, I was a lot less keen, but I didn't know how I'd get out of it.

"Maybe. It's quite pricey. I'll have to see what David says."

Secretly, I had no intention of telling him I'd been there.

"I know what we'll do," said Donna, enthusiastically, "I'll ask Johan to suggest it to him."

"Oh, that's not necessary." I said, feeling a little panicky.

"It's no trouble," said Donna, decisively. "Besides, it'll be much more fun coming here with you. Do you play tennis?"

~

My trip to the country club hadn't gone exactly as planned. In fact, it was hard to imagine how it could have been worse. Despite my feeble objections, I had Donna's cast iron promise that her husband would speak to my husband about a membership.

I sat in my hot car in the club's parking lot, surrounded by expensive foreign cars, and rubbed my forehead, trying to ward off an incipient headache.

The whole situation was ridiculous—even hilarious—although not to me.

I sent Sebastian a quick message.

Sorry. Not the surprise I'd planned. Cx

I waited a few minutes but there was no reply—he was probably still working. I drove home, determined to sketch out some more ideas for *City Beat*. There was no point in letting the day be a complete wash-out.

As the hands on the kitchen clock crept toward 6PM, I put away my laptop and notebook, and turned my thoughts to making dinner. Risotto wasn't David's favorite but it was quick and easy.

The moment the hands on the clock were aligned vertically, I heard David's Camaro pull up outside. I hurried to set the

table and waited anxiously. Would he fight with me about the missed colposcopy before or after we'd eaten?

His face was impassive although I'm sure mine was a little paler than usual.

"Something you want to tell me, Caroline?" he said, his voice unnervingly even.

I felt my courage shrivel under his chilly gaze.

"Such as?"

"Don't be obtuse. I was talking to Captain Vorstadt today," he said, emphasizing the title 'Captain'.

I frowned. Where was he going with this?

"Apparently you were out at the country club this afternoon."

"It was just a silly thought, David," I said, hurriedly.

"You have many silly thoughts, Caroline, but if people like the Vorstadts are members at the country club, we should certainly join. I'm glad to see you're making more of an effort for a change."

I gaped at him.

"In fact, Captain Vorstadt suggested we dine there together tomorrow night," he continued smugly, "so I can see the facilities."

David looked sickeningly pleased with himself, presumably because a senior officer had invited him—or rather us—to dinner.

He tossed his cap onto the couch and didn't even ask about the exam I'd skipped. I knew the reprieve was temporary but I was happy to take what I could get.

I spent the evening with anxiety twisting my stomach but nothing more was mentioned. When David finally headed to the bathroom to get ready for bed, I switched my phone back on. Sebastian's response made me smile:

You always make my heart beat faster. Tomorrow?

Yes, tomorrow.

CHAPTER EIGHT

David was almost cheerful as he left for work. The prospect of dinner with a superior officer had put him in a good mood and kept him there.

"Wear something nice tonight: a cocktail dress. And heels, of course. In fact, buy a new dress."

"David, that's really not necessary. I've dry-cleaned the green one."

I'd thought he'd be pleased with my frugality, but, as usual, I was in the wrong.

"For God's sake, Caroline! I can't have the Vorstadts thinking I can only afford to buy my wife one decent dress. Get a new one."

"I had plans for this morning..."

"Such as?"

"Well, writing..."

"You can do that anytime. Buy a new dress. But no more than $150. You don't want to look like you're trying too hard."

Like you're *trying too hard, you mean.*

I sighed. There went my plans to spend the morning at the beach with Sebastian. Well, maybe if I went to the mall, I could be done in an hour.

I watched David drive off then picked up my phone to text Sebastian.

**I have to go clothes shopping. Pick you up later?
Sorry. Cx**

Immediately my phone started ringing.

"Why are you going shopping? Don't you want to see me?"

"Don't be..." *Rephrase.* "It's not that—the Vorstadts have invited us to dinner tonight. David is insisting I buy a new dress."

"I wish you wouldn't say that."

"Say what?"

"When you talk about you and ... him. You say 'us'."

There was a long silence as I tried to frame a response but Sebastian spoke first.

"Can I come with you?"

"Where?"

"Can I come clothes shopping with you?"

I was nonplussed. "Well, I guess ... if you like."

"Great! See you at the park at our usual time. Love ya!"

I shook my head as he ended the call. I couldn't help thinking of all the times I'd seen pitiable men, waiting outside women's changing rooms, looking for all the world as if they'd been there since the dawn of time. But I was also intrigued, and if Sebastian wanted to come with me, well, I wasn't going to argue.

He was sitting on the curb with the hood of his sweatshirt pulled over his head, as if he was some punk looking for trouble. The thought made me smile—it was the polar opposite of Sebastian's personality which was so warm and thoughtful and caring, although I was beginning to recognize a reckless streak in him, too.

"Hi!"

"Hi yourself!" he answered happily as he scrambled in and fastened his seatbelt.

I longed to lean over and kiss him but we couldn't risk it here.

"So where are we going?"

I shook my head. "I don't know: a mall somewhere."

"Mom goes to Mission Valley. They've got all those brand name stores out there."

I screwed up my face at the suggestion.

"That's not really me. Besides, I want to avoid going somewhere I might run into your mom!" What a horrifying thought. Sebastian clearly agreed because I saw him wince.

"I thought maybe we could head up toward Miramar—there's that mall at Westfield UTC."

"Whatever."

"So, do you make a habit of this?"

He looked puzzled.

"Going shopping for women's clothes?"

He grinned widely.

"It's my new hobby, especially if you're buying underwear?"

I laughed, blushing slightly.

"Well, I ought to—I seem to keep losing mine."

He sniggered. "Yeah! That's fun."

His happiness spilled over and I felt my spirits soaring—six uninterrupted hours with the man I loved. Six stolen hours.

"Did I tell you I was a member of the surf life-saving club at school?" he asked, changing the subject.

I could tell he had something on his mind.

"No, but I guess I'm not surprised."

"Well, my manager at work, Miss Perez, she said that they'd get me certified for CPR and First Aid so I could be a trainee lifeguard at the pool. And I can start studying for the Open Water course, too, although I won't be able to take the test until I'm eigh— until later. It'll make it easier to get work in NYC."

"Oh. Okay."

"And I was thinking," he continued quickly, "if I take a course to be a personal trainer, I could earn maybe a hundred bucks an hour once I'm qualified. You know, while you're getting your journalism career going. I was looking at some apartments on the internet: they're pretty expensive. I couldn't find anything less than $2,000 a month unless we live in one of

the outer boroughs, and we'd take a train or a ferry to get to work and school. It's a little slower, I guess, but a lot cheaper. But by the end of the summer, I'll have enough for the first month's rent wherever we live."

He looked at me anxiously.

A powerful swell of emotion swept through me. Here he was, 17 years old, planning for our future, determined to make it happen—and what had I contributed? Nothing. David had steered my life over the last 11 years, now I was letting—expecting even—that Sebastian would do the same. I felt ashamed.

"What do you think, Caro?"

"I think you're extraordinary," I said honestly.

He blinked, surprised by my unexpected answer. Then he grinned.

"Extraordinary, huh? I can live with that. And you called me 'God' the other night—that was okay, too."

"I like your plan," I said, deliberately ignoring the second half of his reply. "But we need to make sure you can fit your college courses in, too. I don't want you giving up a university education. Besides, I could look for some translation work or maybe even teaching Italian—conversation classes—nothing too formal as I'm not a qualified teacher."

"Well, you know, I looked at that, too. You could be a translator for the courts in NY—you can get $125 a day. Federal Courts pay even more." He reached out and took my hand, then kissed it. "I can't wait for us to be together."

Neither could I.

"Well, that's definitely a plan. If I could earn that sort of money ... although they probably wouldn't want Italian interpreters that much, but even so ... are you still planning on a joint major in English Lit and Italian?"

"Sure!"

"Do you know what you want to do after?"

He nodded slowly. "I'd like to go to Europe. I have this image of you and me on a motorcycle traveling through Italy. I don't know, teaching English, picking grapes—I don't care. I've never been outside the US."

"That sounds wonderful! We could go to Capezzano Inferiore—it's a small village in the hills above Salerno—where Papa was born. I've always wanted to go."

"Then we'll go," he said, simply.

I was grinning from ear to ear, smiling from the inside out.

"Do you have family there?" Sebastian asked thoughtfully.

"I'm not really sure—some second cousins, I think. Why?"

"We should try to find them," he said. "If they're as crazy as your dad, it could be pretty wild."

I laughed out loud, delighted with the picture he was painting. And I decided that as soon as I went home, I would start planning our escape in earnest—no more taking a back seat in my own life.

"There's the sign for Westfield," said Sebastian, bringing my attention back to the road.

I took the exit ramp and followed the signs.

The mall was a vast sprawl of boutique shops and places to eat with a Sears at one end and Macy's at the other.

"Where do you want to start?"

"I have no idea. Let's just make it quick."

"I thought all girls liked shopping?"

"Not this one."

"You look beautiful whatever you wear."

I stared at him. "You always say the sweetest things! How do you do that?"

He shrugged and looked embarrassed. "What about this shop?"

"You're changing the subject."

He smiled and towed me inside.

"May I help you, ma'am, sir?"

Seeing as it was a women's clothing store, I wasn't entirely sure how the sales assistant was going to help Sebastian, although going by the look on her face, I could make a damned good guess. And, of course, she was younger than me.

An unaccustomed desire for sudden violence flooded through me.

"I'm looking for a black cocktail dress," I said coolly. "Size four."

It occurred to me that I'd never once been jealous of another woman looking at David—maybe that should have told me something. I couldn't work out how much of what I was feeling now was to do with my own insecurities. I didn't want to spoil today, so I pushed the wretched thought aside.

The assistant picked out a couple of dresses and I took them into the changing room.

I could hear her chatting to Sebastian through the curtain. Well, I could hear her trying to hit on him.

"Are you from the Base?" she said.

"Yeah, but..."

"Are you, like, a pilot?"

"No, I..."

"But you're a Marine, right?"

I pulled back the curtain sharply, and the assistant jumped.

"What about this one, honey?" I said, throwing a few poses, for her benefit as much as Sebastian's.

"Wow! You look great, Caro!"

I had his full attention. From my peripheral vision I saw the sales assistant pout. Hmm, shopping was proving a lot more fun than I'd expected.

"You want to see the other dress, honey?" I said, doing another slow turn.

"Yeah!"

I smirked and ducked back into the changing room, throwing a look at the assistant that dared her to resume her conversation with Sebastian. Sensibly, she declined the challenge.

The second dress was even more fitted and skimmed the top of my knees.

"Can you zip me up, honey?" I whispered through the curtain, still enjoying my performance.

I gazed over my shoulder at Sebastian, trying to play

seductive. His presence alone made me feel sexy. His expression immediately heated, and suddenly the confines of the changing room seemed unbearably hot. He pulled up the zipper with aching slowness, brushing a soft kiss over my bare shoulder.

"You look beautiful, baby," he said quietly.

Suddenly, we weren't playing anymore. The assistant coughed, embarrassed.

"How's the size, ma'am?"

"Fine, thank you."

"It's perfect," said Sebastian in a low tone.

I wandered out of the shop in a daze. Sebastian insisted on carrying the bag and wrapped his free hand around my limp fingers.

"You want to get some lunch?"

"Sebastian, it's only 11.15AM!"

"Yeah, well I'm hungry."

"You never stop eating. You're going to be enormous when you get older."

"Nah. I'll have you to keep me fit."

Dear God, I hoped I was up to the challenge. A few hours with Sebastian was yoga, Pilates and aerobics all rolled into one delicious workout.

"Donna said I should get Mitch to teach me to surf," I commented slyly.

Sebastian wasn't pleased.

"I can teach you! You don't need him."

"Are you pouting at me?" I laughed. "You are! You're pouting."

I brought our twined hands up to my mouth and kissed his fingers.

"I'm just teasing you."

He still looked hurt and I rather regretted trying to make him jealous. I suppose it was a childish tit-for-tat—that sales assistant had upset me more than I was willing to admit. But it wasn't fair to take it out on Sebastian. It wasn't his fault girls were throwing themselves at him.

"Come on, I'll buy you coffee and a Danish."

He settled on pastrami, lettuce and tomato on ciabatta bread, a regular black coffee with two sugars, and a Danish pastry, as promised. I had a large espresso and watched him wolf down the food. Our grocery bill in New York was going to be huge.

"Where else in Europe would you like to go?"

He swallowed his mouthful and drank some coffee while he thought.

"Well, everywhere, but I'd really like to go to Southern Spain—see all the Moorish stuff. I saw a picture of the Alhambra palace once—it looked, I don't know, like 'One Thousand and One Nights'."

I was surprised and I realized how little I knew of him, his hopes and dreams. The more I learned, the more fascinated I became.

"You've read 'Arabian Nights'?"

He cocked his head to look at me. "You don't remember, do you?"

I was confused. "Remember what?"

"You gave me the book to read—when I was a kid. I must have read it a hundred times. I used to think you were Scheherazade."

Scheherazade: the princess who told a different story every night to keep the king from beheading her. I wasn't very keen on the comparison. Except then he fell in love with her and married her.

"Just because you were such an amazing storyteller," Sebastian said, intuiting my reaction. "I guess I'm not surprised you became a writer."

I smiled gamely. "I'm trying to become a writer."

"You will," he said, certainty coloring his voice. "You are."

I struggled to hold back the tears that threatened to betray me. His encouragement, his certainty that I had the ability to achieve my dream, it meant more to me than I could ever express.

"What about you?" I asked, trying to speak naturally. "After our road trip..."

He shrugged. "I don't know. Mom and Dad always expected me to go the military route."

"Is that what you want to do?"

I managed to suppress a shudder at the thought of being pulled back toward living on military bases.

"No, I don't think so. I mean, parts of it would be great—but I'd like to travel."

"Traveling isn't a job," I laughed. "Unless you want to work on a cruise ship."

"Maybe," he said smiling. "You could be a travel writer and I'll ... carry your bags."

"That sounds like a plan."

He leaned over and kissed me so I could feel the smile on his lips.

This kiss was different somehow: more relaxed, less desperate—just sweet and loving. I stroked his cheek and he sighed happily, leaning into my hand.

"I know," he said, suddenly sitting up. "I'm going to take you surfing. You said you wanted to learn..."

"No, no! It was Donna who said I should..."

"Are you chicken?"

"Yes! The water's too cold."

He laughed. "They've invented wetsuits. You'll be fine. I know a place just north of La Jolla where we can rent boards. Come on! We've got a couple of hours. You can drop me off at work on the way back. We've got time."

I really had no desire to immerse myself in chilly Pacific waters but his enthusiasm was contagious. Maybe it was his recklessness that was catching, his unbreachable zest for life. Maybe I was just no longer afraid to live.

"Okay, let's go!"

We abandoned the car next to a shabby-looking surf shack that perched precariously above a small, secluded cove. The water was turquoise, and I imagined it to be the color of the Mediterranean, wondering if that was something I'd ever see—the sea my dear Papa had lived by as a small child.

"Hey, man," said the owner of the shack. "Long time no see."

I immediately felt anxious. It hadn't occurred to me that Sebastian would take me somewhere he was known. My eyes flickered to him nervously and he squeezed my hand reassuringly.

"Yeah, can we get a couple of shorties, rash vests and a spongey board?"

"Sure, man. Come on through."

Sebastian let the owner go ahead then whispered in my ear.

"Don't worry. He says that to everyone. He hasn't got a clue who I am. It's cool."

I tried to relax, but the shot of adrenaline was still working its way through my body—I smiled wanly.

The owner sized us up expertly and handed over a couple of cropped wetsuits, silky rash vests to wear under the neoprene and a large, heavy foam-covered surfboard. I was glad that Sebastian tucked it under his arm—it was too wide for me to be able to carry easily.

"That'll be twenty bucks," drawled the owner.

Before I could stop him, Sebastian pulled out his wallet and handed the man a couple of bills.

"And I'll need a credit card for security, dude."

Sebastian's eyes flickered uncertainly to me. I knew he didn't have a credit card and I wasn't really keen on the idea of handing one over that described me as 'Mrs. Carolina M. Wilson'.

"How about we give you our car keys?" said Sebastian, thinking quickly. "We're parked right over there."

He pointed at my old Ford.

"Dude, that piece of shit isn't gonna pay for anything!"

"Ah, come on! What are we going to do? Go running down the highway carrying a spongey?"

The owner held up his hands in defeat. "Okay, okay, but only because your girlfriend has such a cute smile, man!"

I thanked him quickly as I dragged a suddenly angry Sebastian out of the door.

"He was hitting on you," he grumbled.

"Hardly!"

"He was."

I shook my head. "Are you going to teach me to surf, or what?"

Sebastian grinned. It really didn't take much to put him in a good mood—how very different from David.

Neither of us had swimming costumes. I just tugged on the wetsuit over my panties, sand unhooked my bra when I'd pulled on the rash vest, so I was half-dressed. Sebastian watched in fascination. I didn't think it warranted *that* close a scrutiny. He caught my expression and winked, pulling his borrowed wetsuit over a pair of tight-fitting gray briefs that soon had my mind wandering.

He carried the board down to the sand and gave me a quick lesson on how to pop up using a rocking motion. He made it look easy—probably something to do with his well-developed upper body strength.

The heavy beginner's board was covered in soft foam to help prevent injuries among the uninitiated, but it was also impregnated with sand, and the palms of my hands soon began to feel sore.

"You're getting it," said Sebastian encouragingly. "Let's try you on a few waves. I'll push you onto them and tell you when to pop up."

The waves in the cove were small and well ordered—perfect for learning on. I lay face down on the board and felt the cold water splash around me.

"Get ready! Paddle, paddle, paddle. Now!"

Sebastian pushed me onto a small wave and as the board began to tip down onto the green-water, I popped up, wobbled for a few feet then fell off sideways. I managed to close my mouth but felt seawater gush up my nose. My head broke the surface of the water as I coughed and rubbed my eyes. My long hair hung like seaweed over my face.

Sebastian was laughing but he looked at me proudly.

"Wow, Caro! You just rode your first wave! That was awesome!"

He kissed my salty face and hugged me tightly as the water rippled around our waists.

"Try again!"

We spent another hour playing in the ocean and, by the end, I'd managed to ride a wave for several seconds and even put in a small turn.

Sebastian hadn't got bored or shouted at me or shown any signs of impatience. I was slightly in shock, but elated, too.

"So, how do you like being a surfer dude?" he said, smiling at me proudly.

"I love it, but I'm exhausted. It's almost as tiring as spending the night with you," I teased him.

He laughed happily then sighed. "I'd like to do that again, but we can't, can we? Not for a while." He frowned and squinted at the sun. "I have to get to work soon—we'd better head back."

We hadn't planned the surf trip so I didn't have a towel in the car. Instead we had to pull our clothes back on over damp, salty bodies, and my hair dripped chilly drops of water down my shoulders.

It was easier for me to get dressed since sI was wearing a skirt, but I enjoyed my private ogling as Sebastian pulled off his boxer briefs, only partially hidden by the car door, and grabbed his jeans. I loved watching the flex and ripple of his muscles under his golden tan, the way his jeans dropped down from his waist to hang on his hips, and the way two tiny lines appeared between his eyebrows when he was concentrating on something.

He grinned as he saw me watching him, and with deliberate slowness pulled his t-shirt over his damp chest, so the washed-out fabric clung to him.

I really wanted to pull it off him again but he had to get to work and I wanted to spend a couple of hours working on my next *City Beat* story.

I'd decided to write about what it was like for military

families to move around the country from base to base. I had some experience of that, and I knew that Donna had lived in at least three other states. She and Johan had also been stationed overseas twice already with the possibility of another stint in Germany on the horizon.

"Time to get back to the real world," Sebastian said wistfully. "Maybe I'll see you tonight?"

"I rather hope not," I said, truthfully.

Sebastian looked hurt.

"It's too hard to act normal when you're there," I explained softly.

He nodded slowly. "I know what you mean ... but I'd still like to see you."

I sighed and shook my head.

"Well, can I come to your house tomorrow?"

"Sebastian, I don't think so. You know what people are like around here—all it would take would be for you to be seen coming in or leaving. Or if someone came to the door because they'd seen my car in the driveway and I ... we..."

He knew what I was saying and he knew as well as I did which risks were acceptable and which weren't. We were making up the rules as we went along, but there were still rules.

"When *can* I see you?" he said, sulkily.

"I'm still free tomorrow. Maybe we could go surfing again?"

"I want to make love to you, Caro," he muttered, gazing at my fingers as he squeezed them gently.

I took a deep breath as the familiar flickering tongues of love and lust swept through me.

"We could find a motel," I said, softly.

He looked up, his eyes wide.

"Do you mean it?"

"Yes," I said. "I want to be with you, too."

He closed his eyes and breathed deeply, a glorious smile spreading across his face.

He pulled me into a hug and leaned his head into my neck. I reached up and stroked his hair, which was nearly dry already.

I dropped him off at the end of the long driveway leading to the country club and watched as he waved once, then jogged along the avenue and out of sight.

I drove home with the sun beating down and all my car windows open. A brief glance in the mirror told me I looked like a cavewoman, with wild, salty hair hanging in clumps. I don't know how Sebastian managed not to laugh at me.

I showered quickly and sat in my robe to tap out the first few hundred words of my article, keeping one eye open for David's return.

As soon as I heard his car in the driveway, I snapped the laptop shut and headed to the bedroom to at least look like I was spending time getting ready. David imagined that all women took hours doing their hair and makeup before going out—it was one of his favorite stereotypes. It came in useful when I wanted an extra half-hour of peace and quiet.

I slipped on the new dress, remembering Sebastian's scorching look as he'd zipped it up. It was a soft chiffon hung over a fitted bustier top and clinging skirt, so plain, it was almost severe, but also elegant and sophisticated.

I dug out my simple, gold necklace that my father had given me and matched it with a pair of plain, gold hoop earrings.

I was just sweeping my hair back to pin it up when David walked into the bedroom.

He stopped and did a double take.

"Is that it?"

"My new dress? Yes."

"We're going out to dinner, Caroline, not attending a funeral."

Once his words would have hurt me, that evening I just stared at him impassively in the mirror.

"It's a classic little black dress, David."

"It's dull."

"It's all I have."

He scowled.

"For fuck's sake, Caroline. Do I have to supervise everything you do? You can't even buy a fucking dress that's appropriate for dinner."

I didn't reply. There was no point. Unfortunately, it meant the evening would now start on an awkward note. I hoped he'd be able to hide his annoyance from the Vorstadts—I didn't want Donna throwing any more pitying glances my way.

Johan's car arrived outside with typical military precision. David was wearing a dark blue suit with matching tie. If it hadn't been for his permanently sour expression, he would have been good-looking.

Johan stepped out of the car to open the door, and blinked when he saw me.

"Good evening, Caroline, David."

"Hello, Johan. Hi Donna."

"Caroline, darling. Don't you look gorgeous," gushed Donna. "Johan, doesn't she look amazing?!"

"I'll say!" agreed Johan enthusiastically.

I saw David frown. It was going to be a long evening.

David sat up front with Johan, while Donna and I chatted in the back. I freely grilled her about her experiences of moving around the country, explaining it was for a new article.

"I can introduce you to some of the other wives," she said. "Well, you know Shirley Peters—she's moved around even more than I have."

"I've spoken to her on the phone, but never actually met her," I admitted.

"I'll set something up," she said. "Shirley is a member of the country club, too. Why don't we all meet over there tomorrow afternoon? I'll drive."

Oh no! Not tomorrow—I'd promised Sebastian.

"Could we make it Friday? I have one or two things on tomorrow."

"Why sure! I'll phone Shirley and set it up."

I found myself looking forward to it and I was curious to meet Mitch's wife. The fact that David would be torn between his disapproval of Shirley and his desire to encourage my friendship with Donna only added to my pleasure. *But how the hell was I going to get through the next three-and-a-half months with this man?*

First we had to get through dinner.

Johan gallantly offered me his arm as we walked up the front steps, much to Donna's obvious amusement and David's sullen irritation.

The maitre d' fussed around our table, pulling out chairs for Donna and me before introducing our waiter for the evening—a familiar face was grinning down at us.

"Oh, hello, Ches," said Donna, pleasantly. "What a nice surprise! So you'll be our waiter. How are you?"

"Very well thanks, Mrs. Vorstadt." Then he turned to Johan. "Hello, sir. Hi, Caroline!" he grinned at me.

I smiled back. "Hi, Ches, how are..."

But before I could finish the sentence David snapped, "Her name is 'Mrs. Wilson'."

Ches's smile vanished, while Donna and Johan looked embarrassed.

"David," I said softly. "I've met Ches before: he and his father were kind enough to help me with my surfing article."

"I know who he is, Caroline," said David sharply, "and it's not appropriate that he addresses you by your first name."

Donna hid a look of disgust behind her menu, and I saw a hard look pass over Johan's face. David had screwed himself royally this time. I didn't care about that, but I was mortified by the way he'd treated Ches.

"Perhaps you can tell us what the specials are, Ches?" said Donna coolly.

"Sure, Mrs. Vorstadt," said Ches, with a chastened tone.

We placed our orders and I tried to think of some way to apologize for David's appalling rudeness.

"By the way, Ches," I said, "the surfing article will be published in *City Beat* tomorrow. There's a photo of you and your dad in it. I'll buy a copy for each of you. Will you tell your dad for me? And Sebastian and Fido. I never did find out his real name."

He grinned at me. "Okay, thanks, Mrs. Wilson, I'll do that."

He walked away smiling but David pursed his lips. "Don't be over-familiar with the wait staff, Caroline."

"He's our neighbor," said Donna, raising her eyebrows to make the point.

"Of course," said David after half a beat.

Johan cleared this throat and threw a warning look at his wife.

It was a wonder we didn't all have indigestion before we started. But then our wine waiter arrived and the talk devolved into a discussion of how well New World reds stacked up against Old World. I kept my mouth firmly shut—now was not the time to irritate David even further.

Johan picked a soft Californian Merlot and ordered a jug of iced water.

Our entrées were very slow arriving and Johan's eyes began flicking back and forward toward the kitchen. The maitre d' came out to apologize, saying that two members of staff had suddenly gone sick and that they were short-staffed but trying to remedy the situation.

That's when I saw Sebastian.

He wasn't in his usual sports assistant uniform. Instead he was dressed in long, black pants, a white button down shirt with a black bow tie. He was walking purposefully toward our table, carrying a basket full of small bread rolls.

No! No! No!

I then had to endure the hideous spectacle of my lover serving my husband, while I tried to stop myself from screaming and running.

Donna smiled as I studied my linen napkin.

"Hello, Sebastian. We've already seen Ches this evening. It looks like you boys are running the place tonight."

I didn't dare look up to see his face but I could tell from his voice that he was nervous as he tried to laugh.

"Not really. They're just very short-staffed—I haven't done this before."

"I'm sure you'll be fine, dear. You look very handsome, doesn't he, Caroline?"

My head jerked up at the sound of my name.

"Oh, yes. Very."

There was a pause that felt long enough for the world to end.

"Would you like some bread?" Sebastian asked awkwardly.

I shook my head while David reached across me to take two rolls. Donna also declined but Johan looked hungry enough to eat all the rolls and the basket, too. Luckily Ches was close behind bringing out our entrées. I had no idea how I was going to eat anything, my stomach was so tied in knots. And I still couldn't look at Sebastian.

The men dug into their food with gusto. I glanced up to see Donna give me a small wink, I had no idea what she was referring to but I tried to smile back. I probably just looked sick. From the corner of my eye, I could see Sebastian waiting on other tables and Ches hurrying to and fro.

"I wonder if those boys will both enlist," said Donna, musing aloud, "you know—following in their fathers' footsteps."

"The Hunter boy is going to," said David confidently. "I don't know about the other one."

"Really?" said Donna. "I'm quite surprised—I rather thought Sebastian might do something else."

"No," said David with finality, "Donald told me. Estelle has talked him into letting the boy have a year at college first," he sniffed disdainfully, "but that's all he's prepared to pay for, the boy will enlist after that."

"That seems a little harsh," said Donna frowning. "Surely they'd let him get his degree once he's started?"

David shrugged. He really wasn't that interested.

I was shocked yet again by Donald and Estelle's callousness, I knew for a fact that Sebastian was unaware of this plan. I was even more determined that he'd get his degree if I had anything to do with it.

The conversation moved onto other people we knew in common and for me at least, into safer territory.

"Where did you get your fabulous dress, Caroline?" Donna asked while Ches cleared away the entrée plates.

"Westfield. I went this morning."

"Oh! I wish I'd known. I was there this morning, too. We could have gone together. What a pity I didn't see you."

I shuddered internally at the thought of a disaster had so narrowly been avoided.

"I don't know why she had to pick black," David complained. "It's so funereal."

Donna stared at him in astonishment then turned her sympathetic eyes to mine. I glanced away and caught Sebastian watching me. He looked angry—he'd obviously heard David's unkind comment.

"Do you have any plans while David is away?" said Donna.

"Excuse me?"

"While he's at the conference ... you know, the thoracic surgery symposium in Dallas?"

I stared at her in bafflement.

"For God's sake, Caroline!" muttered David. "What is the point of me filling in a schedule if you never look at it?"

"When are you going?"

"They're flying out on Friday evening and back Sunday night," Donna added helpfully.

Johan nodded to David. "Have you read the papers yet?"

I barely listened as they discussed the speakers—my mind was racing through the possible ways I could spend my 48 hours of freedom.

"What will you do with yourself, Caroline?" asked Donna.

"Oh, I don't know. I guess I'll be able to get on with my writing."

"And you'll come to the beach barbecue on Sunday?"

She immediately answered my blank expression.

"It's for all the Service families. It's usually pretty good fun and, as you're by yourself ... do say yes."

With everyone staring at me, I had no choice.

"Yes, of course I'll come," I said.

I felt like some weird internal elevator was rushing up and down with its cargo of emotions—from elation at the thought of David being away for two nights, to come crashing down because precious hours when I could have been with Sebastian would now be squandered at a military picnic. Someone sure had a lousy sense of humor.

***s

I deliberately took my time getting ready for bed once we got back from the country club. I hoped that if I was slow enough David would have fallen asleep by the time I slipped under the covers. So far I had managed to avoid any further confrontations about sex, but I knew it was only a matter of time before David would insist on his conjugal 'rights'.

I closed the toilet lid and sat down with my head in my hands. I couldn't go on like this—the stress was beginning to get to me and it had only been three weeks. *Was that all it had taken for my life to change so completely?* I wasn't cut out for infidelity. Or maybe it was simply that Donna's comment about having been at the mall at the same time as us that had made my anxiety levels spike.

The choices were stark: leave David and set divorce proceedings in action—stay away from Sebastian for another 13 weeks and save money from my writing so we could disappear to NYC together at the end of September—and hope no one put two-and-two together to make four.

Either way people would work out the truth when we both disappeared at the same time—I hoped that once Sebastian was 18 and there was no *proof* of wrong doing, they'd leave us alone. That was my grand plan. And money was going to be an issue. David had his salary paid into a savings account and gave me $1,000 a month for groceries, gas for my car and utility bills. It was only just enough. I had no money of my own. When I'd had my job back east, David had insisted that my wages went into the communal pot. That's what he called it, although I never saw the money again. I didn't even know how much was in our savings account. What a humiliating admission.

But if I could get an article published in *City Beat* every week for the next three months, I'd have over $4,000—enough for seven or eight weeks rent in NYC. It was going to be tight, but when it came down to it, what price freedom?

Although the fact that the age of consent was 17 in New

York was reassuring, I tried not to dwell on it. It didn't change the facts of what I'd done in California, and what I planned to continue doing.

The rumbling sound of David's snores broke through my grim thoughts: it was safe to go to bed.

I slipped carefully under the sheets and tried to think positively. Tomorrow was a new day: my first ever piece of professional writing was going to be published—and I had a promise to keep to Sebastian.

CHAPTER NINE

I COLLECTED SEBASTIAN FROM OUR SPECIAL PLACE NEAR THE park and drove off quickly. He was unusually subdued.

"Are you okay?"

He shrugged.

I really hoped he wasn't going to sulk for long—I'd had enough of that in my life, and in particular from David during the last 24 hours.

"Sebastian, talk to me!"

He sighed. "I *hated* seeing you with that asshole last night. How can you stand it?"

I blanched at the anger in his voice.

"I've got used to it, over the years," I said quietly. "But it's getting harder."

I could feel Sebastian's eyes on me as I drove.

"Sorry," he mumbled.

It was my turn to shrug. He didn't need to apologize—if it was anyone's fault, it was mine. I looked for a way to change the subject and diffuse the tense atmosphere.

"I need to buy a half-dozen copies of *City Beat*. My article is published today—you and Ches will be in it."

"Oh, yeah! I can't wait to see that!" he said, sounding happier.

I pulled up at a convenience store and we both jumped out,

racing each other to the stand of newspapers, suddenly light-hearted.

I tore open a copy of the paper, my heart beating rapidly with excitement. I didn't have to look far—my article was printed on page five with a huge photograph of Sebastian, Mitch, Bill, Ches and Fido.

I felt a sharp pain in my chest as I stared at the photograph of Sebastian. In the picture his sun-lightened hair was still long, and he looked the epitome of young and carefree. I'd taken it just a few hours before his father brutally hacked off his hair, and a few hours after that we had slept together for the first time. But I also felt a great welling up of pride—seeing my article in print with my name beneath it was the first real sense of achievement I'd had since getting my degree at night school three years ago.

"They've spelled your name wrong," said Sebastian frowning.

I scanned the page quickly. "Where?"

"There," he said, pointing at the small, bold type under the heading.

"No, that's correct," I said, looking at him puzzled.

"Your name is 'Carolina', not 'Caroline'?"

"Carolina is the Italian," I said softly, emphasizing the long vowel in the middle. "David—and my mother—preferred the Anglicized version, but the name on my birth certificate is Carolina Maria."

I couldn't help noticing that Sebastian's lips were pressed tightly together and his knuckles where he gripped the newspaper had turned white.

"Why are you so upset?" I asked hesitantly.

Sebastian took a deep breath.

"That bastard has taken everything from you," he growled, "even your name!"

I sighed.

"That's not really true, Sebastian. Everything he's done, I've let him do. Look, this isn't really the place to have this conversation—let me just buy the papers and we'll go. Please."

Sebastian waited outside while I paid for six copies.

When I came out with my newspapers tucked under one arm, he was leaning against the brick wall with his eyes closed. I gazed at him anxiously.

He opened his eyes and looked down at me, forcing a smile.

"Come on, let's go celebrate your first article, Ms Reporter!"

I smiled back, relieved that he was attempting to lift his mood.

"We've got something else to celebrate. David is going away to a medical symposium. He leaves Friday night and doesn't get back until Sunday evening."

A huge and genuine smile spread across Sebastian's face. "*Two nights?!*"

I couldn't help laughing at his obvious happiness.

Without warning, he pulled me into his arms, hugging me to his chest. My free arm wrapped around his neck and I pulled his head down. His lips were warm and soft, his kiss gentle and sweet. Then I felt his lips part and his tongue swept into my mouth. I shivered with desire and I could feel his growing arousal through his jeans.

I tried to remember that we were in public. Reluctantly, I pushed him away from me.

"Let's go to a hotel ... like you said."

His voice was low and rough and he rubbed his hands over his short hair, with evident frustration. But before I could answer, I heard someone calling his name.

My head swiveled to see Ches walking toward us and my cheeks flushed with guilt. *How much had he seen?*

"Hey, man! What's up? Hi, Mrs. Wilson."

I tried to smile. "Hello, Ches. And please call me Caroline. I'm sorry about last night—I hope I didn't embarrass you."

He frowned slightly then laughed it off. "Nah, *you* didn't. It's cool."

Then he turned to Sebastian, a puzzled look on his face, his eyes flitting between us.

"Caroline's article has been published," said Sebastian,

pointing at the pile of newspapers still tucked under my left arm.

"I was going to deliver them," I said smiling more naturally, "but now you're both here."

I handed a copy to Ches and another to Sebastian.

"Awesome!" said Ches. "Dad is going to be stoked when he sees this!"

"I've bought copies for Bill and Fido, too. Can you get these to them for me?" I handed the spare copies to Ches. "By the way, what *is* Fido's real name?"

Ches laughed. "It's Arnold. But don't use it, because he won't answer, and it'll just make him want to break my face if he finds out that I've told you."

His attention returned to Sebastian. "So what you doing, man? I'm going to take off and get a surf in before work—they'll probably want us to start early anyway because they're still short-staffed—whatever, it's more gas money for the van. You want to check out some waves or are you *busy* again?"

There was a brief, uncomfortable pause.

"Well, you guys have fun," I said, forcing a smile. "I have some errands to run."

"Are you going to the club later?" said Sebastian, a little too quickly.

I saw Ches's eyes flicker over to him.

"Oh ... I don't know. I'm not a member yet, although Donna Vorstadt suggested we might go there for coffee, but I'm not sure if that was supposed to be today or tomorrow. Maybe I'll see you both later. *Ciao.*"

I tried to convey a message with my careful words but it was hard to tell if it had got through: Sebastian looked pretty pissed off.

I walked away with my copy of *City Beat* under one arm while my stomach played hopscotch.

I was bereft. I'd counted on a few hours with Sebastian and they'd been ripped away. But I wasn't going to waste my time either: not any more.

I pulled out my cell phone and dialed the number for *City Beat*.

"Hi, this is Caroline Wilson. Could I speak to Carl Winters, please?"

I was put on hold for a few seconds before I heard the editor's voice.

"Hi, Carolina, how are you?"

He pronounced my name the Italian way—just like in my article.

"Good, thank you, Mr. Winters. I wanted to say that I thought the article looked really great. Thank you so much for giving me the opportunity."

"Not at all, and please, call me Carl. I was going to call you. Do you have something for the next issue?"

"Yes, I do. I have 1500 words on the work of the Base hospital and I've nearly finished one on military families and what it means to them to move around a lot. That might be a little longer, if it's okay. I have some interviews with other wives set up for that."

"Excellent! Can you email them to me or, better still, can you come on in? It would be really good to meet you in person."

I made a quick decision.

"I'm free now. I could be there in thirty minutes?"

"Great! I'll look forward to it, Carolina."

Next I phoned Donna.

"Hi, Donna, it's Caroline."

"Hi! How are you?"

"I'm good. I just wanted to thank you for last night. It was ... very pleasant."

She chuckled. "I'm glad you enjoyed yourself. Johan was very taken with your dress—I think I should be jealous."

I laughed a little uncomfortably. "I was wondering if you and Shirley were free for coffee later today after all?"

She sounded surprised. "I'm free, but I'd have to check with Shirley."

"It's just I have a meeting with the *City Beat* editor now and it would be great to be able to tell him that I have another article almost ready."

"Wow! That's great! Good for you, Caroline. Look, let me call Shirley and I'll get back to you."

~

The offices of *City Beat* were housed in an orange-stucco, art deco building a couple of blocks from Lincoln Avenue. I managed to park nearby and hurried in with my laptop and notebook. I'd decided to show Carl some of my photographs of Base life. I knew they were pretty amateurish but there were three or four that I thought had come out well.

As I was walking into reception I heard my phone beep. There was a text from Donna arranging coffee at the country club and two missed calls from Sebastian.

I texted him back quickly.

Hi mtg at City Beat. Very exciting. Will meet Donna and Shirley at cc 3PM. Hope 2 cu. But wkend just for us

I turned my phone off quickly and introduced myself to the cheerful receptionist.

Carl Winters was much younger than I'd expected—in fact he was probably only a couple of years older than me. Here he was running a whole newspaper in a major city. It made me feel inadequate. But he was friendly and seemed to go out of his way to put me at my ease.

"It's nice to meet you at last, Carolina," he said shaking hands. "We've had some really good feedback already on the article. What else have you got for me?"

I opened my ancient laptop and while it was slowly cycling through its warm up, Carl started asking me questions about myself. I'd answered three or four before it occurred to me that I was being interviewed.

"How long have you been a military wife?"

"Eleven years."

"Eleven! You must have been a child bride."

"Well, not quite, but pretty young I guess. I know that's not in fashion these days, although you find it more among the military."

"Why do you think that is?"

"Rules!" I said, laughing lightly. "If you want to be able to follow your spouse around the country, you have to be married first. Or, if you want to live in sin, you have to live off base."

"It's quite different from civilian life, isn't it," he said thoughtfully.

"In all sorts of ways, big and small," I agreed.

I showed him the article on the Base hospital and he nodded as he read through it, which I took to be a good sign. Then I showed him my photographs.

"These are really good," he said, sounding surprised. "You didn't say you were a photographer."

"I'm not. I mean, I enjoy taking pictures, but I've no training. I just use my dad's old SLR. It's not even digital—I have to get the films processed at the drugstore."

"Well, they're really good: they definitely capture that sense of ... organized chaos, I guess. Well, Carolina, if we're going to use your photos, too, there'll be an additional fee for you: $450 for an article and photo. How does that sound?"

"That sounds wonderful. Thank you."

He glanced at his watch.

"I'm going to head out and get some lunch now. Maybe if you're not busy I could buy you a sandwich and a coffee?"

"Oh! That's very kind of you, Carl, but I've set up interviews with a couple of wives from the Base and, as I'm sure you'd guess, none of us do 'late'."

He laughed but looked a little disappointed. "Another time then?"

I smiled without answering, thanked him again, and left. He'd seemed very friendly. I hoped that's all it was.

Despite that slight awkwardness, I was walking on air,

thrilled with the response to my articles and with a new sense of purpose. For a few brief moments, I allowed myself to be happy and in love.

Driving out to the country club, I ran through the questions I wanted to ask of Donna and Shirley. Carl Daniel's assessment of my work had given me confidence—newborn and weak, but it was confidence—of a sort.

I parked around the back, as before. It was only two o'clock and I hoped, really hoped, that I'd be able to snatch a few, private moments.

Am at cc

I sat for a minute but there was no reply. I didn't even know if Sebastian was allowed to carry his phone while he was working. I'd just have to be patient.

At reception, I handed in a completed membership form and a check, signed by David, for our first month's membership. David had felt that last night's dinner had gone well—he seemed to be oblivious to how much he'd annoyed Johan and Donna. Empathy was not one of my husband's qualities. I almost felt sorry for him. Almost.

I changed into my bikini and headed out to the pool with my notebook, sketching out some more ideas and refining my questions. I was so absorbed in my work—my work, not my hobby—that it was several moments before I realized that someone was standing over me.

"Your mineral water, ma'am."

I looked up to see Sebastian smiling down at me.

"Hi," I whispered.

"Hi, yourself. Meet me in the women's locker room in five minutes. There's a door at the back that says 'Private'. I'll be waiting."

My mouth was still hanging open as he walked away, desire shooting through my body. I took a sip from the frosted glass and stood up as casually as possible on shaky legs.

The locker room was mercifully empty. I made my way to

the back, glancing over my shoulder every other second, my heart rate accelerating with every step.

I pushed open the door marked 'Private' and peered into the gloom of a large storage closet. I gasped when Sebastian's hands pulled me inside.

He didn't speak, not with words.

His lips burned on mine and I felt his hands everywhere, drinking me in, pulling me in, heating my blood.

I ran my hands down his chest and then around to his back, pushing them up under his t-shirt to feel his taut muscles and the warm, smooth texture of his skin beneath my fingertips.

He gripped my hair jerking my head back, running his teeth across my neck. I don't know if it was the dark, or the confined space, or the sense of danger, but Sebastian's movements were more confident, more assured than ever before, and I was swept away.

I felt the straps of my bikini top suddenly loosen, the thin fabric falling away. His mouth moved from my neck, across my chest and then he ran his tongue between the valley of my breasts and down to my stomach, where he knelt.

He hooked his fingers into my bikini bottoms and tugged them down. I stood naked before him in the dim light while, in his own way, he worshipped my body.

He stood up slowly, kissing me all the way.

I gripped his shoulders, feeling his muscles bunch under my hands as pleasure shot through me. I tugged on the material of his t-shirt, desperate to connect flesh with flesh. He stood quickly and pulled it over his head then crushed me to his chest and kissed me with increasing urgency. I had never felt so desired, never wanted a man as much as I wanted Sebastian at that moment.

He pressed himself into me and I knew that he was as aroused as I was.

My fingers scrabbled at the front of his shorts and I heard his soft gasp. With one, swift movement I pushed his briefs off his hips and reached down to grip him in my hands.

He groaned again, then abruptly brushed my hands away.

He bent down and pulled out a condom packet from his shorts. The sound of the foil tearing seemed so loud, I half expected someone to bang on the door and demand to know what we were doing.

Sebastian straightened up and fastened his hands on my hips, lifting me up suddenly. I wrapped my legs around his waist as he thrust into me, making me cry out. I clung onto his shoulders as he pushed me back against the wall, moving hard and fast, his face buried in my neck, his breathing becoming ragged.

Behind my bare back, I felt the doors of a cupboard. The contents rattled alarmingly as Sebastian pounded into me.

The rawness and urgency of our love-making pushed me over the edge and I climaxed around him, made breathless by the extraordinary turn of events. Four minutes ago I had been working quietly by the pool.

I felt Sebastian slam into me one last time and he cried out softly then sank to the floor with me cradled on his lap.

I stroked his face in the dark. I thought I felt tears on his face but I couldn't be sure.

I laid my hand on his chest, feeling the rapid beating of his heart slowly return to normal.

"I love you," he breathed, placing gentle, loving kisses on my lips. "I love you so much."

We lay there for some minutes, cocooned by the dim light creeping through the cracks around the door.

"You have to get back to work," I said softly.

He sighed. "I know."

"We have the whole weekend to look forward to."

"I have to work all day Friday and Saturday," he said sadly.

"The nights are still ours."

"All night."

"Yes."

I felt his lips turn upwards in a smile and he kissed me.

I slid off him, wincing slightly. I'd enjoyed his aggressive love-making, more than enjoyed, but I was feeling a little sore. I didn't care: it was a small price to pay.

We both had to scrabble around in the dark to find our clothes. I couldn't help laughing to myself—there certainly wasn't much dignity in it, but damn, it was hot!

We listened carefully at the door but at that time of the day the locker room was still empty. I don't know what we'd have done if it had been busy—we could have been stuck there for hours! Hmm, that didn't sound so bad.

Sebastian quickly pressed his lips to mine then snuck out first. He looked his usual, handsome self, although perhaps a little more flushed than usual.

I, on the other hand, looked as if I'd just had rough sex up against a cupboard door in the dark. I stared in the mirror at my reddened face, neck, chest and back, and at my once neat ponytail which was lopsided with half my hair coming loose.

I spent a few minutes splashing myself with cold water, trying to return my skin to its usual olive tones, and combed my hair out with my fingers. Eventually I felt composed enough to leave the locker room. As I walked back to the pool, I imagined that everyone I saw knew *exactly* what I'd been doing. I felt as if I had a sign pointing at me shouting 'Locker-room Slut!'.

I slid onto my sun lounger and gratefully took a long drink of my mineral water. I picked up my notebook and pencil and tried to concentrate but my thoughts were well and truly scattered. I couldn't believe what I'd just done. It had been so intense and exciting and so completely out of character for me. Although I wasn't entirely sure what my character was anymore. I'd meant it when I'd told Sebastian that it wasn't David's fault, that I'd let him take control and allowed him to take away the essence of being me. I'd been a sleepwalker through my marriage: we both deserved better—David as well as me.

I wondered again what David saw in me—had he seen something when I was 19 that was no longer there? Or did he simply prefer a submissive, compliant, bovine wife? And what about Sebastian? Why did he want me? Was it more than just sex for him, or was I being naïve? He said he loved me but...

"I see you've been catching some sun—my, you're looking a little red, Caroline."

Donna's kind face was looking down at me.

"Oh, hi Donna," I said, my voice sounding a little more high-pitched than usual.

"And this is Shirley."

"We've spoken on the phone—it's nice to meet you in person."

I stood up to give Donna a quick hug and to shake hands shyly with Shirley Peters who was short and dark haired, and had mischievous hazel eyes—the resemblance to Ches was obvious.

"It's good to meet you, too, Caroline. I've heard so much about you already. You've made quite an impression on the boys. Ches couldn't wait to show me your article."

She laughed lightly. "My son is certainly a fan and I have my suspicions about Sebastian."

My face froze as she winked at Donna. "It's like having a second son—I swear Sebastian spends more time at our house than he does at his own. Hmm, well, not so much lately: Ches thinks he's got a girlfriend, although I don't know why it's such a secret." She sighed. "Well, maybe I do—I can't imagine him wanting to bring a girl home to meet Estelle and Donald."

Donna nodded sympathetically and settled herself in a deckchair under the large, colorful sun umbrella. Shirley headed for the locker room to change into her swimsuit.

"How was your meeting at *City Beat?*"

I couldn't help smiling at Donna—she really was interested in my writing. I showed her the article and watched her face as she read it in detail.

"You've really caught the spirit of surfing, Caroline," she said. "And that's a super photograph. Oh, look! Sebastian still had his long hair there. I wonder why he cut it? I suspect that his father had something to do with that."

Shirley returned wearing a purple and orange tankini.

"What are you suspecting?" she asked, her voice laced with curiosity.

"Oh, we were just talking about Sebastian's buzz-cut."

"Oh, that," said Shirley darkly. "He wouldn't say anything to

Ches, but we definitely had the impression it wasn't voluntary. All the girls at school were crazy about Sebastian, according to Ches. I think if they weren't such good friends he would have been a little jealous—well, more than a little. There was even something in the yearbook about Sebastian's long hair, if you can imagine that." She frowned. "And did you see that bruise he had on his cheek last week?"

She sucked her teeth.

"Hey, Mom!"

Ches was walking toward us in his shorts and polo-shirt uniform. He grinned at his mother and gave her an affectionate kiss on the cheek.

"Chester, honey! Just in time—Donna and I are about to expire from thirst."

"Hi Donna, Caroline," he smiled, but whatever he saw behind us made his smile falter. "Hello, Mrs. Hunter."

Sebastian's mother weaved her way toward us—it was clear she'd spent some quality time at the bar.

"Donna," she slurred. "And friends." She looked at me, "the won-der-ful Caroline Wilson. I almost expected you to be walking across the water in the swimming pool, not lying next to it."

"You've been drinking, Estelle," said Donna sharply. "Perhaps you should rest on the veranda where it's cooler."

"Yes, let's put the embarrassing drunk where she won't bother anyone, let's hide her out of the way," sneered Estelle. "You sound just like Donald."

Donna turned to Ches and spoke in a quiet voice. "Is Sebastian here? Can you get him, please."

Ches nodded and walked away quickly.

Estelle picked up my copy of *City Beat* and tried to focus her eyes on the photograph. Suddenly she tossed the newspaper into the pool.

"You don't fool me, *Mrs. Wilson*," she snarled. "You were a stuck up bitch nine years ago and you haven't changed, have you? You've just polished up your act. But you don't fool me."

"Estelle! Keep your voice down," ordered Donna, as other

people around the pool began to stare. I was frozen on my sun lounger, terrified of what Estelle might say next.

She scowled at me then turned her glazed eyes to Donna.

"You don't tell me what to do, Donna. I don't even know why you like her. She pretends to be so sweet and pure—but she isn't. Flaunting herself everywhere, ingratiating herself. Well, she doesn't fool me. She's nothing but a..."

"Mom!" Sebastian's voice was tight with anger as he walked toward us. "What are you doing?"

Ches stood behind him, one hand on his shoulder, seeming to restrain him.

"Mom, you're embarrassing yourself," he said, coldly. "I'll drive you home."

Estelle whirled around and slapped him hard. I couldn't help gasping as my hand flew to my mouth and I started to stand up.

Sebastian's eyes were almost black with fury. Ches gripped his arm and tugged him backward.

"Come on, buddy, walk away."

A sudden silence descended, horrified eyes staring at Estelle.

Slowly she came to her senses and her cheeks flushed with embarrassment as she took in the shocked faces turned in her direction. She straightened her purse over her shoulder and staggered off.

"What the hell was *that* about?" whispered Shirley.

Donna sighed. "I don't know: but her drinking is getting worse. Donald will have to do something."

Shirley scoffed at the idea. "Donald doesn't give a shit about her—word is that he's been seeing some young civilian nurse. *Seeing to her,* probably."

Donna shook her head slowly. "God knows those two should have divorced years ago. It would have been better for Sebastian if they had. Poor boy, I hope he's okay."

"He's got Ches with him," said Shirley softly. "He'll be okay, he's used to it."

My heart lurched painfully. I desperately wanted to wrap my arms around Sebastian to comfort and protect him, but I couldn't. It hurt so much. And then a more painful thought crossed my mind—maybe he wasn't running *to* me, maybe he was just running away from *that*. And if he was, I couldn't blame him. Besides, wouldn't he say the same thing about me and David?

I didn't want to believe it, but once the thought was there, it seemed more plausible than to believe that Sebastian would want to be with me.

He had opened my eyes to a world of possibilities, to a world where I could be loved for myself, but would my new life be with him? I was afraid to hope.

After a moment, Shirley stood up. "I'll just go check on the boys."

Donna exhaled deeply and looked at me. "Are you okay, Caroline?"

I nodded, still feeling shaken. Did Estelle *know?*

"That wasn't really about you," Donna continued, "she's just jealous."

"Jealous? Of what?"

Donna smiled sadly. "Never mind, it doesn't matter. Now, what were those questions you had?"

I shook my head. "They seem rather insignificant now." I stared at the sodden sheets of newsprint that some helpful children were fishing out of the pool.

"Please ask me," said Donna. "I need something to take my mind off that awful scene."

We chatted about our shared experiences of living on different bases for several minutes, before Shirley reappeared.

"How's Sebastian?" asked Donna, her concern evident. "Did you see Estelle?"

"Ches and Sebastian got her into the car, he's driving her home."

She shook her head. "If there are any more incidents like that, Estelle will have her membership suspended."

"I'll speak to Johan," said Donna. "Maybe he'll be able to persuade her to … seek some help. She won't be the first Navy wife to … well, she won't be the first."

A subdued Ches returned with thee orange juices. Shirley

rubbed his arm and they swapped brief smiles. It was refreshing to see the close relationship they had—especially after the unpleasant scene that had played out between Estelle and Sebastian.

I bit my tongue as Ches went back to work—I wanted to ask him if Sebastian was okay, but I couldn't.

I turned my attention to finishing my article, as Donna had suggested.

Shirley was incredibly helpful, offering fascinating insights into the world of the military wife.

"Of course, it's hard leaving friends behind, and hard for Chester starting new schools every couple of years, but it's made us closer as a family, too. And the Marine Corps is a second family, we're all pretty tight. It's made Chester good at making friends and he's a very resourceful boy, very self-sufficient. But we did make sure that his last four years of high school were consistent—we felt that was important for his education. I like traveling and the challenge of new places—new countries. To be honest, I'm dreading the day when Mitch retires: I don't know what he'll do with himself. He's so used to the structure and routine of the Marines, I'm not sure how well either of us will adapt to civilian life.

"But what about you, Caroline? If David decided to quit the Navy, what would you do?"

I twitched uncomfortably, not wanting to have the spotlight turned on me.

"I don't think his routine would change that much: he'd still work in a hospital, still work his clinics. It wouldn't make that much difference. Just a different sort of uniform."

Donna smiled. "Yes, you're right. Medicine imposes its own set of regulations and routines. Being the wife of a doctor isn't such a huge leap."

I'd enjoyed talking to Donna and Shirley—it had been a lot like having friends—but I realized the sun had shifted in the sky and I leapt up.

"Oh, I'm so sorry. I have to get back and pack for David.

He's taking everything with him to the hospital tomorrow morning. I have a mountain of ironing to do."

Shirley laughed and Donna smiled sympathetically.

I thanked them again and waved quickly.

CHAPTER TEN

Dᴀᴠɪᴅ ᴍᴀɴᴀɢᴇᴅ ᴛᴏ ꜰɪɴᴅ ꜰᴀᴜʟᴛ ᴡɪᴛʜ ᴇᴠᴇʀʏᴛʜɪɴɢ ᴛʜᴀᴛ evening: my cooking, the clothes I'd packed for him, the way I'd ironed his shirt and pants, probably even the amount of air I was inconveniently breathing.

I tried to think if he'd always been so difficult. I honestly couldn't remember.

He was particularly annoyed because I refused to come to bed with him, insisting instead on finishing my interview notes. During his bombastic huffing, I realized that he didn't have a coping mechanism for dealing with my refusal—he wasn't used to it and he didn't know how to handle it. The thought was oddly liberating.

When he left the next morning, he didn't even ask how I was planning to spend my weekend. Not that 'screwing the brains out of my young lover in your bed' would have figured high on my list of responses to that particular question, but I did think he might have pretended to take an interest.

I'd had one brief text from Sebastian simply saying that he was looking forward to the weekend. He hadn't answered when I'd asked if he was okay.

I spent the day writing and also took a moment to look up possible photography classes I could take at NYU. Carl Winters had praised my snaps—it made me wonder if I could take that side of my work further.

During the afternoon, Donna telephoned to invite me to supper. I appreciated her kindness but I wasn't going to be as alone as she thought. I simply told her I was enjoying the peace and quiet—she understood at once, checking only that I'd be at the annual Base picnic on Sunday.

I felt strangely nervous. I hadn't seen Sebastian since yesterday's ugly scene. It was also the first time that we'd been able to plan to be together for more than a few hours.

It was nearly midnight when I heard his light tap on the backdoor. I'd been dozing on the couch while I waited for him to finish his shift at the country club.

I made sure the kitchen light was off before I unlocked the door.

"Hi."

"Hi, yourself."

We stood staring at each other, and he frowned slightly.

"Can I come in?"

"Of course."

I stood back to allow him to pass, then I closed the door and locked it again. When I turned around he was still staring at me.

"I want to kiss you," he said, sounding uncertain.

"Do you?"

I didn't know why there was so much tension between us.

"Caro, what's wrong?"

"Nothing. Just kiss me."

He hesitated for less than a second then slowly walked forward. He held the palm of his hand against my cheek and lowered his face to me. He kissed me twice, his mouth lightly touching mine, then he wrapped his arms around my waist and leaned down to rest his forehead against mine.

"I've missed you," he whispered.

I smiled and felt my body relax.

"Have you?"

"Yes." He pulled me in more tightly. "I'm really sorry about yesterday, about ... what my mom said."

I straightened up abruptly and his hands dropped to his sides as he gazed at me warily. We needed to have this conversation—now.

"Does she know? About you and me?"

He shook his head vehemently. "Of course not!"

I looked into his eyes. "Because she said some things that made me think she did."

Sebastian looked horrified.

"What did she say?"

I shrugged.

"Please!"

I let out a long sigh, closing my eyes against the unpleasant memory.

"She said I'd been 'flaunting' myself and that I wasn't 'pure', that she *knew better*. Sebastian, what does she know? She must know something or why would she have put it like that?"

He ran his hands over his hair looking angry and upset, but stayed resolutely silent.

"For God's sake, tell me!"

My voice was louder than I'd intended.

He blinked and looked away. "I promise she doesn't know anything, Caro. It's just that..."

He paused.

"Just what?"

"Just some shit my dad was talking. It's nothing."

"Tell me!" I said forcefully.

Sebastian looked at me angrily.

"My dad said you were a hot piece of tail and that you wouldn't be such an uptight bitch if *your husband* had been fucking you properly."

I felt sick.

I walked to the kitchen sink, and leaned over it.

"Is that ... is that what people think of me?" I murmured.

"No! God, no! My father is an asshole, Caro. No one thinks that. Mitch, Bill, Ches—they all think you're great. I mean,

182

yeah, they think you're gorgeous, who wouldn't? But I promise they've never *ever* said anything like that."

I straightened up slowly and turned around to face him. He was standing with his arms out-stretched as if he wanted to touch me but was afraid to.

"Are you hungry?"

He was confused by the sudden change of topic, away from my self-flagellation.

"Hungry?"

"Yes. Did you eat at the club tonight?"

His hands fell to his side and for a second he closed his eyes tiredly, before walking toward me and taking me into his arms.

I tried to resist, still raw from his father's words.

"Caro, don't push me away."

He wrapped his arms around my shoulders and held me.

"I'm sorry, okay. I'm sorry I told you what that asshole said. Hell, you should hear what he calls me sometimes ... well, maybe not. I don't listen anymore. All that matters is that we're together, okay?"

I didn't answer.

"Okay?" he said again, more forcefully.

I took a deep breath.

"Okay," I agreed, quietly.

He kissed my hair and smiled down at me.

We stood there for some minutes, just enjoying a moment of peace.

"So, are you hungry?" I said at last. "Did you eat tonight?"

He rolled his eyes at me and I had to smile.

"No, we were slammed—I didn't have time."

"I'll fix you something to eat: linguini, pesto and pine nuts okay?"

"You don't have to cook for me, Caro," he said frowning slightly.

"I want to. Besides, you haven't eaten ... and you'll need your energy."

I grinned up at him and he gave in with good grace.

"Well, in that case, yeah, I'm starving."

He pulled out a chair and sat at the table watching me.

"So, how was work? Anything interesting happen today?"

I was determined that we would have some normal conversation.

"I did that First Aid training certificate this morning. It was all stuff I'd done at the surf lifesaving club, so it was pretty easy. I'll be mostly working poolside with Ches from now on."

"You don't like waiting tables?"

"Not so much—I'd rather be outside."

"Are you sure it's not just a chance to impress bored, horny Navy wives with your gorgeous body?"

"There's only one woman I want to impress," he said, returning my smile.

"How's that going for you?"

"Well, it was touch-and-go for a while, but she's making me dinner, so I guess it's going okay. How was your day?"

"Good. I finished another article and have planned out three more. I was afraid I might run out of material, but I have enough ideas to write a whole book, I think. Oh, and I looked up some photography courses at NYU. Have you decided which classes you want to take in the spring?"

When he didn't answer, I looked up from the chopping board—Sebastian was sitting, rocking back on the chair, a huge smile on his face.

"What?"

"I love it when you talk like that?"

It was my turn to be confused.

"Like what?"

"When you're talking about stuff we're going to do together: about our future."

I dropped the torn basil leaves and looked directly at him.

"Sebastian, I didn't *have* a future until you got me thinking about one. God knows how long I'd have carried on drifting. But you have to promise me something..."

"Anything: I'll promise you anything."

I took a deep breath.

"I want you to promise me that when you ... when you start thinking about a different future ... without me..."

His expression changed and his eyes darkened with anger.

"Jesus, Caro! How can you say that to me?"

"No, please! Let me finish. We can't ignore our age difference and one day, when it starts to ... change things, I'll understand. I don't want us to sink into indifference and dislike. Been there, done that. When you decide to go, just ... just give me some notice. That's all I ask."

He stared back.

I was glad I'd said it—I'd needed to say it, but Sebastian looked really angry.

"Caro, don't you understand how I feel about you? I love you: you're all I want. I want a future with you—I want our lives to be together. I'm not a kid—I've had to grow up fast. I've been taking care of myself for a long time now. And I want to take care of you."

"I'm just saying that I'll understand when that changes."

"Don't patronize me, Caro," he said, sounding even angrier. "You think I don't know what it means to make this commitment, but I do. You think I'm giving up everything and that I'll regret it later, but you're wrong. I've seen what a bad marriage is like, I've seen how miserable my parents have been. But when I'm with you, I feel ... so incredibly happy, like the world is worth it after all. I know how rare that is, I've *seen* how rare that is. Don't dismiss how I feel just because ... just because I'm younger than you. You're beautiful and kind and talented and you have a gift ... people are drawn to you—and you don't even see it. And it's just one of the things I love about you."

I sighed, feeling his anguish in every word.

"And what about children, Sebastian?"

He blinked several times.

"What about children?"

"Well, do you really want to be saddled with children when you're twenty? No, I don't imagine you do. Well, what about when you're in your thirties and you like the idea of having a couple of kids running around the house and I'll be in my late forties and *too old*."

He shrugged, trying to look casual but I could tell that he was rattled.

"If you want kids we can have kids."

I smiled sadly and shook my head.

"It doesn't work like that, Sebastian: we'd both have to want them—and time isn't on our side. Do you see what I'm saying?"

"Yes, I see what you're saying—and I see what you're doing: you're trying to think of every reason under the sun why we shouldn't be together. But none of that matters—if you want to be with me." He took a deep breath. "Do you, Caro?"

I sighed. I wanted him more than air, but I had to make him think, *really think*, about what we were doing.

"Sebastian, how long do you think these *physical* feelings will last? Six months? A year? Two, if we're lucky. And then what? What about when you make friends at college and you introduce them to your *older* girlfriend? What about..."

But he interrupted me.

"None of that matters. And I think you're wrong anyway—I can't imagine not wanting you—not ever. You're smart and funny and I enjoy being with you even when we don't ... when we're not ... making love. When I was eight years old, I used to imagine that you were my girlfriend and that we'd run away together. And then you left and I'd lost my best friend, too. I used to dream about you coming back. As I got older, I ... I began to understand the ... my feelings for you better. I didn't think dreams could come true—but they have for me, Caro. Why are you so scared? I mean, forget all that legal bullshit ... why do you keep trying to ... I don't know, make me change my mind? What do you think I have here that I wouldn't give up in a heartbeat to be with you? There's nothing to keep me here. I'll go anywhere, do anything to be with you." He sighed. "I know you have more to lose and I hate, *hate* that I'm responsible for that, but ... do you want to be with me? Forever. *Sempre*."

I didn't have any words of opposition or defiance left in me.

The future was unwritten—maybe one day I would be too old for him and he would leave me—it seemed inevitable. But wouldn't two or three years of love be worth having, regardless? I knew my marriage was over: it had been over for a long time before I'd met Sebastian—I'd just been too much of a coward to admit it.

Was I prepared to take a chance on the future ... a chance on love? I looked into his lovely face, tension and fear and anxiety holding him rigid. I thought again about the question he'd asked me: did I want to be with him?

"Yes. I do."

He exhaled deeply as if he'd been holding his breath.

"That's all that matters."

He pushed his chair back and walked over, draping his arms around me. He rested his chin on my shoulder and nestled his face in my neck, his breath warm on my skin.

We stood like that for some moments, allowing the fear and tension to drain away.

"You'll have to let go if I'm going to finish making you supper," I said gently.

I felt his smile as he tightened his grip momentarily and then let his hands slide away. He sat back at the table and grinned at me.

"It's good to know you want food more than you want sex," I couldn't help commenting.

He laughed. "It's about even at the moment, but you told me that I'd need my energy so I'm just following your advice."

I loved to see him like this, happy and relaxed, teasing me. I felt guilty for causing the tension in the first place, but relieved we'd talked it through—for now, at least.

I finished making the pesto and served up the linguini with toasted pine nuts and freshly grated parmesan.

"Aren't you having some?"

I shook my head. "I had mine hours ago."

"It smells great."

He ate rapidly, shoveling in huge mouthfuls. He was clearly ravenous. I thought it was rather poor that the club hadn't ensured that their young staff had had a proper meal break.

"What's this photography course that you're interested in?" he said, between mouthfuls.

"When I met up with Carl Winters at *City Beat* he really liked my photos of Base life. I thought I might try and take a course in photojournalism. What do you think?"

"That sounds great. I haven't seen your photos—I'd really like to."

"Would you?"

He rolled his eyes at me as he chomped through another enormous mouthful.

"Okay, well, I'll show you later if you like."

"Later, like tomorrow," he said assertively.

A thrill of anticipation ran through me at his words. Yes, later.

"I'm going to have a glass of wine. Would you like one?"

"Isn't that illegal," he smirked at me. "Plying a minor with liquor!"

I glanced over my shoulder at him as I retrieved the bottle of red wine I'd opened earlier.

"If I'm going to go to Hell, I may as well do it thoroughly."

He laughed. "I'd rather have a beer, if you've got one."

I pulled a face. "Beer doesn't go with pesto. Here, try this."

I passed him a small glass of red wine.

He tasted it hesitantly then smiled. "That's really good. What is it?"

"It's a ten year old Barolo. It's better when it's not too fruity. Most people like the oakier-tasting ones but I guess I get my old-fashioned ideas from my dad."

Sebastian looked impressed.

"Do you know a lot about wine?"

"A little. Well, only what Papa taught me. His family used to grow Moscato grapes." I shrugged. "Maybe they still do."

"Let's find out!" he said, his eyes sparkling with adventure, "when we take that road trip."

"Can you ride a motorcycle?"

"Sure! Well, I don't have a completion certificate from the motorcycle training course, but I took a few lessons, and I've ridden Ches's. It's cool."

I saw that he'd cleared his plate and was eyeing the fruit bowl.

"Help yourself."

"Thanks!"

I stood up and carried away his empty plates. I liked listening to music when I washed dishes so I put on a CD of my favorite arias.

"Puccini?"

I smiled. "Of course. Do you know this opera?"

Sebastian shook his head. "I recognize it but I can't remember what it's from."

"It's *'O Mio Babbino Caro'* from *Gianni Schicchi*."

"Caro! Like your name, except that's the male way of saying it, isn't it?"

"I don't mind. I like that you're the only person who calls me that."

His answering smile was huge.

"Papa used to call me *'mia cara'*."

The music swirled around us and I was swept up in a deluge of memories.

"What's this song about?" asked Sebastian after a couple of minutes.

"It's an aria sung by a girl to her beloved father, begging him to let her marry the boy she loves."

"It sounds very Romeo and Juliet."

"Yes, except it's a comedy."

He raised his eyebrows. "Yeah, right!"

I laughed at him. "It is!"

He listened to the music some more. "I can pick out some of the words—something about buying a ring?"

"That's right, and if he doesn't let her, she's threatening to throw herself off the Ponte Vecchio bridge."

"Sounds over the top."

"Well, it is opera."

"I'd like to buy you a ring."

He sounded so serious I turned around from the sink. Sebastian was staring at me.

"I want to marry you, Caro."

I gasped and dropped the glass I was holding. It slid down into the soapy water but didn't shatter.

"Sebastian..."

"I mean it. I want to marry you. Will you, Caro? Will you marry me?"

I shook my head. "Sebastian ... I can't talk about this now. I *am* married—to David. And anyway, I wouldn't do that to you—you're too..."

"Too young? Is that what you're going to say, because if you are, don't bother."

He rested his head in his hands then looked up again.

"In just over three months, I'll be 18. I could enlist and a few months later I could be sent to the Middle East. I'll be old enough to fight, to die for my country, but you don't think I'll be old enough to marry you?"

He didn't sound angry, just determined.

My brain had ceased to function—I simply carried on staring at him.

He looked at me accusingly.

"You met David before you were 18—and you married really quickly."

"Yes, and what a disaster that's been," I said, bitterly.

Sebastian looked like I'd slapped him.

I immediately regretted my words.

"I'm sorry, but..."

"But what?"

"Sebastian, we've been together for just a couple of weeks—under the most intense circumstances. Can't we just ... spend some time together? Get to know each other properly. Sometimes I feel that we hardly know each other at all."

"I love you and I want to marry you. What else do you want to know?"

"Everything! What's your favorite book? What's your

favorite movie? What was your best subject in school? Who was your first crush? What CD have you got in your player at home right now? What do you eat for breakfast? Do you prefer football or baseball? Were you a jock at school? Did you ever date a cheerleader? Do you remember your dreams? What's your favorite color? Have you ever cried watching a movie? I don't know—everything!"

He let out a deep sigh.

"Okay, I get it. I'm rushing you."

I frowned.

"That's not it—well, not entirely. It's just ... we've done everything backward."

I walked over to him and laid my hand on his chest. "I want to know everything: inside as well as out. I want to know *you*."

He held my hand and played with my fingers but he still couldn't look at me. He was really upset. I guess being turned down when you ask someone to marry you would get you that way. I'd hurt him—and he was the last person in the whole world that I wanted to hurt.

I pulled my hand free and held his face until he had to look at me.

"Sebastian, I feel like you've woken me from a dream. But I barely know who *I* am, let alone ... I'm sorry I hurt you. I would never want to do that."

I rested my lips on his, two, three times, trying to convey a message with my light touch.

He pulled away and looked at me.

"Old Yeller."

"Excuse me?"

"That was a movie that made me cry ... when he had to shoot his dog."

"How old were you when you saw it?"

"Ten, maybe. I'm not sure. I always hoped we'd have a dog, but Mom said they made too much mess. Do you like dogs?"

"Yes. When I was growing up a neighbor had a little Jack Russell terrier called 'Tano'. He said the name meant 'number five' but I don't remember what language that was. She was so sweet. I cried for three days when she died. Dad wanted to buy me a puppy but Mom wouldn't let him, so I got a goldfish instead."

"A goldfish?!"

I grinned at him. "Yes, not quite the same thing! I called him 'Splash'—not very original."

"We could get a dog."

"What, and take him on the back of our motorcycle through Italy?!"

"Yeah! A biker dog! That would be awesome!"

I laughed.

"What's your favorite movie?" he said.

"I can only think of animal movies now. I don't know, 'White Fang' maybe or 'Call of the Wild'. Oh, but I love 'Gone with the Wind'."

He pulled a face.

"What was the last movie that made you cry?"

"I cry at most movies. Um ... 'Edward Scissorhands'—that always makes me cry."

"Who was your first crush? It had better be a movie star though or I might have to hunt him down."

"Better get your gun then!"

"Why?"

"Anthony Kiedis."

"Who?"

"The vocalist from the Red Hot Chili Peppers."

"You like rock?"

"I like all sorts of music."

He laughed happily.

"God, I love you!"

I couldn't help smiling back at him. "What?"

"Just when I think I know you, you surprise the shit out of me."

I sat on his lap and put my arms around his neck.

"Okay, your turn: favorite book?"

"Heart of Darkness."

"Ugh! Why that? It's a horrible story!"

"I guess because it shows how ... how far a man can go when he's in a place without limits."

"Hmm, I don't think you'll turn me into a Conrad fan. Okay, first girl you ever kissed?"

He reddened and looked down.

"Go on, tell me. I won't be jealous. Well, maybe a little."

"Brenda Wiseman."

"And how old were you?"

"Sixteen."

I couldn't help thinking that wasn't so very long ago for him. And then my overactive brain imagined him making out with her and...

"What happened to her?"

"Nothing."

"Well what happened *with* her?"

He shook his head, clearly embarrassed. I was intrigued.

"Come on, tell me. It can't be that bad."

"We dated for a while..."

"And..."

"We broke up."

"When was this? When did you break up with her?"

He shifted uncomfortably beneath me.

"Four months ago."

I felt like I'd been punched in the stomach.

"You went out with her for two years?"

He shook his head. "No, not ... about ten months."

"Oh."

I stood up and he looked at me helplessly.

"I'm sorry, Caro..."

"No, don't apologize. I'm just ... surprised. I got the impression that you hadn't..."

"We didn't sleep together."

"Why not? Most teenage boys..." the words burned my throat, "most teenage boys would have been desperate to..."

He shifted uncomfortably.

"We were going to—then I heard that she'd been screwing Jack—that guy you met once." He shook his head. "But I'm glad

I didn't—with her. I didn't love her. You're the only woman I've ever loved: it's always been you."

I found it hard to take in. Where did his certainty come from?

"Caro?"

"I'm okay. I'm just … surprised." There was that word again. "What would you have done if I hadn't come back?"

He shrugged. "I don't know."

But I knew. One day he would have met someone his own age, someone special, and he'd have fallen in love, he'd have had a chance of a normal relationship. And if *I* hadn't met *him*? I'd still be sleepwalking through my life.

But I *had* come back and we *had* met again. And I couldn't go back to the way I was. I didn't want to.

I held out my hand to him.

"Come on, it's late. Let's go to bed."

We walked up the stairs, hand-in-hand. He stood awkwardly in the doorway while I turned on the small bedside light.

"You want to use the bathroom first?"

"Okay."

"You can use my toothbrush if you want. The blue one."

He fidgeted for a few seconds then went into the bathroom. I turned down the sheets, wondering if it would have been better if we'd gone to the guest room. But then again, what difference would that really make?

We swapped over and as I cleaned my teeth with the damp brush, I stared at my reflection in the bathroom mirror—the face was familiar but that was about all. Everything else had changed.

When I came out Sebastian was sitting on the edge of the bed, still fully dressed.

"By the way, where do your parents think you are tonight?"

He blinked and looked up, clearly his thoughts had been somewhere else entirely.

"They won't notice I'm not there. They've probably passed out drunk again."

He sneered the words.

"Ches dropped me off at home and I jogged over here—that's why I was late. I didn't want him to know where ... he's picking me up at 10.30AM, so I'll have to be back by then." He sighed. "That doesn't seem very long from now."

"What if your parents see your room is empty and that your bed hasn't been slept in?"

I felt panicky at the thought.

Sebastian gave a half-smile. "I didn't make my bed this morning. If they look in—which they won't—they'll just assume they missed me. Honestly, they won't notice." He scowled. "They never notice anything about me anyway—except my fucking hair."

Unconsciously, he ran his hands over his head as he spoke.

"But it got us here, didn't it," I said quietly.

He looked at me seriously and nodded slowly. "Are you sorry?"

I shook my head. "No. You make me feel ... alive."

I leaned down and kissed him—a soft, gentle, loving kiss. He responded immediately and passionately, kissing me until we were both breathing hard.

"I ... I have to go downstairs," he said, standing up.

"What? Why?"

"I left the condoms in my jacket pocket," he mumbled, embarrassed.

"Oh, well, I meant to say something about that."

He flashed a nervous glance at me.

"I told you I was going to start taking birth control pills—and I did, I have. We don't need to use condoms anymore."

"Really? You're sure?"

I smiled. "Yes, no more playing hunt the lost condom."

He laughed softly. "I kinda liked that game."

"Well, *I* didn't. Anyway, we're good to go," I said, arching one eyebrow. "Oh, but I should mention ... I don't know if this will bother you ... but I got my period. That's why I know it's safe for us to stop using condoms. Does it bother you? I mean, *will* it bother you?"

I felt suddenly anxious—we were reaching for a new level of intimacy and I wasn't sure what his reaction would be.

"Can you? I mean, is it okay to ... while you're...? I don't want to hurt you..."

I stroked his cheek. He looked so worried.

"Yes, we can still make love. I was just checking that you were okay with ... a little sblood."

His eyes were huge. "I want to make love to you, Caro. God, I want to."

"Then I think you're wearing too many clothes."

He responded immediately, kicking his sneakers off his bare feet and tearing his t-shirt over his head. I thought I heard one of the seams rip.

"Hey, it's okay! We've got all night. I want to take it slow with you."

He looked confused for a moment, then smiled shyly.

"Okay."

I pushed him down so he was sitting on the edge of the bed again, and sat astride him. His arms encircled my waist, pulling me toward him.

"Mmm," I said, nuzzling his chin as I wrapped my arms around his neck, "this is my happy place."

Using my teeth, I tugged gently on his earlobe and was rewarded with a soft moan. I let my fingers ripple across his back, enjoying the feel of his skin and the tautness of his defined muscles. I used my fingertips to massage him lightly and he groaned again.

"What's your favorite color?" I whispered against his neck.

"What? Um ... blue. No, green. Red—maybe."

"That sounded definite! So, football or baseball? Or maybe basketball? Hockey?"

"Basket ... base... um..."

"Are you finding it difficult to concentrate?" I teased him.

"Caro, I can barely remember my own name when I'm with you!"

I chuckled quietly. "What do you like for breakfast?"

"Jeez, I don't know!"

"Tell me!"

"I don't usually eat breakfast."

"Well, what would you like tomorrow?"

"You!" he said.

He stood up suddenly, taking me with him, then threw me down on the bed.

"Enough with the slow," he said, his eyes dark and serious.

A pulse of desire and lust and need surged through me.

I sat up slowly, hooking my fingers into his belt loops and pulled him toward me. He trembled as I ran the tips of my fingers under his waistband. With bold hands, I traced the outline of his erection through his jeans. He inhaled sharply.

Watching his face the entire time, I opened his jeans, one button at a time, and pulled them down his long, strong, tan legs. His eyelids fluttered closed and he breathed deeply as I pushed the jeans past his knees.

They tangled around his ankles and he nearly fell over trying to kick them off. I smothered a laugh. Sebastian didn't have an arrogant bone in his body, but he was a man, and all men have their pride.

"Come and lie down next to me," I said, still smiling.

I wiggled out of my skirt and tossed it onto the floor. Tonight was not a night to worry about creased clothing.

We lay facing each other: he in his briefs, me in my t-shirt and panties. He scooted down the bed till our faces were at the same level and he smiled at me.

"Hi."

"Hi, yourself."

"What's *your* favorite color?" he said.

"I have absolutely no idea."

He laughed happily and ran his warm fingers down my arm.

"You're so beautiful," he breathed.

"So are you," I countered, "and so sweet."

He frowned slightly and let his hand drift over my body until he was cupping my backside. He squeezed gently and I responded by hooking my leg over his hip.

He flexed automatically, pushing himself into me and another delicious shiver ran down the entire length of my body.

He rolled gently so I was on my back, and he was hovering over me.

"You still want to go slow?"

I nodded, stifling a chuckle.

He smiled reluctantly. "Okay, I'll try."

He slid down the bed and used his teeth to pull my t-shirt up off my stomach. He ran his nose across my body and kissed me slowly on every exposed inch of skin while he supported himself on his arms.

I ran my fingers over the front of his briefs and he groaned.

"I won't be able to go slow if you do that again," he said in a warning voice.

I laughed quietly, unsure whether or not I wanted his slow, delicious torture to continue.

"I want to get this t-shirt off you."

I sat up briefly so he could pull it over my head. When I lay down again, he nuzzled my breasts, running the tip of his tongue along the junction between my skin and the fabric of my bra.

I stroked my hands over the bunched muscles of his biceps, luxuriating in their hard tension.

Carefully he fastened his teeth over the fabric of my bra and pulled the cup down, then ran his tongue over my nipple, sucking hard. The sensation was exquisite, almost painful.

I pushed the waistband of his briefs over and down his hips. He rolled off me to kick them free and I sat up to undo my bra.

"No, I'll do that," he said confidently.

For several seconds he tugged futilely on the elastic straps. "Fuck! Turn around—I can't see what I'm doing."

Smiling to myself, I turned my back to him. A heartbeat later, my bra was dumped on the floor and I shimmied out of my panties, tossing them down with the rest of our clothes.

"How slow?" he whispered as his body loomed over mine again, lightly pressing me into the mattress.

"How slow can you go?" I asked teasingly.

I pulled my knees up and slid my hand along his erection. He trembled and bit his lip.

"You're not helping!" he said, accusingly.

But I didn't care anymore: I wanted to feel him inside me—all of him.

I pulled him toward me and I felt the mattress move as his weight shifted on the bed. He used his knees to open me wider, then, with aching slowness, he sank into me, pulled out, then sank in again, circling his hips, stimulating me everywhere.

I tilted my hips up to meet him—the movement seemed to push him too far.

"I can't! I can't!" he suddenly gasped and started moving faster.

I wrapped my legs around his waist and gripped his arms with my hands.

His eyes were squeezed tightly shut and I felt his body turn rigid then he collapsed onto me with a soft moan.

"Sorry," he mumbled into my neck a long moment later.

I stroked his hair, smiling to myself. "It's okay. Practice makes perfect. And we've got all night."

He raised himself up and kissed me softly and sweetly. Then he pulled out gently and rolled off of me.

"Oh, wow!" he said, looking down at the blood on his dick. "That really didn't hurt you?"

I shook my head, suppressing a smile. "Do you want to take a shower?"

"Um, yeah, if you don't mind."

He looked stunned.

"I don't mind—not if you let me scrub your back."

He grinned and looked up at me. "Oh, definitely up for that."

I turned on the hot water and led him into the shower.

"Did you have a long day at the office, dear?" I said as I ran a soapy sponge over his back.

He chuckled, stretching out his arms.

"God, that feels so good!" he sighed.

He rested his hands on the tiled wall and let the water rain down on his head and back. When I reached around and ran the sponge over his front he jumped slightly. Gently, I swirled the sponge over his stomach and thighs and everything in between, he groaned loudly.

I felt his erection stir again. I guessed that's what they called a fast re-loader. I was impressed—and shocked.

He turned around and kissed me hard, his tongue demanding access to my mouth. He pushed me back against the chilly ceramic tiles and I almost slipped.

"Careful!"

"Sorry! God, sorry," he muttered, barely moving his mouth from my lips.

I was slipping and sliding all over the place—suddenly shower sex didn't seem like such a good idea.

I left the hot water running and pulled him after me. He looked confused as I leaned over the sink and grasped the rim with both hands.

"From behind," I whispered.

I heard the breath hitch in his throat then a second later his hands were gripping my hips. When he entered me it felt amazingly deep. Truthfully, I'd never felt anything like it before.

"Oh fuck!" he hissed.

I glanced up into the mirror—his eyes were wide with wonder and his lips were parted. Our eyes met—and locked on each other's.

I clenched around him and watched his face as he cursed again.

He rotated his hips slowly and this time I was the one who cried out.

"Hand!"

"What?" he grit out between his teeth.

"Give me your hand!" I half-gasped, half-yelled at him.

He leaned onto me, his weight pressing me into the cold, hard porcelain, and I groaned but he gave me his hand. I pushed it between my legs and against my clitoris. He caught on fast: the thought crossed my mind that he must have got good grades in school. My orgasm began to gather and I felt the delicious trembling inside.

I knew Sebastian felt it, too, because he swore again and started moving faster, his hand in rhythm with his thrusts.

I screamed out his name. The sheer relief of being able to be as loud as I wanted, to show vocally how much he was pleasing me: it felt fantastic.

He kept moving, his hips grinding into me. I could barely stand, my thighs were shaking with the effort of staying upright.

What? No? Surely not! I couldn't believe it! My eyes opened wide as a second orgasm began to build. I was shocked to my core—I didn't even know I *could* have two orgasms so close together. And then I lost all train of thought as my body became nothing but sensation.

I was vaguely aware that Sebastian had stopped moving and that we were both lying on the floor, gasping.

It was desperately uncomfortable on the hard surface but I felt too weak to move. A giggle escaped me—I was, quite literally, well fucked. That expression would never again have the same resonance for me now I'd actually experienced it.

I started laughing.

"What's so funny?"

But I couldn't reply, I was laughing so hard. I pushed up onto my hands and knees, vaguely aware that there was blood on the floor.

"What are you laughing at?" said Sebastian, sounding aggrieved.

I crawled into the shower, slightly hysterical.

"What?!" he said, starting to laugh despite himself.

"I. Am. So. Thoroughly. Well. Fucked!" I finally managed to spit out.

Sebastian was laughing, too, as he came and joined me in the shower.

We sat in the shower tray and I leaned back between his legs, letting the hot water soothe and restore us.

Eventually I managed to stop laughing but I felt too weak to stand.

"That was amazing," Sebastian whispered into my hair.

He sounded slightly awestruck.

"It certainly was. But I can't stand—you'll have to help me up!"

Sebastian laughed and stood up easily, pulling me up by my hands.

I managed to turn off the shower as I staggered out. I grabbed a clean towel and tossed one to him. I made a few quick passes with the towel and, still half-soaked, collapsed face down on the bed.

"Hey," said Sebastian, following me to the bedroom. "You're all wet."

Gently, lovingly, he dried me with the towel, doing his best to get the moisture out of my hair as well.

"I'm so tired. I can hardly keep my eyes open," I mumbled.

"Go to sleep, baby," he said softly.

I rolled onto my side and felt Sebastian's warm, slightly damp body curl up behind me. He wrapped his arm around my waist and I was asleep in seconds.

CHAPTER ELEVEN

At some point, not long after dawn, I woke.

Sebastian's arm was still draped over my waist but I must have turned in the night because now I was facing him. His lips were slightly parted and he was breathing softly. I thought he must be dreaming because his eyelids fluttered and he frowned.

A pale gold stubble covered his cheeks, upper lip and chin. It was soft, nothing like five o'clock shadow and he looked so young and very beautiful.

His tan was deep over his arms, back and chest, then vanished completely, leaving his buttocks and hips a creamy white that changed again to gold on his legs.

The low angle of the sun cast long shadows that highlighted the definition of his muscular chest and stomach and I reveled in the thought that for a few more hours—and for another whole night—he was mine.

I hardly dared to imagine how it might feel to wake up like this every morning, feeling such peaceful joy. And I refused to think about what would happen when our weekend was over.

I spent another minute drinking in his beauty before I tore myself away to use the bathroom.

"Where are you going?" he asked sleepily, blinking up at me.

"To pee," I whispered. "Go back to sleep."

But when I returned to the room, the bed was empty. For a

heart-stopping moment, I thought he'd left. Then I saw his sneakers, t-shirt and briefs, all still strewn on the floor. Only his jeans were missing.

I stared with some distaste at the blood on the sheets. At least I didn't get really heavy periods and they didn't last long. Even so...

I heard soft footfalls behind me and turned to look. Sebastian was carrying two glasses of orange juice and wearing, well, half-wearing his jeans.

He'd pulled them over his hips but only bothered to fasten half of the fly buttons. He was beyond sexy, I felt my face getting hot—and then I remembered I was standing there naked—and blushed everywhere.

I scooted back into the bed and under the sheet.

Sebastian looked at me like I was a little crazy.

"I wanted to make you breakfast," he said, shrugging slightly, "but I can't cook. I can, however, pour a mean juice."

He passed me a glass and I took a long drink.

"Why, Mr. Hunter, you can indeed pour an amazing orange juice."

He smirked, then tipped the rest of his drink down his throat in one swift gulp. How the hell did men do that? It was a complete mystery to me.

"Well, let me make you some breakfast. What would you like? Eggs, pancakes, bacon, omelet?"

"I already told you yesterday," he said.

I frowned.

"You. I want you for breakfast."

He put his glass on the bedside cabinet and slowly walked toward me, his eyes never leaving my face. His expression made me breathless.

"Sex rather than food today?"

"Yes, ma'am."

I looked at the alarm clock. It was 6.45AM.

"We've got about three hours before I have to drop you off. Do you think that's enough time?"

He shook his head.

"Not really."

Then he leapt on the bed, making me shriek with surprise. I spilled orange juice down my chest and onto the sheets.

"Sebastian!"

He ignored me and started lapping the juice from my bare skin. I nearly melted from the heat of his touch, but just about managed to place my somewhat emptier glass on the bedside table.

I scrabbled to pull off his jeans but he was too intent on working his way down my body. It was neck and neck who was going to have their way first.

Sometime later, some *considerable* time later, the alarm went off.

We were both lying on our backs breathless. Again. I felt like I'd just gone ten rounds with Mike Tyson: every muscle ached and I was bathed in sweat. Sebastian had been tossing me around the bedroom for nearly two hours. He lay with his eyes closed and a blissful expression on his face.

The alarm clock had inconveniently been knocked out of reach. I struggled to sit up, crawling the length of the bed and fumbling on the floor to find the obnoxious electronic box.

Sebastian tried to bite my ass, which didn't really help my coordination.

"We need to get up!" I moaned.

He didn't reply.

"Up!"

"I am up," he mumbled against my skin.

Again? Oh, my God!

"Time for a shower. Go! Now!"

He grumbled a little more but eventually rolled off the bed, allowing me to get up and pull on my robe. I glanced around to see him stumble into the bathroom. It was true: he was up.

Smiling to myself, I headed down to the kitchen and rummaged around in the refrigerator. As he hadn't managed to express a preference, I decided to make a cheese omelet with bacon on the side.

I was still grilling the bacon when I heard him running

down the stairs. There was a huge thud and I guessed he'd jumped the last three or four steps. His exuberance made me smile. And where the hell did he get all that energy?

He wrapped his arms around my waist without hesitation and nuzzled my neck. I nearly dropped the spatula.

"What can I do?" he said.

I was surprised. No man had ever said that to me in my kitchen before. I turned and smirked at him.

"Just sit there and look decorative."

He threw me an amused look and stretched his long legs under the kitchen table, rocking the chair back on two legs, just like he had last night.

To have him sitting at my breakfast table felt wonderfully new and wonderfully natural, all at the same time.

When I served up the food, I put most of the omelet on his plate and four out of five of the pieces of bacon. He didn't even seem to notice the uneven distribution, he was so intent on getting the food into his stomach in the shortest time possible.

I was still chewing when he pushed his plate away. He glanced around to see if there was anything else to eat. Really, his appetites were enormous in all sorts of ways. The last ten hours had been a revelation.

"Toast?"

"Please!" he said happily.

I cut four slices off a new loaf and shoved them all in the toaster. "Do you want jelly?"

He pulled a face. "Nah, just butter, please."

"Don't you have a sweet tooth?"

"Only for you."

I rolled my eyes.

"Where do you stand on chocolate? I'm serious! It's an important question!"

"You like chocolate, Caro? What sort?"

I could see what he was thinking. Sometimes he was so easy to read.

"I don't want you to buy me any, Sebastian."

"Why not?"

He pouted and I wanted to laugh.

"Because we're saving our money for more important things."

He sighed. "Yeah, I guess."

"Mind you," I said, slyly, "I wouldn't mind licking some melted chocolate off you—I bet that would taste really good."

For a moment he looked a little shocked, then a huge grin spread across his face.

"Yeah! That sounds *hot!*"

"I'll see what I can do for tonight."

He groaned.

"What?"

"I'll have that image in my head all day now! I'll be a walking hard-on!"

"It's one way of increasing tips at work," I said, laughing at him.

He shook his head and looked embarrassed. He was so easy to tease. I really wasn't being very fair.

I glanced at my watch. It was nearly ten o'clock.

"Time to go," I said, trying not to sound too bereft.

He scowled.

"I'll call in sick."

"You can't do that," I said patiently. "For a start, Ches will be knocking on your door in about 20 minutes, and secondly, word is sure to get back to your mom—do you *really* want her asking awkward questions about where you've been?"

He sighed. "I guess not."

"Come on. Go be a lifeguard."

I cursed the day I'd left those empty packing crates in the garage. Instead of being able to drive my car inside it, so Sebastian could make a discrete exit from the house, I had to reverse the car right up to the front door so he could sneak in the passenger side with the least chance of being seen. By now it was broad daylight and I was anxious. I tried to come up with some excuses just in case—some reason as to why Sebastian was in my house at this time in the morning. Nothing sounded convincing. I just crossed my fingers. How very mature.

Luckily, very luckily, we arrived to the park without incident.

"Text me later?"

"Okay," he promised. "See you tonight. Love you!"

He slammed the door and waved goodbye. I watched him jog across the park and with a last glance, I made an illegal U-turn and headed off to the store. I wanted to make him something special for our last night together. And to buy some chocolate.

I'd just parked outside the store when my phone beeped. Sebastian hadn't wasted any time before texting me. But when I checked the message it was from David.

Flight lands 2115. I need dress uniform dry-cleaned for formal on Monday

And hello to you, too.

The message put me in a bad mood, reminding me that by tomorrow evening I would have to be *that* person again—loyal wife, spineless factotum. I didn't know how the hell I was going to do that.

"Hello, Caroline. How are you? You look a little tired."

Donna stood behind me with a piled up cart and a kind smile on her face. She patted my arm as my brain attempted to click into gear.

"I know, dear," she said. "I never sleep well when Johan's away either. I think I miss his snoring!"

I tried to smile and her face creased with concern.

"Are you all right?"

"I'm fine, thank you, Donna. I just got a message from David—he wants his dress uniform dry-cleaned for Monday. Now I'll have to go back to the house to get it."

"Oh my. Did you forget to look at the schedule again?" she teased me.

I couldn't help laughing.

"Yes! You'd think I'd have learned by now."

"Well, I'm glad I caught you. I was wondering if I could ask you to bring something for the picnic tomorrow. Maybe some of your delicious cold pasta? Just for our group."

"Oh, of course! I was going to bring some sandwiches, too, if you like?"

"How wonderful! Yes, please. I think it's going to be a fun day, and it looks like we'll be blessed with the weather. Would you like me to pick you up? There isn't a huge amount of parking, and the organizing committee has asked us to carpool. Besides, you haven't met my boys yet. They're back from college now."

"Oh, yes, that would be lovely," I stuttered, feeling under pressure. "Thank you!"

"I'll pick you up at 11AM then. And do try and get some sleep tonight, dear. You're far too young to look so tired. You don't want to end up with bags under your eyes like mine. Well, I have suitcases rather than bags."

Truthfully, I wasn't planning on getting much sleep during the night, but maybe I could take a nap later. I wondered briefly if I should let Sebastian get some more sleep—he'd probably only had about four hours last night and he was working all day. But then again, he was young—and I couldn't imagine him agreeing to sleep when I was fairly certain he would have other things on his mind. The thought made me smile.

Damn it! I'd forgotten to ask Donna how many people were part of the 'group' that she'd mentioned.

Moving slowly up and down the aisles, I filled the cart with focaccia rolls, cold cuts and some fresh pasta. I felt guilty buying store-made pasta but figured no one but me would be any the wiser. I also bought some lamb chops, potatoes and salad for Sebastian. And a jar of chocolate sauce. Although that was more for me.

As an afterthought, I picked up a few of David's favorite foods, too. He was always more amenable on a full stomach.

It was getting harder to buy 35mm film, especially in black and white, but I managed to find a few rolls. I wondered if I'd be able to buy a digital camera when we moved to New York. I had no idea how much they cost. I'd be sorry to stop using my dad's SLR, but the price of buying and developing film was an additional cost I could well do without. A cost *we* could well do without.

As I was happily daydreaming about a new life in a new city, my cell phone rang.

"Hi, Carolina! Carl Winters, here. How are you?"

"Well, thank you, Carl. And you?"

"Good, good. Look, I heard that the folk at the Base are having a family fun day on the beach tomorrow. Are you going?"

"Yes, I am."

"Great! I was wondering if you could take some photographs for the paper. We'd need them dropped off on Sunday evening."

"Oh, I'd love to do that but I think I mentioned to you—I don't have a digital camera. I wouldn't be able to get the film developed that quickly."

"No problem. We have a lab on site—just drop off the film and I'll have one of my technicians develop it."

I was silent.

"Carolina! Are you still there?"

"Oh, yes. I'm here."

"Is there a problem?"

"It's just ... what if they're not good enough? I'd hate for you to be relying on me and..."

He laughed.

"Carolina, it's a family fun day. I'm sure the snaps will be just fine. We'll get something usable—we can do a lot with cropping images. Don't worry about it."

"Well, okay. Thank you! I'm really flattered."

"Good. That's settled. I'll see you tomorrow."

He ended the call leaving me puzzled. He was the editor of a weekly paper and he was going to be there on a Sunday evening? Go figure.

Shopping bags filled the trunk of my car, including a jar of chocolate sauce, and I drove home with an unaccustomed smile on my face. It took a while to unload all the extra food I'd bought for the picnic.

But when I went into the bedroom, it looked like a bomb had hit it. With a sigh, I scooped up the sheets lying in a tangled heap on the floor, and wearily stripped the bed. Then I trudged downstairs and loaded them into the machine. I didn't know that having an affair meant more housework.

And then I remembered David's damn dress uniform. Muttering bad-temperedly, I shoved it into a plastic bag and drove to the dry-cleaners.

I nearly fell asleep at the wheel driving back and when I stumbled into the living room, I couldn't help thinking that the couch looked inviting. Perhaps just five minutes...

My cell phone alerted me that I had a message, waking me from a very interesting dream that involved a shower of chocolate instead of water ... and a naked Sebastian.

Feels like a long day. Missing you. Can't wait for later. Did you get chocolate? Sxx

I smiled and sent a text back.

Yes to choc. But how slow can you go?

He replied immediately.

Let's find out x

I had a huge grin on my face when I flipped my phone shut. But then I glanced at the time and was horrified to see I'd been asleep for more than three hours. I had a mountain of food to prepare for the picnic tomorrow and I sure as hell wasn't going to be wasting my time doing it while Sebastian was here.

Despite the rude, very rude awakening, I felt better for my extended nap and set to work with a will. I had so much food, I had to drag out some cardboard boxes that I had stashed in the garage and stack it inside. I couldn't help thinking about the morning Sebastian had come over to help me empty our moving-in crates. It seemed a lifetime ago—I wondered how it seemed to him.

I hunted through the kitchen cupboards for some candles. I'd bought them in case of a power outage—they'd certainly never been used for a romantic interlude with David. I wanted what I'd never had. I wanted tonight to be perfect.

The table looked so pretty, laid with proper linen napkins and decorated with candles and a small posy of flowers that I'd picked in the yard. I headed up to change into the little black dress that Sebastian had helped me choose, and matched it with elegant, suede pumps—I wanted to look beautiful for him.

After I unlocked the kitchen door, I curled up on the couch with a book. I must have fallen asleep again because it was dark when I next looked up. I was shocked to see that it was nearly one o'clock in the morning. *Where was he?*

The first thing I did was to check my phone, but there were no messages and no missed calls. Uncertainty vied with panic—had something happened to him or had he just had enough of me? I wondered if I should risk calling him. In the end I decided to send a text—just in case. And it was also our more usual form of communication.

r u ok? I'm worried

I sat on the edge of the couch, anxiously waiting for a reply. When I couldn't take the tension anymore, I stood up and started pacing.

Another half an hour passed and I still hadn't heard from him. I was pondering the wisdom of getting in my car and going to look for him when I finally, *finally* heard a soft knock on the door.

I flew into the kitchen, yanked the door open and, to my dismay, I burst into tears when I saw him standing there smiling at me.

"Hey! What's wrong? I'm sorry I'm late. Don't cry, Caro. Please don't cry, baby!"

He held me in his arms, stroking my hair, letting me cry myself out, all the fear and unreasoning anxiety, the stress of having to split myself in half, the intensity of the last three weeks, the hope for more that was so tender and fragile—it all poured out of me.

"Sorry," I choked out. "I was just so worried. You didn't answer your phone and I didn't know how to contact you."

"We got a flat on the way home," he said, soothingly. "It took forever for me and Ches to put the new tire on in the dark."

"I texted you!"

"I couldn't charge up my phone yesterday—it died on me a few hours ago. I didn't think it would matter. You were really worried about me?"

I nodded miserably. I felt such a fool getting myself into that state because of a dead phone battery and a flat tire. I wanted to yell, *keep your phone charged, you jerk!* But I didn't—I was just glad he was here with me and safe.

He wiped my tears away with his fingers.

"I like that you were worried about me," he said, softly.

He glanced over my shoulder at the kitchen table.

"Is this for me, too?"

I nodded again and tried to smile. "Surprise!" I muttered.

He laughed quietly. "I love it. Thank you. And ... you look beautiful, Caro."

"Red-eyed and hideous is more like it, but thank you for saying so."

"You always look beautiful to me."

"Yes, well that must be because you're wearing those rose-tinted glasses again."

He sighed and shook his head. I couldn't tell if he was irritated or amused—maybe a little of both.

"Are you hungry?"

"God, yes! Right now my stomach is thinking that someone cut my throat."

"They really ought to feed you at work," I grumbled.

He shrugged. "We were busy. But I have tomorrow off."

He looked at me expectantly but when he saw my dismayed reaction, his face fell.

"I thought ... I just hoped we could spend the day together, but ... it's cool ... if you're busy."

I swore. He looked surprised, I wasn't much given to cursing.

"Oh, I wish I'd known! I've told Donna I'd go to the family fun day at the beach—you know, the big picnic?"

He scowled. "Can't you tell her you've changed your mind?"

"I wish! But I've agreed to take photographs for *City Beat*, too. They're counting on me. Oh, Sebastian, I'm so sorry! If I'd known you had the day off..."

"It was a last minute thing," he muttered. "They gave Ches the day off, as well. Probably because so many people will be at the fun day."

The possibilities presented by being able to spend a whole day alone with Sebastian now drifted through my mind, as substantial and certain as mist.

I wrapped my arms around his waist and laid my head on his chest again.

"There'll be other days," I said, my voice sad.

"Yeah, I know. It's just that every day ... every moment with you..."

"...is precious," I finished the sentence for him.

"Very."

I kissed him softly. "I'll go make dinner."

"I'll light the candles."

I was surprised when he pulled a lighter out of his pocket, I'd never seen Sebastian smoke and I'd certainly never smelt tobacco on him. Odd.

I switched off the overhead electric lights so the only illumination in the kitchen was from the candles. The flickering lights threw weird images onto the walls, like some freakish shadow play. A shiver ran through me—someone must have walked over my grave. I shook off the superstitious notion and concentrated instead on the way the candlelight played across Sebastian's face, highlighting his cheekbones and making his eyes glitter. He smiled up at me and in the dim light, his irises looked coal black. I could lose my train of thought just by looking at him.

I served up the grilled lamb chops and Sebastian ate heartily, I merely picked at my food. I felt resentful of tomorrow's wasted opportunity and, stupidly, I was letting it spoil this evening, too. I made an effort to pull myself together.

"How was work today?"

"Busy. There was some big golf tournament: a lot of out-of-towners."

"Any pool-side incidents?"

He laughed as he remembered something.

"Yeah! One of the guests dropped her cell phone in the deep end. I dove down to get it for her."

"Was she grateful?"

"I think she was more pissed, but she gave me ten bucks ... and her cell phone number."

"You're kidding me!" *How dare she? Was she pretty? How old was she?*

Those were the questions that I couldn't ask.

"I mean, how dumb can you get?" continued Sebastian. "She just dumped her damn phone in the pool and that's the number she gives me!"

"Sebastian," I said, pointing out the blindingly obvious, at least to me, "the number will still work—she'll just have to buy a new handset."

He looked at me.

"Really?"

"Yes!"

He shook his head. "Well, it doesn't make any difference—I threw her number away."

"You did?"

"Of course I did!"

He looked annoyed. "I wouldn't cheat on you, Caro!"

I couldn't bear to point out the irony in that statement. Instead, I changed the subject.

"Do you want some dessert?"

His expression changed in an instant—from righteous indignation to the most scorching look of lust.

"Chocolate?" His voice was low and seductive.

"I ... I made a polenta cake ... but I bought chocolate sauce, too."

He didn't take his eyes off me and his voice didn't waver.

"Just the chocolate."

He stood up, his chair scraping across the kitchen floor, and he held out his hand to me. I took it wordlessly and Sebastian pulled me into his arms, then kissed me until I stopped breathing.

"I want to make love to you," he said, his voice hoarse. "I've been thinking about it all day. Fuck! I couldn't think of anything else." He blinked and his eyes danced with amusement. "People could have been drowning in that pool and I don't think I'd have noticed."

"Let's go to bed."

"Oh, yeah, baby!"

Suddenly he scooped me up off the floor and flung me over his shoulder. The surprise made me cry out. He practically ran up the stairs and threw me on the bed. I couldn't help laughing at his eagerness, at the sheer joy I saw on his face.

"Damn! We forgot the chocolate."

"No, we didn't." I pointed to the bottle of chocolate sauce by the alarm clock and watched his eyes light up.

He twisted the lid and the jar made a soft popping sound as it opened. He stuck his index finger in and pulled it out covered in chocolate. He held it out toward me.

"Suck," he said.

So I did.

～

At some point in the night we must have fallen asleep. It hadn't been a conscious decision, more a sort of acknowledgment of sheer exhaustion.

Waking up was a struggle. My eyes were gritty with

tiredness, and my body ached so much, I didn't know which muscle to favor first. *And there was chocolate everywhere!*

Oh, the chocolate! Mmm, that had been good. No, that had been *great*. That had been *fun*.

We'd laughed so much. I couldn't remember laughing so much, not ever.

And the way we'd explored each other's body. I remembered again the touch of his fingers, the way his skin warmed against mine, the soft, wet heat of his lips, everywhere. The passion that had smoldered for hours, blazing suddenly into flames that burned.

I rolled over to find his eyes open, a smile of wonder on his face.

We didn't speak, we just gazed at each other. I think I was smiling, too.

His fingers stroked my arm slowly, rhythmically.

I reached up to rest my hand on his cheek, but he pulled it to his lips and kissed the palm. I nestled into his body and his hand moved down to stroke my bare back.

I listened to the quiet, steady beat of his heart.

"We have to get up," I said, sadly.

He nodded slowly but neither of us moved.

"When will I see you again?" he murmured.

"Today, at the picnic," I said, trying to sound upbeat.

"You know what I mean."

I sighed. I did know what he meant, I just didn't have an answer. There was no tomorrow for us.

"We'll figure something out," I said, trying to sound reassuring.

"I hate this," he said sulkily. "All the sneaking around, all the lies. I want everyone to know we're together."

"Fine!" I snapped. "Go ahead! Tell everyone! And then I can spend the next God knows how long in prison, or stuck on the sex offender registry and not able to get a job."

I knew I was behaving badly, childishly, but I couldn't seem to stop.

He gasped in shock. "I didn't mean it like that," he mumbled.

"Then what did you mean?" I said, my voice beginning to rise in volume. "Do you think I find this easy? Do you think I enjoy betraying people, lying to decent people like Donna and Shirley? Deceiving everyone? Do you think this isn't hard for *me*? This isn't a game, Sebastian!"

"I know that!" he yelled back. "It's my life, too!"

I closed my eyes and took a deep breath. "I'm sorry. I'm just ... a little tired. You've worn me out."

That brought a slight smile to his lips but his eyes were still hurt and angry.

I knew I shouldn't take my constant anxiety out on him.

"I'm sorry, it's frustrating for me, too."

"I don't want to fight with you, Caro. I just want to be with you all the time. You're all I think about."

We lay there for a few more minutes, wishing the hands of the clock to slow in sympathy.

"Donna will be here in an hour," I said quietly. "We have to get up."

Our shower was over too quickly and my hands reluctantly let him go. We dressed in silence, the ache of separation already billowing between us.

I glanced at the bed where he had made such sweet love to me, the chocolatey sheets a reminder of a carefree night.

"Do they have other flavors?" asked Sebastian, following my gaze.

"I don't know. Psrobably. Maybe we should investigate?"

"I like peanut butter," he said, wistfully.

I raised my eyebrows. "Crunchy or smooth?"

He laughed, a little sadly, and pulled me into a hug.

"I'd better get going."

"You don't want breakfast?" I was surprised.

"You can't risk driving me to the park today—half the neighbors will be outside in their yards. I'll go through the back."

At least one of us was thinking clearly.

"I'll see you later?" he said, tentatively.

"Yes," I said simply.

He smiled.

We walked down the stairs in silence.

In the kitchen I pulled him toward me and we kissed hungrily. I held him as long as I could, but too soon, it was time for him to go. He kissed me lightly on the forehead and then ducked out through the kitchen door.

I'd forgotten to remind him to charge his phone.

Feeling miserable, I threw the chocolatey sheets in the washing machine and made up the bed with clean ones. I removed every piece of evidence, every trace that there'd been anyone in the house but me—the doormat wife of a bullying man.

I was disgusted with myself—and the list of reasons was endless.

CHAPTER TWELVE

DONNA WAS ON TIME. OF COURSE.

"Good morning, Caroline. How are you today?"

"Just fine, thank you, Donna. Are these your sons?"

Two attractive men in their twenties with Johan's Nordic looks were getting out of Donna's station wagon.

"Kurt, Stefan—Caroline Wilson."

"Hello, nice to meet you. I hear you're down from college for the summer break?"

We chatted easily while the boys loaded up Donna's trunk with the boxes of food stashed in my kitchen.

"My goodness," she said. "There's enough here to feed the five thousand!"

"Too much?" I asked anxiously.

She laughed. "I'm sure it'll all be eaten, it looks delicious."

I grabbed my notebook and camera, shoved the spare films in the pockets of my shorts and we headed off.

"How many people do you think will be there today?"

"Oh, well, probably a couple of thousand in total—it's mostly folk from the Naval Medical Center but quite a few families come from the Marine Corps, too. The Peters will be there, and I think Shirley said the boys had been given the day off work, so I expect they'll tag along ... especially if they know you'll be there—with food."

I stared out of the window, hoping my burning cheeks wouldn't give me away.

I hadn't realized the picnic was quite such a big deal. Of course, if I hadn't been so preoccupied, I might have been a little more aware. But then again, I'd never gone out of my way to be involved with family life on the Base, not having had a family.

I'd been to Harbor Beach just once before. It was a wide, flat esplanade of fine sand, perfect for families. Lifeguard towers ran the length of the beach between the jetties, where a couple of surfers were catching some small waves. A playground on the sand was a major attraction for the younger children and Donna informed me that some of the older ones—and their parents—would be making use of the volleyball courts: just supply your own ball and net.

The beach was already getting crowded, the military personnel stood out a mile with their crew cuts and buzz-cuts. The parking lot was a cheerful, chaotic crowd with mountains of food being ferried to the fire pits that ringed the beach.

The tide was way out, it would be quite a hike for anyone wanting to go for a swim. But most people seemed intent on playing and eating their way through the day.

I saw volleyballs, soccer balls, Frisbees, footballs, numerous body boards, and lots and lots of kids carrying colorful kites— several in the shape of airplanes. One group of mothers was organizing a sandcastle-building contest for the kids—and whichever of the adults felt like joining in, and a group of Marines was planning a pie-eating competition. Something I personally found rather gross—watching grown men shove as much pie in their faces in the shortest amount of time was unpleasant, to say the least. I couldn't understand why anyone would want to do it. It seemed a waste of good food.

Despite the fact that alcohol was not allowed on the beach, I saw several men openly carrying six-packs. It wasn't really taking that much of a risk—I knew that you would be hard-pressed to find a police officer willing to give a ticket to someone in the service. I suppose you'd call it a sort of brotherhood. I'd lost count of the number of tickets David had gotten out of because of his 'Fly Navy' license plate and his military service window stickers.

There was a real holiday feel to the day—I felt cheerless by comparison despite knowing that I'd see Sebastian later. Nevertheless, I had a job to do, such as it was. I pulled out my camera and started snapping some candid shots of the military at play. To my surprise, I began to enjoy capturing the varied scenes of happiness: games of football that seemed to be rule-free, small children chasing their burly fathers, kids running around in swimsuits, and enough food to feed an army—which it was, of course.

Although it had been advertised as a 'family' fun day, there were lots of singles there, too, men (and a few women) adopted into the family of the unit they served with. There was no doubt that putting your life in the hands of the other guys in your unit created a bond.

It dawned on me that I was one of the 'singles', and that Donna had adopted me into her family for the day. There were worse ways to be treated.

I heard Ches's van before I saw it, but I studiously kept my eyes on the boxes of food that Kurt and Stefan were carrying to the spot where Donna had staked her claim.

She looked up at the noise and waved furiously to attract their attention. The van rumbled to a stop nearby and I saw that Mitch was driving, with Bill and Shirley sharing the front seat.

My heart began to beat a little faster because I knew that Sebastian was now just a few feet away from me, although he may as well have been on the moon because I wouldn't be able to touch him. I would hardly dare to look at him.

I didn't know which was worse—to see him and not touch him, or to not see him at all.

Shirley jumped out first followed by Bill who winked at me, much to Donna's amusement. Mitch went around to open the back of the van. I kept my eyes on the trunk of Donna's car and continued unpacking.

"Can I help you with that?"

Sebastian's soft voice made me jump. He was wearing a fresh white t-shirt and colorful board shorts, with a pair of wrap-around sunglasses pushed up onto his short hair. He'd also shaved. I felt dizzy just seeing him, but quickly dropped my eyes.

"Oh, thank you!" I managed to mutter.

He grinned at me and took the box from my nerveless hands, following the convoy of Donna's sons, Bill and Mitch. I picked up the polenta cake, still untouched from last night, and gingerly joined the line.

"I really liked your article, Mrs. Wilson."

I turned around to see Fido smiling at me. I was surprised, I'd never heard him speak before.

"Thank you! I'm glad you enjoyed it—and please, it's Caroline."

Sebastian must have overheard because he turned around and frowned, throwing an angry look at Fido. Fido merely grinned back and insisted on carrying the polenta cake. I tried to keep my smile bright, but inside I was dying—wasn't this day going to be hard enough without worrying about whether or not Sebastian would be jealous of anyone who spoke to me?

I didn't think it was a coincidence that Sebastian chose that moment to pull off his t-shirt, baring his chest, flaunting his golden skin, naked in the sunshine. He knew I wouldn't be able to stop myself from having a quick ogle. Of course, the other men immediately followed suit and I was soon surrounded by a surfeit of taut, tanned and toned flesh. I pulled my sunglasses over my eyes and tried to think cooling thoughts.

We settled in a loose group around our fire pit, Sebastian securing a spot opposite me, but every time I stood up to get some more of the food, or pass something around, he'd stand up, too, and 'help'. Then he'd brush up against me: seemingly innocent little touches. Each time my skin blazed with need and I wanted to yell at him to stop—or to not stop but do something about the heat that was rising within me. Somehow I managed to follow a conversation with Shirley about her idea to keep chickens as a way of making some extra money. I knew nothing about poultry so it was a fairly one-sided discussion.

Bill and Mitch kept up a friendly banter of profanities as they proceeded to char vast quantities of meat. I resolved to stick to cold cuts and salad as I helped to lay out the rest of the provisions.

Several Marines from Mitch and Bill's unit wandered over to pass the time and help reduce the mountain of food. All the men were eating like their lives depended on it, and my concern that there was too much quickly vanished.

Donna introduced me to all the visitors and I could read surprise on the faces of several when she explained I was the wife of Lieutenant Commander Wilson. Clearly, David's reputation had gone before.

Kurt and Stefan regaled us with tales of college life, each trying to outdo the other. They were attractive, intelligent young men, good company and entertaining. Stefan was following in his father's footsteps and studying medicine at UCLA. Kurt had chosen civil engineering and went to school at McCormick in Chicago. Unfortunately, the brothers seemed to have a well developed rivalry which, on this occasion, they were using to take turns flirting with me. It was beyond embarrassing, particularly as I could see Sebastian's murderous looks from across the fire pit, and Ches's amused expression. Fido just stared at me, which was more than a little unnerving.

During the course of the afternoon, Sebastian became quieter and quieter, and I sensed that his temper was beginning to fray. Worse still, Fido's dog-like devotion to me was also becoming more apparent. Every time I reached for something, he leapt up to hand it to me. I had never been so popular—and it had never been less well timed.

I couldn't help wondering if all the sex I'd been having was giving off some sort of invisible signal, some sort of scent, a pheromone, perhaps. Could that happen? I'd never before been in a position to need to ask the question.

As unobtrusively as I was able, I stood up, determined to slink away by myself for a while.

"Are you okay, Caroline?" asked Donna.

I cringed as every eye focused on me.

"Oh, I'm just going to go and get some shots of the volleyball game and sandcastle competition," I said lightly.

"I'll come with you," said Sebastian immediately.

"No, no! I'm fine. Stay and enjoy yourself," I said, just one shade too forcefully.

His eyes darkened with anger and he slumped back to the sand, a surly expression on his face.

Honestly! Did he want to make it so obvious?

I hurried off to take some photographs, including the ghastly pie-eating competition. Even though I ached for Sebastian's company, there were too many eyes everywhere. I returned half an hour later, when my blood pressure had returned to normal, and avoided meeting his too ardent gaze. But I did see Donna raise her eyebrows and smile. The woman was just too damned observant. It made me nervous.

Ches was interested in my old SLR so I showed him how to change the focus and how to read the built-in light meter. I let him take a few snaps of our group. Bill, of course, bombed the photograph, scooping me up into a huge hug, which earned him a furious look from Sebastian. Then Ches insisted on taking one of me. I didn't mind—it wasn't like I'd have to look at it—all the photographs would be developed at *City Beat*.

"I had an old SLR once," said Bill. "I wonder what happened to it—I used to love taking photographs."

"First I've heard of it," said Mitch, raising his eyebrows.

"Hey! I do have one or two secrets, buddy!" replied Bill, raising a bottle of beer in salute. "So, what else do you like taking photographs of, Caroline?"

"You mean other than pictures of fine figures of men like you, Bill?" laughed Shirley.

"Too right!" said Bill, flexing his biceps. "You want to take some photos of me, Caroline? *Private* photographs? Anytime, honey—but you'll need a long lens!"

I laughed, trying to seem as if I was enjoying the joke. It was kind of hard when Sebastian looked like was about to punch Bill.

"I do like taking photographs of people," I said, trying to change the direction of the embarrassing conversation, "but when they're not aware I'm watching—just candids of people carrying on with their lives. I'm not into landscapes that much —I always admired people like Robert Capa and Cartier-Bresson and..."

"Oh, I love it when you talk French to me, Caroline!" said Bill, winking at me.

This was getting beyond embarrassing.

Ches's head was swiveling between Bill and Sebastian as if he was watching some sort of tennis match.

I saw Shirley throw Bill a warning look. His only reply was to smirk at her and take another swig of beer.

I wondered if he was deliberately trying to tease Sebastian. Heaven forbid, but it seemed to be some sort of open secret that Sebastian liked me. It was obvious from the way that everyone's eyes were drawn to him whenever I became the subject of conversation that they knew *something*. Thankfully, no one had guessed that his feelings were more than reciprocated.

I wanted to shake him or send him for acting lessons or something that made it less damn obvious how he felt about me.

Not only did it make me anxious, but it made me question how successful my own attempts were to act like I didn't notice him, or didn't give a damn. The whole thing was giving me a headache and I longed for the picnic to be over. It really wasn't living up to its billing of a 'fun day'.

I began to have quite violent thoughts toward Donna—I wished more than anything that I hadn't accepted her misplaced kindness and instead gotten here in my own car.

The mountain of food continued to diminish and Donna was encouraging me to serve up the lemon polenta cake when I became aware that the eyes of every male in our group had swung to a spot just behind my right shoulder.

"Hi, everyone," said a female voice.

"Hi, Brenda," said Ches, his tone friendly but cautious.

I saw him glance at Sebastian.

Oh. The ex-girlfriend.

Brenda Wiseman was undeniably lovely: a perfect, willowy figure, stick-straight blonde hair that she flipped over her shoulders, pale blue eyes, and the smallest bikini I'd ever seen outside of a men's magazine. Irritatingly, she certainly had the figure to wear it to its best advantage.

While everyone stared at Brenda, Bill's eyes about popping out of his head and Donna's lips pursed in apparent distaste, I saw Sebastian glance nervously toward me. I dropped my eyes to the polenta cake and continued to cut it, gripping the handle of the cake-slice tightly. It was bad timing on Brenda's part that I happened to have a weapon conveniently at hand.

"Hi, Sebastian," she said.

"Hi."

His reply was short and unenthusiastic.

I couldn't help wondering if that was solely for my benefit.

She hesitated for a moment, as if waiting for an invitation. When none was forthcoming, she sat down next to him anyway, stretching out her long tan legs and leaning back on her hands.

"I haven't seen you since graduation."

Sebastian stared at the sand. It was clear he had no clue how to handle this.

It was quite funny—if you weren't me.

"Where have you been hanging?" she persisted, her voice unnaturally cheery.

I wondered if she'd been rehearsing.

"I've been busy."

"Ches said you guys have jobs out at the country club," she prompted him.

Sebastian glared at Ches who guiltily shrugged his shoulders.

"So, what do you do there?"

"Lifeguarding," replied Ches quickly, "and some waiting on tables when they're short-staffed."

"Cool!" said Brenda, flipping her hair over her shoulders *again*.

I wanted to leap across the barbeque pit and make her eat sand.

The men looked amused as Sebastian became increasingly and obviously uncomfortable, his cheeks reddening with each awkward second. Shirley and Donna looked sympathetic and politely tried to maintain a separate conversation. I hated to think what expression was leaking out onto my face.

"Hey, you cut your hair," said Brenda, reaching out to run one hand across the nape of his neck.

I wanted to snap her fingers off at the wrist.

Sebastian flinched away from her and looked annoyed. I hoped that Brenda would take the hint but she hadn't deployed her primary weapons yet.

"Well, it suits you," she said, hitching up her bikini top.

I could have sworn her tits had magnets attached to them the way the men's eyes seemed to be drawn toward her impressive cleavage. Even Sebastian's.

"Although I always liked your hair long, but then you already knew that, didn't you?"

"I cut my hair, too," said Ches in a farcical attempt to protect his friend from Brenda's relentless onslaught.

She glanced at him with humiliating brevity.

"Nice."

"Have you decided where you're going to school in the fall?" asked Stefan, trying to attract her attention.

"I've been accepted at UCLA—and UCSD," she said, her eyes fixed on Sebastian.

"You should go to UCLA," said Stefan. "It's a really great school. What's your major?"

But she completely ignored him and he crashed in flames, much to his brother's amusement. Brenda drew up her knees and nudged Sebastian's arm with her thigh.

"Can we talk?" she said softly.

"I thought you'd be *talking* to Jack," he said coolly.

She blushed.

"Please, Sebastian? In private."

The sudden timidity in her voice made me look up. She was staring at Sebastian, a worried little pucker between her eyebrows. I had to hand it to her: she was good. And she had guts. She was making a very public statement that she still had feelings for him. In fact, speaking from recent experience, I'd say she was crazy about him.

The burn of jealousy in my throat got worse, running all the way down to my gut. She was gorgeous, sweet, rather brave, *extremely* determined, and had her eyes on the prize. Oh, and they were the same age. She was perfect for him, she was the sort of girl he ought to be with—assuming she wasn't really the man-eating tramp she seemed to be channeling.

It was unfair of me to hold onto him, it was wrong.

I felt my eyes began to fill with tears. I hoped I was near enough to the smoking barbeque pit to have a believable excuse.

I waited for Sebastian to tell her that there was nothing to talk about.

Except he didn't.

He pushed himself to his feet in one graceful move.

"Okay," he muttered.

I don't know if he looked at me because my gaze was locked on that damn cake—I'd never be able to eat lemon polenta ever again.

"She's a nice girl," said Shirley sympathetically, as Brenda walked away with Sebastian. "I was so surprised when they broke up." She glanced at Ches, who wouldn't meet his mother's eyes. "I don't know what happened between them."

I stabbed the cake viciously.

"She's a hottie!" declared Stefan.

"I remember when she was skinny and wore braces," said Kurt. "Now look at the size of those bazookas!"

"Kurt!" said Donna in a warning voice.

Mitch and Bill laughed.

I handed around the cake, a painful smile plastered to my face. I told myself that it was wrong to watch Sebastian and

Brenda and that I wouldn't try to see what was happening—it was just coincidence that when I sat down again after helping everyone to cake, I had a clear view.

From what I could see she was using every trick in her well-thumbed manual. Nice girl, my ass!

She pretended to stagger slightly, losing her balance so she could bump against him and take his arm, she played with the strap of her bikini to draw his gaze and show him what he didn't necessarily have to go on missing. Then she tossed her hair over her shoulder and tucked a strand behind her ear. I was desperate to know what they were saying. Sebastian was shaking his head and she was standing too close and stroking his arm. Then they seemed to be arguing. She was pleading with him, her arms outstretched, he was shaking his head vehemently, his hands on his hips. I don't know how it happened but then she had her arms wrapped around his neck, her cheek on his bare chest, and he was holding her, rocking her gently, the same way he'd held me last night.

"I have ten bucks says we won't be seeing Seb till tomorrow morning," said Stefan, gesturing obscenely with his hands.

"You won't get any takers on that bet!" laughed Kurt. "She's all over him!"

Ches looked disgusted, and threw the remains of his sandwich into the fire pit.

"Boys!" said Donna in a warning voice.

I'd seen enough. Seen enough and heard enough.

"Caroline? Are you going somewhere?"

Donna's attention was directed back to me.

I smiled stiffly, forcing the words out.

"I'm just going to go and take some more photographs before I lose the light—I want to make sure I have everything covered." *And to get the hell away from all of this.*

I wandered along the beach, feeling numb even though traitorous tears were leaking from my eyes. I snapped photographs at random, barely aware of what I was looking at. There was only one picture in my head—the one where

Sebastian held his ex-girlfriend. His beautiful, sexy, *young* ex-girlfriend.

I was angry! So it seemed my hypocrisy knew no bounds. I was angry because Sebastian had left me and gone off with Brenda—the slut who'd screwed his friend Jack. Yes, I was cheating on my husband; yes, I was an unfaithful wife. But I'd risked everything for Sebastian—everything. The life I'd known, jail time, a record.

I had to watch him walk away and smile and smile while he played the villain. I was choked with jealousy and anger and more hurt than I could easily take.

I found myself at the ocean's edge. The tide had turned and was beginning its slow journey back across the sun-warmed sand. The gentle lapping of water at my feet was soothing. I let my mind wander among the dizzying memories of the last three weeks—a ridiculously short amount of time during the course of a life. And yet ... and yet I had never felt so alive. Fear—as much as hope—had colored those weeks but I realized I didn't have to go on like that.

I had expected too much from Sebastian: it wasn't fair. He was so young ... too young to be expected to take on everything I represented, with all my ridiculous insecurities and emotional baggage. If I truly cared for him, I would make it easy for him to go. Of course, it didn't seem as if he'd need my blessing, the way Brenda had clung to him and the way he'd held her, too.

Much as my body, my whole being ached for his touch, I had a revelation—I was strong enough to make it on my own. He'd shown me how to be strong. Perhaps he'd given me his own strength, I didn't know. One thing was certain—I couldn't be with David anymore. And if Sebastian didn't want me, there was no reason for me to stay.

But it hurt. It hurt badly. I'd opened myself to the possibility of love and now love had slapped me down. Down, but not out: not quite.

I felt a dull tearing inside my chest—part of my heart was breaking, knowing that in all probability I wouldn't see

Sebastian again. I took a deep breath and stared toward the horizon—time for me to grow up at last.

I glanced at my watch. I hoped Donna was ready to leave because I needed to get over to *City Beat* and drop off the films. Oh, and pick up David's dry-cleaning. I quailed at the thought of facing him, or rather, telling him that I was leaving. I needed to clear my head and decide how I was going to do that. Just thinking about it made me feel sick. So much for being strong. I was definitely going to have to work up to it. Somehow.

By the time I'd wandered back to the barbeque pit, Donna and Shirley were alone, slowly packing up the remains of the food—women's work, it seemed. I hurried to help them.

"Did you take all your photographs?" asked Donna.

"Yes, I think so. Are you heading back now? It's just I need to drop these films in at *City Beat*?"

"Tonight?" Donna was surprised. "The paper doesn't go out until Thursday."

"I know, but the editor asked for them, so..."

"Well, Shirley and I are heading back now anyway. The boys are getting a ride with Mitch. I expect they'll be rather late."

She raised her eyebrows and shook her head in a way that suggested *boys will be boys*.

With everything piled into Donna's station-wagon, we drove away from the beach. I glanced over my shoulder once, as the sun had begun its slow descent toward the horizon. I don't know what I was looking for—a soft hiss of steam as the sun touched the ocean, or perhaps a glimpse of someone silhouetted on the sand. Of course, there was neither.

It felt like the end of something, but maybe it was a beginning, too.

"That went well, didn't it?" said Donna, cheerfully.

For a moment I couldn't think what she was talking about. Oh, the fun day. Right. So much fun.

My lonely thoughts burned like acid. I was so stupid to have expected anything different.

Shirley smiled. "Yes, I think everyone had a good time. Of

course, the boys are planning on extending the fun. I hope Mitch keeps an eye on them."

I didn't want to think how Sebastian might be extending the fun at this very moment.

Donna smiled, "I'm sure he will."

For a moment I wasn't sure if she was answering my unspoken thoughts.

"Hmm, well, he won't let them drink too much, but I dare say there'll be a few sore heads in the morning. Mitch did say that there was a possibility they were going to sleep in the van tonight if they didn't make it back, although I'm not sure how they'll all fit now Stefan and Kurt are with them."

Donna shook her head and smiled. "I doubt they'll care. You know what they're like when they all get together." Then her serious look was back. "Although they really shouldn't be drinking on the beach—Chester is still under age. And Sebastian. And that other boy—Fido."

Shirley laughed. "Don't you remember when you were that age, Donna? You've told me you bent a few rules in your time—in fact, I distinctly remember you saying that Johan climbed in your dormitory at that private girls' school of yours."

I threw a surprised look at Donna. She was a lovely lady, but she'd always struck me as rather formal.

"Oh, yes," said Shirley, smiling at me, "Donna has her fair share of secrets, don't you?"

"You'll be giving Caroline the wrong impression of me."

"Or the right one," laughed Shirley. "Yes, Johan used to climb into her dormitory to steal a kiss or two. She nearly got expelled, didn't you, Donna?!"

"Yes, I admit it all," smiled Donna.

"Well, now you know where your boys get their wild streak from," said Shirley with a wink.

"Yes, well ... and who would you say Chester takes after?"

"His father!" asserted Shirley. Then she sighed. "I don't know who Sebastian takes after—luckily the poor boy isn't like either of his parents. I sometimes wonder if Donald is really his father."

"Shirley!" said Donna, looking shocked.

"Well, you've said yourself he doesn't take after either of them—he certainly doesn't *look* like either of them. Then there's Estelle's *reputation*. And it would explain why they're always so ghastly toward him."

"Well," said Donna, quietly, "I don't think we should speculate on that. Not without facts."

Shirley shrugged and for a moment there was an awkward silence in the car.

"You're very quiet, Caroline. Are you okay?" asked Donna, her eyes inquiring.

"Just thinking about the week ahead," I replied, my words deliberately bland.

The week. The month. The rest of my life.

In truth, I'd been fascinated to hear Shirley's speculation about Sebastian's heritage. I wondered if there was any shred of truth in it, or perhaps it was just the useless, baseless gossip that percolated through so many military facilities.

With a painful jolt I reminded myself that in all reality, it wasn't any of my business, Sebastian wasn't any of my business. But I couldn't resist torturing myself a little more.

"What happened to Sebastian this evening?" I asked innocently, while nearly choking on my words. "They'd all vanished by the time I came back."

"I think he left with Brenda," said Shirley, confirming the thoughts that tormented me.

"Oh, I don't know," disagreed Donna. "He was talking to Chester for a while, wasn't he? Or was it before that girl arrived? I thought she was rather ... underdressed."

I definitely agreed with that point of view. Tramp.

Shirley smiled. "All the young girls dress like that, Donna. And, frankly, if she wanted to catch Sebastian's attention, which she obviously did, she certainly went about it the right way!" She paused. "Although, to be fair, I was a little surprised, she'd always seemed rather sweet when they were dating, hardly the siren of today's little show and tell. But who knows: they're probably off having mad, passionate sex behind the pier."

I could have quite cheerfully stuck Shirley's head in the passenger door and slammed it several times. It wasn't that she was saying anything I hadn't been thinking, but to hear it confirmed by a third party was a new source of humiliation and hurt.

"I should hope not!" said Donna, severely.

"Oh, come on, Donna. You were young once. You've got two sons: you know what teenage boys are like. They think about sex every other second—or more often than that. You saw their faces when Brenda arrived—and what she wasn't wearing. I wouldn't be surprised if every dick within a hundred yards leapt to attention and saluted when she fiddled with her bikini strap. Which of them can say no when it's offered up on a plate like that? I mean, I've tried to talk to Ches about waiting until he's in love and respect for women and all that, but I'm definitely swimming against the tide there—I'm probably too late anyway. Mostly, I hope he's being safe. I don't relish the thought of being a grandmother just yet."

Donna shook her head but it was clear she didn't agree with Shirley's more liberal views. "I think I'd be a nervous wreck if I'd had daughters instead of sons. And their father would have kept them locked up until they'd graduated college ... or possibly longer."

Just then my phone beeped. I decided to ignore it. Donna glanced at me, a quizzical expression on her face.

"It's probably David making sure I've collected the dry-cleaning," I said, trying and failing to keep the bitterness out of my voice.

She smiled.

"Yes, Johan said something about a formal dinner at the mess tomorrow. I don't think he was very keen, having been away for two nights. But who expects the military to be sympathetic to us poor wives?"

Shirley nodded in agreement, and the topic moved on to other wives and partners who had dropped by to say hello during the course of the afternoon.

"I think Bill enjoyed himself today," said Shirley. "I haven't seen him like that since before he and Denise divorced."

"How long have he and Mitch been friends?"

"Oh, ever since we came to San Diego, so it must be at least four years—we wanted Ches to have some consistency through high school."

I leaned back in my seat as the conversation continued, letting the tiredness wash over me. I was almost asleep by the time Donna pulled up outside my house.

"Did David mention that I was picking them both up at the airport?"

"Oh, I probably should have read David's text," I said, guiltily.

"Never mind," she said, smiling at me. "You've got enough on your mind remembering the dry-cleaning."

I laughed, although I knew the tone was a little off.

"And I have to get into town. Well, thanks for a lovely day, both of you. And thanks for the ride—and for looking after me."

I gave Donna a quick hug and blew a kiss to Shirley.

"Our pleasure, Caroline," said Donna.

"We must have another coffee soon," agreed Shirley. "Maybe at the country club?"

I had no intention of ever going near the place again but I smiled wanly. I waved goodbye and watched them drive out of sight. They really had been very kind to me. I'd be sorry to leave them behind.

Tiredly, I got into my own car and headed to the dry-cleaners. My phone beeped for a second time but I ignored it.

David's uniform was ready, the woman at the dry-cleaners proudly informing me that it was their patriotic duty to give precedence to the military. I smiled thinly and thanked her, tossing the plastic-wrapped uniform into the trunk. I was so tired I was about ready to fall asleep at the wheel.

I parked as close to *City Beat* as I could and jogged the block and a half to the offices.

The reception was in darkness and the door was locked. I

rang the buzzer for the intercom and was just considering the wisdom of dropping the films into the mailbox when I saw Carl striding toward the door.

"Carolina, hi! Good to see you! You look well—you've got some color on your beach day."

I realized too late that appearing in a shorts and a skimpy t-shirt wasn't the most professional attire.

"Oh, yes," I agreed awkwardly. "It was a lovely day—everyone enjoyed themselves."

"Did your husband enjoy it?"

His question threw me off balance.

"Um, well, no. He's away at a medical symposium at the moment."

"Oh, that's a pity," said Carl, although if his expression was anything to go by, that was the opposite of what he really thought. "Well, perhaps you'd like to join me for a quick drink? I was just about finished here anyway."

I'd definitely given him the wrong impression by wearing my beach shorts.

"That's kind, Carl," I replied quickly, "but actually I have to go pick him up at the airport now."

He looked disappointed.

"Are you sure you haven't got time for one quick drink?"

"Sorry. I really have to go."

"Okay, well ... I guess I'll see you."

"Sure. Have a good evening. I'll be interested to see how the photographs turn out."

"Drop by any time."

I waved hurriedly and made my escape. My beat up old Ford made a good stand-in for a sanctuary.

I decided I'd better check my phone to see what commands from on high David had sent this time.

But the texts weren't from David, they were from Sebastian. My heart shuddered, an intense mixture of pain and pleasure. With trembling hands I opened my phone. To my surprise, there were three texts, each one more urgent than the last.

Where are you?
I need to talk to you. Where are you?

And the last one.

I'm going to your house NOW

I gasped and, although I tried to beat it back, hope flared suddenly and brilliantly. It was so confusing—I was still burning with anger and jealousy. *He'd left me at the picnic for that girl.*

I glanced at my watch—it was just after 9PM. Donna would be at the airport by now. Another 30 minutes and David would be walking through our front door. It would take me more than 20 minutes to drive home. I did the math.

Fuck.

By now my hands were shaking so badly it took me three attempts to scroll through to find Sebastian's number on my cell.

The phone rang, and rang, and rang. And then it switched to voicemail.

I hung up and tried again. This time it went immediately to voicemail. This time I left a message.

"Sebastian, do not, repeat DO NOT go to my house. I'm downtown and David will be home any minute. Please, please don't go."

I had no idea if he'd get the message or, if he did, whether he'd do as I asked. And then I started to feel angry—really angry. *He* was the one who'd gone off with his ex-girlfriend, *he* was the one who was threatening to go to my home just as David was due back.

Maybe my anger was unreasonable but it didn't feel like it, and right there and then, I needed it.

I drove home as fast as I dared. I didn't have those get-out-of-jail-free military plates on my car, and I couldn't risk getting stopped for speeding now.

I screeched onto the driveway, relieved that the house was dark and silent. I'd beaten David home, at the very least.

I nearly leapt out of my skin when I heard Sebastian's voice in the darkness.

"Where were you?"

"Sebastian!" I hissed. "You can't be here! David will be home any second!"

"I'm not going anywhere until you *talk* to me."

His voice was tight with anger.

Well, fuck him! I was pretty damned angry, too!

I shoved the key in the lock and pushed the front door open.

"Get in!" I snarled. "Before someone sees you!"

He pushed past me and I slammed the door shut behind him.

"You can't be here!" I repeated.

He didn't answer but suddenly grabbed my waist and pulled me toward him. Without warning, he kissed me fiercely, forcing his lips against mine.

My body started to respond, but anger and fear had the upper hand. I shoved him hard in the chest. He let go, his hands dropping to his side, his face shocked.

"Caro!"

"I mean it, Sebastian. I want you to go. Now!"

His voice turned pleading, the words tripping over themselves.

"I need to talk to you, Caro. You just disappeared. I didn't know where you were. I know how it must have looked ... with Brenda ... but it was *nothing*. I promise. She was upset and I couldn't ignore her, could I?"

Yes, you could! I wanted to yell at him.

"Why did you just go? Why didn't you talk to me? You could have called me! Please! I love you!"

I didn't know what to believe. I did know what I'd *seen*.

Blue-white car headlights suddenly flooded the hallway and I heard the sound of Donna's station wagon pulling up outside.

"For the love of God, Sebastian! Just go!"

"When will I see you? Caro, please!"

"I don't know. Just go. Just get out!" I yelled.

He gave me one, last, tortured look, then turned and ran into the kitchen. I heard him fumbling with the lock on the back door as I moved swiftly through the house turning on lights.

My heart was hammering so loudly in my chest that I barely heard the sharp rap on the front door.

Breathless, I snatched it open.

"You *are* in then, Caroline. I was beginning to wonder."

His tone was brusque. It was just what I needed to hear—and I snapped out of my funk.

"I haven't been in long—I had to drop off some films I took at the fun day to *City Beat*. How was your flight? Can I get you a coffee?"

"You know I can't drink caffeine at this time of night, Caroline."

"A glass of wine, then?"

"I don't need to drink every day—not like you."

I blinked. This was a new and interesting development. Now I was an alcoholic? I almost laughed. And then I had an epiphany: I wasn't scared of him anymore.

"Well, I'm glad to see the flight didn't affect your good mood, David. I'm going to have a glass of wine. Let me know if I can get you anything."

I left him gaping in our hallway.

Eventually, I heard him stomp up the stairs with his bags. My adrenaline rush over, I felt a little shaky. I hadn't eaten much at the picnic but now I was ravenous.

Scrabbling through the fridge, I found a jar of peanut butter. I'd bought it for David, not really being a fan, but right now it was just what I needed. I found a dessert spoon and dug in.

I remembered that only this morning Sebastian had told me that he liked peanut butter. Was that really just this morning? It seemed a lifetime ago. In some ways it was.

I started to feel bad for the way I'd spoken to him. I'd thought he was behaving recklessly to insist on coming to my house and taking such a huge risk. Yes, that was foolish, but, truthfully, I was the one who'd behaved badly. He looked so hurt when he left. No, damn it! I was right to be angry.

My emotions whirled around, reeling from sadness to anger and back again. It was sometime later when I realized that David was being unusually quiet.

I walked upstairs and found him already under the sheets, his dirty clothes scattered on *my* side of the bed.

When it came down to it, I had to admit that David had Sebastian beaten in childish behavior.

I headed for the guest room. It was cool and calm and untainted by any association with David or any memory of Sebastian. Before I set my phone alarm to wake me in the morning, I wondered briefly about texting Sebastian, but I wasn't sure what I wanted to say.

I fell asleep with the pain on his face burned into my eyes.

CHAPTER THIRTEEN

DAVID WAS SULKY AT BREAKFAST. WHAT A SHOCKER.

Without comment, I served him bacon, pancakes and eggs, pointed out his dry-cleaned uniform and calmly sat down with a slice of toast at my laptop.

I could feel his eyes on me, a silent castigation. Well, as long as it remained silent, that was just fine by me.

True to form, he flounced out of the house without speaking to me. I noticed he took his dress uniform so, with luck, I wouldn't see him until tomorrow. A twenty-four hour reprieve I could definitely use.

Before I faced David, it was time to man up and face Sebastian. I sure as hell wasn't going to apologize for what I'd said last night but we needed to talk. At least, I thought we did. Whatever had happened between him and Brenda, or not happened as he'd insisted ... whatever the rights and wrongs of him risking our exposure by coming here last night, I was supposed to be the adult in this relationship. I decided I was going to let him go with a few shreds of my dignity intact.

I pulled out my phone to text him.

Texts were such a useful medium: they could say so much or so little—and yet they side-stepped all the screwed up emotions of a face-to-face encounter. I could see why dumping someone by text was so popular. It was the coward's correspondence method of choice. Well ... perfect for me, then.

I was about to type a message when I heard a soft tap at the back door. It seemed Sebastian had beaten me to the punch. At least he wasn't going to dump me by text. I supposed that was a good thing.

God, he was so beautiful. I couldn't help taking one long, last, devouring look.

Even if this was goodbye, I felt lucky to have had him in my life. Knowingly or not, he'd been the catalyst for changing my life. I'd always be grateful.

"Hi. You want to come in?"

He nodded silently and I pushed the door open wide to let him through.

"I'm just having a coffee. Do you want one?"

"Why are you being like this?" he whispered.

"Being like what?" I said, coolly.

"Like ... *this!*" he gestured helplessly.

His voice pierced my carefully constructed façade—he sounded so bruised. I sat at the table, warming my cold hands on my coffee mug. I began my pre-prepared speech.

"I'm sorry I disappeared without saying goodbye. I didn't mean for you to worry. I saw you with Brenda and ... I thought it was better for me to go."

"I knew it! I knew that was it! Fuck, Caro!"

He sat down opposite me and rubbed his hands over his face.

"It was nothing with Brenda. Nothing! Why are you being like this?"

Oh no, he didn't get to be the injured party.

"It didn't look like nothing," I hissed, my careful control sliding away. "You say you love *me* and then you just walk off with Brenda? Do you have the slightest idea how much that hurt? Do you? You entered into a relationship with me knowing that I'm a married woman. But it's okay for you to get mad with my husband, and it's okay for you to sulk when Bill pretends to flirt with me, and you tell me how upset you are that you can't be with me in public at the stupid fun day ... but you know what, Sebastian? This is what you signed on for. With me. I sure didn't sign on to see you going off with some girl. Did you really think it was okay for you to take a nice, romantic stroll along the beach with your ex-girlfriend who obviously has feelings for you and wants you back? Did you? Because it isn't okay. It really isn't."

"Wow. You're ... you're really angry. Caro..."

No shit!

I glared at him and he dropped his eyes to the table, sighing heavily.

"I'm sorry. I am. It's just ... Brenda is ... was ... I guess I knew she might be there yesterday. Her dad's a buddy of Mitch. I should have said something ... I get that now ... but I didn't know what to say ... I mean, I broke up with her months ago before I even met you again so I didn't think it would matter if she did ... but I didn't know she was going to... I'm not interested in her, so it didn't ... how can you..."

He took a deep breath.

"Caro, I've said to you over and over again that I love you. You never say ... why don't you believe me? Why don't you trust me? I'd never, *never* do anything to hurt you. I love you."

"You did hurt me, Sebastian," I said, gravely. "You hurt me a lot. You say you'd never do anything to hurt me but then you go ahead and do something like this."

I thought he was going to reach out for me, but then he closed his eyes, shaking his head slowly.

"God, Caro, I'm so sorry. I didn't mean to hurt you. I just ... I didn't know what Brenda was going to say and I didn't want you to have to sit there and listen to it. I thought ... I thought I was doing the right thing—getting her out of the way. And ... she was upset and I guess ... I felt like I owed her or something. She's been having a really tough time since..."

He stopped. It was probably the look on my face. I *so* didn't want to hear him telling me how he owed his slutty ex-girlfriend and that he still cared enough about her not to want to upset her. But it was okay to upset me.

I sighed. I knew that wasn't what he'd intended. He'd obviously thought that getting her out of my way was the best solution if she was going to start babbling about wanting him back. Sometimes he was just too damn nice for his own good.

"Caro, I'm sorry. Please, please don't be mad at me. I love you."

His voice trembled and his eyes begged me to believe him. And I did. I just wasn't sure I believed in us.

I reached over and took his hands in mine, my resolve a little shaken by his renewed declaration.

But it was a mistake: the warmth of his skin, the touch of flesh on flesh—my whole body flushed with desire. The prepared speech died on my lips.

"You looked so good together." I choked out the admission.

He shook his head slowly, his scared eyes fixed on mine.

"And then ... the others were saying how nice she was—and pretty—and that you'd made a great couple and ... I couldn't help agreeing with them. And I *saw* the way she was with you. She made it pretty damn obvious she wants to get back with you. I guess I couldn't blame her. Or you. And ... you don't need all ... all my emotional baggage. You *should* be with Brenda—or someone like her ... someone your own age. And ... I *saw* you! I *saw* you with her—how you were with her—holding her like that."

He pulled my hands to his face and kissed the palms gently.

Then slowly and deliberately he sucked the tip of each finger. He could see on my face what that did to me.

"I want to make love to you," he whispered.

I tried to snatch my hands back but he held onto them.

"Don't give up on us, Caro. Because I haven't."

I tugged my hands free and this time he let them go.

"Sebastian, I'll be honest with you—I don't know what to do for the best so I'm kind of making this up as I go along. But ... all this ... this craziness—we're getting swept away by it. Making love with you is extraordinary. I've never, *never* felt anything like this my whole life. But it was wrong of me to ... to start this relationship with you—and I don't mean because of what the law says, although that's certainly an issue ... but because it's not fair to you."

He tried to interrupt me but I was determined to finish.

"Please, I need to say this. I've had a lot of years of feeling inadequate, of not being good enough—I don't need to paint a picture, I'm sure you can guess why. And every time, *every time* I see you with a younger woman, whatever the circumstances, it's going to rip me up. I don't want to see the best thing I've ever known soured by my insecurities—I couldn't bear that. You've brought me to life—and you'll never know how much I owe you because of that. But you're only just starting out in your life. It's not fair to burden you with me. You deserve better than that. I *have* to let you go."

He stared at me in silence for some seconds as if to make sure I really had finished. He took a deep breath—and I held mine.

"You want honesty? Well, answer this: if I was 25 and you were 38, would we still be having this conversation?"

I shrugged helplessly.

"About you going off with your ex-girlfriend? Yes. Definitely."

He shook his head impatiently.

"No, the age thing."

"Maybe," I said, cautiously.

"No, I don't think so and nor do you—not really. That's what I'm saying, Caro. Nobody would blink twice. It wouldn't matter. It *doesn't* matter. Don't you think that I don't feel the same, that I'm not good enough for you? Hell, what can I give you? A shitty apartment and working two jobs while you try to put me through school. You think I feel good about that? Because it fucking kills me! I want to take care of you, not ... I don't care about going to college, I don't care about leaving San Diego. I only care about being with you. And we have this same fucking argument over and over. You're driving me crazy! I love you! If you left me now..."

But he couldn't finish the words. He scrubbed away tears from his cheeks and looked down.

"Every time something goes wrong, you give up on us. You're killing me, Caro."

I sat with my hand over my mouth, unable to move or speak, appalled at what I'd done to him.

He looked up.

"You want honesty? Well, I don't know what will happen ... but neither do you. Maybe we'll make it ... maybe we won't. But you're giving up before we've even tried. I don't understand. Why won't you take a chance?"

Is that what I was doing? Had I found yet another way to be a coward? I'd thought I was setting him free, but he saw it as my refusal to take a chance ... on him, on us, on love—maybe even on myself.

"What do you want to do?" I said, softly.

"Try. Just try."

Yes. I could do that.

"Okay."

"Okay?"

"Yes, I'll try."

"You've got to mean it, Caro. *Promise* me."

"I promise I'll try."

His shoulders slumped with relief.

"I missed you last night," he said.

I tried to smile but my face still felt stiff from our most recent fight.

"Should we go to our favorite coffee shop?" I suggested, thinking neutral ground might be a good idea.

He shook his head.

"I don't want to share you."

We stared at each other across the kitchen table.

"Can we go to bed?" he asked. "I ... I really need you, Caro. To touch you ... to show you how much I love you. Please."

It was breaking all my carefully constructed rules. What if someone saw my car in the driveway and came around? What if someone had seen Sebastian arrive? What if they saw him leave later? What if? What if? But I was tired of being afraid, and right now, I didn't care. I needed him, too.

I stood up and held out my hand. For a second he continued to stare at me, then a huge smile lit his eyes.

We walked up the stairs hand-in-hand, each step measuring the distance from our argument.

He was surprised when I turned left into the guest room. He threw me a questioning look.

"I sleep in here now," I said simply.

I saw him try to suppress a triumphant smile. He almost managed it.

Slowly we undressed each other, taking our time to reconnect.

He unbuttoned my shirt, pausing to kiss my chest, a little lower each time. He undid the cuffs and kissed my wrists, then let the material slide over my shoulders. I ran my hands down his chest, then tugged lightly on the hem, pulling his t-shirt over his head. I slid my hands over his skin, burying my face in his chest, breathing him in. He smelled of sunshine and the ocean.

He watched me, his eyes dark, filled with desire, as I slowly unzipped his jeans. He pushed them down his legs and stepped out of them, quickly sliding his briefs over his hips, so he stood naked before me, his love exposed.

He sank to his knees, and rested his hands on my waist, his eyes still fixed on mine. Then his eyes closed, and he kissed my stomach, nuzzling me gently.

I rested one hand on his shoulder, and stroked his head with the other.

He smiled up at me then turned his attention to my zipper. Carefully, he helped me step out of my jeans and panties. He kissed my body briefly, then stood up and pulled me into a tender hug.

"Do you know how much you mean to me, how much I love you?" he whispered into my hair. "I hate fighting with you."

"I hate it, too. Just kiss me."

His mouth rested gently on mine and I felt the softness of his lips as they moved against me. His fingers drifted over my shoulders and down my spine where both his hands cupped my behind.

My hands trailed up over his ribs until they were twisted behind his neck, pulling his head down to deepen our kiss.

Here in this room, with our bodies entwined, I felt that I could trust this fierce love that had shattered and rebuilt my life. But outside, the world was a cold and dangerous place. I didn't know if love would be enough, but I'd promised to try.

He bent down suddenly and quite literally swept me off my feet so I gasped. He cradled me in his arms and kissed me again.

"I've been meaning to do this for ages," he said, his voice a soft murmur.

"Sebastian, you swept me off my feet our very first night together."

He grinned.

"Yeah, but I've been wanting to do it properly ever since."

Gently, he placed me on the bed and stood looking down at me, his gaze soft and loving.

"I want to kiss every inch of you," he said.

"That sounds nice: which end are you going to start?"

He laughed lightly.

"Hmm ... choices, choices. Today, I think I'll start with your toes."

"My toes?!"

"Sure, why not? You have beautiful feet."

And, to make his point, he picked up my left foot and sucked my big toe, nipping the end playfully.

Why that was so erotic, I couldn't say, but it made me desperate to feel him inside me. I reached out for him but he leaned away.

"Nope! You're always saying you want me to go slowly ... your wish is my command."

"But...!"

"Nope—slowly."

He kissed the front of my foot and ran his tongue up my shin. He sucked my knee, gazing up at me through his lashes, a wicked gleam in his eye. Just when I thought he'd be moving up to my thigh, he put my foot back on the bed and started again on my right foot.

Why the hell had I ever asked for 'slow'? This was torture. Slow, delicious, unbelievable torture. Boy, he was a good student.

This time he didn't stop at my knee, but hooked my leg over his shoulder and kept on going. And going.

My back arched and I gasped as his tongue flicked up to my sweet spot, then circled around and around.

I moaned his name and clutched at his shoulders but he just pressed harder and I felt myself begin to build.

"Sebastian," I moaned again. "Please!"

I wasn't even sure what I was pleading for: me, him, us.

Then he started teasing me with his fingers, slowly circling, massaging me inside and out. I didn't think I could take much more and tried to push his hands away but he was relentless. My body shuddered and he sat up. I glimpsed a satisfied expression on his face between my frantic breaths.

"Slow enough for you?" he muttered, as he continued his kisses up my body, finally reaching my breasts, which he sucked and teased with playful bites.

I pulled my knees up and felt his erection pushing between my thighs, but he didn't try to enter me. I ran my hand up and down him and he squeezed his eyes shut, momentarily losing his concentration.

"Don't," he said.

"But, I..."

"You have to wait, Caro."

"Why?!"

"You wanted slow. I'm giving you slow."

"I've changed my mind," I whimpered. "I want fast. Please. Now."

He arched his back away from me and grinned.

"No. I like slow. Who knew?"

And to make his point, he grabbed both my hands and held them above my head so I couldn't touch him and he carried on kissing my breasts.

That made me mad. I didn't like not being able to touch him.

"Let go my hands!"

He ignored me so I bit his neck and pushed against him with my feet.

"Wow, you want to fight me? I like it!"

"Stop teasing me!"

"I thought you wanted slow?"

"No!" I said forcefully, and he laughed.

"What do you want then?"

I shook his hands off me and grabbed hold of his erection, placing it at my entrance. *If that wasn't enough of a clue, I really didn't know what was!*

Thankfully he took the hint and allowed himself to slide into me. I was so turned on it was a relief and pain and pleasure when he was finally inside me. And that's when his plans to go slow completely unraveled.

"Oh, fuck!" he hissed. "You feel so fucking amazing! Oh, Caro!"

I tilted my hips up and he started to really move—long, hard strokes that rocked the whole bed and sent the headboard banging against the wall.

I clenched around him, and that tipped him over the edge. He rammed into me urgently one last time, his muscles rigid, his breath hot and rapid on my neck. He rested his head on my shoulder and gently pulled out of me, collapsing onto his side.

Breathlessly, I inched back down the bed and nestled into him. He wrapped his arm around me and we lay there wordlessly.

Finally, we lay peacefully. My head was on his chest, listening to his heart beating, his breath rising and falling, and the distant sounds of the world outside our window. His fingers drifted rhythmically up and down my back.

I felt so content, I began to fall asleep. Then Sebastian brought me crashing back to the here and now.

"Did David say anything to you when he came home?"

I sighed. I really didn't want to talk about him.

"Not much."

"He must have said something."

"He implied I drank too much."

"What? Why?"

I laughed mirthlessly. "I think, because I offered him a glass of wine. I was trying to be ... civil."

Sebastian muttered an oath under his breath.

Well, now that he'd started this line of questioning ... here was my starter for ten.

"How did you get home last night? I understood from Shirley that everyone was sleeping in the van."

"Hitched," he said, shortly.

And now for the six million dollar question.

"What did Brenda say to you, when you went off with her?"

He sucked some air in through his teeth. *Yeah, should have seen that one coming.*

"She wanted us to start dating again."

I'd guessed as much. Hell, she couldn't have been more obvious if she'd sky-written it with scarlet letters, then ripped his clothes off and mounted him on the sand in front of everyone.

"And what did you say?"

"I said I didn't feel the same ... I told her I'd met someone else."

I inhaled sharply. "Was that wise?"

He shrugged. "I thought that would make her back off."

"But it didn't?"

He shook his head. "Not at first. She kept on and on asking me who it was."

"And?"

"She kept naming all these girls we knew in school..." he sighed. "Then she said the thing with Jack was a mistake ... and she started crying."

All those girls...

I couldn't help feeling he wasn't telling me the whole story. Did I want to know? If he didn't tell me, I'd probably just imagine something worse.

"How did you leave it with her?"

"What do you mean?"

"Well, when she started crying, what did you do?"

"You *saw* what I did," he said, sounding annoyed.

"Yes, but after that. sShirley and Donna said you'd been gone ages."

He didn't answer straight away.

"We went for a walk," he said at last. "Brenda was ... embarrassed. She didn't want to go back to her friends looking like she'd been crying."

"She's very pretty."

He looked uncomfortable. "Yeah, I guess."

"What happened next?"

"That's it. I walked her back to her friends. She seemed fine. I went back to the fire pit, but you'd already packed up and gone. I texted you," he said accusingly.

"I didn't look at my phone."

I could see he wasn't fully convinced but he didn't press me either. I was grateful for that.

"Why were you downtown so late?"

"I was dropping off the films I took of the fun day."

"On a Sunday?"

"Yes, the editor wanted them early. I don't know why."
Although I had a pretty good suspicion what the reason was.

He paused. I was glad he'd decided to let it go.

"Bill's an asshole."

Ugh. He wasn't letting *everything* go. Now I was the one who should have seen that coming.

"You shouldn't let him wind you up so easily."

"I hated the way he spoke to you!"

"I know how that feels," I said, calmly.

We lay quietly for a few minutes, letting the twin specters of our jealousy spiral further away.

I think Sebastian must have finally decided to try and put yesterday behind us, because he suddenly said, "I never asked: have you ever been to New York before?"

"Yes, a couple of times. You?"

"No. Mom and Dad went sometimes but they always left me with a neighbor."

His voice was bitter. I wondered again if Shirley's speculation about his parentage was accurate.

"What made you want us to go there then?"

He shrugged.

"Same reason you want to go back East—to get as far away from here as possible."

"What should we do when we get there?" I said, happy to try and imagine our future. "I mean, is there anything special you'd like to do?"

"Have sex. A lot."

I rolled my eyes. "That's a given. Anything else? Perhaps of an outdoor nature?"

"Have sex outdoors."

I laughed.

"I don't think they have a lot of beaches in New York City."

"Yeah, they do! I checked. Well, not the city exactly but there's a surf community at Rockaway Beach. If we lived in Brooklyn or Queens, we'd be less than 10 miles from it."

I had to smile. "You've been doing your research."

"Sure! And a guy I know who used to surf Long Beach said that it can get pretty gnarly."

"I think you should write me a glossary of surfing terms so I know what you're talking about."

"Well, you've gotta know about Sex Wax, baby."

"What?!"

"Yeah, you rub it on your stick."

"Okay, you've got about five seconds to explain that or..."

"Or what?"

"No peanut butter for you!"

"Wow! You really do play rough!"

"You'd better believe it."

He laughed and tugged my hair gently.

"Sex Wax is a brand name for the kind of wax you put on your board—your stick. It helps give you traction. Not as much fun as it sounds."

"*Preferisci una inceratura a caldo ... o a freddo?*"

"What does that mean? Because it sounded really dirty!"

"I said, 'Do you like it coated in hot wax ... or cold?'"

"Oh man! That sounded so hot!"

"*Si è alzata l'onda, o sei proprio contento di vedermi?*"

"Huh?"

"Is the surf up or are you just pleased to see me?"

"Fuck! It makes me so horny when you say stuff like that."

"Sebastian, I could read a bus timetable and you'd say it made you horny!"

He smiled. "Yeah, you're right. I have a tide table in my jeans' pocket. Will you read that to me?"

"You want a bedtime story? Does that sound good?"

"*Supra la luna!*"

"You're learning!"

"You're a good teacher," he murmured into my hair.

His stomach rumbled loudly, interrupting the mood somewhat.

"Are you hungry?"

"Hungry for you."

"That is *such* a cheesy line, Sebastian!"

"Yeah, but it's still true."

I kicked the sheets off the bed and pushed him away, grabbing my robe.

"Come on. I'm going to feed you. A little lesson in Italian cookery."

"Pizza?" he said hopefully.

"That's not proper Italian food. Papa would turn in his grave! No, we'll make some fresh tortellini."

"Will it take long?"

"It can be a little tricky."

He sat up, propping himself with a pillow.

"We don't have that much time," he said, his tone solemn. "I have to be at work at 2PM."

I held back a sigh as I pulled on my robe.

"Oh well. Something quick then. How are you going to get there? Ches?"

When he didn't reply I looked over at him.

"What's wrong?"

"I was going to ask Mom to drive me."

"Oh, why?"

He blew out a lungful of air and fiddled with the sheet.

"Ches is kind of mad at me."

"I can't imagine that. He seems so easy going."

Sebastian looked uncomfortable.

"I guess. But ... he doesn't get why I won't tell him who I'm ... dating."

I couldn't help sniggering. "I'm sorry, really. It's just ... dating?!"

He gave a half-smile and ran a hand over his hair.

"Whatever. He said that I shouldn't expect him to cover for me with my folks if I don't trust him with the truth."

I felt a shiver run through me.

"Has he had to cover for you?"

He didn't reply.

"Tell me!"

He grimaced.

"Mom ... she noticed that I wasn't there for two nights. She ... she kind of made a big deal out of it."

I groaned. "I knew it!"

"She phoned Ches's mom and Ches said that I'd stayed over. I guess Mrs. Peters is covering for me, too. She knew I hadn't been there."

"We'll just have to be more careful," I whispered.

"Maybe ... maybe I could tell Ches. He'd keep it a secret, I know he would."

I was appalled. I understood why he wanted to tell his friend but I couldn't let that happen.

"We can't risk it, Sebastian. *I* can't risk it. And ... if anyone found out, he'd be complicit in ... in a crime. You do understand, don't you?"

He shrugged and looked down. "Yeah, I guess."

He obviously wasn't happy with my answer.

I sighed. "Do you want me to run you to the country club? I

could drop you at the entrance and get there before you. No one would be any the wiser."

"Okay," he muttered. "Thanks."

A thunderous knocking at the front door made me jump.

"Fuck!"

I heard Sebastian's oath as if from a great distance but I couldn't move.

The banging on the door started again.

"Caro!"

Sebastian's panicked voice unfroze me. He was thrashing about, dressing as quickly as possible. There was nowhere to hide. He couldn't get down the stairs and out through the back without being seen. This was every nightmare I'd imagined, played in fast forward.

I pulled my robe around me more tightly.

The pounding started again.

"Caro! Get the fucking door!" mouthed Sebastian.

I ran down the stairs and stumbled to a halt. I took a deep breath and pulled the door open.

"Delivery, ma'am," said a man in a red and yellow DHL uniform as he handed me a large parcel. "Sign here, please."

I started giggling. I couldn't help it.

"Are you okay, ma'am?"

"Yes!" I gasped, wiping tears of relief from my face.

He gave me a strange look and headed back to his van shaking his head. *Hysterical woman alert: just walk away.*

I sank to the floor and began to cry in earnest, more from shock than anything else. Sebastian came down the stairs and sat on the floor next to me.

"Fuck! That scared the shit out of me! Don't cry, Caro. It's okay."

He wrapped his arms around my shoulders and rocked me slowly.

Eventually, he pulled me up off the floor.

"Come on. Let's get some breakfast. I'll make you one of my special omelets."

"I thought you couldn't cook," I said, my voice still shaky from the rush of adrenaline.

"I can't—that's why it's special."

He sat me at the kitchen table and started rummaging through the fridge.

"How many eggs do I need?"

"How hungry are you?"

"Starving!"

Of course.

"Then get six. And you'll need to add a drop of milk in the mixture."

He peered at me from around the door.

"Really? Milk? Oh, okay."

He frowned and disappeared back inside the fridge.

I stood up to fetch the frying pan and mixing bowl but he waved me back to the table.

"I can manage," he said, confidently, as he turned on the stove and placed the frying pan on top.

I waited for a moment, twitching in my chair. I had to speak.

"Um, Sebastian?"

"What?" he said, staring intently at the eggs as he whisked them sloppily.

"The frying pan is getting really hot and you haven't put any oil in it..."

"Oh, fuck!"

He pulled the pan off the stove and swore as the hot metal burned his wrist.

"Quick! Run your hand under the faucet!"

He stood with his hand under the running water cursing softly. He really was adorable and I couldn't help grinning at him.

"What?"

"Will you let me help you now?"

"Okay," he said reluctantly. "You can help."

In a calmer, more organized fashion, I showed him how to make a plain omelet, seasoning it with black pepper and a little salt, fried some tomatoes to go on the side, put on a pot of coffee, and then sbreakfast, or rather brunch, was ready.

"By the way," I said, a thought occurring to me, "what were you planning on doing—you know, if it had been someone ... else at the door?"

"Fucked if I know," he said honestly. "Climb out the window, hide under the bed? Any suggestions?"

"Not the window—you could fall and get hurt. Besides, that window is right above the front door—it would have been kind of obvious."

"I could have flattened the bastard," said Sebastian easily.

While I went back upstairs to shower, Sebastian insisted on clearing away the dishes, which was a novelty for me. I hoped he would manage not to break anything.

I'd just finished rinsing the conditioner out of my hair when the shower door opened and Sebastian pressed his chest against my back.

"Mmm, you smell great," he said approvingly.

"Sebastian!" I said, my voice a warning, as he ran his hands over my breasts and kissed my neck. "We don't have time for this."

"I'll be quick," he mumbled into my skin.

I didn't even try to resist him.

Which made us horribly late.

"I told you!" I said crossly, as the highway traffic congealed in front of us. "You're going to be late *and* get fired!"

"It was worth it," he grinned, reclining his seat all the way back and pulling his sunglasses over his eyes.

He was acting like he hadn't a care in the world. *How did he do it?*

"Look, I'll drop you around the back of the country club, you haven't got time to run down from the entrance."

"Whatever," he said, carelessly.

I shook my head, a little irritated, even though I was just as much to blame.

I drove too fast down the avenue leading to the club and skidded into my favorite parking lot at the back.

"When can I see you again?" he said, curling his fingers into my hair.

"Tomorrow morning?"

"That's ages away. Can't you sneak out tonight? I mean, you're in the guest room—he'll never know, right?"

"Sebastian, I don't think so. It's too risky. We've just got to be careful for three more months and that's it. After that you'll see me every day and you'll soon be sick of me."

"That's not funny," he said frowning.

"Sorry. Bad joke."

He sighed. "Okay, tomorrow, then."

Instead of getting out of the car, he pulled me toward him and we kissed with the desperation of our imminent separation.

For a moment, he leaned his forehead against mine, and then pushed open the passenger door. And froze.

Ches was staring right at us—and from the shock on his face it was obvious he'd seen everything.

The floor dropped away and I stared back at him in horror.

"Fucking luck," said Sebastian bitterly. "Let me go talk to him—it'll be fine, Caro, I promise."

My hands locked on the steering wheel as Sebastian walked toward his friend. For three of the longest minutes of my life, I watched them talk. Well, Sebastian seemed to be doing most of the talking, in fact it looked like he was pleading with Ches. It was a twisted replay of yesterday's scene with Brenda, except this time it was Sebastian who was doing the begging.

Ches's body language was hostile, his arms folded across his chest, his face stiff and angry. Eventually,s I saw him nod curtly then stalk off in the direction of the clubhouse.

Sebastian looked upset as he climbed back in the car and pulled the door shut.

"He's cool," he said, an expression of pain on his face.

"What did he say?" I whispered.

"He promised not to say anything."

"He didn't look very happy about it."

Sebastian sighed. "He wasn't."

"What did he say?"

Sebastian shook his head.

"Please tell me," I said softly. "I'd rather know."

"It doesn't matter—the important thing is that he won't tell anyone."

"Please tell me," I repeated, quietly.

"Why?" said Sebastian, angrily. "What difference does it make? He's just pissed at me generally."

"I thought you wanted us to be honest with each other," I reminded him gently.

His temper exploded.

"Why do you do this, Caro? Why do you have to drag out every last fucking, miserable word? Why can't you just let it go?"

"How the hell am I supposed to 'let it go'?" I snarled, my fear and anger getting the better of me. "I'm the one who'll be prosecuted if Ches tells anyone!"

"He won't!" shouted Sebastian.

"Well, I'm glad you trust him so much!" I yelled back, "Because he's the loose-lipped idiot who told Brenda that you got a job here!"

"What the fuck has Brenda got to do with this?"

"Nothing! Everything! I don't know! Just tell me what Ches said—I *need* to know!"

"He said I was a stupid fucking asshole for screwing a married woman who probably just wanted to get her rocks off for the summer, and he hoped the fucks were worth it because my dad would beat the shit out of me when he found out. Happy now?"

He looked away from me and slammed his fist against the car door.

I dug my fingernails into the palms of my hand, refusing to cry.

We sat there in silence for several minutes, the atmosphere tense and angry.

"You'd better get to work," I said at last in a low voice.

He stared at me coldly then flung open the door and stormed off.

I kept waiting for him to turn back or turn and look at me —some slight acknowledgement. But he didn't.

Bile rose in my throat and I hurriedly leaned out of the car and vomited, watching my brunch slowly sink into the gravel.

I drove home feeling weak and shaky.

All afternoon I waited for Sebastian to text me, but he didn't. A dozen times I picked up my cell to send a message, but I didn't.

When I couldn't stand it anymore, I tapped out five letters.

Sorry

Why had I forced Sebastian to repeat Ches's angry words? Why did I continue to allow my pathetic insecurities to spoil the best thing that had ever happened to me? Was it some form of deliberate self-destruction, some way of proving that I didn't deserve Sebastian's love? And it must be love—why else would he put up with my ridiculous outbursts and lead-weighted emotional baggage? Because it sure wasn't for the *fun*.

Feeling wretched, I tidied up the guest bedroom, *my* bedroom, and contemplated the sorry state of my life. I really had an amazing talent for making a complete fuck-up of everything. If the military could bottle that negative energy, they'd have one helluva weapon of mass destruction.

As I hung up my robe, a thought occurred to me—something I'd forgotten about in the whirlwind of the last three weeks. I reached into the pocket and pulled out the lock of Sebastian's hair that I'd saved from the bathroom floor the night I'd found him at the park, the night we'd made love together that very first time. His hair was light brown near the root, bleached by the sun to a golden blond at the ends—the surfer boy he'd been when I first met him.

I took an envelope from David's study and carefully sealed the lock inside, simply writing Sebastian's name and the date across the corner. Then I placed it between the pages of my copy of *Lolita*—a book so profane that I knew David would never so much as touch its dust jacket, it was also my private joke—not that I felt like laughing. In fact it was everything I could do to keep from crying.

And I knew I was on borrowed time with David—he wouldn't take another night of me sleeping in the guest room without some sort of explanation.

I had two choices. I could lie:

'I'm fine, I just need some space'.

Or I could tell part of the truth:

'Our marriage is over and I want a divorce. No, there's no one else'.

Either way, I was scared of what he'd do. His temper was so unpredictable, I didn't know what would happen if I pushed him to extremes. Discussing divorce certainly constituted 'extreme' in anyone's book.

I wandered into the kitchen to make something for his supper. Without even being aware of my movements, I threw together a lasagna and tossed it into the oven.

It was a quarter after six and I was beginning to wonder where David was when I suddenly remembered it was his formal dinner at the officer's mess. He was right: I really should check the schedule more often.

I pulled the lasagna out of the oven and dumped it on the side. I considered throwing it in the garbage but I hated to waste food. David could have it reheated in the microwave tomorrow. He was going to have to get used to microwaved meals once we were separated—I figured he may as well start getting in some practice now.

The thought made me feel a little better. I decided to risk checking my phone. Maybe there would be a message from Sebastian, or maybe I could just torture myself a little more by seeing that he hadn't responded.

But he had.

Me 2

God, I loved this man.

I sent another quick message.

Can I c u tonite? I can get away for a while if u can. What time u finish? Pick u up?

His reply was immediate.

10
I'll be there
:)

With those few words, happiness flooded through me.

And then I remembered Ches—I hoped I wouldn't have to face him again today. It had been bad enough seeing the look on his face this morning, and it had been beyond horrible fighting with Sebastian. I just wanted to be able to see him and touch him and have him hold me and utter the sweet lie that it was going to be okay.

It really wasn't my day.

He was waiting for me: 'he' being Ches, not Sebastian.

He was leaning against his van in the rear parking lot where he'd seen us earlier in the day. He folded his arms as I drove up and threw me a look of such contempt and loathing that my stomach gave an unhappy lurch. I wanted nothing more than to hit the accelerator, drive in the opposite direction and get the hell out of Dodge.

Gathering strength from some unknown place, long hidden, I took a deep breath and got out of the car to face him.

"Hello, Ches."

"Mrs. Wilson," he said, emphasizing the 'Mrs.'.

He scowled at me, challenging me to speak.

"I can guess what you think of me," I said softly.

"Can you?" he said coolly, raising an eyebrow in disbelief and disgust.

"You think I'm just using Sebastian, but it's not like that."

"Then tell me what it is like," he sneered, "because I'd really like to know. Seb is my friend and you..."

"I don't want to hurt him," I said, forcing the words out as my throat began to constrict.

264

"Yeah? Well, you're doing a really great job there! His head is completely spun, he doesn't know what the fuck he's doing. You've messed him up real good."

I choked on my reply but he wasn't going to give me time to recover.

"You've met his dad. Do you know how many times he's beat the shit out of him? Have you any idea what he'll do to him when he finds out about this?" His voice was bitter. "Yeah, the military hero will really freak out, his son bringing shame on the good family name of Hunter and all that crap, by banging a married woman."

I had no words.

He glared at me.

"And what about when your husband finds out? I suppose you'll dump Seb so fast that..."

"I'm leaving David."

I spoke so quietly I wasn't sure he'd heard me at first.

"What?"

I looked up. "I'm going to ask David for a divorce."

He stared at me, then shook his head.

"I don't believe you."

"It's true. We ... I ... as soon as Sebastian turns 18."

"You're full of shit."

"No, she's not."

Sebastian's voice came out of the darkness and I closed my eyes in relief. He walked up and put his arm around my shoulders, kissing me quickly on the lips.

"Hey, baby."

Then he turned to his friend.

"We're just waiting till I'm 18 and then I'm legally free of my family. We're going to go to New York." He pulled me closer and nuzzled my hair. "I've found us an apartment. It's in Bensonhurst—it said on this website that they call it Brooklyn's Little Italy. I thought you'd like that."

He smiled at me then looked back at Ches who was staring in outrage and astonishment.

"What the fuck you talking about, man? New York?"

"Yes, as soon as we can, and as far away as we can get."

"But ... *New York?*"

"Caro's going to work while I go to school. And I'll get a job, as well. We've got it all worked out."

"Are you crazy, dude?"

I thought Sebastian would lose his temper, but he just carried on talking, his voice even.

"We know it won't be easy but we want to be together. It's the only way."

Ches blinked, opening and closing his mouth several times. "Why didn't you tell me, man?" He sounded hurt.

"We didn't want to tell anyone because ... we couldn't. Caro is breaking the law by being with me."

It was clear Ches was in shock. He stood and gaped at us.

"I'm under age," continued Sebastian softly. "If anyone found out ... if anyone reported us, it's a felony—because of ... the age difference." He shrugged. "Caro could go to jail. That's why I couldn't tell you."

"Wow, I'm sorry, man. I didn't know!" said Ches helplessly.

"She's taking a huge risk. She wanted us to wait but ... I couldn't stay away from her. So if anyone is to blame, it's me." He looked Ches directly in the eye. "I think you owe her an apology."

I touched his arm. "It's okay, Sebastian. He was just looking out for you. I understand."

Ches looked mortified. "I didn't know! I just thought ... is it that serious? I mean, what could happen to her?"

He seemed to be having a hard time taking it in. I couldn't blame him—I still had a hard time with the concept of being loved so much, of being so much in love that it hurt.

Sebastian nodded, and I stared at the ground feeling a mixture of pride and shame in our confession.

"I'm sorry, Caroline," said Ches, shaking his head. "You guys ... wow ... I..."

"Thank you," I said quietly. I looked up at Sebastian. "I'll go wait in the car."

They talked for a few more minutes while I sat and waited

and watched. Eventually Ches pulled Sebastian into a bear hug and then patted him on the arm. I guessed he was telling him it was going to be all right.

Sebastian opened the passenger door and slumped down onto the seat.

"Everything okay?" I asked, tentatively.

"I guess," Sebastian said wearily, rubbing his eyes. "He ... he gets how much you mean to me but..."

But?

"He still thinks it's kind of crazy. He's cool though. He won't tell anyone."

I hoped he was right.

Sebastian raised his hand to my cheek. "Don't worry: Ches is my best friend—he's my brother," he said simply.

I leaned against him, feeling the warmth of his body through his thin t-shirt. I stared out at the stars in the night sky, wondering if one of them might be our lucky star.

I traced Sebastian's silhouette in the darkness, his straight nose, his full, sensuous lips, his strong chin, the graceful profile of his head.

He leaned back in the seat and turned to smile at me.

The most incredible feeling of love welled up inside me. I was so lucky. He was kind and thoughtful and caring. He was fun to be with, beautiful inside and out. I didn't know a lover could be a friend, too. And he loved me.

Me.

But was I really strong enough to follow my heart and to hell with the consequences? Could I expect a 17 year old boy ... man ... to be strong enough for this? No, that wasn't right. I was the one who had to be strong for both of us.

And at that moment, I knew the question and the answer. Was I strong enough? Yes, I was.

CHAPTER FOURTEEN

"I NEED TO HOLD YOU," SAID SEBASTIAN, SOFTLY.

I scrambled onto his knee and we clung to each other in the dark of the country club's parking lot.

All our hopes and fears had been explored in those tense few minutes with Ches. Sebastian was strong in so many ways, but he was also so young. And now he needed me and I wanted to give him comfort, to reassure him, to protect him from the world. He needed me—and I needed him.

I held him tightly, pulling him closer. Gradually his body began to relax, the tension leaking away.

"So," I said, breaking the heavy silence, "you found an apartment in Little Italy?"

I felt him smile against my neck.

"Yeah, I thought you'd like that."

"I do. Tell me about it."

He let out a long breath and settled me more comfortably in his arms.

"It's got one bedroom and one bathroom and is on the fourth floor of an apartment building on 82nd Street. We've even got an elevator."

I smiled. I didn't care how many elevators it had, I just wanted it all to be real.

"From the top of the building you can see Staten Island and the Statue of Liberty. We can walk along the Belt Parkway Promenade, or ride bikes—people go kite-flying there, too..." he paused. "And the rent is only $1,250 a month, but that's unfurnished, and we get 875 square feet."

"So much room."

I couldn't bear to tell him that despite the tiny size of the apartment, the rent was still more than twice the amount I currently had in my checking account.

"Yeah, well..." he continued. "But it says it's near the train and we can walk to Coney Island in about 30 minutes. Oh, and it's only four blocks from a park."

"It sounds perfect."

He sighed. "I almost phoned the rental agency but..."

"Too soon."

"I know," he sighed again. "Jesus, Caro. How the hell are we going to get through three more months like this?"

"Because we have to," I said in a steady voice. "And we will."

A look of admiration flickered across his face.

"God, I love you!" he said.

He kissed me lightly on the lips but his touch was like an incendiary device going off inside me. I kissed him back deeply, pouring all the angst and fear and passion I could into that one moment, showing him how much I loved and needed him, too.

His body responded immediately and I felt his arms tensing around me.

"Let's go somewhere," he said, his voice low and rough.

"I don't want to go to my place," I said, a shiver running down my spine. "I don't know what time David will be back. We can't risk that."

"Where is the bastard?" Sebastian spat the words out.

"At a mess dinner."

"Oh, yeah. I forgot about that—Dad went, too. They're usually pretty late though," said Sebastian thoughtfully.

I shook my head. "No, I'd rather go to the beach. Anywhere but *home*."

The word sounded like a lie on my lips. It wasn't my home, not anymore.

"We could drive out to the beach? But it's pretty cold tonight—no cloud cover. I guess we could stay in the car."

He sighed. I knew what he was thinking. After the luxury of a bed, neither of us really wanted to revert to an awkward backseat fumble.

"We could find a cheap motel," he said doubtfully.

"We can't afford it," I reminded him. "Let's just drive out to the beach and..."

"We could go to my place," said Sebastian suddenly.

"Excuse me?" *Had I heard him right?*

"Yeah! Dad's out at that officers' mess dinner with the asshole. He always stays over—he usually passes out in a bachelor room," he said, the disgust clear in his voice.

"What about your mom?"

He pointed to the clubhouse with his chin. "Drinking."

"How's she getting home?"

"Like I give a damn? Taxi, probably. But she won't come in my room. She never does—she stopped coming in my room when I was ten." He paused, his lips curling with contempt. "Anyway, she usually can't even make it up to their room—she just sleeps on the couch in the den."

"I don't know, Sebastian..."

I felt freaked at the thought of being in Donald and Estelle's house, but now Sebastian had suggested it, I was burning with curiosity to see his room.

"How will I get in without being seen?"

"There's an empty lot next door and we'll go in through the backyard. No one will see us."

He sounded excited.

"Okay," I said, shaking my head in wonder at what the hell I'd just agreed to.

He grinned at me, a beautiful, wide, beaming smile.

We drove back listening to *Lucia di Lammermoor*—the tale of a girl caught in a feud between her own family and that of another powerful clan. And then she went mad. I hoped it wasn't portentous.

I parked my car behind the vacant lot, making sure it was as well hidden as it could be on a public street.

"Okay?" said Sebastian, squeezing my hand.

I laughed nervously at my own recklessness.

He led me through the darkness, following the line of a high fence. When we arrived at a large and beautiful Japanese maple that grew close beside, he stopped. The tree partially obscured the fence.

"How are you at climbing?" he grinned at me.

"You're joking?" He just smiled at me. "You're not joking?!"

"I'll help you."

He climbed the fence easily, his strong arms pulling him up and over. He'd obviously done it many times before. He disappeared from sight briefly, then reappeared, balancing his torso on the fence as his arms reached down for me.

"Jump! I'll pull you up!"

I took a deep breath and ran at the fence, jumping as high as I could. Sebastian grabbed my wrists and pulled me up but our combined momentum was too much, and we were pitched over the fence, crashing down onto the turf below.

The air was forced from my lungs and I lay there winded for several seconds. Sebastian struggled to sit up, which wasn't easy as I'd landed mostly on him.

"Caro! Are you okay?"

I couldn't answer.

"Caro!"

I gasped for air and started to giggle.

"Shit! You had me worried there for a minute. Seriously, are you okay?"

"Ow!" I sat up slowly, still slightly hysterical. "If I have to come in through your backyard again, I'm going to buy a ladder."

Suddenly he pulled me to his chest and kissed me fiercely.

"What ... what's that for?" I gasped.

"You're just so ... brave!" he said, in awe.

I was pretty certain he had me confused with someone else.

"You are!" he insisted. "You always take that leap, whatever it is. God! I love that about you!"

I flushed at his unexpected praise—I really didn't think it was justified, but I loved that he'd thought it, and loved it even more that he'd said it.

"Come on," I whispered. "I want to make out in your bedroom."

"Definitely up for that," he agreed, laughing quietly.

He pulled me to my feet.

"Wait here a sec. I'll make sure there's no one around."

I watched as he climbed onto a water barrel outside one of the rooms and levered himself in through a narrow window. I had the distinct impression that he was enjoying himself.

I stood alone in the darkness, knowing that I was being swept along by all the craziness, or maybe, finally, I'd just dove right in and stopped fighting it.

I saw a light go on upstairs and a moment later Sebastian was unlocking the back door.

"Coast's clear," he said grinning. "There's no one in."

From what I could see in the gloom, the Hunters' kitchen was sleek and modern and well equipped. But everything had a pristine look about it, as if most of it had never been used. I remembered Sebastian saying that his mother never cooked. I could have gone to town in a kitchen like that—it was almost to a professional standard. I wondered why a woman, why anyone, would want to have a show-kitchen like that and not be tempted to use it. Maybe the answer was in the description: a show-kitchen, a kitchen for show—like everything else in Estelle Hunter's life. Despite excessive opulence of design, the room had a neglected air: the trash can was overflowing with pizza boxes, and a large number of empty wine bottles, beer cans and hard liquor bottles had been tossed haphazardly into the recycling box.

Sebastian towed me quickly down the hallway and up the stairs, eager to get me into his room. An unpleasant thought crossed my mind—how many times had he brought Brenda here, maybe to make out in his bedroom?

I tried to ignore it, but the idea was like a worm in my brain, wriggling, wriggling, burrowing away.

On the upper floor, we passed several empty rooms that looked like guest suites before Sebastian opened a door at the end of the corridor. From the layout of the house, I guessed that this room, his room, must overlook the backyard. The fact that his parents had put their son as far away from their own room as possible had worked out well for Sebastian—in the end.

He'd turned on his bedside light and drawn the curtains, I could feel the suppressed excitement coursing through him.

His bedroom was small, barely bigger than a box room, with a narrow, single bed pressed against one wall. Several old surfing posters were tacked to the only free wall space, the rest were covered by unmatched bookshelves, crammed with a mixture of CDs, paperbacks, a few hardcover books, with what looked like surfing trophies jammed in among them.

There was a large chest with one of the drawers partially open, and a couple of t-shirts hanging out.

My eyes were drawn back to the bed, currently strewn with a pair of jeans, shirts and the boardshorts he'd worn to the beach yesterday. The sheets and cover, however, were neatly folded, almost with military precision. I shivered as I imagined Donald 'teaching' his son how to do that.

Sebastian cleared away the clothes hurriedly, tossing them onto a small, wooden chair that was festooned with t-shirts.

"It's pretty small," he said, sounding embarrassed.

"It's very you," I said, watching him throw more clothes on the chair. I turned to examine some of his books. I always thought you could learn a lot about a person by the kind of books they had on their shelves. David didn't have any books, he only read the newspaper and occasionally medical journals.

Sebastian had a whole shelf of Conrad, several Allan Quatermain paperbacks, Jack London's *The Road*, countless travel books. *The Red Horse* by Corti in translation caught my eye.

"Wait, what's this?" I pulled out a heavy book, bound in cloth, and ran my fingers over the cover. I stared at him in disbelief. "You still have this?"

He nodded, his face serious.

I flicked through the pages depicting Hansel and Gretel, Rumpelstiltskin, Rapunzel ... all the gruesome stories from the Brothers Grimm.

I turned to the frontispiece, knowing what I'd see,

To Sebastian, from Caroline

And a date, nine years in the past.

"You kept it."

"Of course," he said simply. "You gave it to me."

I didn't know what to feel, standing there with the evidence of his childhood in my hands, the grown man in front of me.

"It's always been you, Caro."

I continued to stare at the book, at my handwriting, evidence in black and white, of our innocent and childish friendship.

His voice became anxious.

"It doesn't mean anything, Caro, not like that."

But it did, to me at least. It had been a horrible mistake coming here.

"I think I'd better go now," I said quietly.

"It's just a book, Caro, just a damn book. Please don't go!"

He grabbed me by the shoulders and forced me to look at him.

"Caro! Stop it!" he said, almost roughly. "I was a kid, we were friends. That's all. You haven't done anything wrong." He shook me, making me grab onto his arms. "I'm younger than you: so what?! It doesn't mean *anything*."

Suddenly my knees gave way and I sat down on the bed hard. I felt sick. I hadn't eaten anything since the omelet I'd made earlier, and that had ended up on the gravel of the country club's parking lot.

"Caro?"

"Could I have a glass of water, please?" My voice was shaky.

"Sure! Sure!"

I heard him running down the stairs. I put my head down and tried to breathe deeply.

He was back a moment later with a large tumbler of cold water. I took the glass from him and drank a few sips gratefully.

"Are you okay?" he asked anxiously.

"Yes, I'm fine. Sorry. It was just..." *Disturbing? Shocking? A devastating reminder?*

My hands were still trembling and I was in danger of tipping the rest of the water onto his pillows. He took the glass from my hands and placed it on the tiny bedside table.

"Come and lie down with me," he said, tugging gently on my hand. "Just lie with me. I'm not going to do anything you don't want, you know that."

He pulled me down and held me in his arms, softly stroking my hair. We lay there peacefully. Somewhere in the room I could hear a clock ticking—my life was passing with every second.

He continued to soothe me, kissing my hair, stroking my back and my arms, threading his long legs through mine.

"Do you want to hear a bedtime story?" he said, quiet humor in his voice.

"Not funny," I muttered into his chest.

He laughed gently. "You'll like this one. It starts with a girl and a boy, a motorcycle and a full tank of gas."

"Very romantic."

"Told you you'd like it."

"Well, the boy says to the girl, 'Hey, baby, let's go see the world.' And do you know what the girl says?"

"'I'm washing my hair'?"

"Ha! No, not quite. She says, 'Let's go see Italy because the whole world starts there'."

"She sounds like an idiot."

"Hey! This is *my* bedtime story."

"Okay, I'll be quiet."

"Is that even possible?"

I punched him lightly on the arm and he laughed.

"Okay, so the boy says, 'I have an idea. Let's fly to Switzerland...'"

"On the motorcycle? Because I should explain to you..."

He put his hand over my mouth, so I kissed the palm and snuggled in some more.

"'Let's fly to Switzerland, drive over the Alps and then we'll go to Milano and see *Il Trovatore* at La Scala'."

"That's the opera where everyone ends up dying."

"You said you'd be quiet."

"Sorry."

"So, then they stay at this amazing hotel where they have breakfast in bed, served on silver plates..."

"And they *scappati* in the morning because they can't pay the bill?"

"Yeah! Then they ride off on their trusty motorcycle and go to Verona, one of the most romantic cities in the world..."

"It's not romantic—that's where Romeo poisons himself and Juliet stabs herself to death."

"Shh! Then they drive down the spine of Italy, stopping to eat pasta ... and have *a lot* of sex..."

"This story is NC-17."

"Yeah, that's because it's *my* bedtime story. Then they ride to Salerno and take this little mountain road to a tiny village called Capezzano Inferiore and they meet all these wonderful, crazy people who turn out to be cousins and aunts and uncles of the girl, because she's kinda crazy, too..."

"And then what?"

"They live happily ever after."

I sighed. "Okay, that was a pretty good story after all."

"Told you you'd like it."

I felt very comfortable lying in his arms and my attack of guilt and disgust was slowly passing.

He didn't speak after that and neither did I. We drifted to sleep, wound around each other.

A loud crash woke me suddenly. I sat up, disoriented and panic-stricken in the darkened room.

"Oh, fuck. Mom's home," said Sebastian sullenly. "Are you okay, Caro? Don't sweat it, she won't come up here."

My heart was pounding, it was so loud I felt certain he must be able to hear it knocking against my ribs.

"Are you sure? Is your door locked?"

"I don't have a lock—I put the chair up against it when I want some privacy."

I couldn't believe how casual he sounded. I almost leapt out of my skin when he reached out to stroke my hair.

"I'll go see if she's passed out," he said, reading my mood.

I nodded, nervously twisting my wedding ring around my finger.

He frowned, then rolled off the bed and gently opened his bedroom door. He was gone for less than a minute while I waited anxiously.

"She's out cold—like I said. No problem."

He pulled the chair up against the door, letting all the clothes slide off into a heap, then wedged its wooden back tightly under the handle.

He turned slowly, staring down at me.

From the look on his face, I guessed he wanted to cash in the rain check on the make-out session I'd promised him. I definitely wasn't on the same page, the adrenaline rush caused by Estelle's noisy return had freaked me out.

I pulled my cell phone out of my jeans pocket and flipped it over to check the time; it was after 1AM.

"It's late," I whispered. "I should get back."

"Stay. Please."

He sat down next to me again and ran the tips of his fingers down my arm.

"We don't know when we'll have another night together," he said persuasively, kissing my shoulder. "What difference does it make if you go now or in a few hours?"

When he didn't meet any resistance, he pushed me gently back onto his bed and used his body to press me into the thin mattress. I could feel that he was already aroused. Boy, it didn't take much. I still felt shaken, but at the same time it thrilled me that I could make him feel that way, make his body respond that way.

"Stay," he whispered as he ran his tongue up my neck and tugged at my ear lobe with his teeth.

His right hand rode up under my t-shirt and cupped my breast, circling his thumb over my nipple. "Please stay."

For that moment, his touch pushed away all my concerns, all the dull considerations of a rational mind and I wrapped my hands around his neck to pull him closer.

My tongue swept into his mouth and I raked my nails down his back, making him cry out.

"Ssh, you have to be quiet, *tesoro*," I reminded him.

I tugged on the hem of his t-shirt and he immediately yanked it over his head, throwing it across the room. Mine soon followed and the cold metal of his pants button pressed into my belly making me shiver.

I lay on my side so he could unhook my bra, this time he didn't fumble—within seconds it had joined my t-shirt on the growing heap. In fact, there wasn't any floor space that *wasn't* littered with clothes, his and mine.

He knelt up to watch me as I undid my zipper and shimmied out of my jeans and panties. He ran his hands down my body and then slid his fingers back up along my inner thighs. I closed my eyes and sighed deeply with pleasure and desire.

His body hovered over mine again and I enjoyed the rough feel of his denim against my bare flesh. I pulled his waistband toward me and slipped my hands inside, running my fingers over his fine, sculpted ass. A tremor ran through him and he leaned down to kiss me again.

Hastily I unzipped his jeans, pushing them down over his hips. When he sat up to kick off his pants, I reached up to run the nail of my index finger from his chest to his stomach, watching the faint white mark I left behind quickly fade. His eyes fluttered closed and he sucked in a deep breath as his body quivered.

"Now you've got me here," I said teasingly, "what are you going to do with me?"

His eyes opened wide with surprise. "What do you mean?"

"Well, what do you want to do?"

"I want to make love to you," he said, sounding confused.

I laughed gently. "Yes, I can see that! But will you be on top, or should I be on top, or maybe you'd like to do it from behind again? Or perhaps I'll let my mouth do the talking? You choose."

He licked his lips as he hesitated, his eyes blazing.

"From behind," he whispered.

"Your wish is my command."

I knelt up on the bed and, with deliberate slowness, turned around and sank to all fours. Then I glanced at him over my shoulder, flicking my hair out of my eyes.

I heard him suck in a deep breath and the springs of the bed protested loudly as he climbed up the mattress. He knelt behind me, holding my hip with one hand and positioning himself with the other. He sank into me slowly and groaned loudly.

"Fuck! Oh, fuck!"

I pushed my hips back toward him and his whole body convulsed.

I could tell he was trying to control himself, to move slowly, but his body was winning the battle over his mind. I wasn't even trying for control. I wanted all of him. Now.

I ground back against him again and Sebastian lost it completely, gripping my hips with both hands and pounding into me. The bedsprings squeaked loudly with every thrust. A breathless giggle escaped me—it couldn't have been more obvious what we were doing if there had been a neon sign over his door saying, 'sex in progress: do not enter'. Although I was rather enjoying the entering. And exiting. And entering.

His hand moved to my sweet spot the way I'd shown him

before, and, at that point, I lost all cogent thought as exquisite and uncontrollable sensation lanced through me. He'd gotten so good at finding my weak spots: mentally and physically. He was a hell of a fine student. I let my elbows fold, taking our combined weight on my forearms, so I could sink my face into his pillow, attempting to muffle my increasingly loud moans. Between us, we were making enough noise to wake the dead— luckily not enough to wake Estelle.

I felt Sebastian shudder into me with one last, powerful thrust—he gasped, biting back a mangled sound that could have been my name.

We sank down and lay full length on his narrow bed together. After a moment, he shifted onto his side and pulled me with him so my back was half-resting on his chest.

"That was ... fuck, Caro! I didn't know..."

He paused.

"Didn't know what, *tesoro?*" I asked, still breathless.

"Nothing."

He sounded embarrassed.

"Go on. I'm curious now." I stopped and shook my head. "Sorry ... I'm doing it again, aren't I?"

"Doing what?"

"Forcing you to speak when you don't want to. Sorry."

"Fuck! Don't be sorry, Caro. I was just ... okay, but don't get mad at me. I just didn't know girls really liked it like that."

For a moment I was taken aback and then I started to laugh. "What? You thought only porn stars liked it from behind ... doggy style?"

"Well, yeah!" he sounded rather shocked.

I turned around awkwardly in the narrow bed so I could look at him. I stroked his face, but I couldn't stop grinning.

"Sebastian, women like sex just as much as men ... if it's good."

He tried to smile but still looked uncertain, his forehead creasing with worry.

"Am I...?"

He bit his lip.

I knew what he was trying to ask me.

"Yes, you're good. In fact I'd say you're amazing in so many ways." I didn't mean to tease him—well, maybe just a little. He was just so unbelievably sweet. "Besides," I continued, "the whole orgasm thing is a clue that the woman is really enjoying it. In case you were wondering."

"Yeah, I was. Kind of. I mean, it always feels amazing with you, but I wasn't sure if you thought so, too."

"Well, I do. So stop worrying." I considered for a moment. "I could make score cards if you like: grade you on required elements, presentation, and technical merit—like in ice skating."

He laughed. "Okay! So how did that score?"

"Three sixes."

He didn't reply for a moment, then said quietly, his tone hurt, "Only six?"

I nearly choked, I was laughing so hard. "The score is out of six!"

He laughed, too, but the sound was a little embarrassed. "Oh, okay then."

He reached down and pulled a sheet up to my shoulders. I was warm and comfortable in his little bed and could easily have fallen asleep.

When I felt my eyes closing I nudged his chin with my nose. "I should go now. It'll be getting light soon."

He pulled me tighter. "Five more minutes."

"Okay, but I'm going to count: 300, 299, 298..."

"Okay, okay! I'm moving."

He pulled back the sheet and shivered slightly. He knelt down, fumbling around on the floor trying to find our clothes.

"Hey, can I keep your bra?"

"Excuse me?"

"I haven't got anything of yours, Caro, please!"

"Sebastian!" I shook my head in disbelief.

"Please, Caro!"

"Fine! But you owe me, Hunter. That's the second bra that's gone missing in action on your watch."

He grinned and threw my t-shirt at me.

When we were both dressed, he pulled open the door and we tiptoed down the stairs. Well, I tiptoed, he walked normally, glancing at me and shaking his head like I was a little crazy. I'd never snuck out of a boy's bedroom before—it was more fun than I'd imagined.

Once we were out of the confines of the house and in the yard, I began to breathe a little more easily. Sebastian insisted on rolling the water barrel over to the fence to make it easier for me to climb over.

There was the faintest hint of gray light in the east, and the air was cool and scented with pine.

We leaned against the car, holding each other before the inevitable division that always came.

"Your buzz-cut is growing out," I said, absentmindedly running my fingers through his hair.

"Yeah, I guess."

It was clear his mind was elsewhere. "Can I come over tomorrow morning before work?"

"It *is* tomorrow," I reminded him.

"Can I?"

"I guess so, but let me text you." I frowned when it occurred to me that I had to face David now—or at some point soon. "Just in case."

He sighed. "Okay. Love you, Caro."

I hugged him more tightly then let him go. "I'll see you later."

"We're always saying goodbye. I hate it, Caro."

"It won't be for much longer," I said, with as much conviction as I could muster.

Getting in my car and driving away from him was one of the hardest things I'd ever done.

～

A few minutes later I was home—or rather, at the house where my soon-to-be-ex-husband slept. I certainly hoped he was asleep as I crept through the back door.

But then I froze. From the kitchen I could see a leg hanging off the end of the couch, it was clad in dress uniform.

Shit!

I took off my shoes and slunk past him barefoot, hardly daring to breathe. His snoring remained deep and regular, so when I reached the top of the stairs without incident, I gasped, feeling faint with relief.

Glancing into our ... *his* bedroom, I noticed that the bed hadn't been slept in. He'd come home so drunk he'd never even made it up the stairs.

Just like Estelle.

The clock on my bedside table informed me that it was 6AM, I still had an hour before the alarm. I peeled off my t-shirt and jeans and slid under the cold sheets. I missed Sebastian's warm body next to mine and couldn't relax, instead of sleeping, I found myself staring dry-eyed at the ceiling for the best part of an hour.

Five minutes before the alarm was due, I gave up and headed for the shower. The hot water soothed and revived me, and then I spent a few minutes rubbing in moisturizer and body lotion. I'd better start looking after my skin more carefully if I was going to have a boyfriend who was so much younger than I was. It didn't seem likely that a little palm oil could help *enough*, but I was prepared to try pretty much anything—anything that I could afford—which wasn't saying a lot.

As I stared in the mirror, examining the fine lines around my eyes and searching for any gray hairs, I noticed a small, oval bruise above my left breast. Oh, my God! A hickey! I hadn't had one of those in years! Well, make that over a decade. In fact I wasn't completely sure that I'd *ever* had one. What was that boy's name who'd asked me out the semester before I met David? Kevin? Colin? I remembered he'd tried to make out with me in the movie theatre, but I'd been more interested in watching the screen.

I made a mental note to remind Sebastian that biting was out until we'd got to New York. Pity.

When I'd finished drying my hair with the towel, I laid out David's uniform for work. I hoped it would avoid, or at least delay, the next fight for as long as possible. Needs must.

He was just beginning to stir when I started making breakfast. I banged around the kitchen as loudly as possible, taking out some of my frustration on the frying pan and kitchen sink, feeling his whiskey-soured eyes glaring at me balefully.

"Good morning, David. Are you feeling up to some breakfast?" I asked breezily.

"Just coffee," he said sulkily, then added, "Thank you."

I nearly dropped the plate I was carrying, staring at him in disbelief. I couldn't remember the last time he'd thanked me for anything. I wondered what had brought on that outbreak of civility. It was too weird. Still, it was better than being snarled at, which was usually how he behaved when he was hung-over. Wonders would never cease.

The polite entente was fairly short-lived. He left the house without speaking to me again, for which I was inordinately grateful.

The sun had broken through a layer of thin cloud and the gloom of San Diego in June was promising to be another glorious day. My heart felt curiously light—and I knew what would be perfect. I texted Sebastian immediately, knowing he was waiting to hear from me.

Park in 20? Bring your boardshorts!

His reply made me laugh.

Isn't it bedtime?
No! 20 mins?
ok :)

I changed into my bikini and pulled on a pair of shorts and

strappy t-shirt, then ran downstairs to make an *enormous* picnic. I knew he wouldn't have gotten himself any breakfast or, even if he had, he'd still be starving by lunchtime.

As an afterthought I picked up my laptop and notebook and tossed them in the trunk of the car. I still had some notes to type up and, more than ever, I needed the money from the articles that *City Beat* was prepared to pay me for. Besides, now I had a membership to the country club, I may as well use it. Of course, there were also the ancillary benefits of the locker room to be considered, if it happened to be empty again, well, who knew what might happen.

Sebastian was sitting on the curb in his usual place, my dear sweet punk.

"We're going surfing?"

The hope and surprise were equally evident in his voice.

"Why not? It's a beautiful day. Maybe you can teach me some more moves."

"I liked the moves you taught me last night."

"Sebastian!"

He shrugged. "It's true."

"Well, maybe. We'll have to see if that locker room is free later."

He groaned. "Oh, man, that was hot!"

I couldn't disagree with that assessment.

We drove with the windows down and Sebastian chose another jazz station to listen to. I was fairly sure that his interest in opera was just to please me. It was really rather cute.

I parked next to the same surf shack just north of La Jolla. It was aptly named, being so ramshackle, it looked as if it might tip over the cliff with the faintest gust of breeze.

The owner recognized us immediately—either that or he used the same patter on everyone.

"Hey, sugar, long time no see! You want to rent another board?"

"Yes, please," I said politely, elbowing Sebastian in the ribs as he scowled at the man. "And two shorties."

"I'm good," muttered Sebastian. "Just a shortie for her."

"Aw, that sucks," said the owner, sizing me up, "I bet you look great in a bikini."

I paid quickly, leaving my car keys again as surety, and pushed Sebastian out of the shop before he decided to start something. The owner grinned at me and winked. When he slid me my change, I saw that he'd written his phone number on one of the bills.

Classy. Ugh.

What kind of guy hit on someone when they were with their boyfriend? You wouldn't find a woman doing ... and then I thought of Brenda. Yes, she was definitely the kind of woman who would do *exactly* that.

I wondered if it was worth keeping the surf shack man's number to pass on to her, he was quite attractive in that so-laidback-he-was-almost-horizontal sort of way. And I knew for a fact she liked surfers. I really wished he hadn't written his cell number on a ten dollar note. Oh, well, I'd just have to use it for a tip somewhere. A large tip.

Sebastian carried the heavy board down to the beach and swam out with me. I didn't know how he could stand the water without a wetsuit—it felt cold to me. He just laughed and said he was used to it.

I wobbled about and fell off more times than I could count, but I also managed to get several rides where I rode the board all along the green water in front of the breaking wave. Sebastian was wonderfully encouraging and I felt very proud of myself.

We'd been playing in the surf for nearly an hour when a familiar looking van parked alongside my battered old Ford and Ches strolled down to the beach, his sleek, lightweight twin-tail thruster under one arm.

I nudged Sebastian and his happy expression vanished.

"Let's go say hi," I suggested.

He shrugged, but followed me as I caught a wave to the beach.

"Hi, Ches," I said pleasantly, as I dragged my heavy board onto the sand.

"Hi, Mrs. ... Caroline," he said, looking warily at Sebastian. "I didn't know you could surf."

"Sebastian is teaching me."

"Yeah, we don't spend all our time fucking," Sebastian said aggressively, folding his arms across his chest.

I cringed and felt my cheeks redden. Apart from anything else, he was such a hypocrite.

Ches winced and fiddled with the leash on his board.

"I still have trouble making the turns," I said, desperately trying to lighten the tense atmosphere.

"Yeah, well, you were looking pretty good out there," muttered Ches.

"Why don't you guys go have some fun, I'm ready for a rest. Sebastian, take my board."

I thrust it toward him, giving him very little choice in the matter. He gazed at me mulishly then snatched up the board and paddled out.

Ches stared helplessly for a second, murmured something inaudible, and followed him. I watched for a while, hoping that they'd work it out somehow, then peeled off the wetsuit and stretched out on my beach towel. The sun was deliciously warm on my chilly skin and I was soon dozing peacefully, full of happy non-thoughts. Besides, I hadn't been getting a lot of sleep lately.

I was woken abruptly by something very cold dripping on me. I squinted into the sun to see Sebastian grinning down at me. My heart lurched suddenly—it was so much like the first day we'd met. So much had happened since then. I was barely the same person. Was he?

At least Sebastian looked happier now.

"Hey, baby, did I wake you up?"

"Sort of—not really. Did you have fun?"

He shrugged. "It was okay. Waves aren't great today. Wind's onshore, so it's pretty mushy. It was more fun with you."

I shivered as he lay down next to me.

"Ugh! You're all cold and clammy!"

"I could warm you up," he said suggestively, running his hand across my stomach and leaning over me.

I pushed him off.

"Not here!"

I glanced up to see an embarrassed Ches desperately trying to find something else to look at other than his best friend getting it on with a married woman.

"Behave!" I said severely, frowning at Sebastian.

He just grinned at me with the same irritating air of insouciance. God! He could be infuriating.

I sat up and flicked his wrist away as he tried to lay a possessive hand on my thigh. I reached into my bag and pulled on my t-shirt. I thought Ches might feel slightly more comfortable if I was wearing a few more clothes, and there was that damn hickey, too. In truth, Ches's level of comfort mostly depended on whether or not his friend would quit behaving like an ass.

"Ches, would you like some sandwiches? I've made more than enough."

"Yeah, that would be great, Caroline," he replied quietly.

His eyes flickered nervously to Sebastian who was acting like a sulky teenager. Okay, maybe he wasn't acting—he *was* a sulky teenager. I sighed. He was spoiling our lovely day. It wasn't Ches's fault that he'd turned up at the same beach as us. We should just be thankful it was Ches and not any other of Sebastian's surfing buddies.

Over lunch, relations began to thaw. Sebastian stopped trying to show off, and Ches began to relax. Food was proving to be a universal panacea for men's ill tempers. I was relieved— the last thing I wanted to do was come between Sebastian and his best friend. And, if things went badly, he'd need all the friends he could get. I shivered at the thought.

After our increasingly enjoyable picnic, Sebastian insisted on returning my board and shortie to the surf shack, and *I* insisted that he ride to the country club in the van with Ches.

"I'll see you there soon enough," I pointed out, cutting off his protest. "Please, *tesoro!*"

He kissed me hungrily and this time I knew it wasn't an act. When we could bear to stop, he leaned his forehead against mine.

"Bye, Caro," he said softly.

I kissed him on the lips and watched him climb into Ches's van.

He was right about one thing—we were always saying goodbye.

When I arrived at the country club, my grim mood turned into something much darker. A girl in a *very* skimpy bikini was lying on a sun lounger by the pool.

Brenda fucking Wiseman.

CHAPTER FIFTEEN

BRENDA LOOKED UP AND FROWNED AS I SETTLED MYSELF AT A table under a sun umbrella and fired up the laptop.

It was clear from her confused expression that she recognized me, she just couldn't remember from where. I didn't have any plans on helping her out with that—the less she connected me with Sebastian, the happier I'd be. In fact, the smart thing to do would be to pack up and go home for that very reason.

Even though I'd only just arrived, I should leave—maybe if I could just pretend that I'd forgotten something, I could go without drawing too much attention.

Quietly, I closed the laptop's lid and slipped it into my shoulder bag even though the poor machine was still grumbling through its start-up routine. I stood up to go but I was ten damn seconds too late. Sebastian was walking toward me in his country club uniform, a huge smile on his face. You would have thought he hadn't seen me in days, not just a few minutes. I felt exactly the same.

I flicked my eyes to Brenda then stared at the floor, but he didn't seem to be able to read my mind, which, at that precise moment, was extremely inconvenient of him.

"Hi!" he said, happily. Then he frowned. "Are you going somewhere?"

I was like a deer caught in headlights from the juggernaut that was Brenda Wiseman—and I was about to get squashed flat. Her eyes swiveled toward us and, from the look on *her* face, I was pretty certain that *she* had super-powers, probably X-ray vision, the way she was ogling his body.

"Hey, Seb!" she sang. "Oh, I *love* your uniform! It's, like, so cute!"

Her hysterical cheerleader whine made me want to hold her head in the pool's deep end and watch until her pedicured feet kicked out a tarantella.

Sebastian's expression morphed from happy to irritated and then to slightly worried. He was right to be concerned—his acting abilities were even worse than mine. The two of us being in the proximity of the preternaturally observant Brenda, was a sure recipe for disaster. Possibly hers, as I might be forced to rip her tongue out of her head and feed it to the nearest tiger shark as bait.

I still thought that my best plan was to exit stage left at a convenient moment, although that meant leaving Sebastian in the clutches of the harpy. Unobtrusively, I sank back down in my seat and retrieved the confused laptop from my bag.

"Um, no," I said softly, trying not to look too befuddled, "I was just going to get … a coffee."

For a second Brenda glared at me then her gaze became rather condescending.

"Oh, I thought I recognized you—you were at the picnic on Sunday, Mrs....?"

"Caroline Wilson," I supplied politely. "And you are...?"

"Brenda Wiseman," she said, raising her eyebrows, clearly believing she was unforgettable. How right she was.

Sebastian's haunted eyes pedaled between us.

"Nice to see you again, Brenda," I said, matching her for insincerity.

She adjusted her tiny bikini top, her tried and tested method for attracting Sebastian's attention. This time it failed spectacularly, he was still staring intently at me. God, I hoped somebody tried to drown themselves soon—maybe that would snap him out of it—although it was doubtful.

Brenda's eyes narrowed—she sensed competition, so now she was going in for the kill. While Sebastian's gaze was still fixed on me, I saw her fiddle with one of her earrings and slip it into her purse. What was she up to?

I was about to find out.

"Seb?" she whined. "I lost an earring, I think it came off in the deep end. Would you, like, dive down and find it for me?"

Wow, she really was shameless! She'd deployed the poor, helpless female act to get her own way *and* she was about to make him take his shirt off—all in one short sentence. I would never have thought of that: I had a lot to learn.

Sebastian frowned at her.

"Are you sure you lost it in the deep end?" He stared at her accusingly. "Your hair is dry."

She flushed. "I've been here a while ... I was swimming when I noticed it had gone. Please, take a look?"

"Okay," he said, staring down into the pool.

I saw a look of triumph in her expression which soon changed to lust as Sebastian pulled off his t-shirt and stepped out of his flip-flops.

It was really hard to imagine that they'd dated for ten whole months. Even harder to imagine that she hadn't ripped off his clothes and stolen his virginity at some point during that period. Had she only become so obviously desperate once he'd broken up with her or had she always been like this? I reminded myself of the reason why they'd broken up in the first place— she'd slept with someone else. Perhaps Sebastian had a good grasp on his self-control when he was with her—just not with me, I concluded smugly.

Across the pool, I saw two women of Shirley's age nudge each other and adjust their sunglasses for a better look.

Big tips from horny, older women.

Jealousy was such a new and unaccustomed emotion, that I had to remind myself my homicidal thoughts were something of an over-reaction. Except, perhaps, where Brenda was concerned.

I was relieved that the nail marks I'd inflicted on Sebastian last night—or very early this morning—had, mostly, faded. Hes wasn't the only one who had to be careful not to get carried away.

With a grace that took my breath away, he dived into the deep end and stayed under for half a minute, searching for the earring that Evil Brenda pretended she'd lost. He came up for air then dove down again. Twice more he swept the bottom of the pool but, of course, found nothing.

Eventually he gave up and pulled himself out of the pool, right next to where Brenda was sitting, the vixen trying to look all helpless and grateful. His swim-trunks clung to his body as the water poured off him, and his skin sparkled in the sun, droplets reflecting light off his chest and arms.

Brenda looked like she'd died and gone to heaven. Although ... a thought occurred to me, hadn't she seen it all before? Hadn't he ever taken her surfing with him? I'd have to remember to ask him. Then I slapped the idea down—I'd promised myself to quit plaguing him with questions that were only going to piss off both of us.

The two women across the pool were grinning at each other and I swear they gave each other a high five. I could see Sebastian was going to have a long afternoon of being asked to retrieve lost jewelry from the pool. Or maybe, if those cocktails the women drank were alcoholic, he'd end up having to save them both when they threw themselves in the deep end, hoping that he'd give them mouth-to-mouth resuscitation.

"I'm sorry," he said at last, "I couldn't find it. It probably got sucked into the filter system. I'll report it to the manager and he can ask the pool guy to look out for it. But it won't be until tomorrow morning now."

Brenda shrugged.

"Whatever. So, did you decide which school you're going to go to yet? UCSD, right? What classes are you taking?"

"I'm working, Bren," he said, not very subtly.

She pouted. "It's not *that* busy."

He frowned. "I'm not supposed to chat to members."

"I won't tell if you won't," she said, smiling up at him.

I felt desperately sorry for Sebastian, he was utterly hopeless at trying to blow her off. He really didn't have a clue. He was far too nice for his own good.

I wondered if he'd appreciate my help—maybe if I attacked her with a pool chair and beat her into putty, she'd be distracted enough to leave him alone. On the other hand, that would definitely draw unwanted attention.

Instead, I tried to focus on the small screen in front of me, but I couldn't help noticing that Sebastian's eyes kept flicking nervously in my direction.

Brenda was getting irritated that her wiles weren't working, and she was bound to notice that he kept looking at me, not her.

At that moment Ches walked over to Sebastian and spoke to him quietly. Whatever he said, Sebastian was hugely and obviously relieved. He picked up his uniform polo-shirt and pulled it over his still-wet body, slipped on his flip-flops and walked off, glancing just once at me and smiling.

But it was enough: Brenda had seen the look.

Her eyes narrowed dangerously and I couldn't help a nervous swallow. Then I straightened my back and decided that I wasn't going to roll over and let her walk all over me.

"Where's he gone?" Brenda snapped at Ches.

"We've been told to swap duties," he lied casually.

I knew for a fact that Sebastian was supposed to be poolside his whole shift.

"They want him in the gym," continued Ches, sounding utterly convincing. I was glad he was on our side—on Sebastian's side.

Then he looked at me and grinned, "Hey, there, Mrs. Wilson! How are you?"

"I'm just fine, thank you, Ches," I said, smiling at him gratefully. "How's your mom and dad?"

We slipped into our double act as if we'd been practicing it all our lives.

"Good, thanks. Are you writing another article?"

"I thought the staff weren't supposed to chat to members," Brenda muttered in a sulky tone.

Ches pretended not to hear her and spoke to me for several minutes before taking up his place in the lifeguard's chair.

I was totally unprepared for Brenda's next line of attack.

"So, you're, like, a writer?" she said, coming and standing next to me, one hand on her hip.

I glanced up and saw Ches's fleeting look of sympathy.

"Trying to be," I said politely.

"Aren't you, like, kind of old to be starting out?"

I was astonished by her rudeness.

"I don't think it's ever too late to try something new."

She sniffed and started reading my notes over my shoulder. I'd had enough.

I closed the laptop and looked her in the eye. "Is there something I can help you with, Barbara?"

"It's *Brenda!*"

"Oh, is it?"

"You knew Seb when he was a kid, right?" she said, not the least bit perturbed by my overt hostility.

"Slightly," I acknowledged.

"So, you've known him, like, forever?"

If she said 'like' again, I might have to beat her over the head with a book of English grammar. Or I might just do it anyway—the idea was undeniably attractive.

I smiled coolly at her and she looked a little confused. "Oh, sorry, Barb ... Brenda. Was that a question?"

She nodded briskly.

"No, not really," I replied shortly. I wasn't going to give her any information I didn't need to.

"You know his parents, right?"

"Slightly," I repeated, knowing that would aggravate her more than anything.

"Seb and I have been dating since tenth grade," she lied blandly.

"How nice," I said, grinding my teeth. "Dear me! Shirley must have been mistaken when she told me you two had broken up."

She flicked her honey blonde hair over her shoulder. "We were on a break, but he wants to get back with me."

She spoke with such an air of conviction that I was rather in awe of her. How did she lie so easily and with such confidence? I should take lessons from her—especially as I had another three months of living with David to get through.

The reminder was a sharp one, and I'd had enough of her games.

"How nice for you. Well, it's been lovely chatting, but if you'll excuse me, I have deadlines."

Now she looked mad. It turned out that I was much better at blowing her off than Sebastian was. What's more, *it had been fun*.

She huffed angrily, grabbed her towel and headed indoors. I suspected she would be stalking Sebastian in the gym. I looked up at Ches. He shrugged and shook his head helplessly. Nope, he didn't know what to do about Barbara ... um ... Brenda either.

I decided to wander in to get that mythical coffee after all. I left my laptop on the table and Ches cheerfully acknowledged that he'd keep an eye on it. Pulling on my t-shirt and shorts I headed for the bar area but before I got there I could hear a woman's angry voice.

"It's not appropriate for you to be chatting to your girlfriend while you're working, Mr. Hunter."

"She's not my..."

A middle-aged Hispanic woman in a neat pant-suit was chewing a piece out of Sebastian. My immediate reaction was to rush in and defend him. Instead, I watched silently from the sidelines. Story of my life.

"We have rules here for very good reasons. We don't want our members injuring themselves when they're in the gym—

that's why we have staff on hand to instruct them in the correct use of the equipment. If you're chatting to your girlfriend, Mr. Hunter, that's when accidents will happen. I take a very dim view of that ... a very dim view indeed."

"She's not my girlfriend, ma'am, she's a member and..."

"Well ... I've made my views clear, Mr. Hunter. And should any other of your *friends* decide to come and chat, I'm sure you'll dissuade them from that. Am I making myself clear?"

"Yes, ma'am."

"And may I ask why you are working the gym right now and not Mr. Peters?"

Sebastian flushed and dropped his gaze to stare directly over his manager's shoulder.

"I ... I asked to swap, ma'am."

"*I* arrange the rosters, Mr. Hunter, not you. Kindly go back to your lifeguarding duties and send Mr. Peters to see me, please."

"But Ches..."

"*Now*, Mr. Hunter."

"Yes, Miss Perez."

Sebastian turned on his heel and strode back out to the pool area.

Luckily, he was unaware that I'd overheard the humiliating little scene. I could cheerfully have smacked Brenda into the middle of next week for causing so much trouble.

I lingered to order a coffee and the young barista offered to carry it out to the pool for me when it was ready. Now Sebastian was back outside, it was the only place I wanted to be.

Happily, Brenda seemed to have disappeared. Which was lucky for her, the way I was feeling.

Sebastian was slumped in the lifeguard's chair when I emerged into the sunshine from the gloom of the clubhouse, but beamed at me as I resumed my seat under the sun umbrella. I really was going to have to talk to him about playing it cool. I gave him a quick smile and went back to my laptop. Now

Brenda had gone, I had a reasonable chance of actually managing to put some words on the page.

It was surprisingly soothing to have Sebastian sitting there while I worked. I wrote steadily for some time, sipping at the thin coffee that had been brought to my table, becoming more and more absorbed in describing life on a military Base, with its odd mixture of discipline and play, rules and separation that marked us out as different from the world beyond the walls. It made me realize how much I'd come to rely on that sense of orderliness, togetherness, of family, even. I'd felt so alien in this world for so long, I hadn't even noticed my slow absorption into this isolated, alternative way of life. I wondered if I'd miss it once I left. I didn't think so, but it was all I'd known for 11 years. Now, at last, Sebastian was offering me something different.

I looked at my wristwatch, astonished that it was already after 5PM. I had to get home—and face David. Twelve more weeks of feeling like this, I didn't know how I'd manage. And I'd be without the warmth of Sebastian's body beside me tonight. That thought alone made me feel bereft.

I looked up to see him watching me, a small frown creasing his forehead. I smiled quickly and subtly tapped my watch. The corners of his lips turned down and he nodded fractionally.

With a sigh, I packed up my notebook and laptop, and left him behind.

≈

At 6PM I heard David's car pull up. I made sure that his dinner, reheated lasagna and salad, was ready.

As he walked in, I fixed a smile to my face and pulled his steaming plate out of the microwave and placed it on the table next to the salad bowl.

But he didn't look at the food—he looked right at me, his face stiff and angry, sitting bolt upright at the table.

"Have you got something to tell me, Caroline?"

I'm sure my face was drained of color, because I suddenly

felt very faint. I tried to speak but the words wouldn't come out.

"Well?"

"I..."

"I saw Dr. Ravel today," he snarled at me, "who reported to me that you *missed your appointment!*"

I felt a sudden desire to laugh. Was *that* all that was bothering him.

"That's right," I said, feeling brave now that I was sure it was nothing to do with Sebastian.

"Would you like to explain that?" he hissed.

"I felt no need for an appointment, David. You made it without consulting me. If you had, I would have reminded you that I had a Pap smear six months ago and that there were no problems. And I certainly am *not* experiencing an early menopause—I'm quite sure of *that*."

Silence filled the room and our eyes locked.

"And what the hell is Dr. Ravel doing discussing me—her patient—with you? Hasn't she heard of HIPPA?"

"If it's not physical, it must be psychological," he said, coolly ignoring my comment. "I'll arrange for you to see the Base psychiatrist and..."

"No, you won't, David," I replied, trying to match his sanguine tone, but with little luck. "I am not seeing a shrink, there's *nothing* wrong with me."

"Then why are you sleeping in the guest room?" he yelled, all attempt at any control gone. "*That* is going to stop tonight. I want you back in my bed where you belong!"

"No!" I yelled back. "I fucking well won't!"

David's face was comically shocked. "Yes, you will," he said, with far less force.

I stared back at him and folded my hands across my waist.

"No."

We glared at each other across the kitchen table.

"What the fuck is wrong with you?" he shouted suddenly, making me jump.

Adrenaline and mounting anger sharpened my tone.

"Nothing! There's nothing wrong with me! I wash your fucking clothes, I iron your fucking pants, I cook, I clean, I..."

"That's your job! That's what you're here to do!"

"I'm NOT a fucking servant!"

"You're being hysterical, Caroline, I think..."

"I don't give a rat's ass what you think, David! I'm tired of you bullying me, putting me down, patronizing me, treating me like some sort of simpleton. I was supposed to be a *partner* in this relationship—that's what I signed up for. *Not this!*"

"You're acting like a child, Caroline."

"Then stop fucking treating me like one! I'm thirty fucking years old!"

"And please stop using that vile language."

"Aaaaaaaagh!" I screamed at the top of my lungs. For a moment he actually looked scared.

Then he stood up abruptly and forcefully shoved the lasagna and salad away from him. The plate slid right across the kitchen table and crashed to the floor, sending a shower of steaming hot sauce and scalding vegetables over my bare feet and legs.

I cried out and jumped back, trying to scrub off the burning food.

"You bastard," I screamed at him. "You fucking bastard!"

He looked shocked.

"Caroline ... I ... I didn't mean for that to ... are you hurt?"

I ran to the sink, trying to splash cold water over my burning legs and feet.

"Caroline!"

Tears sprang to my eyes and my voice was shrill.

"Go away, David. Leave me alone."

Instead, he hovered guiltily while I cleaned myself up in silence. The hot food had left blotchy, red burn marks down my thighs and shins and across the front of my feet. I thought I'd got the hot sauce off quickly enough to prevent any blistering or real damage.

David watched me helplessly. It was clear he hadn't a clue what to say or do. Just as long as he didn't try to touch me—if he did, I wouldn't be responsible for my actions. The great doctor didn't even offer to get the First Aid kit.

Carefully, I rubbed large dollops of antiseptic cream over my legs and, without a single glance in his direction, I left the room. The pool of lasagna was still spread out over the floor like a crime scene.

I walked upstairs stiffly and lay down on the bed in my room. I wanted to curl into a tight ball but my skin was too tender to stretch like that. Instead I lay on my back and stared at the ceiling. David had never ever hurt me before—not physically. I knew it was an accident but the hate I felt for him at that moment raged through me. All the years of being belittled and bullied, all the times he'd made feel stupid and inadequate, it all came boiling up inside.

The fury I'd felt when Brenda had flirted too openly with Sebastian was nothing, an insignificant annoyance, compared to the way I felt now.

I was *glad* I was having an affair behind his back. I was *glad* I'd taken a younger man into his bed. I was *delighted* thinking of the humiliation he'd suffer when he finally knew the truth. I wanted to yell it to his face and watch his whole fucking world fall apart.

Even after I heard the front door slam and his car screech out of the driveway, I continued to imagine the fierce joy I'd feel when I finally told him what a pathetic little man he truly was.

I lay on the bed as the house sank into darkness. Outside I could hear the small sounds of the day's end, people's lives continuing down the same, certain paths. I'd been like that once—moving from hour to hour, sleepwalking down a road that had been chosen for me—not awake, not aware.

It was all ashes and dust.

∼

I must have fallen asleep because when my cell phone buzzed with a text message, I jerked awake. I struggled to sit up, wondering why I felt so sore and then the memories came flying back like locusts. The skin on my legs felt raw, or rather, the hot tightness of bad sunburn. I was astonished to find that my face was wet. I didn't know it was possible to cry in your sleep. It wasn't from the pain—at least, not the physical pain.

I turned on my side to reach the bedside light. The little alarm clock told me it was after 11PM, I'd been asleep for nearly four hours.

I expected the text to be from Sebastian and it was—but not the goodnight message I'd anticipated.

Am outside. Is he there? There's no car? Can I c u?

I leapt out of bed and immediately regretted moving so quickly. Even in the weak pool of light from the little lamp, my legs looked horrible. I needed to find something to cover them up. I found an old hippy skirt at the back of the closet. It was dated and faintly ridiculous, but it was the only fabric I could tolerate right now. Best of all, it was floor length.

Moving carefully, I made my way down to the kitchen. I stared in disgust at the vomit-like pool of cold lasagna on the tiled floor. That bastard hadn't even tried to clear it away. I hesitated, thinking I should clean up before I let Sebastian in— he'd only ask questions which I wanted to avoid. But it was too late, he'd seen my silhouette as soon as I'd walked in the kitchen and I could see his shadow rocking impatiently on the balls of his feet.

His smile vanished as soon as he saw my face. My attempt to fool him for even a second had obviously been in vain.

"Caro, what's wrong?"

I just shook my head and he pulled me into a tight hug. His jeans pushed against my legs, rubbing my skirt fabric against my burns. I winced and he felt me shudder.

"What's the matter? Did something happen? Tell me!"

I sighed into his chest.

"David and I had a fight," I said.

He froze as soon as I'd said the words.

"He knows?"

I shook my head slowly. "No. It was nothing to do with you —just a stupid fight."

He breathed a sigh of something like relief.

"What was it about then?"

He wasn't going to let this one go.

"He was pissed because I refused to sleep with him—I mean, sleep in his bed, not ... I told him I'd be staying in the guest room."

"That asshole! Fuck, Caro! I really want to..."

He didn't finish the sentence but it didn't take a genius to figure out what he was thinking.

"Has he ... gone out?"

I nodded. "Yes, he's been gone a while. I've no idea when ... or if, he'll be back."

"Can I come in?"

His voice was hopeful.

"Okay, for a minute."

He frowned at my unenthusiastic reply. I was so tired and wrung out, I couldn't handle a jealous and angry Sebastian right now.

He halted in his tracks when he saw the mess on the floor.

"Did *he* do that?"

I nodded silently and fetched a cloth to start clearing it up.

Without speaking Sebastian took the rag from me. I was too weary to argue even though I wanted to. It was just all wrong to have my lover clear up the mess my husband had made in our kitchen over a fight about the matrimonial bed. My brain was tied in knots just trying to keep all the pieces in the right place. Somehow everything had gotten so mixed up and confused.

Finally, the floor was clean and the remains of David's dinner had been dumped in the trash can. Sebastian washed his hands and dried them on the back of his pants.

He sat down at the table and put his arm around me. I leaned my head against his shoulder and closed my eyes. He wrapped his other arm around my waist and pulled me to his chest, just holding me. Every now and then I felt his light kisses in my hair.

His kindness was the thing that broke me, and tears began to slide down my cheeks.

"Don't cry, Caro," he said softly, his voice aching with sadness. "Don't cry, baby."

He repositioned one arm under my knees and gently lifted me up. I whimpered once from the pain, then bit my lip to stifle any more sounds.

Slowly and carefully, he carried me up the stairs and laid me down on my bed, placing his body alongside mine.

We lay together as I sobbed quietly. We didn't speak.

When my tears finally dried, he kissed me on the cheek.

"Come on, let's get you undressed."

His hands rose to my waistband but I pushed them roughly away.

"No, don't!"

He looked hurt. "I wasn't going to do anything, Caro. You're exhausted. You need to get some rest. Come on, let me help you."

I tried to push him away, but my body felt like I weighed a thousand pounds, and he'd pulled up the hem of my skirt before I could stop him.

I heard his gasp and then he swore.

"What the fuck, Caro? What happened? Did ... did *he*...?"

"It was an accident," I said tiredly. "He didn't mean to."

Sebastian was furious, as I knew he would be. I could see cords of tension on his neck, his eyes were blazing with fury.

"That *asshole!*"

He bounced off the bed and balled his fists as if he wanted to hit something—or someone. He was trying to rein in his temper, but he wasn't having much luck with that. Then he saw my face, fresh tears breaking out.

"Shit, I should take you to a doctor!"

I shook my head slowly. "I'm okay. They're just ... mild burns ... from the pasta sauce. I'm okay."

"You should fucking report this! You can't let him get away with doing this to you!"

"It was an accident," I repeated quietly. "Please, Sebastian, just drop it."

"Drop it?!" he shouted. "Look what that sack of shit has done to you! Fuck, Caro!"

I put my hands over my ears and squeezed my eyes tight shut, trying to stop the new tears from leaking out. His rant stopped in midstream.

"Oh God, Caro."

I felt the mattress tremble and he lay back down on the bed and hugged me to him. That was all I needed, his arms around me.

After a long while it was Sebastian who broke the silence.

"What do you want to do?"

His voice was soft, unnamed emotions making his tone raw.

"I don't know."

"You can't stay here anymore, Caro. You know that, right?"

I let my breath out in a long sigh.

"I don't have anywhere to go."

"Maybe Mitch and Shirley? They'd help, I know they would."

I shook my head slowly. "I'm not taking my troubles to their door." I sighed. "I'm still ... in an illegal relationship with a minor—I wouldn't do that to them."

He didn't argue so I knew he'd taken my words seriously.

"What about your mom's? I know you're not close, but..."

"No. She practically kicked me out when I was 19," I said bitterly. "Why do you think I married David so quickly?"

He was silent for a moment but I felt his body tense, he did that every time I so much as mentioned David's name. Some sort of primal response, I guessed.

"What about friends back east?"

"Same problem," I whispered. "I'd be involving them in ... well, you know."

He hugged me closer and I could feel his warm breath on my neck.

"There's a women's shelter near Park West ... I ... I heard Mom mention it once. Maybe..."

"I can't because..." My whispered words shuddered to a halt.

"Because of me."

His voice was bitter.

"You can't go to any of the places that would help you ... because of me."

I knew why he thought that, why he would say that, but I couldn't let him blame himself.

"It's not your fault, Sebastian," I said gently, stroking his arm. "You're the one good thing I have in my life. I wouldn't change that for anything. Not for anything. I finally feel ... alive."

I heard him gasp and he pulled me closer.

"I feel the same, Caro. You've taught me everything I know."

I blinked in surprise.

"You have. You've taught me who I can be, you've made me stronger. You make me want to see the magic in the world. I ... I didn't know falling in love could be ... like this."

Was that really how he felt? Is that how he saw me—someone who could make him stronger? How did that happen? I was so weak and cowardly. But, and I felt a small flowering of hope inside me, I *had* changed, hadn't I. I was getting stronger —not yet strong, but getting there.

It felt as if he'd been the one to teach me. Perhaps we had learned together.

He held me carefully, making sure his legs didn't accidentally brush against mine.

"I don't know what to do," he said softly. "I want to be with you so badly, but you just end up getting hurt every time I come near you. Why is it so hard for us to be together? It's so fucking unfair!"

"I know, *tesoro*."

He was so hurt and confused and there was so little I could do to help either of us.

I let out a long sigh.

"I think you'd better go now."

"No!" he gasped. "No way!" He raised his voice. "I'm not leaving you alone with that asshole!"

"I can't fight with you, too, Sebastian," I whispered. "I don't have the strength."

"No! I didn't ... what if he ... I *can't* leave you here alone!" he said, desperately.

I turned carefully to look at him.

"This isn't something you can fix, Sebastian. I'm the one who's screwed up, I have to fix it. But you're right about one thing—I can't stay here." I took a deep breath. "There are lots of empty rooms around the university now all the students are on vacation. I'll check out the listings for people wanting roommates. There are places for less than $500 a month. I can manage that."

I didn't tell Sebastian I had no idea how I'd afford to eat and put gas in my car at the same time.

"And there's a Motel 6 up by San Ysidro that's only $50 a night. That can be my last resort, if necessary."

Sebastian's face was grim. "I have nearly $700. That'll buy another month, food and gas."

Maybe he could read my mind.

I stroked his cheek. "I can't take your money."

"Yes, you can! I want you to, please, Caro. Let me help you. I want to take care of you. This is all my..."

I laid a finger over his lips. I couldn't bear to hear him so desperate, trying to look after me the way a man looks after a woman.

He kissed my finger and pulled my hand away from his mouth.

"You should go see a lawyer, Caro. Take half of everything that bastard has."

I shook my head. "No, Sebastian. I won't be doing that."

"Why not?" he said, hotly. "You deserve..."

I interrupted him gently.

"I don't *want* anything of his. Do you understand? Nothing. But there's another reason ... if I make David fight a divorce,

I'm afraid he'll find out about us. I *know* him: he'll keep digging and digging and digging until he finds the reason why I left him after all this time. His ego will demand that there's a reason other than ... other than himself. And then he'll take me down."

I could feel the tension and stress in Sebastian's body—all his muscles were rigid and he was only just holding onto his temper. He pulled me tighter against his chest, his hands trembling, but he couldn't speak. He buried his face against my neck and we held each other as the night slipped past.

I stroked his back and gradually his body began to relax, his breathing becoming deep and even.

I couldn't sleep but I was glad that Sebastian did. I listened to the soft sounds of breath on his lips, and watched his face relaxed and peaceful. I felt such crushing guilt when I looked at him, so beautiful, so sweet and young. All he'd done was to love me and now he was in danger of being swept away in the floodwaters of my failed marriage.

The right thing for me to do was to leave quietly and head for New York. That way David and I could conduct our divorce with some dignity—I hoped—and my relationship with Sebastian would stay hidden. Once he was 18, and with me already on the east coast, he'd be able to escape. People would talk and maybe even guess the truth, but there would be no proof—and we'd be safe.

Two things held me back from making that decision: firstly, I knew that Sebastian would never agree and it would mean another fight, and secondly, I felt responsible for his fragile soul and I didn't want to leave him unprotected.

I knew Shirley and Mitch would look after him as much as they could—they already thought of him as a second son—but they didn't have the legal power to support him against the wishes of Donald and Estelle. Not unless they were prepared to swear to the historic and ongoing abuse. And, despite everything, Donald was one of *them*—part of the military family. That worked two ways. The military looked after their own, but the other mantra that was drilled into them had a darker side: 'snitches get stitches and wind up in ditches'.

I couldn't see Mitch wanting to go down that road—it would be the end of his career. If Sebastian had been younger, then maybe, but not now he was so near his eighteenth birthday, legal adulthood and emancipation.

So that was the reasoning behind my plan—spend the next couple of days finding a room, then work up the courage to tell David I was leaving him.

I knew my husband well enough to feel confident that his guilt over my accident would keep him silent for the few days I needed.

At least, that's what I hoped.

CHAPTER SIXTEEN

At dawn, I gently shook Sebastian awake.

I'd listened all night for the sound of David's return but the house had stayed silent and kept its secrets.

He yawned and stretched, giving me the most glorious smile.

"God, I love waking up with you, Caro. I want to do it for the rest of my life."

His words squeezed my heart painfully. I badly wanted to believe them.

Then his smile faded and I saw the weight of memories flood back. He frowned.

"How are you? How are your legs?"

"Not too bad. Pretty good really."

In truth, they were more than a little sore, particularly so when I flexed my knees, but nothing I was going to worry about. The worst area was the top of my right foot and that *was* painful. From a few exploratory prods, I could feel that it had blistered over night. It was going to be hellish trying to wear shoes, even flip-flops would rub in all the wrong places.

He looked at me skeptically.

"Really?"

"Sure," I said, not meeting his eyes and sitting up.

He reached out and pulled me back down, forcing me to look at him. "Really?"

"My right foot is a little sore," I conceded. "I just need to put a band-aid on it, that's all."

This time he let me get out of bed and lay there watching me.

I couldn't help noticing that he'd kicked off his jeans in the night and was wearing just a t-shirt and boxer briefs—with a large bulge showing clearly. Although my body tingled with Pavlovian response, I really wasn't in the mood to do anything about it, and Sebastian didn't even seem to be aware. Perhaps he woke up like that every morning. I smiled to myself, considering that soon I'd be in a position to answer that interesting question.

When I came back from the bathroom, he was fully dressed. He'd even taken the time to make the bed and turn back the sheets nicely.

I crept downstairs in the pale, gray light of dawn, checking that David's return wasn't imminent. We'd have about two minutes after hearing his car in the driveway—just enough time for Sebastian to make an escape through the back door. I'd liked to have made breakfast for him but there was a good chance that David would return soon to get a change of clothes.

We stood in the kitchen, the scene of so much drama, so many key moments in our lives, and held each other.

"I'll miss you every minute," he said, softly.

I sighed into his chest.

"I'll see you at the park at 9AM?"

"Yes," he said, simply.

And then it was time for him to go. It seemed to me like it was always time for him to go. I knew he felt the same.

But David didn't return. Instead I spent the hours before I could be with Sebastian again wandering around the empty house, letting my fingers drift over the old, familiar furniture and through the old, familiar memories.

I decided what I would take with me from the marital home.

When it came down to it, there was very little: my clothes, the jewelry my father had given me, my ancient laptop, a few books, and my favorite CDs which were already in the car. The ugly wedding china that my parents had bought us had been my mother's choice—I was more than happy for David to keep it. It wasn't much to show for 11 years of marriage, but with a new life ahead of me, I didn't care either. That, by itself, said everything.

When I'd still lived in North Carolina, some friends and I had had a rather drunken evening and we'd all had to choose which three things we'd save in a house fire. One woman that I didn't know very well said, and I remembered this clearly, "My dog, my handbag and my wedding album."

"What about your husband?" we'd asked, laughing.

"He can get his own damn self out," she'd replied.

I had one other job to do before I left the house—I scoured the rooms-to-rent websites and made a shortlist of five places to check out. I didn't much care what the room was like so long as it was cheap and reasonably clean. It wasn't going to be for long.

Despite my lack of sleep, I was filled with a nervous, restless energy. I'd made my decision and now I was ready to get on with my life. The last month had raced by, but the next few days seemed destined to drag.

I headed back up to the bathroom and gritted my teeth through a tepid shower that stung my too sensitive skin. All the burn marks were ugly but only my foot really bothered me. I dug in the closet and eventually located a pair of long, loose pants and found some old sneakers that were bearable once I'd made a gauze pad to cover the large blister. Not my most elegant look but hell, Sebastian wouldn't care. And that was all that mattered.

He was waiting for me, of course, and just seeing him made my day a little brighter.

"How are you?" he said again, peering anxiously at my face.

"I'm ... surprisingly good," I said, honestly.

He smiled that beautiful smile and I saw his shoulders relax.

"How are you?" I grinned back at him. "Are you hungry?"

"Yeah, starving!"

"Did you skip breakfast again?" I admonished.

His smile died. "Yeah, I guess."

"What is it?"

He shrugged. "No food in the house."

I felt so bad for him, knowing I'd sent him away hungry. "Is ... is it usually like that?"

He carried on staring out of the window. "I guess. Although it's gotten worse lately. All they do is fight. I don't know why they stay together—it damn well isn't for me. Probably to protect their reputations—as if that were even possible. God, I can't wait to get out of there."

I reached over and gently squeezed his thigh. He looked down and a moment later carefully twined his fingers through mine.

"I thought we could go to our coffee shop," I said, softly.

He was still gazing at our joined hands, when he replied.

"Yeah, that would be good."

"I'll spring for breakfast," I said, hoping to make him smile. "I saw on their menu that they do fresh *zeppole* and three different *crostata*."

"Only three?" he said, his lips lifting upwards at last.

"Hmm, well! I think a taste test might be in order."

The Benzinos welcomed us back with open arms, berating us vociferously for having stayed away so long. I made the mistake of mentioning that Sebastian had skipped breakfast and the little old *nonna* scolded him for five minutes solidly, rattling off her rebukes in quick-fire Italian while Sebastian wilted under her stern gaze—then she turned her attention to me, wagging her finger and telling me I was a bad wife for not feeding my man. I agreed with every word. If only she'd known.

Almost every item on the menu was soon delivered to our table and I couldn't help smiling as Sebastian's eyes bugged out at the vast quantity of food. But then I remembered the reason he was always so hungry, and my smile faded.

He ate everything in sight with the exception of one *crostata* that he insisted I have for myself.

"Oh wow, that was amazing!" he said, replete at last. "I'm going to get so fat when we go to Italy."

"If you carry on eating like this you'll be enormous long before we make it to Italy," I laughed at him. "There's nothing on the menu here that I can't make."

"You're kidding? Wow, really? Jeez, I knew there was a reason I loved you!"

And he leaned forward to kiss me.

The little *nonna* clapped her hands together with feeling, then darted over and peppered me with questions, her quick, squirrel-brown eyes darting between us. I shook my head, more than a little embarrassed. She sighed heavily, pointed at her watch and shot off to serve some newly arrived customers, still shaking her head.

"Was that about what I think it was about?" said Sebastian, raising his eyebrows.

"How much did you pick up?" I asked, curious to know how good his Italian was getting—as well as avoiding answering the question.

"Something about babies and the time?"

"Well, yes," I agreed, feeling flustered. "She wanted to know when we were going to start a family." I tried to smile. "She was pointing out that time waits for no woman."

He lifted my hand from the table and frowned as he stared at my wedding ring. "I'll do whatever makes you happy, Caro. I reckon I could handle the idea of a couple of *bambinos* running around. We'd make a helluva better job of it than my folks, that's for sure."

I tried to smile but I didn't want to dare let myself think that far ahead. What was the point? He was far too young to be talking like this. And when he *was* old enough...

The conversation was making me feel despondent so I thought quickly how to change it.

"What time are you working today?"

"Not till 4PM," he said, smiling again. "What would you like to do?"

"Not much," I admitted.

"Do you want to go to our beach?"

My smile faded. "I don't think that would be a good idea—I don't want to get my feet wet or sand in my blister." My words stalled, seeing the venomous look on his face.

He made a visible effort and reined in his rising temper.

"Maybe we could check out some of these rooms to rent that that you've seen advertised?"

"No, that's okay, thanks. I'll do that this afternoon while you're working."

He thought for a moment.

"There's a jazz band playing down in the Gaslamp Quarter today. We could go listen if you like?"

"Jazz again!" I teased. "And here was me thinking you were devoted to opera."

"I like both," he said, looking a little sheepish.

I smiled at him. "Me, too."

He stood up, stretching his tall frame and held out his hands to pull me up.

We hid some bills under our plates and tried to sneak away before the Benzinos saw us but the *nonna* must have had her eagle eyes trained our way because she sent her son darting after us with the money, remonstrating about our underhand trick and reminding us that family didn't pay. Then he kissed us both, thrust the notes into Sebastian's hands and hurried back to his business. How they ever made any profit was beyond me.

We wandered through the Gaslamp Quarter, admiring the Victorian architecture and old world charm, enjoying the sun and warm air, people-watching and relaxing in a way that was new and rather wonderful to me.

We heard the sounds of jazz filling the summer morning long before we saw the band. Strolling out of an alleyway into a large plaza, I could see that one side had been converted into a mini stage where the musicians performed, decked out in black jeans and t-shirts, and wearing dark sunglasses, presumably to show that they were jazzmen, if the music didn't already prove it. They looked young enough to be students and were playing a sort of hyped up version of Dixieland jazz mixed in with a more modern, fusion sound and some Latin rhythms. A couple of girls in their late teens were already dancing, losing themselves in the music. Soon, other people were joining them and the crowd steadily grew.

We didn't want to waste any money by sitting at one of the café tables that ringed the plaza, so we joined a group sprawled out on the sidewalk. Sebastian gallantly pulled off his sweatshirt so I wouldn't have to sit on the dusty ground.

He did these things so naturally, with no fuss or embellishment that my heart expanded with delight and pain each time. Sebastian always put me first. I wasn't used to that.

We sat shoulder to shoulder and he casually draped his arm around me, turning every now and then to kiss my hair. I wished the moment could last forever.

I couldn't help noticing that his feet and hands moved constantly with the music, keeping up a contrapuntal rhythm, his fingers drumming on my arm.

"Have you ever learned a musical instrument?" I wondered.

He smiled. "No, but I always wanted to play guitar."

"We should get you one when we get to New York. Not electric, though, please! An acoustic guitar."

"I thought you were a rock chick at heart. Which reminds me—I still have to go beat up Anthony Kiedis!" He paused. "Did you ever learn to play anything?"

"Not really. I had piano lessons when I was eight. I hated them. Mom wanted me to do it but I begged Papa to stop the torture and he did."

He hesitated for a moment. "Will you tell your mom...?" His words trailed off.

"When I leave David? Yes, I suppose so. Eventually."

He held my hand tightly and kissed my fingers. "At least you had your dad—that's one more good parent than I had." He considered for a moment. "But I have Shirley and Mitch—they've been more like parents to me than my mom and dad. I hate not being able to tell them about you."

He frowned and I stroked his arm, trying to soothe away the hurt, or, if that were impossible, to show that I understood.

"I know, I hate it, too. But when this is all over, if ... if they forgive me, maybe we can..."

He lifted my chin with his fingers to make me look into his eyes.

"There's nothing to forgive," he said, his voice forceful. "We fell in love: it's not a crime."

But I still felt like a criminal. Sometimes.

He kissed me on the lips, trying to lighten our suddenly bleak mood.

"Come on," he said, pulling me to my feet. "Let's dance!"

"What? You can't dance, can you?"

"Oh, yeah? Is that what you think? Let me show you, baby!"

And he could, he really could!

He placed my arms around his neck, wrapped his around my waist and pusheds his right leg between mine so we were joined at the groin. If it hadn't been for the fact we were practically welded together, I would have fallen over from shock. No one had *ever* danced with me like this before. It was so good I was sure it must be illegal. In fact the way he wove our bodies together I was quite certain it would have been banned in several states.

David's idea of dancing was to sway slowly, usually to a different tune from the one that was being played, and circle carefully on the spot. The only other man I'd danced with had been Papa—and that had been a waltz. I hadn't even gone to my high school prom because I was already dating David so I hadn't seen the point.

But this! This was more like sex to music but without the messy sheets. And in public.

He ground himself against me, our bodies undulating with the music. Then he spun me around and pulled me tightly against him again. I caught glimpses of envious faces of other women as we moved. Then his hands slid down to my ass and he pushed my hips into him, fingers splayed out over my buttocks.

When the tune finished I was red-faced and hyperventilating and so damn aroused! He grinned at me wickedly, knowing exactly what he'd done. He dipped me almost to the floor, then swept me up and kissed me hard.

The watching crowd gave us an ironic cheer and several yelled at us to get a room. It was the best suggestion I'd heard all day. Instead, Sebastian saluted the amused audience and grabbed my hand, towing me in the direction of the car.

"Where ... where did you learn to do that?" I gasped.

"Shirley and Mitch," he said, walking so fast I had to trot to keep up.

"You're kidding me!"

"Nope! Base salsa champions, four years running."

He pulled me down the street, a determined look on his face. When we got to the parking lot, I saw his eyes scanning the rows of parked cars until he found my Ford. I tried to fish my keys out of my purse but he was walking so quickly, it was hard to keep up and do anything else.

When we got to the car, he slammed my back against the door, his hands in my hair, his teeth on my throat .

"I want you so bad," he breathed into my skin.

"Empty lot."

"What?"

"That empty lot—you remember."

"Fuck, yes!"

With shaking hands, I climbed into the driver's side and fiddled with my seatbelt. Sebastian reached across me and snapped it into place, letting his fingers drift across my stomach as he did so, his heated expression made my mouth dry up.

I don't know how I drove without having an accident—my whole body was on fire for him. Sebastian leaned back in the passenger seat, his eyes closed. He looked calm, but his too rapid breathing gave him away.

I swung into the weed-covered space of the empty lot, slammed on the brakes and the car screeched to a halt. I'd only just managed to take off my seatbelt before Sebastian was unzipping his pants and showing me just how much he wanted me. I was so turned on seeing his need. I crawled onto his lap and thanked my lucky stars I'd chosen to wear loose pants with an elasticized waistband. I pushed them over my hips, ignored the pain from my sore skin and sank down on to him.

There was no finesse, no gentle touches—it was hard and raw and urgent. Sebastian grabbed my hips, pumping me up and down even faster. His eyes were tightly closed and his head was buried in my chest, every muscle rigid. He came hard, shuddering into me. I whimpered as my body exploded from the inside out and, without meaning to, I bit down on his neck.

His arms tightened around me and we sat there, trying to adjust our shattered breathing.

Finally, the pain from my sore skin broke through the post-orgasmic miasma and I shifted awkwardly back to the driver's side.

I glanced over to see Sebastian zipping up his pants, a huge grin on his face.

"We should name this empty lot," he said.

"Like what? 'Emergency Room'?"

"Yeah!" he laughed out loud. "I hope they never build on it."

"Maybe they'll build one of those Japanese Love Hotels and put a plaque on the wall in our memory."

"What's a Love Hotel?"

"Places where courting couples can go for some privacy. You can pay by the hour."

His eyebrows shot up. "Seriously? Do they have them in San Diego?"

"I can see what you're thinking, Hunter, and the answer is no way!"

He narrowed his eyes and then with a lascivious leer, leaned toward me. He ran his finger down my throat, over my t-shirt, between my breasts and all the way down to my stomach.

"You sure about that?"

My eyelids fluttered. I couldn't remember what my reasoning was.

Suddenly he swore. "Fuck!"

A police officer was walking toward us.

He tapped on my window and I rolled it down. If he'd been two minutes earlier ... I really didn't want to think about that.

"May I see your license, please, ma'am?"

He was stocky, in his fifties, and had a weathered face that was not unkind.

"Yes! Yes, of course!"

I reached over to the back seat to grab my purse. I felt a little shaky, Sebastian just looked pissed.

The officer glanced at my ID and then over at Sebastian. "You from the Base, too, son?"

"Yes, sir."

"Hmm, well. This is private property. So you and *Mrs. Wilson* should find somewhere else to ... park."

"Yes, sir. We'll do that. Thank you, sir."

The officer handed me back my license and watched while we buckled ourselves in and I drove off.

Sebastian blew out a long gust of air and grinned at me.

"That was *so* embarrassing," I whined.

He laughed and shook his head. "It was worth it."

"Where should we go now?" I said, still feeling grumpy.

"Somewhere we can get some food."

"You're hungry *again?*"

He gave me a wicked smile. "Sure! It must be all the ... exercise."

I slapped his leg. "You are a bad influence!"

"Yeah, baby, but you love it."

I couldn't argue with that.

I drove us back to the I-5 and then took a turning toward Mission Beach, heading north up the coast road until Sebastian told me to pull over.

"There's a place here we can get some food," he said, quietly. "This cove is real pretty—we could just sit and chill for a while."

"Sounds great," I said smiling at him. "Although I'm more thirsty than hungry."

"You should eat something," he said seriously.

I just adored the way he tried to look after me—so, so sweet.

"Okay, I'll have a sandwich. Anything, whatever they've got."

I wandered down the steps to the small cove and cautiously laid out the picnic blanket as near to the concrete steps as possible, without being so close that people would actually trip over me.

It was soothing being by the ocean. I imagined how blissful it would be to hear the sound of the waves rolling in until they were as familiar as breathing. I felt so full of hope for the future —I hadn't even realized it had been missing from my life until Sebastian had opened my eyes.

I didn't need to turn around to recognize his quiet footsteps coming down behind me. He had a bottle of water and a can of Coke in one hand, and two packages of sandwiches in the other. He flopped down next to me with a grin and kissed my shoulder.

"Tuna or BLT?"

"Tuna, please."

He handed me the package and I took a huge bite. It was freshly made and very good.

"Hungry?" he said, raising an eyebrow.

"Must be all the exercise," I said, glaring back with my mouth full.

He laughed and unwrapped his own sandwich.

He finished before me, of course, and pulled off his t-shirt to lean back on his elbows and soak up the sun. His smooth skin gleamed in the sunlight, utterly distracting me from finishing my sandwich. I ran my eyes over his flat stomach and muscled chest and decided I'd much rather eat him.

I laid the remains of the sandwich to one side and pushed him down onto the picnic blanket.

His eyes flashed open in surprise and then he let out a long sigh as I kissed his chest and teased his nipples with my tongue. Mmm. He tasted way better than any sandwich, no matter how freshly made.

I stroked the flesh just below his waistband, running my fingers along the edge of the denim, knowing that he was primed and ready for action. He groaned.

"Caro, what are you doing to me?"

"Saying thank you for the sandwich," I murmured against his stomach.

"You're driving me crazy! How am I supposed to think about anything when you've got me like this?"

He gestured weakly toward his zipper.

"That's the point," I said, smiling against his chest. "You're not supposed to think about anything."

"It's working," he muttered, then ran his hands down my back, pulling me closer.

I wanted him very badly and I only had myself to blame. I wondered briefly if the storage closet at the country club's locker room had a 'vacancy' sign on it. But he had work to do and I had room-shares to check out.

I ended our mutual torture, planting a loud kiss on his belly button, then snuggled into his shoulder, resting my head on his chest.

"When did you get to be such a bad girl?" he asked, stroking my hair.

"Oddly enough, around the time I met you," I said, digging my fingers into the ticklish spot around his waist.

"Okay, okay! I give in! Jeez, you play rough."

"I got the distinct impression you like it rough," I said, leaning up to look at him.

His anxious look was back immediately. "Oh, God, I'm sorry, Caro! I didn't hurt you, did I?"

"Of course not! And believe me, I enjoyed our illicit car sex just as much as you."

"You're sure?"

"Yes! How many orgasms do I have to have for you to believe me?"

He smiled and looked smug. "Five is the record."

"What?! You've been counting?"

He shrugged and looked a little embarrassed, as if he'd been caught out in a naughty secret, which he had.

"Can't help it—it's a guy thing."

"You ... you haven't said anything to Ches, have you? Because if you have I wouldn't be able to look at him..."

"Of course not!" He sounded angry. "I would never say anything to anyone about us. Ches knows as much as he needs to."

"Has he said anything else?"

Sebastian sighed. "He's worried, I guess, but he won't tell anyone."

I decided to let it drop. If he trusted Ches, well ... there was nothing I could do about it one way or another.

"By the way, did Brenda find you again yesterday?"

He scowled. "That stupid bitch nearly got me fired."

While I wasn't sorry that Brenda was annoying him, I was shocked to hear him talk about his ex-girlfriend like that.

"Did she ... um ... try again after I left?"

He sighed. "Kind of, but..."

"But what?"

"I told her I was seeing someone and that there was no way I was getting back with her after..."

Now he had my complete and undivided attention.

"After what?"

"Nothing," he mumbled.

I bit my tongue, determined not to press him if he didn't want to talk. But, wonder of wonders, my silence seemed to have the opposite effect.

"Ches told me some stuff ... after I broke up with Brenda, she started hanging out with some of the guys we used to surf with. She was ... partying a lot."

"Oh."

From the expression on his face I guessed that was a euphemism for sleeping around. I could see Sebastian wasn't impressed with that.

I sighed to myself. Men were so good at double standards— here he was, having an affair with a married woman, and he was dismissing his ex-girlfriend because she'd slept with other people *after* they'd split up. I knew he didn't think of what we had as an affair, but that was just his insider view, and if he'd have asked Ches to tell it like it was, that's exactly what his friend would have said.

I felt almost sorry for Brenda. Almost.

"You know, I just don't see you two together. Was she always so ... pneumatic?"

"Pneumatic?!"

He smirked then a shadow crossed over his face.

"Not always. I mean, she could be pretty full on—she liked being the center of attention, Homecoming Queen, all that kinda shit. It wasn't really my scene—it was one of the things we used to argue about. But she could be really sweet and fun, too."

It was my own fault for asking, but I really didn't want to hear her described that way. My sympathy for her took an early bath.

"What happened?" It was none of my business but now I *really* wanted to know. "Why did she change?"

He shrugged and lay on his back, folding his hands under his head.

"Some of her friends were sleeping with their boyfriends and she thought we should, too. I just thought it was lame to do it just because her friends were."

"And you were never tempted?"

"Yes and no. I thought about it a lot..." Then he smiled. "Not as much as I think about having sex with you, but yeah, I thought about it. We got close a couple of times. I'd pretty much made up mind I was going to..."

"Hence practicing with the condom?"

He reddened and didn't reply.

"So what stopped you?"

"Ches told me he'd seen her making out with some other guy. He wouldn't tell me who so I figured it was probably someone I knew ... I thought maybe Jack ... she denied it—at first, then blamed it on having too much to drink. But that just finished it for me. I thought ... I thought I must be something special if she wanted to ... with me, but ... I guess not."

I leaned over and kissed him gently on the lips.

"Well, I think you're *very* special, and Brenda's loss is my gain. Although, I'm surprised she thought you'd take her back after that."

He smiled. "She said she didn't believe I was seeing anyone —that I was just making it up to get back at her."

"Well, hopefully she'll go on thinking that."

He frowned. "Why?"

"Because as long as she's thinking that, then she's not suspecting me. I mean, let's face it, you couldn't have been more damned obvious yesterday!"

He looked hurt. "I hardly even spoke to you!"

"Sebastian, you were staring at me the whole time. Even when she heaved up her enormous tits in her bikini top, you didn't look at her. She must have thought you'd gone blind."

"Enormous tits!" He laughed loudly. "Yeah, I guess they are kind of hard to miss. But I prefer yours."

"I thought all men liked women with big breasts?"

He nuzzled my hair. "I'm more of an ass man," and he ran his hands over my backside, squeezing gently, to emphasize his point.

"Well, I'm glad to hear it, because I definitely can't compete with her on ... chest volume."

He chuckled quietly and continued stroking my back as I snuggled closer.

Then his hands stilled and he seemed deep in thought.

"I was wondering," he said softly, "can I ask you something ... about you and David."

Uh oh.

"What were you wondering?"

"How you got together in the first place. You don't seem to have much in common."

Or, in fact, anything at all.

"He was stationed at the Base near where I lived. I'd gone to the drugstore to pick up something for my mom and he drove up in this cute little sports car—a Corvette—electric blue. He was in uniform and he just came up and started talking. I couldn't believe he was interested in me—sophisticated older man."

I rolled my eyes.

"I just saw what I wanted to see—and I was desperate to leave home."

He nodded. "I totally get that."

"I was in my senior year, so ... when he proposed, I said yes."

"Did ... did you love him?"

"I convinced myself I did—at first. But I soon realized I'd made a mistake. I just didn't have anywhere to go back to. Mom made it pretty clear I'd made my bed, and Papa—he just did as he was told. Besides, I got to travel some."

He was silent for a moment but I could tell he still had more questions. Eventually he cleared his throat and tried to sound casual.

"When did you and ... him first ... um...?"

"First have sex?"

"Well, yeah."

He had a right to know—he'd told me all about Brenda.

"It was a week before my eighteenth birthday. There'd been some event up at the Base—my first big formal. I'd loved all the dressing up—it seemed so glamorous to me." I took a deep breath. "We did it on the passenger seat of his car. It was ... unpleasant. It hurt."

"Have you...?" He bit his lip, unable to finish the question.

"Have I what?"

"I know I have no right to ask, Caro, but since ... since me and you ... have you ... slept ... with him?"

I could tell this was a question he'd wanted to ask me for a while.

"No, *tesoro*. I haven't let him touch me since our first night together."

I didn't think he needed to hear that I'd jerked David off instead.

"Sorry."

"Don't be sorry, *tesoro*. It's only since I've met you that I've known what it's like to make love, *really* make love."

And I kissed him, desperately, passionately, to show him

that I meant every word. He held me to him, our mouths locked together, breathing each other in.

"Don't go back to him tonight, Caro, please."

"I have to, Sebastian. After I drop you off at the club, I'm going to check out those rooms. I'm sure one of them will do. I'll put down a deposit and move my stuff in tomorrow. Then, when I have somewhere to go, I'll tell him that I want a divorce —tomorrow evening. I'll be able to go straight away."

"I don't like leaving you with that asshole! You don't know what he'll do! He could hurt you again!"

Sebastian's body filled with tension and his hands were balled into fists at his sides.

"He won't hurt me. Yesterday evening was an accident. Yes, he's a bastard, but he's not like *that*."

It was clear that he didn't believe me. Perhaps he needed David to be as big a bastard as his father.

"I can come over tomorrow morning and help you pack," he offered, rubbing his eyes with his knuckles.

"There won't be much—just my clothes and a few bits and pieces."

"I want to help."

"It's probably best if I do it myself after he's gone to work tomorrow. I'll meet you after I've moved into the new place."

He scowled, unhappy with my plan.

"Sebastian, I have to do this by myself. It's my mess—I don't want you anywhere near him."

"If he lays one finger on you, I'll fucking crucify him!"

"He won't. I promise. I'll be fine." I glanced at my watch. "Look, we should go now. You have to be at work in half an hour."

"I mean it, Caro, I'll rip his fucking arms off!"

I didn't think there was any point replying so I picked up my empty bottle and Sebastian's can and shoved them in my purse, and waited for him to get off the picnic blanket so I could fold it.

He stood up and pulled his t-shirt on but his expression was still angry.

"Hey, come here!"

I dropped my bag on the floor and wrapped my arms around him, willing his tension and anger away.

"We've just got one more day to get through and then I'll be free of him. One more day, *tesoro*. Just one more day. We can do it."

After that we walked back to the car in silence but I could tell his mind was still mulling over everything I'd told him. I hoped it would be busy at the club to help distract him.

As I drove, my right foot started to feel very sore. I glanced down and noticed that the dressing was wet. Damn. The blister must have burst. I really needed to re-do it before I started traipsing around the city or it would be a lot worse. I decided to ask at the club's reception to see if they'd let me use their First Aid Kit, once I'd dropped Sebastian at the parking lot. I really didn't want to give him another reason to imagine doing violence to David.

"Can I see you tonight?" he said, his eyes already knowing my answer.

"No, I need to pack and sort out a few things. I'll text you tomorrow when ... I've moved."

He sighed and got out of the car, then stood, waiting for me to leave.

"I ... have to go and check up on something in reception," I said. "I'll text you later."

"Promise?"

"Yes, I promise."

He walked away, his hands jammed in his pockets. I could tell he felt miserable from the set of his shoulders—and because I felt exactly the same way.

I waited for him to disappear out of sight, then headed to reception where I explained my predicament.

"Of course, ma'am," said the helpful receptionist. "I'll just send for one of our first aiders."

"Oh, that's not necessary, I can do it myself."

"Sorry, ma'am," she said, not sounding at all sorry. "I have to call it in."

She made a call and a few moments later Ches came striding over, a look of surprise on his face when he saw me.

"Hi, Caroline. How are you?"

"Good thanks, Ches. You?"

"I got a call that someone needed first aid?"

"Yes, this lady here needs some help," said the receptionist, obviously having one ear tuned to our conversation.

"It's nothing, really," I said hastily.

"I'll take Mrs. Wilson to the med room, Nancy," said Ches, to the receptionist.

She nodded and returned to her computer screen, having already lost interest.

Reluctantly, I followed him. If I'd known what a fuss was going to be made, I'd have waited until I could have gotten to a pharmacy in town.

It felt awkward being alone in the small room with Ches. He looked uncomfortable, too, shifting around from foot to foot. Maybe he thought I was going to leap on him.

"I just need to change a dressing on my foot," I said quietly. "Do you have some gauze and tape?"

"Sure. You want me to do that?"

"No, that's fine, thank you, Ches. I'll be fine."

I sat down on the low hospital bed and rolled up my pants leg to my ankle, then tugged gently on the gauze. It was stuck fast. I was going to have to yank it off—and it was going to hurt.

I took a deep breath and pulled hard—a huge flap of skin came away with the gauze. My foot looked like raw meat.

"Wow! That looks bad," said Ches, his eyes anxious. "I think maybe a doctor should see that."

Then he blushed, remembering that I was married to a doctor.

We heard voices outside and Sebastian burst in, a worried looking Nancy hot on his heels.

"Caro! Are you okay?"

Damn it! Hadn't he listened when I'd told him to be more discreet?

329

"I'm fine, thank you," I said as calmly as possible. "Ches is looking after me."

Perhaps noting my chilly reception, or Ches's panicked look, Sebastian took the hint and closed the door in the face of the nosey Nancy.

"Dude, that looks pretty bad to me," Ches said quietly to Sebastian, pointing at my foot.

"I'm fine," I repeated, not at all happy to be the subject of their combined attention. It was like being a particularly ugly zoo exhibit.

"What happened?" said Ches.

"Just a silly accident."

"It wasn't an accident," snarled Sebastian. "Her bastard husband did that to her. Show him the rest of your burns!"

He yanked up my pants leg and Ches's eyes scrunched up in horror.

"It was an accident," I whispered again, pushing his hands away.

I couldn't take the pity I saw on Ches's face and the anger on Sebastian's.

To the accompaniment of their silent stares, I cleaned the wound with some saline, applied a thick layer of antibiotic cream and covered it up again. Sebastian's eyes watched every move I made. Ches was desperately ill at ease, I decided to help him out—and reduce the excess of tension in the room.

"Ches, could you give us a moment, please?"

"Sure, sure. Seb, I'll see you later, man."

Sebastian nodded but didn't look at Ches as he ducked out of the room.

"I want to kill him!" he said between gritted teeth.

"Sebastian, please don't."

"Don't what?" he snarled.

"Make things harder for me."

He blinked, his expression changing from fury to hurt.

"How am I making things harder? I just want to help. I love you!"

"I know that, but right now what I need is for you to be

calm and in control. If you keep charging in on your white horse to save me, people will start to notice." *If they haven't already.* "And the last thing, the *last* thing I need right now is for *anyone* to see you treating me as anything other than just another member here. Do you understand?"

"Of course I understand—I'm not a fucking idiot!"

"Good. Then please tell me why you're here, making a scene in front of that receptionist, when Ches was looking after me?"

Every emotion was transparent as it scrolled across his face: surprise, anger, hurt—again—and then understanding and shame.

"I'm sorry. It's just ... I go a little a crazy when I think you're hurt."

"I know, *tesoro*. I understand, but can you see how that makes things harder for me?"

"Yeah, I get it. Sorry."

"Okay. Then just hold me."

He pulled our bodies together and we stood in silence, feeling the tension ebb and flow.

"Okay?" I asked, stroking his cheek.

He took a deep breath. "Yeah, I'm fine."

He didn't look fine: he looked stressed out and worried.

"Okay. I'll text you later—hopefully to tell you that I've found a room."

He forced a smile.

"Stay out of trouble till then?" I said, softly.

"I'll try," he said, forcing a grin, "but I'm not making any promises."

I kissed him gently and walked back through the lobby, avoiding the over-curious eyes of Nancy.

I was so distracted that I narrowly avoided colliding with Brenda as she sashayed through the main doors.

"Hi, Barbara!" I called cheerfully as I walked down the steps.

"It's *Brenda!*" she snarled.

It really is the little things in life that matter.

CHAPTER SEVENTEEN

THE FIRST ROOM TO RENT WAS A SHITHOLE THAT I WOULDN'T even have let David sleep in. Well, probably not.

Apart from the fact that the landlord answered the door in a knit undershirt that looked like it had last month's breakfast down it, and talked to my cleavage rather than my face, the room he showed me smelled of cabbage and cat wee, and the carpet was tacky under my shoes. I didn't even want to think about the stains on the bare mattress that was introduced to me as the bed but in fact was nearer to something that had been plucked from a landfill site sometime during the last year.

The second room in a hip part of downtown was perfect— small but clean, in a house shared with two mature law students, Phyl and Beth. I put down a $60 retainer and drove away two parts happy, promising I'd be back tomorrow.

They hadn't probed too hard into why I was looking for a room, but they were bright women and I was sure they'd put two and two together during our brief conversation.

When I got home (and I wouldn't be using that word for much longer), I was surprised to see that David had been back —the evidence being dishes in the sink and a full basket of his dirty clothes next to the washing machine. He'd obviously waited until I'd gone out to make a stealthy return. That made two of us then. Two cowards locked in a loveless marriage.

But not for much longer.

I ignored the laundry, faintly amused to think he'd have to learn how to clean his own damn clothes, or continue living in some hotel, as I guessed he must be doing.

I filled my suitcase with all the clothes I could squeeze into it and shoved everything else into black garbage bags. What I removed from the house made almost no difference—it was only if David looked in my closet that he'd notice any major changes. That my 11 years with David had made such a small indentation was a sobering thought. I hadn't been a bad wife, but I hadn't been a companion to him either. Although it seemed doubtful that he'd ever wanted one. Still, it was a lonely way to live—for both of us.

Six o'clock came and went—still no sign of David. I wasn't quite sure how I was going to tell him I was leaving him if he wasn't even around himself: leave a note, send a text message, call his office, or even ... drop by in person? None of them seemed particularly palatable. When I'd imagined telling him, I'd always assumed it would be in the privacy of our own front room.

Just after 10PM I got a text from Sebastian.

How's it going? Did u get a room? Is the a$$hole there?

I knew if I told Sebastian that David was AWOL, he'd want to come over. But without knowing where David was, or his intentions, it was risky. The smart thing was to wait another 24 hours. But being smart and being in love, well, that was oil and water.

By myself. Can Ches drop you downtown? Need to get out of here.

He replied immediately, as I knew he would.

30 mins, jazz plaza. r u ok?

I didn't know how to reply so I just sent a quick text agreeing to meet him where we'd seen the jazz band earlier in the day.

The city felt very different at night. Once the sun had disappeared the laidback aura was tinged with a frisson of excitement, and an intangible air of possibilities. I was so close to being free, so close to restarting my life—it was a heady feeling. I was dizzy with unaccustomed recklessness—and I was going to see Sebastian.

We had three more months before we could escape to New York—it was going to be a time of austerity, not that I cared about that, but I thought we deserved one night to really celebrate. So when I found myself outside a low- to medium-priced hotel, I hesitated less than the length of a heartbeat, reserved a room, paid cash and put the keycard in my purse with a sense of abandonment.

My impulsive decision made me slightly late getting to the plaza. My phone started ringing just as I spotted him scanning the crowds and running a hand through his hair.

I watched him from a distance, enjoying that moment of seeing before touching. Dressed simply in washed-out denim and a plain, black t-shirt that emphasized his strong, slim build, he was a still point of light, surrounded by the swirling crowds.

"Hi!" I said into my cell phone.

"Where are you?" he said, sounding worried.

"On my way," I said, softly as I snuck up behind him and ran my hand over his toned ass.

He jumped and turned around with a scowl on his face which broke into a huge, sexy smile when he saw me.

"I have to go now," he breathed into the phone, "a beautiful woman is feeling me up."

"Is that right?"

Hidden by the crowd I ran my hand up the front of his jeans.

"Yeah," he said into his cell phone, "I don't know what she wants."

"She hasn't given you a clue?" I asked, rubbing my hand over him again and feeling his body respond.

"I think I'll have to call you back," he said, and snapped his phone shut.

We stood staring at each other as I slowly lowered my cell phone.

He took a pace forward so our bodies were nearly touching then he ran his hands lightly over my arms and rested his mouth on mine. I felt his warm breath wash over my face and his lips parted.

It was hard to remember we were in a public place as he deepened the kiss, his tongue sweeping into my mouth. Tasting him, touching him, losing myself in him—the world fell away. Eventually I pulled back, aware that there was a time and a place—and tonight we had both.

"God, Caro!" he whispered and closed his eyes, just holding me to his chest.

"Come on," I said, after a long moment, "let's go for a walk."

He frowned, looking puzzled. "Are you okay?"

"Sure, why?"

He shrugged. "I just wasn't expecting to see you tonight. I mean, I'm glad you're here, but..."

"Well, I have everything packed up in my car. I ... I just need to tell David. I was going to do it in the morning, but, well, he didn't come home. And I wanted to see you."

"Good," he said happily.

I smiled up at him.

"Are you hungry or is that a dumb question?"

He laughed. "Yeah, I could definitely eat something."

"Let's head to Little Italy."

"Yeah! We can pretend we've got that motorcycle and we're on our road trip!"

We didn't get quite that far before we found a small Sicilian café serving *couscous al pesce*, one of my favorite dishes—I was finding it hard to walk on by.

"I don't know, Caro," said Sebastian, scanning the menu hanging up outside, "it's not that cheap."

"I know it's not, but tonight I don't care—tonight I start my life over. Thanks to you."

He smiled down at me and his eyes glowed with love.

"Really?"

"Truly. We're celebrating ... and I have another surprise. But that's for later."

I tried to tug him into the café but he resisted. "Tell me!" he said his voice suddenly husky.

I shook my head and smiled. "No, it wouldn't be a surprise if I told you."

"Caro, you're driving me nuts! Please!"

"Well, okay, as I don't want to be the cause of your insanity ... I've reserved a hotel for us."

His breath hitched in his throat and his eyes widened. "A hotel?"

I nodded and had to swallow when I saw his expression change from love to lust.

"Let's go now," he said, pulling on my hand.

"No, I want to eat—and you said yourself that you're starving."

"We'll get take-out!" he growled, tugging me down the street.

I planted my feet and tugged back. "Sebastian, no!"

He stopped, staring at me in hurt surprise.

"Why not?"

I couldn't help but smile at the expression on his face, but my voice was serious. I'd spent quite a while thinking about this.

"Because after tonight we won't be able to afford to do this again for a while, and for tonight, at least, I don't want to hide. I just want to have a nice meal in a nice café ... I just want to have ... a date. With you."

He grinned. "A date? Yeah, I'd like that. With sex after?"

I laughed. "Oh, yes. *A lot* of sex after."

We sat at a table in the window and the elderly waiter lit a candle and stuck it in an old wine bottle encrusted with wax.

I spoke to him politely in Italian and he smiled hugely.

His accent was very strong and he explained he was from Trapani on the toe of Sicily. I could tell Sebastian was finding it hard to follow the conversation so I switched to English.

"We hope to visit Sicily one day soon," I said, throwing a quick glance at Sebastian who grinned back.

"Ah, then you must visit my home town and wish her well for me," said the old man, "and you will weep before the beauty of our Madonna di Trapani."

He wandered away, happily chattering to himself, as he reminisced about his home town. I smiled at Sebastian as he held my hand across the table, but then his eyes widened in shock.

"You took off your rings," he whispered.

I nodded silently.

It was true: earlier, while I was pacing around the house, I happened to glance down at my hand and saw the rings—I mean really saw them, and everything they stood for. I slipped off my engagement ring, three small diamonds in a channel setting, and then took off the plain, gold wedding band. I held them in my hand, wondering what to do with them. I considered leaving them on the kitchen table, or on the cabinet next to David's side of the bed, but in the end, I dropped them into my change purse.

My hand felt so light without my wedding rings, it was as if it could float away, but Sebastian held my left hand to his cheek and closed his eyes. When he opened them again, his eyes glistened with unshed tears.

"You're really leaving him," he said and I wasn't sure if it was a statement or a question.

"Yes. You didn't think I would?"

He looked ashamed. "I did and I didn't. I kept hoping but ... I knew how much you'd be giving up. And ... and I knew I couldn't offer you anything..."

I held up my hand to stop him.

"That's not true, Sebastian. You've already given me so much—you just don't realize it."

He shook his head impatiently. "Don't try to make me feel better because…"

I interrupted him again. "I'm not! You've given me back my self-esteem and you've given me hope for the future. You've given me love. You've given me yourself. There's nothing else I want."

He reached across the table and held his hand against my face. I leaned into him and closed my eyes.

"I love you," he said.

The waiter interrupted us with a polite cough, a smile and a wink at Sebastian who grinned back.

Sebastian refused to order *antipasti* and I couldn't tell if it was because he was anxious about the cost or because he wanted to get back to the hotel as quickly as possible. Either way, I couldn't persuade him to change his mind so I had to abandon my thoughts of *caponata* and ordered the couscous for *secondi* with half a carafe of the house red.

I didn't mind. He wasn't the only one who was thinking about a king-size hotel bed with crisp, white sheets and a double shower. Hmm, sheets I wasn't going to have to wash— what a treat. Hmm, soapy, wet Sebastian in a double shower. Wait! Wasn't there a large bath, too, or did I just dream that? Damn! I couldn't remember. That was really going to bug me.

"What's the matter? You look kinda pissed," he said, worriedly. "I don't mind if you have a starter."

I looked up, confused, then I smiled at him.

"No, that's fine—I was just trying to remember whether or not there was a bath in the room."

"That's what you were thinking about?"

For a second he looked slightly shocked then a wicked grin lit up his face.

"Cool!"

I was distracted momentarily when I caught sight of someone turning away from the window, a glimpse of long blonde hair…

"What were you thinking of doing if there is a bath?"

I raised an eyebrow. "Well, I thought I'd start with getting really dirty. And then getting really clean."

He swallowed and blinked several times. "How dirty?"

Now he had me on the back foot because I really didn't know. David was nothing if not traditional. It was only over the last few weeks with Sebastian that I'd begun to explore the possibilities of pleasure.

I looked directly at him. "Let's find out together."

His answering smile was glorious.

The waiter arrived with our half carafe and poured a glass for each of us. I could see Sebastian was taken aback and then I remembered his age. How ridiculous that I could forget it, given the unusual circumstances of our relationship. Clearly the waiter was quite prepared to believe that Sebastian was over 21—he hadn't even given us a second glance. It made me feel—hopeful.

Sebastian picked up his wineglass and ran his finger around the rim. For a second I imagined him dressed in a black tux and white shirt, sitting in a private box at La Scala. I picked up my glass and angled it toward him.

"Salute!"

He smiled and clinked his glass against mine, "To us."

A much better toast.

I leaned across the table toward him and whispered conspiratorially, "Of course, you're too young to drink that legally."

He smiled and took a long sip.

"I'm too young to do a lot of things," he said, then dipped his finger into his wine and held it toward me.

I took his finger in my mouth and bit it gently then sucked hard.

A hiss escaped him and he closed his eyes. When he opened them again the black of his pupils had eclipsed the sea-blue irises.

I shivered, releasing his finger.

He smiled, a slow, sexy, seductive twist of his lips. I wanted to run my tongue over those lips, feeling their softness, their fullness, their wetness when he parted them. I imagined letting my tongue taste every inch of his firm, taut body, drinking in his scent and tasting the salt on his skin.

He hadn't taken his eyes off me and I'm sure mine revealed each and every thought. He licked his lips and swallowed.

The waiter broke the spell by discreetly placing our dishes in front of us and ignoring our heated gaze. Perhaps it was something he saw all the time although if he did, I couldn't imagine why the restaurant hadn't gone up in flames.

Sebastian leaned back in his chair and I took a deep breath.

"Is it always like this?" he said, suddenly looking lost and vulnerable.

I knew what he was asking me and I didn't have an answer. I shook my head. "Not for me ... not until now, until you."

What did I know of the kind of love that made it hard to breathe, where your body ached day and night for that connection with another, physically, mentally, spiritually? It was utterly new and terrifying and exhausting and wonderful. I was dazzled by the light that spilled from him into the shadow of my previous existence. He eclipsed everything, erased everything that had gone before. I was reborn—not just to him, but to myself. And I was ready for the adventure.

I took a deep breath and pointed with my chin toward his food.

"Eat: you'll need your energy."

Without breaking eye contact, he picked up his fork and lifted some pasta, holding it out toward me. "Want to taste it?"

I took the food in my mouth and felt the creamy sauce drip down my chin. Sebastian grinned and cleaned up the drip with his finger, putting it into his own mouth.

The rest of the meal went the same way, tasting each other's food, turning ourselves on, stoking the flames, with each new sensory assault. I wanted to crawl over the white tablecloth, tear off his shirt and take him where he sat. I imagined running my hands through his hair and thrusting my tongue into his mouth, clenching on his body when it was inside my own. I licked my lips.

He threw down his fork suddenly and rubbed his hands over his face.

"I can't concentrate on eating when you look at me like that!" he complained.

"Like what?" I said, feigning an innocence I most definitely wasn't feeling.

"Like *that!*"

Tauntingly, I pushed my fork into the couscous and carefully lifted it to my mouth, chewing with insolent slowness, as I kept my eyes on his face. Then I licked my lips and sucked the fork clean.

He made a sound deep within his throat that was halfway between a moan and a growl and my eyes opened wide.

"Caro, I mean it! If you do that again..."

His warning amused and aroused me. I wanted to know his limits—and I was curious about mine.

Again, I pushed my fork into the couscous, again I lifted it to my mouth and slowly sucked the fork clean, a challenging look on my face.

He slammed his chair backward, startling the waiter and the elderly couple who were sitting across the room from us drinking their after dinner Sambuca. He strode around the table and pinned me to the chair, one hand on each side of my seat and kissed me roughly, his frustration and ardor all poured into that one, spellbinding moment.

My hands reached up to his chest and fastened into his t-shirt. I didn't know if I was pulling him toward me or pushing him away. My whole body was flushed and heated.

I was dimly aware that the waiter was hovering over us and Sebastian stood up reluctantly.

"Ah, sir," the poor man said nervously, "we have other patrons, sir ... ah..."

"Wrap the food to go," Sebastian ordered.

"Certainly, sir," replied the waiter, gratefully scuttling away with our dishes.

"You're impatient tonight," I said, taking a much needed drink of wine.

He scowled at me. Jeez, even his anger turned me on.

"How the fuck can I eat a plate of carbonara when you're looking at me like that and I'm sitting there with a boner that's as hard as Mount Rushmore?"

I nearly spat my wine out and couldn't help laughing.

"Mount Rushmore?"

A reluctant smile made his lips twitch but I could tell he was still a little mad.

"Come on, then, let's go. You can finish your cold carbonara later." *Ugh.*

I paid for our abandoned meal with cash, disappointed that our date hadn't quite gone as planned, although it was my own damn fault. I should have realized that Sebastian wasn't the kind of man who played games. I didn't think of myself as that kind of woman either—I just hadn't realized that a little flirting with food would have such a gratifyingly immediate effect.

Once we'd left the relieved waiter behind and were strolling down the street, Sebastian draped his arm possessively around my shoulders, every now and then stooping to kiss my hair.

"Maybe I should just buy you energy bars next time and skip the whole dinner-date idea," I teased him. "I could tie you to the bed and feed you Gatorade."

He stopped so suddenly, I almost skidded past him. He turned and stared at me, then swallowed, his expression burning.

"What would you tie me up with?" he said, his voice full of unexplored longing.

I blushed beet red as he pulled me to his chest and stared down into my eyes.

"Stockings?" I whispered uncertainly.

He squeezed his eyes closed and tightened his grip on me almost painfully.

"And garter straps?" he choked out.

"If you like."

"In black?"

"*Tesoro*, for you I'll wear a different color for each day of the week."

He let out a low moan.

"Where's this fucking hotel?" he muttered, then towed me down the street at the quick march.

It took a moment to orientate myself and remember the direction for the hotel. Sebastian was so frustrated I was half expecting him to toss me over his shoulder and make a run for it. He was a man on a mission and he'd had as much foreplay as he could take.

When we reached the hotel, he yanked open the glass door and hauled me across the lobby while the bemused reception desk clerk blinked in surprise.

"Which floor?" he snarled, his fingers drumming impatiently next to the elevator's call button.

"Fourth," I stuttered, a little awed by his suddenly commanding behavior.

The doors slid open silently and I almost ran to the back, gripping the handrail, certain I needed something to hold on to. Sebastian took one step inside and let the doors close an inch behind him. He glanced over the buttons and stabbed number four with his finger.

My heart rate spiked as he stared at me, a hungry, desperate, utterly focused look on his face. I licked my lips but my mouth was suddenly dry.

I struggled to think of something to say but my mind was blank, totally without thought—just a raging need to consume.

The elevator started to rise and Sebastian took a pace toward me. Then another. And another. Until he was standing in front of me but still our bodies weren't touching. Then he reached out and placed one hand above my left shoulder, and his other above my right. I was trapped between his arms. And *still* he didn't touch me. He leaned forward and I held my breath. Then slowly, deliberately he nuzzled my hair out of the way and ran his tongue up the side of my neck.

I could feel his warm breath on my cheek, his wet tongue teasing my ear. I took another, deep lungful of air and breathed in his scent: some spicy soap, salt, and his own sweet smell.

Perhaps he was getting his own back for my distractions in

the café or perhaps he was learning to take his time, I couldn't say.

I pushed my hands into the back pockets of his jeans and heard his breath catch in his throat. He let out a long sigh and let the full weight of his body rest on mine.

The doors hissed open, an almost welcome distraction.

He stood up straight and I pulled my hands out of his jeans' pockets, then he stepped back so I could exit the elevator first.

The corridor was silent and our feet sank into the plush carpet soundlessly. The gilt sconce lights cast pale shadows on the patterned wallpaper, and twenty wooden doors stretched in each direction. It took me a moment to remember which way to turn. I fished in my purse and pulled out the keycard.

"It's room 429," I said, softly.

Wordlessly, Sebastian took it from me then led me by the hand down the corridor, his eyes glancing at the discreet numbers on each door.

Toward the end of the corridor, he stopped, pushed the keycard into the lock, and let the door swing open.

I'd left one small sidelight on and my overnight bag was still on the large bed.

I heard Sebastian turn the catch on the door, locking it behind us. When I turned around, he was standing watching me.

He kicked off his sneakers and tugged his t-shirt over his head as he padded toward me barefoot. I stood limply, frozen to the spot, mesmerized by his predatory gaze. When he reached me, he rested his hands on my arms and breathed in deeply, his fingers tightening around my biceps.

I laid my head on his chest and kissed him just above his heart. He sighed and wrapped his arms around my back. We stood there in silence, just holding each other.

Then I kissed his chest again, and ran my tongue across his torso, remembering that I'd wanted to taste every inch of him. I let my hands drift down, pushing them inside his jeans, beneath his briefs, stroking his skin and digging my fingers into the flesh of his buttocks. A soft sound escaped his lips and his hips pushed forward.

Still without speaking, I pulled my warmed hands free and stepped back, giving myself room to undo the button of his pants and pull down the zipper, opening his jeans and pushing them over his hips. I ran my hands lightly over his briefs and felt his body quiver, his erection evident beneath my gentle fingers. Carefully, I pushed the briefs down so he could step out of them.

He was beautifully, gloriously naked and I drank in his beauty and his strength as he stood before me, unembarrassed, eyes soft with love.

"You are my world, Caro," he said.

"And you're mine."

He smiled and pulled me into his arms then walked me slowly backward toward the bed.

I sat down and wrapped my arms behind his thighs, pulling him closer. I placed a soft, wet kiss on his tip and watched as his eyelids fluttered.

"Do you still want me to tie you up?"

He blinked several times then smiled again and shook his head.

"Not tonight. I want to be able to touch you—all of you."

He grabbed the hem of my t-shirt and gently pulled it over my head.

"You're so beautiful."

He kneeled in front of me, resting his hands on my hips. He leaned forward to kiss my breasts, playful little nips, and then his tongue was washing over me, laving my cleavage. I arched my back, letting my head hang backward and suddenly his hands were urgent. He pushed me onto the bed and leaned over me, his mouth, breath, tongue, hot against my skin. He groaned loudly then stood up. I struggled to sit but he slid one arm under my knees and the other behind my back, picked me up bodily and slung me higher up the bed. I was so surprised, the breath whooshed out of my lungs. He stretched out alongside then reared up to hover over me, his erection pointing confidently toward my belly. Before I could reach out for him, he knelt across me, lifted me up with one hand and with the other expertly unhooked my bra. *Jeez! Had he been practicing?*

I knew what was coming next but before he could reach for my pants, I pushed him away and rolled onto my side, struggling to turn off the bedside lamp. The curtains were still open but the dull, orange illumination of the streetlamps was the only light.

"What are you doing?"

His tone was surprised.

I had my reasons. The marks on my legs were no longer painful, with the exception of my right foot that throbbed relentlessly, but they were unsightly. And I didn't want him distracted, not by that. I had other distractions in mind.

I shimmied out of my pants and panties while he watched me, and tossed them randomly, not caring where they landed.

I could see his silvery gold outline on the bed next to me as my eyes adjusted to the dim light. I sat up and found that my skin was too tender to kneel across him. Instead I seated myself in his lap and stretched my legs out in front of me.

"Sit up," I said, my voice high from tension.

I wrapped one hand around his neck as he raised himself off the bed, and then held his length in my hand to position myself over him. I stroked him several times and he took a deep, faltering breath. As I sank down onto him, he groaned and I felt him tremble.

It was an extraordinarily intimate moment as our bodies joined together, our faces just inches apart.

His eyes were wide and wondering and I pulled his head toward me, breathing a soft kiss onto his lips. Then his mouth locked onto mine and our tongues moved in a new rhythm as our bodies thrust together. I pulled my knees up slightly and he did the same, almost lifting me off the bed with each powerful movement of his hips. He wrapped his arms behind me, pulling me still closer.

I needed to take a breath and Sebastian mirrored my actions. His eyes were fixed on mine and in a moment of utter stillness, I stroked his face, letting my fingers whisper across his cheek, his eyelids, along his soft eyebrows, down his nose, across the slight flare of his nostrils, along his jaw and fluttering across his lips, where he kissed them.

We were joined together as one, it was impossible to be closer, more intimate—all the barriers between us were finally down. We were equal and open and unafraid.

I ran my hands down his back and felt him move inside me. I pulled back and leaned away from him, changing the angle of connection, and he groaned again and began to pump faster.

I clenched around him, unable to control the waves of sensation pulsing through me.

He called out and I felt him shudder into me with one, deep thrust. He gasped, pulling in lungfuls of air and then he gathered me to him, crushing me to his chest so hard I could barely breathe myself.

We sat like that, still joined together, and I felt a small giggle bubble up as I wiped a bead of sweat off my forehead.

"Who needs gym classes," I said, stroking his face.

He laughed softly. "You don't need anything, Caro, you're perfect."

"Oh, I'm far from perfect, but I'm very happy that you think I am. I'll have to keep you in a darkened room forever."

"Suits me."

"You might get hungry," I pointed out. "You'd starve to death."

"We'd order take-out," he said pragmatically.

I eased myself off him gently and lay back in his arms as he stroked my hair.

"Hey, did you check out the bath situation?" he said.

"Hmm, what? No. I was too busy checking you out."

He laughed. "Seriously! We could take a bath together."

"Oh, okay," I said, reluctant to move from my semi-comatose position. "If you go run it. See if they've put out any bubble bath."

He kissed me quickly and leapt off the bed. He had so much

energy. I was exhausted already and I sensed it was going to be a long and wonderful night.

I heard the sounds of the faucet running as if from a great distance while I felt myself drifting asleep. But then a strange, unfamiliar sound reached my ears and suddenly, unexpectedly, I was wide awake: Sebastian was singing to himself. I strained to hear the words. When I did, my heart broke open, filling with the love that poured from those faint, heartfelt words. Peace and joy and a sense of wholeness that I'd never known utterly overwhelmed me and I began to cry softly.

> *When I hear her voice, the world disappears*
> *When I hear her voice, I have no more fears.*

I had never believed it was possible to cry from happiness.

Quietly, I slipped off the bed and moved silently to the bathroom door, standing half hidden, watching him. He was leaning over the tub, testing the water with his fingers, the steam weaving through the air like ghosts.

He'd switched on the light above the shaving mirror and the yellow glow bathed his skin with gold. I watched the ripple and play of his muscles as he continued to reach into the bath, drawing pictures with his fingers in the hot water.

> *She takes away the sadness, she takes away the pain*
> *She takes away the darkness, she takes away the rain.*

He stretched up to pull down two white towels, placing them carefully at the side of the bath.

> *When I'm traveling from so far away*
> *She's my path, she's my sun, she lights my way.*

Then he turned and saw me standing in the shadows.
"Caro! Why are you crying?"
"Because I love you."

CHAPTER EIGHTEEN

HE STARED AT ME, THEN ONE, LONG SECOND LATER HE STRODE toward me and took my face in his hands, kissing the tears as they trickled down my cheeks.

And there we were, two fools in love.

"I waited and waited and waited," he stammered. "You never said it ... you never told me ... and now you have. I love you I love you I love you. Oh, Caro, so much."

A sob escaped his throat and I felt ashamed of having held back for so long, not realizing how much he'd needed to hear me say the words.

I wrapped my arms around his waist as he took long, shuddering breaths. My own tears soon dried, overwhelmed as I was by my own happiness and my need to protect and comfort this beautiful man-child who had known so little love in his life.

Skin to skin, my head to his shoulder, we stood, drinking each other in. Finally his breathing slowed and he kissed the base of my neck. A smile lifted my lips and I opened my eyes.

"Sebastian, the water!"

The bath was nearly full and in danger of overflowing—like me.

"Oh, crap!"

He leaned down to turn off the stream of water and pulled

out the plug to let some escape. He continued to stare into the water and I sensed he was using the time to compose himself.

When he looked up again, his focus was slightly to the left of my shoulder. He couldn't meet my eyes and the expression on his face was sheepish.

"Sorry for spazzing out on you."

I laid my hand on his cheek, forcing him to look at me.

"No, Sebastian! Don't *ever* be embarrassed about how you feel—not with me. Not ever. I love that you're so open with me, I love that you show me how you feel every moment of the day and night, it drives me crazy when you do it in front of other people but I love it, too, because it's part of who you are. I've never known anything like it and I don't want it to stop. Because I feel the same."

He gasped slightly then beamed at me.

"Okay," he said softly.

I smiled back and all the tension drained from the room leaving us calm and replete.

"Should we have a bath now?"

He nodded, then his forehead creased as he glanced at my right foot that was still swathed in thick gauze.

"Can you? You don't want to get that wet," he said, and his expression darkened to something quite intimidating.

"I'll hang it over the side," I said, trying to stop him from brooding on my injury, "but I'll need to lean on something: I had you in mind."

He smiled. "You think I'll make a good pillow?"

"Well, you're a little hard..."

He grinned at me salaciously, then looked down at his dick.

"Not at the moment, but I could be..."

"Can't you get your mind off sex for two minutes?!"

"Nope, don't think so."

I sighed, pretending to be annoyed, but it was hopeless—a huge smile cracked my face.

He grinned back and even as I looked at him, his dick twitched. It really did have a life of its own.

"Oh no! I'm not ready for round two yet! I want a nice, relaxing bath. I've used muscles that I didn't even know I had."

"Okay," he said, still smiling, "but it'll have to be a quick one."

"'Quick' and 'relaxing' aren't words that really go to together," I pointed out.

"Oh, I don't know—I can think of an occasion when they'd go together."

His eyes seemed to darken and I couldn't help it as my gaze dropped to below his waist, it was apparent that he wasn't just having a rush of blood to his head.

"Can I take a rain check?" I said, my voice a little shaky.

"Nope, don't think so," he repeated, pacing toward me.

"I want to take a bath."

"We will. Later."

I backed into the vanity unit and had nowhere else to go.

He caught me by my hips, pressing himself against me and nuzzled my neck.

"I really want to take a bath," I gasped, gripping onto his wrists.

"Mmm," he replied, as my body arched at his touch. "You're definitely not dirty enough yet."

I watched, speechless, if not completely soundless, as he slowly sank to his knees. His mouth followed the general downward direction and I swallowed hard.

His tongue traced around my left nipple then he bared his teeth and pulled against the heated flesh, tugging not very gently while his hands continued to knead my hips, his fingers digging into my ass. Then he turned his attention to my right breast, sucking and kissing and grazing it with his teeth.

My blood was thrumming through my veins and my knees began to tremble. Then his right hand slid down from hip to my calf, and started a slow ascent back up to my inner thigh. My breathing sounded loud and seemed to echo around the bathroom. The volume was almost embarrassing but it seemed to turn Sebastian on even more because he began to bite harder, making me shudder and call out. Then he began to rub me, gently at first and then harder, circling around and in and out.

He glanced up, giving me one quick look, a slight smile on his face, then his head disappeared between my thighs and I felt his tongue and fingers working me, playing with me, stroking me inside and out.

I thought my legs would buckle but then he hooked my right knee over his shoulder and pushed his tongue deeper inside me. I could barely stand on two legs, let alone one, I hung onto the vanity unit behind me for dear life.

I came loudly and had a brief glimpse of his grinning face before my eyes squeezed shut. He placed my right leg back on the floor and spun me around so I was facing the mirror. I was still quaking from my orgasm when he bent me over and pushed in from behind. He circled his hips, pulled out slowly and plunged in again. My face in the mirror was unrecognizable, my mouth hanging open, my eyes wide, my breasts seemed larger, the nipples flaring outwards, engorged, standing rigid. He pulled out again and sank in achingly slow, rolling his hips, massaging every part of me, all the way in and in. Just as the thought flashed across my mind, *He's learned to do slow*, he started moving hard and fast, increasing the pace as his breathing began to turn to gasps.

He reached around to the front of my legs and pressed hard, sending me plunging into the deep end where I couldn't even remember my own name. I think I actually passed out for half a second because when awareness trickled back, his arm was around my waist holding me up as my hands flapped limply by my sides. His hips pumped hard and he bit the back of my neck as he came.

We sank to the floor and I lay curled up on my side, grateful for the bathmat beneath my hip. Sebastian's chest was against my back and his knees flexed behind mine, his arm still around my waist.

Neither of us could speak for several minutes.

I felt lightheaded and flushed all over, superheated from the inside out.

"What is it with you and bathrooms?" I gasped.

I heard his quiet chuckle. "I think it's the mirrors—I fucking love watching your face when you come—I can see you from all angles. And I can see myself fucking you." I felt his shoulders shrug. "It turns me on."

I wasn't quite sure what to make of that. I realized we still had a lot to learn about each other—and I was so ready for that voyage of discovery.

I pressed my hand to my chest, feeling my heart rate beginning to return to normal.

I struggled to sit up—Sebastian was still lying on the floor, curled around me. I reached down to stroke his hair and a wicked sea-green eye blinked up at me.

"Can I have that bath now, please?" I said in my most persuasive voice.

I would have got up and crawled into the bath myself—except I didn't think I could stand.

Sebastian bit my ass-cheek making me yelp then he pulled himself to his feet.

"You'll have to help me up," I mumbled petulantly.

He grinned then bent to scoop me into his arms.

"Bed or bath?" he said, raising one eyebrow.

It was a tough choice but I was half afraid that if I said 'bed' it would mean more sex and I really needed a rest.

"Bath," I said, at last.

He grinned and carefully lowered me into the hot water, making sure that my right leg hung over the side, keeping the dressing on my foot dry.

It felt wonderful. Not that I needed to relax—my body was so limp I was nine-tenths unconscious already. Two orgasms in two minutes might have had something to do with it.

"Are you going to join me?"

"In a minute—I want to wash you first."

Slowly and methodically he soaped me all over using the small bar provided by the hotel, cupping his hands to rinse me off. No one had washed me like that since ... well, I guessed the last time must have been when I was a young child because I couldn't actually remember it ever happening.

His face was serious as if he was concentrating hard, revealing a small frown as his eyebrows pulled together. He moved my hair off my shoulders and massaged soap into my neck.

"Your eyelashes are really long," he said quietly.

I squinted up at him and waved my fingers indicating that he should come and join me, I was almost too tired to talk.

He smiled and helped me scoot forward so he could climb in behind me. The water lapped perilously close to the edge as he sank down.

I leaned back against him and he kissed the top of my head, letting his left arm rest on the ledge alongside the bath while the right wrapped around my shoulder and across my chest.

"This is nice," he said softly. "I could get used to this."

"We might not be able to afford an apartment with a bathtub *and* a shower in New York," I pointed out.

"I'll get an extra job to pay for it," he said casually. "It'll be worth it."

His optimism made me smile, it made me a little sad, too. I didn't think life was going to be as easy as he seemed to expect. We might be moving across the country but we'd be taking a whole heap of our problems with us. *No, time enough to think about that tomorrow.*

"What will we name our first child?" he said, in a dreamy, offbeat voice.

"Excuse me, what?!"

I was so shocked I jumped, causing a small tidal wave to cascade over the side of the bath. Sebastian didn't move, he just kissed my hair again.

"If it's a boy, we could call him Chester—Ches would get a kick out of that. Or maybe Chesney if it's a girl."

I struggled to sit up but he wouldn't let me go.

"What are you talking about?" I said, my voice rising about four octaves. "We can't have children!"

"Why not?" he said challengingly. "You said you wanted to have kids, so let's do it. We'll find a way."

My head was about to explode with the impossibility of what he was saying. We had nowhere to live, no jobs, no money, he'd only just got his high school diploma and was thinking about going back to study at college and *he was still only 17!* And then, that sneaky little voice in the back of my head said, *Why not? What are you waiting for? He's got all the time in the world but you haven't. You want to wait till you're middle-aged to be pregnant?*

His body had tensed up and I could tell he was waiting for my reaction. I tried to make light of the situation.

"Fine. But let's talk about it when you've got your degree. I'm not going to rob you of a chance to go to school. We can wait three years—we're not in *that* much of a hurry. Besides, we want to see Italy first, don't we?"

I felt his body relax again and he kissed my shoulder.

"Yeah, I wouldn't want to miss that. Okay, when I'm 21. That would be cool. Hey, do you like the name 'Orlando'? I went to school with a kid who was named that—he said it was after some character in a play."

I smiled.

"What's so funny?"

"You are. The name 'Orlando' is the Italian form of Roland. It's also used in Shakespeare's 'As You Like It'—but I always think of the book by Virginia Woolf."

"What's that about?"

"A time-traveling man who becomes a woman."

Sebastian was speechless for exactly three seconds—then he started laughing.

"You're kidding me! Seriously?"

Small waves started washing over the side of the tub as laughter rippled up through him.

"Sebastian! You're causing a flood!"

But he couldn't stop laughing. I twisted around to look at him, adding to the water spilling over the edge.

Tears were squeezing themselves from the corner of his eyes and there didn't seem to be much chance that he'd gain control of himself anytime soon. I shook my head, a smile pinned to my face. *Hopeless!*

I climbed out of the tub awkwardly. Sebastian made a half-hearted grab for me but was too weak from laughter and I slipped out of his grasp.

I picked up one of the towels he'd laid aside and started drying myself while he lay helpless in the now tepid water.

"Are you quite finished?" I said, raising one eyebrow, as his laughter turned to wheezing.

He grinned up at me then slid completely under the water and sat up quickly, rivers of bathwater pouring off his face.

He leapt out of the tub and tried to grab me again.

"Oh no! You're all wet, mister, and I only just got dry!"

I threw a towel at him which he caught before it hit his chest.

He made a few quick passes then tossed it on the floor where it started to soak up the spilled water.

The look on his face had me backing up into the bedroom.

"Sebastian! It's nearly 2AM. We have to be up in less than six hours."

"Plenty of time," he said, his voice a growl.

Unbelievable!

When I finally woke up Sebastian's heavy arm was pinning me to the bed and daylight was pouring into the room. I screwed up my eyes to see the time by my wristwatch. It was already 10AM: check-out time.

"Damn it!"

I pushed his arm off and sat up in alarm.

"Caro! What's wrong?"

He was awake immediately.

I threw myself back on the bed helplessly, angry with myself and frustrated at the lateness of the hour. No, I was angry with *him*. If he hadn't kept me up half the night—if he hadn't *been up* half the night—I wouldn't have slept in: not today.

"Caro!"

"I wanted to get home early," I grumbled.

He pulled me over to face him.

"Why? What's the big rush?"

"I just wanted to catch ... David ... before he went to work. Assuming he went home last night. Now I'll have to put off telling him *again* ... unless I go to the hospital. I guess I could do that."

Sebastian scowled.

"Why don't you just leave him a note? You don't owe that asshole anything."

I disagreed but I didn't want to get into a fight over it either.

"I guess I'll find him later," I said almost to myself.

"Can we talk about something else?" said Sebastian, mirroring my own thoughts.

I forced a smile.

"Sure. What do you want to talk about?"

"Well," he said, suggestively flexing his hips, "I woke up feeling horny and I have this beautiful woman in my bed..."

"Sebastian!" I whined.

But he was already burying his face in my chest and nuzzling my breasts.

"I have to pee!" I moaned.

"Later."

I guess that answered my question about whether he woke up every morning with a hard-on. There were definitely dangers to having an inquisitive mind.

Ten minutes later I had my head thrown back while Sebastian reared into me.

"Fuck!" he hissed, collapsing back onto the bed. "That was so intense! Jeez, Caro! You just about wrung me out there! What *was* that?"

"I told you I wanted to pee!"

He looked at me, utterly bemused.

"Yeah, and?"

"Well," I said blushing a little, "it makes the, um, orgasm

more intense if you have to, you know ... don't look at me like that—I read it in *Cosmo*."

"Wow! Really? Have you got any more trade secrets?"

I slapped him on his chest and stomped off to the bathroom, listening to his laughter roll out behind me.

Damn him!

I insisted that we get dressed, fearing the hotel staff would come at any moment to throw us out, so I put an absolute ban on shower sex on the basis that: a) I'd probably slip and knock myself out or break something, especially as I had a plastic bag covering the gauze on my right foot, and b) I just couldn't take any more.

Sebastian had a full on pout, which made me laugh, and a full on erection, which didn't. But we found a suitable compromise that satisfied us both, although my knees were red and sore afterwards.

I turned over the room key to the clerk as we checked out, embarrassed to think of the state of the place and grateful that I wouldn't have to face whoever had to straighten it up.

I'd tried to tug the sheets into better order and mop up the worst of the spilled bathwater, but it still looked like a wild animal had been rampaging through the room, which, when I thought about it, rather summed up the way Sebastian had behaved all night.

I smiled, remembering the way our bodies moved together, the way his eyes told me he was mine and I was his, the love that my starved heart had craved for so long. The way love had turned to lust, and lust turned to need—raw and ready, sometimes soft, sometimes hard, sometimes gentle, sometimes rough. Our bodies coming together, melding as one, two pieces fitting together, over and over.

I remembered.

It was a beautiful day as we strolled out of the hotel, the early morning gloom was long gone and the heat of July was beginning to build. As usual, Sebastian was hungry and even though he'd eaten the cold carbonara and the remains of my couscous sometime between my fourth and fifth orgasms, he was ready for more food.

We grabbed coffee and rolls to-go and wandered along to my car feeling relaxed, if a little tired. Maybe that last bit was just me because Sebastian seemed to be fizzing with energy, talking happily about all the things he'd got planned for us in New York (going to baseball games seemed to figure rather more than I was expecting), but also walks through Central Park and, of course, checking out all the east coast beaches.

Here on the west coast, the surf was pumping and Sebastian gazed longingly at the barreling surf as we drove along the ocean road.

"Why don't you call Ches and see if he wants to catch some waves?" I suggested.

Sebastian's face brightened.

"Really? You don't mind?"

"No, go ahead. I'll meet up with you later. What time do you have to be at work?"

"I'm on four till ten again."

"Okay, well, I could pick you up after? We can go to my new place—you can meet my roommates."

"Sure, that would be great. You really don't mind?"

"Course not! Go have some fun."

And I had some business to take care of, too.

Sebastian picked up his cell.

"Battery's almost dead but I should have enough juice for one call." He scrolled down to find Ches's number and dialed. "Hey, man, what's up? No, I'm with Caro. We've just driven past Silver Strand and it's pumping. You wanna go take the boards out? No, she's cool." He grinned over at me. "We'll hook up later. Yeah, okay." Then he frowned. "What? No, we didn't yet. Yeah, okay, okay. See you in twenty.

He ended the call. "Ches says *City Beat* printed your article. I dunno, he sounded weird."

I'd forgotten about the article. It was rather irresponsible of me—after all, it was supposed to be my future source of income.

"I'll pick us up a copy on the way back. Where are you meeting Ches?"

I dropped him off on Seacoast Drive. Ches was leaning against his van waiting for us. I smiled and waved but stayed in the car. Things were still a little tense between me and Sebastian's best friend—I didn't want to push anything.

"I'll see you later, baby," said Sebastian kissing me hard.

I kissed him back and felt the now familiar electricity surge through me. I pushed Sebastian away and tried to calm my pulse rate.

"Fuck!" he breathed, closing his eyes. "I just can't get enough of you, Caro."

I smiled and shook my head to clear it.

"Go, before Ches drives off in disgust. I'll text you later."

He kissed me quickly and leapt out of the car, a huge grin on his face.

"And charge up your cell phone!" I called after him.

He waved and jogged over to Ches.

I stopped by a convenience store and picked up half a dozen copies of *City Beat*. As soon as I turned to my article I could see why Ches had acted a little weird. As well as six pictures of different events from the Base's fun day, there was a half-page photograph of me—with Bill's grinning face, his arms wrapped around my waist, and kissing my cheek. *Shit!*

That must have been one of the pictures Ches took when he was messing around with my camera. No wonder he was acting weird: *he damn well should!* Worse still, the way the photo was captioned made it look like Bill was my husband: 'The author, wife of Lieutenant Commander David Wilson'. *Double shit!*

Carl had known damn well that David hadn't been at the fun day. Was it a mistake, or was this his way at getting back at me for refusing to go for a drink with him?

I was getting paranoid. I was sure it was just an honest

mistake, probably the sub-editor wrote the caption—nothing to do with Carl at all.

But an ominous feeling chilled me. I was about to leave David and, looking at this photograph, people would assume I was having an affair with Bill. But ... just maybe I could work this to my advantage—it would certainly deflect attention from Sebastian. Probably too well.

I drove home chewing on the inside of my mouth, deep in thought. I'd do one more check of the house to make sure there was nothing else I wanted and then I'd go find David at the hospital. That was the plan. It seemed callous to just leave a note although a large part of me would have preferred it. Come to think of it, maybe David would prefer that, too.

But when I got home, I was out of choices—David's car was parked in the driveway.

I sat in my car and took several deep breaths to calm myself. It didn't help in the slightest—my heart was still slamming against my ribs.

Pull yourself together, Venzi. You can do this.

My legs were shaking as I got out of the car. I dropped my key twice before I managed to open the front door.

David was sitting at the kitchen table as I walked in, his face tight with anger ... and a copy of *City Beat* laid out in front of him.

I felt like running.

"Hello, David."

My voice was so soft I could barely hear it myself.

"Would you care to explain this ... this nonsense, Caroline?"

His tone was clipped, his anger under control—for now.

I sat down at the table opposite him and tried to stay calm.

"I assume you're referring to the article, David, there's nothing in there that needs explaining."

His face was a dangerous shade of purple.

"And this ... *man* who seems to be draped all over you! Are you *trying* to make a fool of me?"

I took a deep breath.

"David, he's just a friend of the Peters. He was fooling

around—the newspaper editor got the wrong idea, that's all. Look, this isn't important..."

"It most certainly is, I have a reputation at the hospital and..."

I interrupted him quietly but I was proud that my voice didn't tremble.

"No, David, it's not important. But we do need to talk. At least, I do have something to say to you."

"I can't think of anything more important than finding out why *my wife* is flaunting herself in this disgusting way ... and where she slept last night!"

"I might well ask you the same question, David, but I dare say we would both answer 'in a hotel'."

"Don't you fucking start that!"

I paled at the undisguised anger in his voice but I'd gone too far to turn back now.

"I want a divorce."

He stared at me in shock, his face draining of color as the words sank in.

"What? Are you crazy?"

You mean, crazy not to want a controlling bully like you?

"No, David. I'm not—just unhappy. I've been unhappy for a long time and ... I know I haven't made you happy either. I think it's best if we both just go our own way."

"Because of this ... this *ape!*" he snarled, jabbing his finger at the newspaper.

I sighed. The picture of me with Bill was an unnecessary distraction.

"No. I was telling the truth about him. He's just someone who happened to be there that day. I've only ever met him twice in my entire life. David, this is about us. Well, there is no 'us', there hasn't been for a long time—if there ever was. Look, I'm sorry this seems to have come out of the blue, but surely it can't have escaped your attention that our marriage has been over for a while now..."

He glared at me and gripped the table until his knuckles were completely bloodless.

"Are you screwing this man?"

I looked him in the eye—I was so grateful he'd asked *that* question. I wouldn't have to lie to him. Yet.

"No, David, I'm not."

He took a deep breath and it seemed as if he believed me.

"This is about that silly accident the other night, isn't it? For fuck's sake, Caroline, it was just an accident!"

He sat back, his arms folded across his chest, a supercilious expression on his face. I could tell what he was thinking—the storm was blowing over. If anything, this was the eye of the storm.

"I know it was an accident. But the fact remains: I'm leaving you and I want a divorce."

"Don't be ridiculous! You can't leave me!" He stared at me then added, "You haven't got anywhere to go—your mother certainly won't take you back."

God, he was arrogant.

I was beginning to get angry: angry was good.

"I've already moved my things out. I guess you haven't noticed yet. I've rented a room downtown until ... until we get everything sorted legally. Then I'm going back East."

He stared at me, utterly speechless.

"I won't make it difficult," I continued, "I don't want anything from you."

He looked like I'd punched him, he was deflating in front of me, all bombast gone.

"You're leaving me?"

"Yes, David. It's for the best."

His head sank to his chest and I felt an unfamiliar pang of pity for him.

And then there was a loud and insistent banging on the door. I tried to ignore the knocking, but it was relentless.

Who the hell was this? What absolutely appalling timing.

With the habit born of a decade of domestic drudgery, I was the one who walked to the front door and pulled it open.

"There you are, you little bitch!"

Estelle pushed past me into the main room and Donald

363

followed close behind. I could smell alcohol on his breath as he leered at me. The door hung open as I fell back weakly against the wall.

There could be only one reason for them coming here, only one reason for Estelle to speak to me like that...

They knew.

"What's going on?" shouted David, his temper fraying with this new incursion.

He stood up and glared at Donald and Estelle.

"Estelle, this isn't the time or place. Donald, what's going on?"

"Your little whore of a wife has been fucking my son!" spat Estelle. "My *underage* son!"

David recoiled and stared at her as if she'd grown two heads.

"Don't be ridiculous! Have you been drinking again, Estelle, because from the look of you..."

"Ask her!" she taunted him. "See if she denies it!"

David's disbelief turned to shock: one look at my face was evidence enough.

"Caroline, is this ... is this true?"

My knees gave way and I sank onto the couch.

David stared at me, his mouth opening and closing like a goldfish.

"You're such a limp dick fucking pencil pusher, Wilson," snorted Donald. "If you'd been servicing your wife properly she wouldn't have come sniffing around my son."

David was helpless to reply, adrift in a scenario he didn't understand.

"Caroline?"

David's voice pleaded with me to deny what Donald was saying—but I couldn't.

"Caroline?" he stuttered again.

"Come on, Wilson," sneered Donald. "Be a man for once in your life—if you can remember how."

"I just wanted to see you deny it," Estelle hissed at me. "I knew I was right about you, pretending you're so prim and proper. People like you make me sick. Who are you to judge *me* when you go around getting your kicks with *children?* Sneaking around behind your husband's back—or did he know?"

"It's got nothing to do with David," I said, tiredly. "He and I are getting a divorce."

"Oh, so that's the plan, is it?" sneered Estelle. "Trying to blame my son! My *seventeen-year-old* son! Do you think I'd let you implicate him in your divorce? Do you think for one moment we'd let even a hint of a scandal like that sully our reputation? Or maybe you think you can *blackmail* your way out of this? Over my dead body, you stuck up little slut. I suppose you'll say that he attacked you now? Is that it? Blame someone else? Pretending you're so much better than everyone when you've really been putting it out for all the boys, no doubt you've fucked half the Base by now. Well, no, missy! You're not ruining *our* name."

"Shut up, Stell," said Donald coolly. "I'm running this show, not you."

Estelle fell silent, her eyes narrowing at me, her expression vicious.

Where did so much hatred come from? I felt myself drowning in their ugly accusations. I didn't have the strength to think about that: all I could do was try to protect myself. I had to go—now.

"I'm leaving anyway," I said, quietly, leaning forward in a weak effort to get up off the couch even though I was afraid I was going to be sick. "I won't bother you. You'll never see me again."

David's head jerked up. I saw hurt and pain in his expression along with something else. Was it fear?

I needed to get away—I'd done enough damage already.

I could go straight to New York, Sebastian could catch up with me later. It was only three months—only three months.

I was vaguely aware of the sound of car doors slamming outside and angry voices.

"Oh, that's much too easy!" snapped Estelle.

She marched over and slapped my face hard. My head

rocked back and tears sprang to my eyes. She raised her hand again. I didn't try to stop her.

"Mom! Leave her alone!"

Suddenly Sebastian was standing in the room, placing his body between me and his mother who still had her hand raised to hit me. I didn't understand where he'd come from. I felt sick and confused and so dizzy I was afraid I might faint.

At first I thought Estelle was going to hit Sebastian instead, but she backed away when she saw the appalled faces of Ches, his parents and Donna standing at the entrance of the room watching the ghastly drama unfold in front of them.

Sebastian sat down next to me and pulled me into his arms.

"It's okay, baby. I'm here now."

I leaned against him, a half-sob escaping from my chest. It felt good to be held: it felt safe, protected.

"How ... how did you know...?"

"My *mom*," he sneered, "she called Shirley to tell her good news."

"And how did she...?"

His head dropped.

"Brenda told her. She saw us ... last night at the restaurant. She followed us."

The blonde at the window.

"Yes, apparently you were very cozy going into a hotel last night," Estelle added, triumphantly. "And he was missing for two nights without a word. And you," she said, pointing to Shirley, "you hypocritical bitch—you lied to my face to cover it up! I wouldn't be surprised if you knew about it all along."

Shirley gasped and Mitch looked angry.

"Not to mention the box of condoms I found in his room," continued Estelle, enjoying her moment in the limelight. "And a woman's bra—yours, I presume. In my son's bedroom! Slut!"

Sebastian stared at her, his face curiously blank.

Silence crept across the room like ice. I started to shiver and seemed unable to stop.

David's face was frozen in a mask of shock.

"This boy?" he whispered. "You're leaving me for this *boy?*"

Sebastian shot him a look of pure hatred, while Donna held her hand over her mouth as if trying to push back words that sprang to her lips. Mitch shook his head and Shirley took a step forward seeming to reach out toward us. Ches looked as if he wished he could be anywhere but here—I understood that emotion very well. I was watching my life implode in slow motion.

"It's okay, Caro," Sebastian crooned, kissing my hair over and over. "It's okay now. I love you, baby."

It was Donald who broke the spell.

"It isn't fucking okay," he said in a low voice, full of loathing. "It really isn't fucking okay. She's been screwing half the Base and now she's got her claws into you. You're so fucking naïve you can't even see it. Christ! Why did I have to have a son with shit for brains?"

Sebastian was on his feet in seconds.

"Don't you dare talk about her like that! You're so fucking wrong! You think everyone is like you, but they're not! You think it's a secret that you've been fucking that little nurse all those nights you've been working late, *Dad?* You're just a fucking joke and you don't even see it!"

Donald hit him so hard that Sebastian flailed across the room and crashed to the floor. He struggled to his feet, blood pouring from his nose and launched himself at his father.

Ches and Mitch ran forward trying to pull him off. Sebastian had got in several good body blows before they peeled him away. He was incoherent with rage, shouting and swearing at his father.

Donald rubbed his ribs, and seemed to grow calmer as Sebastian's fury increased.

"Sebastian!" I breathed. "Don't, please."

He turned and stared at me and his face softened. His body went limp but Mitch and Ches hung onto him.

"*Tesoro*, please!"

I reached out for him and he stretched his hand toward me. Cautiously, Mitch let him go and nodded at Ches for him to do the same.

Sebastian swept me into his arms and pulled me to his chest.

"Don't listen to that fucking asshole, Caro," he mumbled, his bloodied nose making his voice thick. "He's nothing. Nothing."

"Is that right?" said Donald, nastily. "I've supplied your life with everything you've got: the clothes on your back, the roof over your fucking head! I'm the poor sucker who has a half-wit for a son, but that's the point, isn't it? You're still *my son*—and that whore of yours has been fucking an underage boy. All I have to do is call the police and that bitch will be in jail so fast, she won't have time to say a prayer."

There was a horrified silence and I closed my eyes, fear and disgust burning through me.

"Hey, come on, man," said Mitch, quietly. "There's no need for that."

"No, indeed," said Donna, sounding appalled. "There's no need to involve the police. I'm sure we can sort this out without resorting to anything so ... so serious."

But Donald was too far gone in his anger and hatred to listen. Or maybe he was finally saying what he'd come to say, to find another way to bully and belittle his son, to control him.

"And you know what?" he said, viciously, "She *will* get jail time—I'll see to that. Corrupting a minor at *her* age: that's not a misdemeanor, it's a felony. She's been plying him with alcohol, too, did you know that? And when she finally gets out of jail, after being finger-fucked by every hairy-assed lesbian in the slammer, she'll have a reputation as a pedophile. Try getting a job with *that* tag around you, bitch! I'm going to make you fucking pay."

The whole world came crashing down. All my worst nightmares coming true in one foul-mouthed rant from an evil man who had bullied and beaten up on his son for years.

Sebastian's face was chalky white under his tan.

"You can't do that!" he whispered.

"Just watch him!" sneered Estelle, her eyes glittering. "Your little whore of a girlfriend will get what she deserves."

I hung my head, unable to shake off the weight of her despising words.

"Just because you hate me," said Sebastian, his voice tight with emotion, "there's no need to take it out on her."

He wiped the blood from his face with his jacket sleeve

"Oh, listen to you!" spat Estelle. "Do you think you're some sort of white knight who can charge in and save the day? You're so pathetic! You ruined my life from the day you were born, mewling and puking, always hanging around my neck, a pathetic child! You don't know anything!"

Shirley gasped and Mitch grabbed her arm, Donna was pale with shock and anger, the horror of Estelle's admission washing over them both.

"I'm not a child!" yelled Sebastian. "I've been looking after myself since I was eight years old because *you* were too drunk to look after your own kid. How many times did I have to help you up the stairs because you were too shit-faced to walk, *Mommy*? How many times did strangers drop you at the door because you couldn't even manage to call a cab? And as for *my father*, you're just a fucking joke. Everyone here knows that you're just a pathetic hole-chaser with an alcoholic slut for a wife. Caro is the best thing that ever happened to me. We're going away together and you'll never see us again."

Sebastian stared at his parents triumphantly. Estelle looked winded and turned to Donald.

"No, you're not," said Sebastian's father, with chilly finality. "You're not going anywhere with that whore."

"You've said that enough times now, buddy," Mitch interrupted with a warning tone. "No need to say it again. And you reel it in, too, Seb."

"Butt out, *Sergeant*!" snarled Donald. "This has fuck-all to do with you. It's hanging around with your loser family that started all this in the first place. He's *my* son and what I say goes. So listen good, *boy*: if you go anywhere near that bitch, I'll call the police and she'll be finished."

Sebastian tried to throw himself at Donald but Mitch and

Ches held his wrists and Shirley wrapped her arms around his waist trying to calm him down.

Donna gasped. "Donald, no! Think of the scandal!"

Donald smiled and turned to me.

"If you contact *my son* in any way: email, text, phone, letter, flying fucking carrier pigeon, we'll prosecute. It's a felony—you'll go to prison. At the very least, you'll be on the sex offender's register for the rest of your fucking life—you'll never work again. And the same goes for that fucking asshole of a son of mine if he tries to contact you." He turned his eyes back to Sebastian. "Ever."

Sebastian was yelling obscenities, trying to get to his father, Mitch, Shirley and Ches were desperately holding him back.

"And as for you, *son*," Donald continued, "you can kiss goodbye to any idea about going to college, I'm not wasting another penny on you. But I'll tell you what you will do—as soon as you turn 18 you'll be enlisting. Do it, or your bitch will be facing jail time."

I was still sitting on the couch, white-faced and shocked, body trembling, barely able to take it in.

Donna spoke in a shaky voice.

"Donald, really! There's no need for this. Surely if Caroline promises to leave quietly, we need say no more about it. Sebastian will be 18 in a few months and…"

"You're such a fucking hypocrite, Donna. You'd really do anything for the reputation of this shit-hole of a Base, wouldn't you?"

Donna's mouth opened and closed several times but she seemed unable to speak again.

"And another thing, you fucking whore," said Donald, glaring at me again. "The statute of limitations is three years: *three years*. You come anywhere near my son in that time and you know what will happen to you. Same goes if he contacts you. *I'll know!* If you're so much as in the same *state* I'll make sure you get what's coming to you."

Three years. Oh, God.

I turned to Sebastian, love and loss filling me as my eyes started to blur with tears.

"Don't listen to him, Caro!" gasped Sebastian, desperately. "He won't do it, he won't! He doesn't care enough about me to bother. Don't listen to him!"

"You're right, you little shit," smirked Donald, rubbing his ribs again. "I don't give a damn about you, but believe me, it would give me a great deal of pleasure to send your little bitch to jail, if only to wipe that smug look off your fucking face."

Shirley gasped and Donna looked disgusted.

David was lost and shattered, his gaze drifting around the room as if he couldn't recognize anyone.

But it was Sebastian's face that I couldn't take my eyes off. All the fight had gone out of him and he sagged in Mitch's arms.

I did this. I did this to him. All my rehearsed excuses flew away: I despised myself. And it was time to let him go.

"No, Caro!" breathed Sebastian as he read the decision on my face. "Don't let him win."

Like a sleepwalker rising to Judgment Day, I stood.

Mitch dropped his hands, releasing him, and Sebastian was in my arms for one last time. He held onto me so tightly I could hardly breathe, burying his face in my hair.

"I have to go now, *tesoro*," I said softly, stroking his neck.

His grip tightened around me. "No!" he gasped as if he was in great pain.

"Yes. Sebastian, listen to me. I want you to have a good life, *tesoro*, a big life. I want you to be happy, to fall in love..."

"No, God, no, Caro! Don't say that!"

"Yes! Do it for me."

"I'll always love you, Caro. Don't give up on us. Please don't give up. I'll wait for you. It's only three years. I love you!"

But it wasn't just three years, was it? I knew that now.

"I love you, too," I whispered so softly I didn't know if he'd heard me. "*Ti amo tanto*, Sebastian, *sempre e per sempre*."

I tried to peel his hands away from my body but he wouldn't let go.

"No!" he cried over and over again. "No!"

"Oh, for fuck's sake!" snarled Donald in disgust.

Somehow Mitch and Ches managed to pull Sebastian off, he tried to fight them but his spirit was broken.

I turned to Shirley and Donna, their faces filled with pity.

"Look after him," I said softly. "Ches, I ... just be his friend."

Ches nodded, unable to speak.

"Oh my dear, dear child," said Donna, tears in her eyes.

I looked at my husband, whose silence was more eloquent than a thousand words.

"Goodbye, David," I whispered. "I'm sorry..."

He stared at me blankly, then dropped his head into his hands.

I turned to go, my eyes sweeping over Estelle's malice, David's bewilderment, Donald's triumph, the sadness in the expressions of Donna and Shirley, and the anger darkening the faces of Ches and Mitch.

Then my eyes rested on the man I loved, the man I vowed I would never see again because he'd been hurt enough—by me.

"Caro, no!" he cried again, tears falling down his face, mingling with the blood.

"I love you, Sebastian. So much, *tesoro*."

And then I walked away, leaving behind all the goodness and beauty that I'd ever known in my life.

～

Despite what happened that day, despite what happened later, I can't bring myself to regret the events of that summer, because Sebastian taught me how to love.

END OF PART ONE

THE EDUCATION OF CAROLINE

Ten years later...

When a woman turns forty she is no longer young, but not yet old.

At least, that's what I was told by friends who had reached that milestone some years ahead of me. I wasn't concerned, although perhaps I should have been: my work as a freelance journalist was always uncertain, my mortgage large, my pension minute, with the future unwritten. So, yes, turning forty should have bothered me, or at least sparked my interest a little, but you can't force yourself to feel, can you?

I never dreamed that my past would catch up with me, and that I'd be drawn back into the erotic madness of a decade ago.

But then again, perhaps life is what happens when you least expect it.

Download The Education of Caroline

REVIEWS

Reviews are love! Honestly, they are! But it also helps other people to make an informed decision before buying my book.

So I'd really appreciate if you took a few seconds to do that.

Thank you!

MORE BOOKS BY JHB

Series Titles
The Education Series
An epic love story spanning the years, through war zones and more...
*The Education of Sebastian (Education series #1)
*The Education of Caroline (Education series #2)
*The Education of Sebastian & Caroline (combined edition, books 1 & 2)
Semper Fi: The Education of Caroline (Education series #3)

The Traveling Series
All the fun of the fair ... and two worlds collide
*The Traveling Man (Traveling series #1)
*The Traveling Woman (Traveling series #2)
*Roustabout (Traveling series #3)
*Carnival (Traveling series #4)
*Gypsy (Traveling series #5)

The Justin Trainer Series
The bodyguard and the billionaire
Guarding the Billionaire (Justin Trainer series #1)
Saving the Billionaire (Justin Trainer series #2)

The EOD Series
Blood, bombs and heartbreak
*Tick Tock (EOD series #1)
* Bombshell (EOD series #2)

The Rhythm Series
Blood, sweat, tears and dance
*Slave to the Rhythm (Rhythm series #1)
*Luka (Rhythm series #2)

Standalone Titles

Contemporary Romance
The Lilac Cadillac
Battle Scars
One Careful Owner
*Lifers
At Your Beck & Call
The New Samurai
Exposure

New Adult
*Dangerous to Know & Love
Dazzled
Summer of Seventeen

Paranormal
*The Dark Detective: Venator (Book #1)
*The Dark Detective: Paukúnnum (Book #2)

Novellas

Playing in the Rain
*Behind the Walls

Anthologies of Short Stories

*The Year Book Volume 1
*The Year Book Volume 2
*The Year Book Volume 3

Audio Books
One Careful Owner
(*narrated by Seth Clayton*)

On the Stage
Later, After: Playscript
Trailer

With Alana Albertson
Father Figure

* These titles are published in languages other than English.
Please check Jane's website for details—and receive **a free
short story every month** when you sign up for her newsletter
:)

QR code for Jane's website

ROMANCE WITH STUART REARDON

My love co-author with these titles

Two book series - contemporary romance
*Undefeated
*Model Boyfriend

Three book series - romcom
*Gym Or Chocolate?
*The World According to Vince
*The Baby Game

Standalone
Survivor Love Island *(romcom)*
*Touch My Soul *(novella)*

WRITING AS BERRICK FORD

Police Thrillers, UK

Dead Water
Dead Man's Dive
Dead Reckoning
Dead Shore

www.berrickford.com

www.ingramcontent.com/pod-product-compliance
Lightning Source LLC
Chambersburg PA
CBHW071200250626
47159CB00001B/149